How Portugal, Holland, France, Germany and England destroyed old Africa and old Brazil in their desperate desire for easy profits and rapid wealth, and paved the way for their heating of the planet to dangerous levels.

THE INVISIBLE BECOME VISIBLE

BOOK ONE

From Congo to Mocambo to Samba

BEN LOWE

First published in Great Britain by Hansib Publications in 2022

Hansib Publications Limited
76 High Street, Hertford, SG14 3WY, UK

info@hansibpublications.com
www.hansibpublications.com

Cover image: A scene from battle that ended Palmares, Brazil's largest Free Slave and Tupi community, after nearly 90 years.

ISBN 978-1-912662-76-0
ISBN 978-1-912662-77-7 (Kindle)
ISBN 978-1-912662-78-4 (ePub)

A CIP catalogue record for this book
is available from the British Library

Design & Production by Hansib Publications Ltd
Printed in Great Britain

In memory of all those colonised, massacred and enslaved by the European powers between 1487 and 1888.

To the planet that the European powers and their wider diaspora have come so close to the brink of overheating.

And to my sons, Max and Miki.

ACKNOWLEDGEMENTS

My thanks to

Kash Ali and Hansib for agreeing to publish these three novels, and for their dedication in preparing them for publication;

Max Farrar, for recommending Hansib, and for your support;

Pam Scobie, who believed in me from my first rough and ready draft, and gave me the confidence to persevere with this mammoth undertaking. I am grateful for her extraordinary patience in urging me to work that much harder in moulding and shaping characters, in stimulating me to improve my sense of place. When she saw me reluctant to learn to write a screenplay, she would not allow me to refuse, in the kindest way. Through turning each novel into screenplays I learnt to focus on the dialogue far more and this became far sharper and more developed as a consequence in the novels.

Metaphorically, it is as though she saw a few scraps of material and some string and realised that a fine kite was possible from these bits, and guided me through until three fine kites were made. I am beyond grateful.

Paul Redgrave for his comments on an early draft of the first novel, which were extremely helpful.

CONTENTS

GLOSSARY

A Brief Explanation of some Words and Phrases used in this volume.

BRAZIL

Pau brazil: tree native to the Amazon rain forest. It is the source of brazilwood, or pernambuco; and a red dye used widely in Brazil. The wood is also very suitable for making bows (for a bow and arrow).

Caiman: a member of the alligatorid species, along with alligators; caimans mainly inhabits swamps, marshes, rivers and lakes, in South America and Central America. Often the length of the largest caiman, the black caiman, can be up to 4.5 metres (15 feet); the smaller caiman tends to be no more than 2.1 metres (6 and a half feet), but some can be 2.7 metres.

Mocambo: fugitive communities of former slaves, and at times also indigenous peoples. They could vary from the very large mocambos – Palmares was 200 miles long at one time, and held 20-30,000 people – to the very small, with just a handful of people.

Quilombo: this is mostly an alternative term to mocambo, a community of ex-slaves and often Tupi and other indigenous people too. The word is from the Kimbundu (Bantu) word 'kilombo' (from today's Angola), meaning war camp.

Tupi: The Tupi people were among the most numerous peoples indigenous to Brazil's territory prior to colonisation and they inhabited almost all the Atlantic coast at that time. It is estimated that they then numbered around 1 million people. There were many other linguistic/tribal groups in Brazil at that time and since that time. I use the term Tupi inexactly as I use it to refer to all people indigenous to Brazil when they came across the Portuguese and their ships. I am acutely aware of the very many terms in the novel unfamiliar to the reader, wished to minimise such terms, and so I have used 'Tupi' generally as I do not wish to use the wholly wrong colonialist term 'Indian' except where this is necessary in Spanish or Portuguese dialogue. The Tupi tribal groups often numbered 300 to 1500. Their names, one or two if which appear in the novel, include Tupinamba, Tupiniquim, Potiguara. I do not report them eating humans as the anthropologists studying their culture are divided on this. They are believed to have been in the territory we call Brazil for some 2,900 years prior to 1,500. Many died from smallpox that was brought to Brazil by the Portuguese, others from influenza , also imported by the Portuguese. Much of the culture of the indigenous peoples, including the Tupi, is part of Brazil's culture today.

INDIA

Zamorin/Samudiri: the ruler of Calicut, a major trading port on the West Coast of India, was called the Samudiri; the term Zamorin is the Europeanised version.
Anjediva: an island in Goa on India's west coast. It is now called Anjadip.
Quilon: ancient fortress in Kerala, now called Kollam.
Cranganore: now Kodungallor, is a historically significant town on the Malabar coast in Kerala, north of Cochin.
Cochin: now Kochi, a major port on the Malabar coast in Kerala.

AFRICA

Ouidah: or Whydah, a city on the coast of Benin
Bonobo: an ape closely related to the chimpanzee
Okavango river and delta: the Okavango river reaches its mouth inland, in a region otherwise characterised largely by grassland, and the river's delta flows into the desert during the rainy season from November to April when the river is in full flow. The whole region becomes richly verdant and full of varied flora and fauna during this time.
Lake Lusiwasi: this is in central province, Zambia
Serenje: this is the name of a town and region in Central Province, Zambia

SOUTH AFRICA

Kraal: a village surrounded by a fence or by thorn bushes; or alternatively a palisade.

Khoikhoi/Khoisan: the Khoikhoi were one of two dominant indigenous peoples in the southern part of Africa at the time they encountered the Portuguese and (later) the Dutch in their ships. Alongside the Khoikhoi were the San people, who had inhabited the region far longer, for tens of thousands of years. The Khoikhoi, who may not have been in the region longer than two thousand years at that time, probably had the first encounters with the Europeans. They had a chief, and there were Khoikhoi who had wealth in cattle or goat ownership, and others who lacked such wealth. The San were far more egalitarian and shared everything. **Khoisan** refers to both the San people alone and (for many anthropologists) the two peoples - the Khoikhoi and San - together. The combined term is by far the most commonly used of the two. The languages that involve tongue-clicking originate from the Khoisan people. The Khoisan people are recognised as one of the earliest distinct genetic groups in humanity.

Chainouqua: a khoikhoi tribe that traded with Dutch settlers in the 17th century and at times conflicted with other Khoikhoi who were unhappy with the Dutch settlers taking land and cattle.

CHARACTERS

Mozambique Island
Nawal – mother of Mahmud
Mahmud – her son
Sohail – mother of Ahmed
Ahmed – son

Mozambique Island, and in Bunyoro and Brazil
The Bantu family (see also separate family tree)
Felani
Mai
Niambi – daughter of Felani and Mai
Katchani – husband of Niambi
Matimba – son of Niambi and Katchani
Aneni
Wotambo – son of Kotani and Aneni
Vimbo – daughter of Kotani and Aneni, wife of Matimba
Barawa – son of Matimba and Vimbo
Otapo – son of Barawa
Atwooki – daughter of Barawa
Maira – wife of Otapo
Mande – son of Otapo and Maira
Caua – son of Otapo and Maira
Tucan – daughter of Otapo and Maira
Rosa – partner of Mande
Tsepo – daughter of Mande
Kanda – son of Mande
Rosalina – daughter of Mande

India, Port of Calicut
Zamorin (aka Samudiri)

Portuguese in Brazil, explorers
Nicolao Coelho – explorer
Bartolomeu Dias – explorer
Miguel – prisoners/desperados
Paolo – prisoners/desperados

Brazil, Portuguese soldiers
Ribeiro
Dias

Portuguese Armadas to East Coast of Africa and India
Bartolomeo Dias
Vasco da Gama
Paulo da Gama – brother of Vasco
De Almeida
Diego – interpreter
Allenquer – crew member

Brazil – Tupi (indigenous people)
Janaina
Anahi
Jaci
Piata
Ubijara
Caua
Tupillola
Minimatu
Cauasan
Ubirrata

Tupi women taken on Portuguese ship
Idoi
Tupilaroma
Aroi
Wai
Udoi
Ulara
Potira (goes to live with Portuguese)

Slave Plantation, Salvador Brazil
Otapo
Mobuka – friend of Otapo
Haram – slave rescuer
Matumbo – slave

Bantu family stories
Old Sage

South Africa (then the southern tip of Africa)(1) Khoikhoi
Akasu
Tsawe Tika

Brazil: Palmares
Mo – leader for brief period
Otapo
Maira
Mande, Tucan and Caua – children of Maira and Otapo

Crew for Haram's ship
Mbeki
Edmundo – carpenter
Mwesu – ship builder
Tyere ship builder
Nyasa
Efe

Brought by Haram to ship later
Aftab
Takana
Bufaso
Sembene
Ngumi
Wakuu
Fey
Nyasa

Otapo helper near his Bunyoro home
Felamani

South Africa (2) Khoisan (17th century)
Doman
Bantu: Maphatusama

Benin (when ship arrives)
Femi

Brazil Plantation, 1600s
Mande
Mtatu
Farka
Sando
Ugglay – foreman
Daewu – assistant to foreman

Brazil: Flores Rosas Mocambo
Mande
Manu – leader of Mocambo
Mkelu
Farka

Brazil: Pau Pau Quilombo
Rosa – leader
Tulapu – friend of Maira
Mtatu

Brazil: Mande's Escape
Tecaua
Lazybones

Brazil late 1600s and 1700s, Tupi fighting Dutch in Brazil
Moacir
Boacir
Potira
Van Hydeck – Dutch captain who meets Potira

South Africa (3) (17th century), Dutch settlers
In fort
Van Riebeeck – captain
Dirk
Piet
Doman – Khoikhoi leader
Itoi – son of Doman

Brazil: Candiro Quilombo
Tupi
Moacir Junior
African:
Kanda
Madingo
Nketi
Sousse
Lakoto

Brazil: Palmares, Final Battle
Free Slaves
Zumbi – leader of free slaves
Manu

Portugal forces
Felipe Dias – Portuguese leader in attack
Domingos Jorge Velho
Luis
General Lopez

South Africa (4) Khoisan v Dutch
Mannema – Khoisan
Gonnema – Khoisam
Sukhoi – Khoisan
Wakhoi – Khoisan

Africa: Rosa and family Journey to Bunyoro
(a) Kisano, Africa
Kamina
Mande
Rosa and family
Farka

(b) Rosa heading to Mande's home
Mina (guide to help Rosa find Mande's family home

(c) New family member, Bunyoro
Tucan's daughter Anulka

South Africa, Hangklip Mocambo
Mahotalese (ley-se)
Farka
Watuso
Bete
Kwame
Wakuu
Reijnier

Free slave women at Hangklip
Chimananda
Safina
Nkuti

Bantu village
Makotele – medicine woman

Khoikhoi at Blombos Cave
Doman Junior

BANTU FAMILY TREE

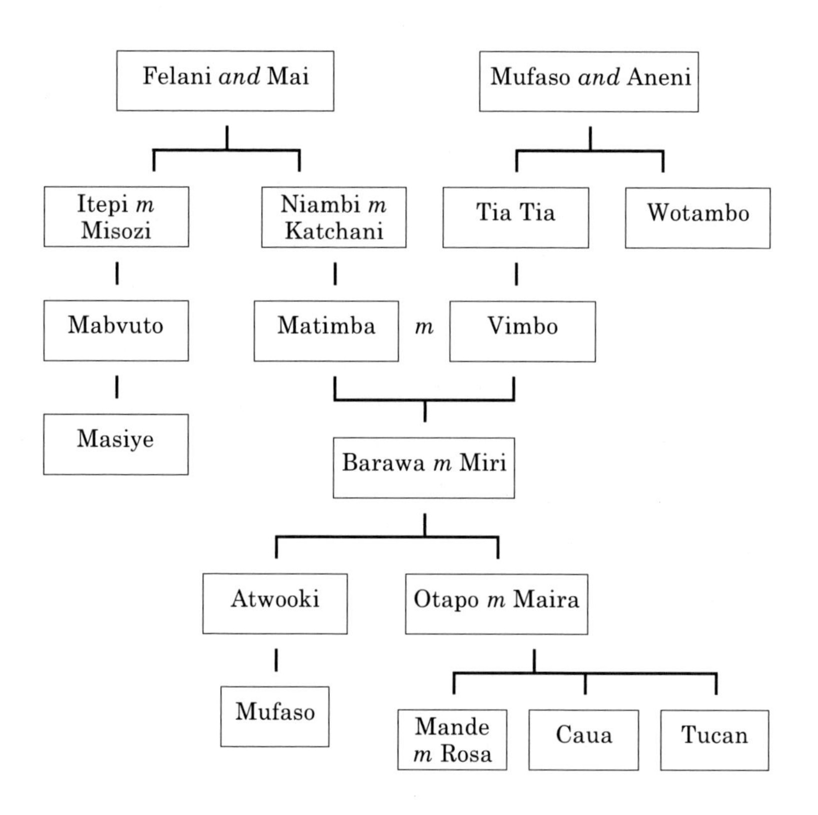

PROLOGUE

Portugal and Spain were part of the Muslim Empire until the 1480s, after several centuries of partial, or at times complete, control by the Muslim Umayyad Empire.

In 1487, with the Reconquista (re-conquest) by Portugal and Spain almost complete, King John II instructed Bartolomeu Dias to find a way around Africa to India. India was the wealthiest economy of the time, and the spice trade the kingpin of the commodity markets. The Ottoman Empire blocked the way by land. King John II's written instruction was for the armada to gain for Portugal a monopoly of the international spice trade and, in addition, to 'make war on the ships of Mecca' and on Muslims generally.

Dias reached as far as Mozambique Island (off today's Mozambique), on the east coast of Africa, before turning back.

Spain, at this time, was also looking to trade with India. When Bartolomeu Dias found the way around Africa to India in 1488, Spain – in 1492 – instructed an Italian from Genoa, Christopher Columbus, to find a way to India across the Atlantic Ocean. When he reached the Caribbean islands, he thought he was in India.

A few decades before Portugal visited East Africa, the Chinese explorer Admiral Zheng He visited a number of ports on the east Africa coast, including Mogadishu (now in Somalia).

1.

China: The Gift of Friendship

Mogadishu

'You have forgotten the chickpeas, Zahra. I can't make humus without chickpeas.'

'Sorry, ma, I will go back for a sack. Did I get everything else we need?'

'Sure.'

Zahra heads out up the street. But there are now so many people in the narrow walled street, all heading for the main square, that she has to just join the throng.

'What is happening?' she asks the tall lanky man next to her, with djellaba and tarbush hat.

'There are foreigners here, with presents for the Sultan. We are all keen to find out who it may be.'

Zahra heads back to tell her mother, Ferida. It is hard, swimming against a human tide, but she squeezes against the wall, and gets home. Her mother is sat by the door, quite intrigued.

'Something big is happening!' she explains. 'Let's go together.'

And she and Zahra follow the enthusiastic throng to the square.

'I wonder who the new foreigners are,' muses Ferida. 'Walid would love to be here. If he didn't have exams in a couple of days, I'd have someone fetch him.'

They head slowly past the tall minaret attached to their local mosque, two white storks nesting there. The mosque's dome is just visible over the dried mud and straw wall, as they inch, tortoise-like, into the main square. The Sultan's majestic grand palace is over to one side.

Through the dense crowd Zahra can detect several rows of soldiers in front of the palace, and the Sultan is held in a sedan chair.

She is able to peer harder as a small gap opens between people in front of her.

'There is an impressive group of foreigners,' she tells her mother. 'One even has his own sedan chair, and he and his entourage wear exquisite silk clothes buttoned high to the neck, mostly a rich blue, with intricate but unusual patterns.'

'Let me see,' pleads Ferida, squeezing her head in next to Zahra's.

'I am amazed! I've not seen the like before. Look! Some of the men have bright cherry red silk outfits, also patterned.'

'The man in the Sedan chair has a refined, thin, long moustache,' says Zahra, as a whisper goes round that the foreigners are Chinese.

"Chinese,' they are saying,' says Zahra. 'What are Chinese?'

'A people from far away, I believe,' replies Ferida. 'By legend they are a mysterious people several moons travelling from us, by sea.'

'How wonderful!' exclaims Zahra.

Four of the Chinese entourage hold a strange banner, with wholly unfamiliar characters, and the entourage is surrounded by the Sultan's soldiers.

A number of underlings in the Chinese delegation kneel before the Sultan's viziers as they proffer their gifts: Ming vases, gold, silver, jade jewellery, silk brocade, silk floss, and silk gauze.

The Sultan confers with his chief vizier, and nods. There is a flicker of a smile. The vizier informs the senior Chinese man in his sedan chair, whose name is Admiral Zheng He, that he and his entourage may enter the royal palace.

The Sultan is carried back into his palace at the front of his entourage. The Chinese men move forward in unison behind their leader's sedan chair. They almost seem to glide forwards.

'It is magical to see Chinese people,' says Zahra. 'One wonders what brings them here. They must have travelled half their lives to get here. Could they be a threat to us?'

'Every sparrow is anxious about the sparrow-hawk, and every sparrow-hawk is worried by the eagle,' opines Ferida. 'We have to be watchful, but in the end, there may be no need to worry.'

'That is reassuring. They are very fetching, with their fine clothes, these Chinese,' says Zahra.

'I agree, quite charming,' says Ferida.

With the Sultan and his entourage and the Chinese delegation inside the palace, the crowd slowly begins to disperse.

Later that day, when Zheng He, the Chinese Muslim eunuch admiral, returns to his ship, a huge crowd gathers at portside to see the gifts offered by Mogadishu.

Giraffes are brought, along with two hippos, a male and a female, and four gazelles, together with large bags of fodder and large crates to hold the gazelles in. Zheng He orders his chief mate to arrange for the beasts to be taken on to his ship, a giant six-masted sea faring monster, larger than any ship that has sailed to Mogadishu hitherto.

The hippos leave large piles of poo on the dock and swing their voluminous arses with pride as they step on to the gangplank to the ship. There is a mighty crack, as the gangplank appears to give way under the hippos' weight, but they continue on, and the simple wood structure seems to bear up.

The giraffes, for their part, have to lower their necks well below the jib as they are led to a place in the hold that has been set aside for them. The gazelles are less problematic, except that one gets a bit giddy as it boards the ship until it is thwacked twice by the mate with his long stick.

Dozens of gulls cackle and squawk as they attack the hippo poo with gusto. Rats emerge from their waterside holes also, but the gulls' beaks are too much for them, and they barely get a morsel before they are sent scuttling away. Just to rub it in, a long snake slithers in from nowhere and takes one of the rats. Camouflaged as a rope coiled around a post, its sudden movement catches the rat by surprise.

With all Mogadishu's exotic gifts on board, including also gold and silver, Zheng He's small fleet leaves Mogadishu and heads down the coast to Malimbi, for a similar visit of goodwill. The fleet then takes the long route, south of India and around Indonesia, to mainland China, at that time under the Ming Dynasty.

A compound outside the town of Mosques (Mozambique Island), 1487

There is the distinctive rhythmic thumping of pestle and mortar as Mai pumps a long pole up and down to grind and pound corn inside the family compound.

Her daughter Niambi is brushing the floor nearby. She is tiny, seven, naked except for a string of beads around her neck, and with a burst of frizzy hair.

A faint whiff of cowpat is carried in by a soft wind, the cows low in the field behind; the goat bleats in its shed, and the smell of goats' milk mingles with the hint of cowpat. The light is bright in the morning sun, the air still.

Niambi's brother Itepi comes running into the compound. He is skinny and also tiny, at eight.

'Four boats with big sails. Never seen boats like this.'

'Are they coming towards us?'

'I think the wind may be guiding them to the town of mosques.'

'I hope it is not bad news. Strangers arriving here with big boats. Why come here?'

'We cannot know. The cow has not had a dead calf. We must wait and see.'

'Our people will not live forever,' says Mai. 'We have been here since the frogs led our ancestors here and told us that there was fresh water here.'

'You have told me the story many times.'

'But the water will not sustain us forever. One day we will need to leave.'

'Let the frogs take us to our next home when we need to.'

'Maybe frogs, maybe gazelles. Will you help me make food? The corn is now ground.'

'I won't say no. I will get the fire going.'

'Our gods will thank you. After our meal, we can sing for peace, sing for life, sing for our village.' Mai is medium height, ebony, and has a bright open face. Her hair in a bandanna, she wears a grass skirt held by a thin beaded belt around her waist. On her back are scarred markings that symbolise a cheetah. Her breasts are still quite pert, in spite of two children. She is in her early twenties.

'A fine idea. While we are cooking, I will visit other compounds with our drum and ask them to join us.'

'You know the Shona family in the new compound? Please ask them too, as I wish to speak to Aneni.'

'I will.'

2.

Portugal: Empire on the Warpath

'The water is dirty. What have you put in it?' complains Nawal. She is petite, chestnut brown, wears a full sari that covers her head and all her body. She has a thin, attractive face, and bony hands.

'It is the water as drawn from the well, as every day,' replies her son Mahmud. He is seven, brown, naked, with just a white cloth wrapped under his groin and round his waist. They are in the cooking area of their small mud-brick home. Mahmud is sitting on a mat on the edge of the cooking area, near the sleeping area. There are red and green rugs on the walls.

'There must be a problem with the well,' says Nawal.

'I will go back with Ahmed and check.'

'Why Ahmed?'

'He is a bit older, and he may see something that I don't.'

Ahmed and Mahmud inspect the well. Each cups his chin with thumb and fingers as he studies the circular wall.

'There is an unusual hole half-way up,' Ahmed says, pointing.

Mahmud looks at the hole. There are a few droppings near the entrance, like a mouse's or a rat's droppings.

'Looks like a rodent to me,' he says.

'The snakes must have missed this one. Or perhaps it is a family of rodents. I will fetch a snake to give us help.'

Ahmed returns with an olive-green night snake, a yellow stripe from head to tail tip, wrapped round his neck. He slips it over his head before putting it on the lip of the well, by the hole.

'Go Simba!' he commands, gently.

The snake slides down and into the hole, and soon emerges with a rat in its throat. Ahmed picks up Simba while the rat passes down its long neck. Mahmud thanks him.

'A rat had made a hole, and some of the dirt pawed out from the hole went into the well,' Ahmed says. 'Simba the snake has now swallowed it.'

'It is a bad omen,' says his mother. 'The mullah's assistant saw sailing ships at sea today. These were not ships from Persia, Arabia or India. They were new.'

'We do not know this is bad,' says Mahmud. 'The billy goat has not lost his horns.'

'They seem to be dropping anchor. The mullah has called us to a special prayer meeting after we have supped. We will pray for peace.'

'As God wills, insha Allah.'

3.

Mozambique Island: Cannon Balls Hurt

Out at sea, Vasco da Gama is speaking to his pilot Pedro de Alenquer on his ship Sao Gabriel. Da Gama is a nobleman with little seafaring experience, with a snowfall of a white beard and a black three-cornered hat. He wears a sleeveless black velvet cloak over a striking, streaked blue and red shirt, with puff adder upper arms and puffed breeches of the same colour, but skin-tight azure blue forearms. Over his chest is a highly ornate silver breastplate. He has leather boots up to his breeches.

'There is a mosque there,' says Da Gama, looking through his eyeglass, 'perhaps more than one.'

'We travel for weeks,' moans de Alenquer, 'having finally driven those mullah-wallahs from our country, and here they are everywhere, ripe for killing.'

'Well, don't shout your feelings too loudly. We still have those two Arab pilots on board to help us avoid unseen rocks and dangerous tides on this coast.'

'Hopefully we'll not need them much longer.'

'We will anchor here and try to stock up a bit.'

A boat starts off from the shore carrying sheep, vegetables and fruit, and a message of goodwill from the Sultan of Mozambique Island.

As the ship slows, and before the Sultan's gifts reach the ship, one of the Arab pilots jumps ship and swims ashore. Da Gama scowls.

'There is something afoot here. I don't like it at all,' he splutters, gruffly.

'I share your concerns. We can't trust any of these people, like rats in a hole,' says Pedro the pilot.

They go ashore in two rowing boats and grab four young Arab men at gunpoint, taking them to the ship. There da Gama arranges for oil to be boiled. He orders that the arms of one of the young Arabs are put into the boiling oil. The youngster screams shrilly, and faints. They throw water over him. Da Gama has an interpreter on board. They ask the young Arab what the Sultan's trick is. He says he does not know. They start to put his arms in the boiling oil again, as he screams and shakes violently. Another Arab shouts at him to stop. He explains they plan to take revenge after a previous attack.

'I will dress as a Muslim,' says Da Gama, 'and you Paulo, and you two,' (he points at his captain and Pedro, the main pilot) 'will do likewise. We will seek out the Sultan and try to discover how he plans revenge. Keep these four rapscallion Moors here for now as hostages.'

'Brother, we do not have Arabic. They will see through our disguise.'

'Diego, translator, you swap with Pedro the pilot. You will be our Arabic speaker.'

'Yes, Sir, of course.'

The four fake Arabs head ashore in a rowing boat with a few gifts for the Sultan. They arrive at the grandest abode in the town, a magnificent high walled villa next to a Mosque.

Three soldiers confront them and ask them for their gifts. They offer these.

The Sultan's men bid the four disguised Portuguese enter, but they are asked to wait in the antechamber while the soldiers take the gifts to the Sultan.

Shortly, a messenger from the Sultan comes through to the antechamber: 'His highness the Sultan is not pleased with your gifts. They have no value in our land. His highness needs more.'

The tone of his voice tells da Gama the content of his comments. He calls the interpreter close to him: 'Tell him we are here to agree a treaty. Our great land Portugal will offer him protection if he signs the treaty and pays a tribute to Portugal in return for protection.'

On hearing the interpreter's words, the messenger returns to the Sultan.

Shortly after, ten soldiers come through with their hands held on the hilt of their swords. The commander says to them to leave, as they are not Muslims, and have lied.

'Your commander,' he says, 'does not know our tongue.'

Da Gama fumes, realising that his ruse was too transparent. He starts heading for the exit, snapping his fingers for the others to follow. They pass between two gold and cream drapes hanging over the entrance and start heading for their rowing boat.

When they reach the ship, Da Gama asks Paulo to instruct his men to fire a volley of cannon balls at the main mosque and the house next to the Sultan's residence.

The town is not fortified.

'They will know better than to insult us next time,' says Da Gama.

Vasco Da Gama then sends off Pedro his pilot to take the four Arabs back and to find two local African men to come on the ship, to help talk to locals further up the coast.

Pedro finds two men cowering with their hands over their heads and their knees fully bent near where a house's front wall has been holed by a cannon ball, causing havoc within.

With the two African men and Pedro on board, and no retaliation from the shell-shocked town, Da Gama's armada is ready to continue.

'The port there seems a good place to return to,' he says. 'There is a quiet harbour, and the fort is not at all well defended.'

'We will no longer have surprise on our side.'

'We will not, but for now, we have a task to complete for the King. We need to ensure that the ships that were tossed and turned off the Cape of Good Hope can now join us. Once the armada is complete again, we will head further up this coast and seek an Indian guide who will take us across the Indian Ocean to India. In the meantime, our two Africans will help us up this coast. We will then discover the route our great king Manuel is most curious about.'

* * * * *

On Mozambique Island, Nawal's neighbour Sohail is distraught and flailing her arms. She screams to Nawal.

'Ahmed was taken on the strangers' ship and his arms are so damaged they may never recover.'

The witch doctor has collected leaves to wrap around his arms, to provide some healing balm while also protecting the arms. Ahmed screams and stamps his right foot with pain.

Nawal says to Mahmud: 'The Mullah has warned that these white monsters from afar may return. The town must prepare itself, he says, and have better fortifications. We will find a place in the hills nearby to hide if they come back. I do not wish you to ever suffer like Ahmed is suffering.'

'As God wills, insha Allah,' replies Mahmud.

The next day, after changing Ahmed's dressing with fresh leaves, they are all preparing for departure for the hills outside the town and on the mainland.

Mombasa

Mai takes Aneni aside as the other neighbours help themselves to coconut milk. Aneni notices a whiff of lily scent from Mai's neck.

'You arrived just two days ago. Have you had a long journey?' asks Mai

'We have travelled for almost a full moon cycle. We come from the city of Zimbabwe.' Aneni is a bit taller than Mai, also full-figured, ebony, and like Mai wears a grass skirt held by a beaded band round her waist. Her face lights up when she smiles. But her face is drawn when she arrives.

'You still seem very weary. Can I offer you something stronger than coconut milk?'

'No, no. Don't worry. The journey took it out of us. There was a big river to cross and towering mountains to get around. But there were highpoints, too, as we saw a wondrous fall of water by a mighty lake.'

'I hear the fall of water sounds like a hundred lions roaring?'

'Like a thousand lions and a hundred hyenas. It took my breath away. My husband Mufaso knelt down and prayed to mother earth. I just knelt and took it all in. But it got worse after that; we encountered lions that seemed to have us in mind for that day's meal.'

'You should have told them that you had not eaten for days either and there was no flesh on you.'

'We did – stared them full in the face – but they didn't seem to believe us. I even shouted to them that I had eaten a bunch of poisonous plants and these would kill them. The lead lion still bared her teeth at us. Fortunately, a herd of springboks appeared in the distance in the nick of time, and the lions went for them.'

'Lucky escape.'

'It was, but two of my children died during the journey. Four survive.'

'That must have been so painful for you.'

'As you may imagine, the heart has too few tears for such tragedy. But how is it you speak Shona?' And she nibbles on a piece of cornbread, raises her eyebrows and tips her head with satisfaction.

'I was born Shona but learnt the local tongue Tsonga when I married my husband Felani and came here. It all sounds like it's been very hard for you. Have you come here to seek work?'

'Life has been very hard for us in recent years. Many are leaving. There has been almost no rain for years. The wells are mostly dry. We had to dig wells ever deeper, but the quality of the water was becoming very poor. Sometimes we had to use coconut milk to wash, but the coconut palms were getting stomach-ache from the drought, and their husks were yielding little drinkable milk.'

'One heard that Zimbabwe was a big city, full of gold.'

'When I was a child, it was full of people, and all families had work. The high city walls stood proud on the Zimbabwe hill. We loved life there. But the gold from the land of the setting sun started to go direct to ports like Sofala and Mombasa, and this undermined Zimbabwe's role in refining and polishing the gold and selling it on as ingots. Things started to go downhill from there.'

'The stripes on the impala's face were no longer pointing in your direction after that, by the sound of it?'

'It seemed that way. After the gold trade had plummeted like a hippo on a mud slide, many left the city. Those who stayed could continue with grain crops and cattle farming, and by selling fine pots and stonework, and maybe foodstuffs and textiles, but the drought was the final straw. Cattle were becoming skeletal, and crop grains became as hard as stone with kernels smaller than a grain of sand.'

'Have most people left Zimbabwe now?'

'Yes. When we were leaving, most were saying they were going a bit further south to Khami, where the stone-working and pottery continue, and where there had been rain. I and my husband thought that we could try Mozambique Island, because of the previous gold trade in part through Kilwa and in part through here. I am used to trading, and I can also sew and cook and so on. The other two of his wives refused to leave, preferring to head south, so he left them.'

'I can ask about work for you. I am a maidservant for a Muslim family in the town. I will see if they know of any opportunities amongst their neighbours.'

'What language do they speak?'

'They speak Arabic, and a little bit of Tsonga. I will have to help you with the Arabic you will need if you work with a Muslim family. For Tsonga, anybody here will help you with it. You should start getting the hang of it after a little while.'

'You have been very helpful, thanks so much. Can I just ask you? How do you make this cornbread so light?'

'I wash my feet and knead with my feet after kneading with my hands – my mother's trick.'

'And timing the baking?'

'I place a little pebble on the sundial at the point where I want the shadow to be to indicate to me when it is ready.'

'I must come here for more cooking tips!'

'Come any time.'

Niambi comes running towards Mai: 'It's pa!'

'What's happened?'

'Gone. The strangers in the ships have him.'

'But he was fixing fascias on buildings in the town, that's all. What can he have done wrong?'

'They just took him and another man from a neighbouring compound. The Muslims say they were just grabbed.'

Mai is distraught and holds her face in her hands. 'Is there nothing we can do? This is terrible. Poor Felani, poor, poor Felani.'

'He is on one of their ships now, and it has sailed away. Oh ma, what shall we do?'

'I really don't know, my darling, I really don't know.' She sits with her head in her hands, with Niambi kneeling next to her, consoling her, and Mufaso sitting by Aneni, consoling her too.

* * * * *

'What's all this for a bunch of bananas?' asks Felani, as he adjusts the manacles on his wrists as much as he can, to reduce the chafing. Felani wears a loin cloth but nothing else. He is quite tall, lanky, ebony, with a handsome but also cheeky face.

'A bunch of rotten black bananas, reckon,' says Kotani, his friend. He is also wearing a loin cloth, and thinner, not quite as tall, cleft lip, ebony. 'How long will they keep us like this, I wonder. The drink is like piss-water and the food like wood. I don't know how they survive on it.'

'Maybe that's why they speak that strange language. All ozh, sozh and mozh.'

'I hope they don't expect us to learn it. It's worse than Arabic.'

'I hate these chains, they grab tenaciously like a hyena. My wrists hurt like mad the whole time.'

'Toothache is less pain! I hope we find out soon what they want us for.'

'We could try a game, to take our mind off that burning sensation.'

'Try me.'

'It's called duck's foot, stone and impala horn. You hold out a flat hand for duck's foot, a fist for stone, and your middle and nose-picking fingers like this for impala horn.' He holds out the two fingers.

'I get that,' says Kotani, flexing his fingers for a moment after pins and needles from the chains, and trying each in turn. 'But then what happens?'

'If I hold out stone, and you hold out impala horn, then I win, as stone bashes impala horn; if I hold stone, and you hold out duck's foot, you win, as the duck's foot covers the stone; and then if I hold out duck's foot, and you hold out impala horn, you win as impala horn pricks through duck's foot. So you have to second guess what the other is doing.'

'Ok, let's give it a try, before we die of boredom. Beady cheeky frog's eye, go!' He holds out impala horn, while Felani holds out duck's foot. 'Hoopla! First one to me, I think.'

'Beginner's bright star at night, my friend. Let's try again.'

They play a while, then Kotani shouts: 'The ship is slowing, perhaps we are stopping here!'

A sailor comes by, rattling keys. Says something in Portuguese as he unlocks their manacles.

A stuttering Tsonga-speaking crew member approaches.

'This is a s-s-s small town, which we b-b-b believe to be called M-M-M Mombasa. We are just s-s-s stopping for f-f-f-fresh water and f-f-f fruit and vegetables. We will s-s-s stock up more in m-m-m Malimbi, which is not far away. You will c-c-c ...'

'Take your time,' says Felani.

'C-come with the chef and m-m me to g-g-g get water and b-b-b bananas. If you try to run away you will be sh-sh-sh shot.'

The anchor is dropped, and they get into a rowing boat. They head for a beach, where there are a few huts under some trees, behind which is the town, which appears to shine a light out to sea in an extraordinary way. Felani and Kotani are carrying a barrel for water.

'Sh-sh-sh shot!' mocks Kotani, with a smile.

Felani frowns at him. At the first hut they reach, Felani speaks to a woman.

'Fresh water?'

She has a word in the ear of a man at the neighbouring hut and he goes off, shortly coming back with two other men, between them carrying some gourds of fresh water and three large bunches of green bananas. The chef pays and Felani and Kotani pour the water into the barrel. They then carry this back to the boat and come back for the bananas.

It is late afternoon when the ships raise anchor and start heading north again, with Malindi now less than a day away.

Malindi

The four ships in the Da Gama First Armada continue up the coast and reach Malindi the next morning.

'We must anchor here,' says Da Gama, 'and I must locate an Indian pilot who knows the route across to the key trading port on the west coast of India.'

'We need some more fresh food for this last leg of the outward journey,' says his brother Paulo. 'We have lost too many to scurvy, and fresh food is the only antidote.'

'Agreed,' says Da Gama, 'it is said we will get a welcome in this port, and no hostility. Do you agree?'

'It is what is said,' replies Paulo. 'They rely heavily on trade with India, Persia and the Arab world, and it is thought that they will welcome a potential new trading partner with open arms.'

'So be it. Ask Franco to keep the two Africans tied up while we are here,' says Da Gama. 'This is an Arabic and Swahili-speaking town. We have two Arabic speakers. We will keep these two for the journey back. I want Simone the stutterer to teach them Portuguese en route, and they can clean decks and scrub dishes to pay for the privilege.'

'Agreed,' says Paulo.

They lower a couple of longboats and climb down.

The sheikh of Malimbi sends out a grander boat with an emissary to greet Vasco Da Gama and his brother and bring the Da Gamas and their entourage to a reception arranged by the Sheikh.

Vasco Da Gama accepts the invitation.

At the reception, Da Gama explains to the Sheikh that he has on his ship a coral pillar, which will be a gift to Malimbi from the King of Portugal, Manuel I.

The Sheikh expresses his gratitude and Da Gama sends orders to his officers to bring the coral pillar ashore. The pillar is later given pride of place on the sea front.

A sea captain, introduced by the Sheikh to Da Gama, explains about the beneficial Monsoon trade winds, that will at the present time take Da Gama's armada across to the main Indian west coast trading port of Calicut at a healthy speed.

Da Gama expresses his gratitude, and asks his scrivener to emphasise this in his report of the voyage, so that the King will be aware that Portugal now has a new route to the spice wealth of India without having to travel across the hostile Ottoman Empire. He stipulates that the report must state that, at the right times of year, especially now, the winds for this last leg to India's west coast will be particularly favourable.

The next day, they return to the ship with an Indian pilot named Sindhu and plenty of fresh provisions, not least oil, water, flour, ships' biscuits, dried pork, fruit, and dried beef, together with gifts from the Sheikh.

Soon they are heading across the Indian Ocean for Calicut, India.

4.

Indian Spice Trade: Insult and Pique

First trip to Calicut

It takes only twenty-seven days to reach the Indian coast, with the powerful Monsoon wind filling the sails.

Vasco Da Gama speaks to Paulo in the captain's cabin: 'Success, my brother. We have achieved the main purpose of this voyage, by locating the sea route to India's west coast'.

'We have, dear brother,' says Paulo. 'However, I hear a 'but' coming.'

'Now we must move on to the King's second purpose – negotiating rights to a Portuguese trading post in Calicut.'

'What presents do we have to offer the chief cock in the hen hutch here?' Paulo asks his servant, who accompanies his master in the cabin.

'We have four cloaks of scarlet cloth, six hats, four branches of coral, a box with seven brass vessels, some sugar, some honey and two barrels of oil.'

'In Europe, this would impress others in most countries, from our King's experience.'

'We are seeing their top man, the Zamorin, tomorrow. We will see then,' says Vasco Da Gama.

As Vasco Da Gama, his brother Paulo and their entourage arrive at the Calicut court, three thousand armed Nairs, or soldiers, are presented to them in full costume, in line with Calicut's customary practice.

When Da Gama offers the gifts from Manuel I, the Zamorin, who refers to himself as the Samudiri, finds it impossible to hide his disdain, and his entourage seek to mask this.

His spokesman asks Da Gama: 'Is there possibly a translation question? Where are the actual gifts from your King to our Zamorin?'

The translator repeats the question in Portuguese.

Da Gama's face and neck go scarlet.

Paulo, seeing this, seeks to defuse the situation, and produces King Manuel's letter to the Zamorin.

As the translator reads the letter to the Zamorin, translated into Hindi, his face brightens.

Da Gama senses progress. He turns the conversation to a Portuguese trading post, but frostiness now returns.

'There will be no Portuguese factor, or trading post,' says the Zamorin. 'This may change if you return with gold and silver, as the Arab nations and Persians bring. This is the currency in Calicut.'

Paulo notices his brother Vasco's ire returning to boiling point, and he seeks to lead him out of the chamber before too much damage is done. But he is not able to act fast enough.

Da Gama screams: 'I will not tolerate this insolence from tinpot popinjays in this puny Court! There will be consequences!' And he storms out of the chamber and orders his soldiers to take five Nairs and fifteen Calicut fishermen by force as prisoners until the Zamorin changes his mind.

When the Zamorin sends his soldiers after Da Gama, the captain orders: 'Stand and fire!' and the Calicut Nairs immediately retreat.

Vasco Da Gama returns to his ship, but returns the next day to the Court. 'I demand an audience with the Zamorin,' he insists. 'I have goods to offer in exchange for fine spices.'

The Zamorin sends his subordinates to negotiate, and Da Gama is able to take a good quantity of spices, mainly pepper and cinnamon, back to the ship, which are exchanged with Portuguese goods of much lower value.

'I must have a trading post in Calicut for the goods we have not exchanged', demands Da Gama.

'His excellency the Zamorin has made it clear that the currency here is gold and silver. If you return with these, we can begin to negotiate,' says the Zamorin's lieutenant.

'Tell the Zamorin that I will return with more ships, cannon, and soldiers, and there will be little remaining of Calicut if he does not compromise with me on the trading post.'

'I will inform his excellency, the Samudiri, or Zamorin as you call him, of what you have said. I must advise you, however, that the Samudiri does not respond to blackmail.'

'He may think differently when I return,' says Da Gama.

'If you propose to depart now,' says the Zamorin's naval adviser, 'you must be mindful of the Monsoon winds. Just as these acted as a flying carpet for you on your journey here, they will act as a magnet attached to our shoreline when you seek to return. You will also encounter violent storms.'

'I think we know the seas,' boasts Da Gama. 'We have navigated around the mighty continent of Africa for the first time in history on our journey here.'

And Da Gama bids his men follow him and they return to the ship and prepare to depart.

The return journey to Malindi takes one hundred and ten days longer than the four week journey to Calicut. Half the crew die, and many more suffer from scurvy.

Somehow, Felani and Korani are still alive, but very ill, when the ships drop anchor at Mogadishu. Here the crew are able to purchase fresh food, and drink fresh water, before heading for Malindi.

Felani feels more himself after Mogadishu. He recites a short poem for Kotani:

'From far away, with their moustache and beard
They think they rule the high seas
They have the ships, they have an arquebus
But they always forget to say please.'

'I like that' says Kotani, 'but keep it to yourself, or we are dead meat.'

'Can I say something before we finish this journey?'

'What's that?'

'You stink to high heaven.'

'Well I can tell you that you stink even worse.'

'But, do you know something? You are the best friend a man could have.'

'And so are you.'

The crew stock up fully in Malindi, although the crew is now much depleted, so less is needed.

After Malindi, Da Gama leaves Felani and Korani at Mozambique Island.

Vasco Da Gama's brother Paulo dies near Cape Verde as they are on the final leg of the return journey to Lisbon. Only two of the four ships, and a small proportion of the men, make it to Lisbon, where Da Gama is feted as a national hero. It is the end of August 1499.

Second Portuguese Armada to India

Large profits were made by King Manuel I on the spices and jewellery brought back by Da Gama, so he was keen to send the Second Armada to India in 1500. Da Gama was still recovering, so a new captain was chosen.

The 1500 trip to Calicut is led by Pedro Alvares Cabral, as captain-major, who is a nobleman and not a naval or military man. He commands thirteen ships, including El Rei, 1500 men (including thirteen captains and one vice Admiral) and is this time laden with valuable gifts and diplomatic letters to win over eastern potentates.

Striking south west from the Azores to avoid the Doldrums, Cabral becomes the first European to find Brazil.

5.

Brazil Discovers Europe

'No, Tiq Taq, no, no no, that beetle is not for you.' And she takes the wriggling black scarab from his grasp.

The baby looks up at his mother, and then looks disappointingly at his curled thick-fingered fist, which is now empty of beetle.

'He is going for a worm,' says sister Janaina

'He can have a worm,' says dad, taller than the others, thin, painted, with yellow, orange and red parrot feathers held by a beaded band at his waist, sticking out over his backside.

'Are we going to up camp and head back for the village?' asks mum Anahi. 'I'm a bit tired now.'

'We could do,' says dad Jaci, 'we have plenty of fish and several guinea pigs, and should be back by nightfall if we head back now.'

'Are the other families coming back?' asks Janaina, whose hair is full of pink and yellow twine, and whose body is walnut brown, covered in red paint. 'I want to go back with Six-toes and Split-tongue. We are intertwining each other's hair with the beautiful twine here.'

'You three are inseparable,' says mum, petite, covered in paint, with just a bead band around her waist. 'Impossible, and inseparable.'

'We're young and happy, are you complaining?'

'No, I am happy you are happy.'

'Can I have some roasted peanuts?'

'You've just had a big meal, what is wrong with you?'

'Just a couple. I am peckish after all that braiding.'

'Go on then. You can pass me one, if you like. Shall we go?'

'I think we will all go back together. There were some big cats trying to get our babies on the way here, and the more of us we have the better we can fend them off,' says dad, responding to mum's question.

The two other families come through the bushes, babies strapped to mums' backs, and smaller children being pulled on a big sheet of bark with twine attached.

'Ooolooooloooolooolooooloooo,' comes a shrill warning from one of the men, Ubijara.

The other adults ask Jaci and Anahi to stay with all the children, and they head off to where Ubijara's call came from. It turns out it is not far from the beach where some of the children had been playing shortly before.

They are all shocked to see the strangest sight: a very large boat in the bay, far bigger than their canoes and as tall as the higher trees. There are men dressed in outlandish outfits, covering most of their oddly coloured blotchy skin, who are approaching in a smaller boat that is now floating on the shallowing waves as they are about to lap the shore.

Only their bearded face and hands seem visible.

The Tupis stand in a group at the back of the beach, puzzled, bemused.

They note that the men have no red stripes across their faces, nothing that may signify their tribe. They wear unfamiliar full-body garments that are not appropriate in the heat and humidity, so that sweat is dripping from the brows of the newcomers like water dripping as beads off leaves after a tropical storm.

The strangers approach slowly, with two of them holding out gifts including Portuguese cloth, a watch, and some necklaces of coral, which they put on the beach in front of the Tupis and leave them.

The Tupis sit down on the edge of the beach and pass the coral necklaces between them.

One woman, Tupilola, looks at her own bead necklace, and the gifted coral necklace, and tries on the coral necklace.

The strangers sit down too. Coelho, the Major-captain, doffs his hat, holds its rim as he draws it behind him in a short arc, and then whips it with a much fuller arc for it to glide in the still air a little way to the side of Ubijara. Coelho points a finger at his own head and points then to Ubijara's head, signalling the throwing action he just used.

Ubijara takes off his headdress, notes all the feathers and the drag they will cause if he throws it, and he walks forward ten paces, half way towards Coelho. He places the headdress on the sand there, before walking back, still facing Coelho.

Coelho walks forward, lifts the headdress to his head, and fixes the band around his crown, with the feathers rising from the band. His crew members cheer, and a beaming smile appears on Coelho's face. His fellow captain, Bartolomeu Dias, nods approvingly.

Coelho beckons Ubijara and the man just behind him, who is Jaci, to follow him to the boat. Coelho mimics supping from a beaker.

Ubijara, Jaci and four of their family get in a huddle.

'We don't know if they want to kill us, or if they wish to talk in a friendly way,' says Jaci. 'What do we do if they kill us?'

'I will send Tupilola to the Tupisisyda tribe past the three rivers, in the direction of the midday sun, and ask them to bring spears and shields and bows and arrows,' says Ubijara.

'If it is only the two of you who go on board their floating thing,' suggests Anahi, 'and the rest of us wait here, most of us hiding behind bushes and near the stream and our boats, then hopefully they cannot do too much harm.'

'If they want to find out a bit about us and the food and water here,' replies Ubijara, 'and if they want to know about our land, they need to talk to us and not murder us.'

'But they could also get the information they want and then murder us.'

'There is a risk. But I agree with Ubijara. Two of us go with them. We prepare to fight if things go bad. For now, we find out what we can about them. We need to know if they bring danger for us, and if so what kind of danger.'

'I agree. Let us do it.'

Coelho again raises up his hand like he is holding a beaker and acts like he is pouring it into his mouth, but now points at the bushes.'

Ubijara holds up his hand, with his eyes signalling recognition. He heads through the bushes and returns with a squash gourd full of water from the nearby stream. He tips some into his mouth, and licks his lips, and passes to Coelho.

Coelho smells it, takes a sip, and then takes a large gulp. He passes it to Bartolomeu Dias, who sups equally enthusiastically. He orders the first mate next to him to take the gourd back to the Tupi to ask for a refill for the crew.

Coelho and Ubijara look at each other with a mixture of curiosity and superstition, but then Coelho nods and smiles. 'I haven't dropped dead on the spot, so it seems OK. Perhaps we can trust these simple people a little bit.'

Ubijara and Jaci move closer to Coelho and his men but stay two to three metres away. They bow. Coelho signals to his men that they are returning on the rowing boats to the ship. He beckons the two Tupis to follow him and Dias. Coelho is still wearing the feathered head-dress.

'It is like a house on water,' says Jaci, as they board.

'But not like any house we have seen,' replies Ubijara. 'They make strange things with wood, and have tall branches and tree trunks to hold a big cloth above us.'

Their eyes pop out at a strange clucking, cackling sound emerging from some cages. They notice some plump birds inside, clawing at the base of the cage and making strange sounds. There are two eggs in one of the cages.

'Only birds, but not like any we have,' comments Ubijara.

'And imprisoned. No bird likes to be prevented from enjoying the freedom of the skies,' replies his friend.

'They don't seem to like our chickens much,' says Coelho to his mate.

They are taken to Coelho's cabin, and sit on the floor akimbo while Coelho sits back in his ornate leather-bound wooden seat. Bartolomeu Dias sits by him on an equally fine seat. Coelho points to the seats behind the two Tupis and encourages them to sit there. They decline.

Dias points to the bright red paint on the chest of each of his guests, and on their faces.

'I like,' he says, and smiles.

Ubijara draws an imaginary tree in the air. He points at the imaginary tree, and then at the red on his face.

'A tree,' surmises Dias. 'We must find out more about this tree that produces red dye.'

Dias offers some honey cake to Ubijara and Jaci. He eats a piece himself and smiles to try to signify it is good. Ubijara breaks off a small piece, looks at it, and places it in his mouth. Jaci follows suit. Suddenly, they are both retching and spitting out what they can.

A little belatedly, Dias offers a spittoon to them.

Bertamoleu Dias picks up a brandy bottle and three small glasses. He pours some for himself and Coelho and takes a sip. He releases a deep sigh of satisfaction.

Ubijara looks at him with curiosity and wonder, and takes the glass offered to him. He smells it and passes it to Jaci, who screws up his nose and passes it straight back. His penis flops out from under his feathers and he encourages it back, for decorum.

'It smells like firewater that has seen too much sun,' he says.

'I sense they want us to lose our senses, and trick us,' says Ubijara, handing the glass back with a brief nod of his head and a smile.

'They don't like our honey cake or our fine brandy,' says Coelho to Dias. 'Hard to please these wild men. Ask the first mate to assemble some more of our beads, as well as iron nails and fine cloth to be offered as gifts. These simple people should appreciate them. Let us take them back to the beach and give them the gifts as a peace offering. We need to find out more about what this land offers before we make enemies of these people.'

'I agree Nicalao.'

'And if you agree, I will ask to have two of our criminals brought from the hold. They can stay with these simple folk and find out more about them. If they learn some of their words, we can converse through this loathsome pair next time we come.'

'You and I are of the same mind.'

The two Tupis are returned to their families by longboat along with the first mate, who takes ashore six other crew carrying the gifts, and two criminals. None are armed.

A further long boat lands further down the shore, with eight crew on board, and with arquebuses unprimed but with eyes alert in case of trouble.

A number of the Tupis come out from the bushes at the side of the beach and greet Ubijara and Jaci. The men have bows raised ready to fire but Ubijara instantly shouts at them to put the spears down. 'They come in peace!' he shouts.

The crew with arquebuses, who had just started to prime them, release the cocks again.

The first mate orders the crew to lay down one of the cloths flat on the beach, and to place the gifts on top. They then draw back and sit down.

Ubijara speaks for a moment to his family and friends, and they all nod sideways to say they agree to examine the gifts.

The women examine the cloth, nails and the new beads. One drapes a fine white cloth around her mostly mother nature body and laughs. Others put beads around their necks.

Soon they are covered with beads and cloths, and giggling, until the Tupi men come and spoil the party, inviting each woman to follow them back to their village. At the first mate's instruction, the two Portuguese criminals, Miguel and Paolo, follow the Tupis, and they head along a path that soon darkens with the denseness of the jungle.

There is suddenly a flutter of red and vermillion feathers and a bird drops to the ground not far from Miguel. A young man with bow in hand approaches, stoops, and retrieves his arrow. He offers the bird to Miguel, putting three fingers and his thumb to his lips to signal eating. Miguel nods, and looks at the bird, whose body is still warm but which has a trickle of blood seeping from its breast. His smile signals to the lad that he is impressed.

They head on a rough path through jungle undergrowth until shortly before nightfall, when they reach a village. All the hammocks here are hung at head height in trees, with branches to reach them, and usually with ample leaf cover in the event of rain, as well as rows of colourful feathers. Further on, the long oval huts holding food are off the ground, on stilts.

'The scent of flowers here is like the most pleasant poems at home,' says Paulo.

'What are you friend, some kind of singer or poet?' asks Miguel.

'I like natural beauty, that is all. I plucked a flower from the pau brasil earlier,' says Miguel, 'this is the scent of this brasil blossom, hung from poles along the path.'

All the people in the village wear nothing, apart from some brightly coloured Macaw or parrot feathers in their hair, and a belt or thong holding more feathers, with similar bright colours that partly shield the backside of the wearer, as with the Tupis who greeted Coelho.

Paulo screams and jumps out of his skin.

A little lad, Minimatu, leaps like a salmon, grabs the black snake by its neck with a forked stick, breaks its head from its body with one swift decisive movement, and throws it down. Paulo is sick for a few moments, then calms down.

Anahi and Jaci encourage the Portuguese men to climb into the hammocks while they put some food out in a hut. A couple more hammocks are slung up for the Tupi families to have enough beds for themselves.

Ubijara, meanwhile, is meeting with elders of the village. He says quietly:

'We have discovered a new people, not another tribe like we are used to, as these ones are far too different, with very strange rags over their blotchy white skin and a boat as big as the trees. Their language is just gobbledegook. I hope it is not bad news. We have brought two of them with us.'

'We will observe them while they are our guests,' says the senior elder, whose feathers are a striking red, like the feathers of the scarlet Ibis. 'I take it they have been brought here to raise our curiosity. We are not looking at collecting up wild garlic, magic mushrooms and fine herbs for a fine feast of their bodies, are we? But we can perhaps offer them simple pieces of cooked armadillo and coconut.'

'If I may be allowed to ignore your jest about the wild garlic soup, I am sure you agree, my elder, that if we look after these guests, we can only hope that they will reciprocate our kindnesses if their masters return.'

'Do you think they will return?'

'I think so. I suspect they will be interested in the tree we call red dye fountain, as they like this red dye as much as we do.'

'Very good, so be it,' says the elder. 'We will be good hosts and add some spice to the roast armadillo.'

'There is also a bird that young Fastarra shot down on the path.'

'Fine, make sure our cooks have the bird to pluck and cook.'

'Will we offer our sisters to these men?' asks Ubijara

'Let us first see how they sleep, how they eat, and how they treat us in the sun's waking hours. We can judge them better when we know them a little better. We will give them monkeys, parrots and amulets for now, to show goodwill.'

'You are wise, elder,' replies Ubijara

He leaves the meeting and invites the travellers to the hut where food is being placed on wild rhubarb leaves. The roast armadillo, with wild chillies added, has a pungent smell, and Miguel and Paolo watch the Tupis eat a few morsels first before tucking in themselves. A girl brings the roasted bird to Miguel, who is impressed.

They each cough at first, with the spiciness of the food, but soon they are enjoying it, and licking their lips. As they eat, Miguel has a word in Paolo's ear: 'I will stay awake for four hours, and you take the next four hours. We need to keep watch so that we don't find that we have had our throats slit in the morning.'

'Agreed,' whispers Paolo.

With daylight now mostly absent, the two Portuguese are suddenly aware of tiny lights that brighten the air all around the village. The numerous lights flicker, move around, die and return, almost by magic.

Ubijara catches one of the lights between his hands and shows it to Paolo and Miguel. It is a tiny fly, with its body becoming lit, and then dying out, alternately. A firefly.

Their meal now over, Ubijara signals sleep with his hands, and takes them back to their hammocks.

Miguel is just settling down to the night-time noise of owls and fruit bats when he hears slapping of thighs and laughter. The next thing, he sees the glint of Paulo's eyes in the moonlight.

'Stop there, Paulo!' he calls, and leaps down from his hammock.

'They are laughing at me!' moans Paulo, half in tears. 'Mocking me as a weak man. I have to defend my honour.'

'Keep a cool head, Paulo. Desist, I say, desist.'

'I agree,' says Paulo, and heads back towards his hammock.

'Besides,' says Miguel, with a big smile, 'it was very very funny when you jumped out of your skin.'

'I don't know,' says Paulo, heading back up to his hammock. 'It was funny but .... Aaagggh!'

And he jumps down in a flash and looks round at the ghoulish, moonlit, laughing faces of the Tupis, and laughs too when he realises it is the same dead black snake now dangling where his head would lie in his hammock.

'Mad, these people,' he says, 'but they have a sense of humour.'

They both now settle down in their surprisingly comfortable hammocks.

The next day

Most of the Tupi village return to the beach the next morning. They are carrying Tupi amulets, spears, and trussed-up live parrots and monkeys, which they place in the spot where the beads, cloth and nails were placed the day before.

A few of the Portuguese crew, who were twiddling their thumbs after having rowed ashore a short while before, walk towards the gifts and examine with interest the trussed-up monkeys and parrots. They then carry them to their boat.

As a second rowing boat is then swept on to the beach by a substantial wave, the Tupis are confronted by another wholly novel site.

Climbing out is a man dressed in a dark grey hooded cassock, with a gold cross hanging from his neck. The hood covers his head, and his long grey beard reaches the size of two fists from his chin.

What they don't know at this time is that this is a Franciscan friar, Henrique Soares of Coimbra, holding possibly the first Catholic mass on American soil.

Fifty of the crew come ashore, including Coelho (but not Dias), and they enthusiastically join in the mass, with around two hundred Tupis, with their feather headdress and tail, observing them a little higher up the beach. Their eyes suggest utter bewilderment, while their uncovered genitalia betray a lack of empathy with the proceedings.

After the mass, Coelho, accompanied by his pilot, beckons Ubijara to approach him. He points to the red on the Tupi man's face, his chest and his legs. He holds out his hands and raises his eyebrows, with furrowed brow, to signal a question.

Ubijara talks to his friends, as they head through the bushes where the children are, with Anahi and Jaci.

He then stops and turns to Coelho. He points to the red on his face, chest and legs and points to a large tree ahead of them on the path. 'Ibiraputanga,' he says.

Coelho's wood-expert pilot says, 'That's the pau brasil tree, I swear on my mother's life, pau brasil.'

Coelho thanks the pilot and shouts to his men a short distance away: 'King Manuel will want this red dye, a very special red dye, appropriate only for nobility. We must take some of this pau brasil tree back with us and send a full report about this island to his majesty.'

Coelho, Dias and their crew stay one further day. On the last day, Coelho orders his men to cut down several branches of the pau brasil tree to take with them to the supply ship and return them to Portugal, while he heads around Africa.

They leave with the sense that the initial contact with the Tupis has been broadly friendly.

The two criminals, or desesperados, remain with the Tupis.

Coelho says to Dias: 'God willing, his majesty our King will ask us to return here within two years and we can then learn more about the Tupi lifestyle from the two criminals we have left here, if they can stay alive.'

'I will ask his Majesty for an audience and make a specific request. I think Portugal has much to gain here. I will also ask that we map the coastline and discover how large this land is.'

'I think we can have too much power for the simple folk here, once we have learnt enough about their land from them.'

'Spears and bows and arrows are no match for our arquebuses, certainly. And I would wager their villages are simple, with no fortresses to overcome.'

One of Coelho's ships, the supply ship, heads directly back to Lisbon under the direction of the supply ship captain. It carries the news of a land previously not known in Europe, and the pau brasil wood containing a special red dye, with samples.

Coelho and Dias continue their journey to the Cape of Good Hope, belatedly re-joining the armada led by Cabral.

There are now eleven ships in the armada.

Soon they are heading to the west of the Cape of Good Hope.

Four ships are lost at sea in a serious storm after Cape of Good Hope, including Bartolomeu Dias' ship. Dias dies in this catastrophe. The armada is now reduced to seven ships.

Kilwa

'Ali, the hole in the thatch on that side doesn't work for me. The wind comes blasting through and blows everything over. I'm forever clearing up the mess.'

'We wanted to have the hole there for a view of the coastline to the south.'

'Well, we were a bit naïve last year, when we built the hut. We didn't know how fierce the wind can be, like a wolf, creeping up stealthily and then aggressively charging.'

'You exaggerate, Wali, but I will block it up later today, and open a hole on the other side. How is that?'

'Thank you, Ali. This will make my daily tasks so much lighter.'

'I need to go to town. The Sultan wants us to clear the road to his palace, as a couple of trees have come down and there are branches, twigs and leaves all over the place.'

'I will wake Sadhu and Kade. The sun has yellowed and is at eyeline now. Here, take a slice of melon with you. Put the peel in your mouth like this to make a smile for your friends.' And she puts a slice with ends upturned across her mouth. 'You can't go off with that scowl.'

He grabs the melon and laughs.

Sadhu and Kade come through.

'What are those huge things out the window?' asks Kade.

'Ghost ships to take us away,' says Sadhu.

Wali looks out to sea and is a bit confused. These are different from the ships she knows. She wonders what their arrival can mean. Then she blocks it from her mind.

She places a coconut on the low table where the children sit munching on melon.

'Sadhu, Kade, this coconut means everything to us. Do you know why?'

'Because it gives us milk to drink?' asks Sadhu.

'Because of its lovely flesh?' asks Kade.

'In part,' says Wali. 'But also, the timbers of this house are made with the coconut tree's trunk; the thatch is made from its leaves, dried out; our baskets are woven with twisted coir from the husk; and the boats that take us to the mainland are made with coconut planks, with the coir used to bind the planks together. Kilwa is a major international trading centre, the largest in this part of Africa. Many of its houses are built with coconut wood. There are so many ways in which the coconut is a blessing.'

Sadhu and Kade gaze at the coconut in wonder.

The boat drops anchor a short way from Kilwa island. Cabral comes ashore with his captain, pilot and three others, one an Arabic speaker. The pilot bears gifts of Portuguese cloth and leather.

Cabral notes with surprise that the centre of Kilwa has fine merchant houses, usually four or five stories high, on either side of the main street. There are ornate wooden doorways, and intricate patterns on the walls on either side of the doors.

Cabral approaches a soldier outside the Sultan's palace, explains that he is the emissary of the King of Portugal, bearing gifts, and wishes to discuss a treaty. The soldier has short black hair, a roman nose and a neat white uniform. He shows Cabral inside the ornate entrance to the palace, with concertinaed red velvet curtains by carved coral pillars

An hour later, Cabral and his entourage emerge with a vizier of the Sultan. Cabral's face is a shock of red. He shouts at the vizier: 'You may spurn King Manuel's offer of friendship and trade now, but you will face the full might of Portugal's wrath later, mark my words.' The interpreter translates.

They return to the ship, and the armada heads north.

Cabral then starts up the east coast of Africa with his reduced fleet. After a stopover at Malindi and collecting an Indian pilot who knows how to cross to Kerala in India, as well as collecting vital supplies, Cabral heads for Calicut.

The visit to Calicut starts more propitiously than Da Gama's, as the gifts from King Manuel I are considered far more appropriate by the Zamorin.

Cabral returns the four Nair hostages taken by Da Gama, and there is an agreed swap of new hostages until negotiations are concluded.

The Zamorin agrees a trading post and a related commercial treaty. Seventy men will be allowed to run the trading post. The new hostages are then released by Cabral, and the process of Portugal's purchase of large quantities of spices commences.

After sufficient spices to fill two ships have been bought, the supply seems to the Portuguese to dry up.

Cabral is convinced Muslim traders, with centuries of trading here behind them, are blocking sales to Portugal. Cabral, like da Gama, is also deeply anti-Muslim.

When the Zamorin refuses to intervene in Cabral's issue with the Muslim traders, seeing it as a purely trading matter, Cabral decides to seize an Arab merchant ship from Jeddah, which is loading up with spices. Cabral claims all the spices from this merchant ship for himself.

The Arab merchants see this as theft, and set the mob on the Portuguese trading post, killing between fifty-three and sixty-five of the Portuguese there.

A few Portuguese manage to jump in the water and swim to the Portuguese ship, where they tell Cabral that the Zamorin's guard stood by and watched as the mob slaughtered the Portuguese traders.

In retaliation, Cabral seizes ten Arab merchant ships in the harbour, taking their cargo, killing the crews and burning the ships. Cabral then orders a day-long bombardment of Calicut, as he blames the Zamorin (with scant evidence) for allowing the massacre to happen.

The city is a trading city, with few fortifications, and is seriously damaged. Around six hundred are thought to have died as a direct consequence of the actions by the Portuguese.

By these actions, a decade-long war between Portugal and Calicut is set underway.

Cabral promptly heads down the coast for Cochin.

The prince of Cochin considers that Calicut has long dominated trade on this stretch of coast and held Cochin back. He sees Cabral's enmity with Calicut as convenient for Cochin and agrees a treaty. The spice market in Cochin is quite small, but the Portuguese start loading up in line with the deal struck.

Nearby Cranganor has a similar gripe with Calicut and offers their ample pepper supplies. Cabral is therefore able to strike another deal.

He also meets Syrian Christians there, and two travel back with him to Portugal.

The Third Armada has a ship battle with the Zamorin's fleet from Calicut, in which the Calicut ships are mostly destroyed. This makes Portugal's relationship with Calicut even more strained. Important and precious naval instruments of the Zamorin are also destroyed.

On the way back, the armada resorts to piracy to steal goods from Arab merchant ships, to ensure the ships are more fully laden for King Manuel I.

Only six ships of the original thirteen return to Lisbon, many months later.

It is a bedraggled collection of ships from the Third Armada that arrives back in Lisbon, and the ships are not as full of spices as the King wishes.

Cabral is congratulated for finding Brazil, but criticised for making things difficult for Portugal in Calicut. He is also in the doghouse with the Court in Lisbon as he failed to locate the gold trading post of Sofala along the African coast from Kiilwa.

1502 trip to Calicut

When Vasco Da Gama is put in control of the Fourth Portuguese Armada in 1502, King Manuel I specifically instructs him to bring Calicut to heel, so that Portugal will be the dominant power in this key trading port on India's spice-laden west coast, regardless of the centuries of trading between Arabs, Persians and India on this spice coast.

The original instruction of Manuel I in 1488 was for the Portuguese armada to gain a monopoly over the international spice trade and to kill Muslims wherever they were found. This remained the policy.

Now, Manuel I instructs Da Gama to ensure that all Arab merchants are expelled from the Indian coast, and that the trade out of Aden is disrupted, by intimidation and the cutting of trade. The King's end goal remains Portuguese control of trade in the Indian Ocean.

With this in mind, the armada is the biggest to date, with twenty ships, and one thousand to one thousand eight hundred men.

Rounding the Cape of Good Hope, Da Gama says to his uncle Vicente, who accompanies him on the Fourth Armada: 'The musulman is a pustule on the face of the planet, the rotting gangrened limb of an animal that needs to be severed.'

'We are in agreement there,' says his uncle Vincente. 'No doubt we will have the chance to bloody plenty of noses on this trip. Are we any nearer finding a resting place after all those tree high waves around the Cape of Good Hope?'

'The pilot says a bay is not far away. We will rest there a while, and check the damage on the ships.'

'Where will we wait for the two that suffered damage?'

'Mozambique Island, further up the coast, is the plan'

There is a familiar cry, 'Land ahoy,' and as they draw nearer the coast, they drop anchor.

South Africa, Mossels Bay

'I'm parched,' says Akasu.

'I've put fresh water in the hidden waterhole as usual,' says his wife Tsawe Tika.

Akasu lifts an ostrich feather and uses his gourd to take water from the hole. He then replaces the ostrich feather as it keeps the water slightly cooler than the warm air of the day.

The children are quiet for once, playing with some round pebbles they have found. Each has a few pebbles and tries to roll one against the other's pebble a few feet away, trying to strike it.

They look out at the ocean, which is quieter than usual today. A whale a little way out spouts water, and another follows shortly after, as though they are synchronising. The first whale then rises up, and dives, heading away from the coast.

'That whale was nearly caught by the reef just then,' says Tsawe Tika. 'It has been a while since our last whale, we need to maintain our vigil here, so that we can spear any that get beached.'

'We can go hunting soon, to keep us going until the next whale.'

'We have our sea lion from yesterday for now. This will do us for a number of days. It's been fully roasted now, so we can feast on it later.'

'What is that huge boat?'

'A boat? Here?'

'Look, just heading towards the bay over there, with a broken pole.'

'I see it now, the storm must have damaged their boat. You are right, it is huge.'

'Very odd creatures on board, all hair and big beards, and the most outlandish things on their bodies.'

'Do you think they are human?'

'They move like humans, but they are nothing like us.'

'Let us move the children to join the other children away from the beach and keep out of the way while these strangers land.'

'I think that is wise.' And they move back towards the back of the beach, joining with the rest of their group, with the children now all playing together, in a form of tag.

Some men climb into three longboats and row to shore. There seem to be about sixteen to eighteen of them.

Akasu says, 'I am worried for our waterhole. These strangers will not know that we guard fresh water like our lives.'

'Let us wait and see what they do,' says Tsawe Tika, 'they are almost on the beach now.'

The Portuguese in the longboats land, with Vasco da Gama at the fore, leading the rest on to the land. They cast around.

'Good bay for resting after the Cape of Good Hope,' says Da Gama.

'Aye Cap'n. Cracking good. We could rest here a while, what do you think?'

'What's this ostrich feather here?' asks the chef, lifting it up.

'Could be a ready-made piss hole,' says the pilot, pulling out his penis.

Akasu bristles at the sight of the man threatening to piss in the tribe's precious waterhole. He starts to make a move towards the Portuguese, but the others hold him back.

'Sir,' says one of the crew, as the pilot pisses into the water, 'there's natives yonder, at the edge of the beach, behind the rocks.'

The Khoikhoi people all come forward, many with bows and arrows in hand, in case they are needed.

Akasu is especially incensed about his water and fires an arrow at the one they call Cap'n, who has the biggest beard.

The arrow hits Da Gama in the leg.

Other Khoikhoi fire arrows too, two or three of them hitting other crew members from the ship.

Da Gama swears against his God and his God's son. He splutters and spits. He orders his men to fire, but they tell him that the guns don't work after being caught in the violent storm.

The Khoikhoi people approach, pointing at the waterhole, and miming as though drinking from a gourd.

Da Gama tells his men to get straight back into their boats and get back to the ship pronto. Only one gun works, and the pilot fires this, to keep the Khoikhoi at bay while they get in their boats.

His pilot shouts, 'We seem to have soiled their waterhole and made them mad.'

Da Gama, already limping, screams, 'Sod them all, the animals. There is poison in that damned arrow! Shout to the ship's doctor to be ready for when we get back on the ship. I'm seriously buggered here.'

The Khoikhoi huddle together.

'Mad people,' says Tsawe Tika

'They will be back,' says the tribal chief, Gulunguri. 'They will come back and seek revenge.'

'They pissed in our water, like they have no civilised manners.'

'They are bad people, but that makes them more dangerous,' says Gulunguri.

'They should only come back when they have learnt how to act like good people,' says Akasu.

'We arrived here with the sands, with the winds, with the great elephants and rhinoceri, at the beginning of time,' says the sire Tsokoi. 'This is our land. The Bantu came to our land, they wanted to share our land with us, and after much strife we found a way to share this great land with the Bantu.

'This land will always be the land that we and the Bantu call our land. But the big ship and its strange inhabitants are a warning. Others may now seek to come to explore here, and they have boats such as we have never seen before that can carry them here.

'The time when the Khoikhoi and the Bantu could say this is our land may soon see the sun start to set. We must prepare ourselves in two ways. We must be sure of where we will retreat to and enjoy our lives the way we have always lived them, if we find a retreat is the sure way to survival.

'And we must prepare to fight these interlopers, who do not feel or see or know or love or caress or understand or romanticise our land.

'One day there will be a great reckoning. Those who do not know how to treasure the beauty of land will conspire to destroy everything that is good. When this great reckoning occurs, only those, like the Khoisan, who truly love and truly know and truly feel the land will offer a way to survive into the future.'

A wounded Da Gama heads for East Africa, where he hopes the fleet will come back together.

He reaches Kilwa, described by the 14th century explorer ibn Battuta as a well-planned city, with the fine ornate palace of Husuni Kubwa, and the great Mosque of Kilwa made of coral stones. There are fine boulevards, and a view of the sea from all directions. There are five storey merchant houses. Those with less wealth live in houses of wood with dried reeds for the roof.

The Sultan is by reputation humble and highly religious, and his authority stretches to Malindi in the north and to Inhambane in the south.

At Kilwa, Da Gama has two objectives: first to bully Kilwa into paying a tribute to Portugal for protection, and secondly to obtain some supplies.

The Sultan Emir Ibrahim contacts Da Gama through an emissary, who apologises on his behalf for not being able to agree a treaty of peace, friendship and trade with Cabral, and offers to talk to Da Gama.

Da Gama invites the Sultan Emir to his ship in light of his badly injured leg, and explains that the terms of a peace treaty are now much more severe, with a substantial tribute to be paid by Kilwa to Portugal for the benefit of not being bombed by Portugal.

The Sultan – who had only come to the ship after guarantees were given of his safety – objects, until Da Gama explains that the town will be obliterated by cannon fire if the Sultan refuses, and no buildings will be left standing.

A treaty is signed, with the help of the interpreter.

The Sultan delays paying the tribute until Da Gama is desperate to move on, and the Sultan finally pays a reduced sum, plus a good supply of provisions for the next stage of the voyage, including millet, rice, poultry and beef.

Da Gama grudgingly accepts the reduced sum, and they move on.

Mozambique Island

At Mozambique Island, Da Gama plans to drop anchor for a few days so that most of the ships damaged by the storms at the Cape of Good Hope can catch up, as well as one or two other stragglers. A report comes that one of the ships had to be scuttled at the Cape as it was beyond repair. Da Gama orders some of the crew to cut down some timber and build a replacement ship while they are waiting on the island.

Da Gama sends out two of his crew to locate Felani and Korani and bring them to the ship. He takes the view that their knowledge of Portuguese will make them even more useful in Malindi, and also knows that they will carry out any task set them when instructed.

He then heads for Sofala, the legendary main port, alongside Mombasa, for trading much of the gold that came through the city of Zimbabwe for many centuries. Da Gama is able to establish a treaty at Sofala, and through this is able to arrange for a trading post to be set up there, with a Portuguese trader, or factor, permanently based there.

Once the delayed ships arrive, he prepares for the armada to move north to Mombasa and Malindi, but he is determined to send a parting shot to Mozambique Island, for not cooperating with the Portuguese on the previous visit, with a blast of cannon fire.

Nawal and Mahmud on Mozambique Island

Nawal is inconsolable. Her son Mahmud's face is barely recognisable, with its whole left side gouged out. His left arm is missing, and his intestines are visible where his tummy should be. He lies lifeless, his friend Ahmed next to him.

Nawal herself has specks of blood on her face, from stones that flew at her when the Sultan's palace was hit. She is aching with pain, but for now can only think of the loss of her son. She had only come to visit, having moved out of town. Next to her, Ahmed's mother Sohail is ululating by her dead son, who has also had parts of his body blown out by the blast of a cannon ball.

The whole market square is in chaos. The ululating of many of the women creates waves of sound that reverberate movingly around the square.

The Sultan moves amongst the women, offering his condolences, with the sign of prayer. The mullah calls for a special service at four in the afternoon.

The whole town mourns.

* * * * *

In the African village, Mai finds herself again distressed at the disappearance of Felani. She knows that she coped somehow last time, with her children helping, but it was nearly three seasons last time, and she fears the same again.

She then hears that Aneni's former neighbour's son has died in the bombardment of the town, and she breaks down in tears.

Niambi walks up to her. Puts her tiny arms around her head. Mai put her arms around Niambi.

Da Gama leaves Mozambique Island, and the Fourth Armada makes good time to Malindi, where his first mate locates a new Indian pilot for crossing the Indian Ocean.

In discussion with the Sultan of Malindi, Da Gama establishes that Malindi dislikes the dominance over East African trade that Kilwa has enjoyed for centuries, and so Malindi would join in an alliance against Kilwa.

Da Gama makes a mental note to discuss practicalities with the Sultan when he returns to Malindi after visiting India.

With the monsoon wind favourable, and having fully stocked up, the armada heads across to Calicut.

6.

Miri

Da Gama confronts the Zamorin on arrival in Calicut, demanding reparations for the treatment of Cabral's armada and negotiations to establish a treaty between Calicut and Portugal. The Zamorin refuses.

Da Gama, who in any event was on a mission from the first order by King Manuel I in 1498 to destroy Muslims where they can be found, decides to take out his anger on an Arab merchant ship taking three hundred pilgrims, men, women and children, to Mecca.

The merchant ship is named the Miri, and it is just heading out of Calicut harbour to head for Arabia.

Da Gama decides that the Miri is to pay for his anger, and no other reason is given for his actions. He orders his ship to confront the Miri, and his pilot steers it round and arranges for the cannons to be aimed at the merchant ship.

The captain of the Miri surrenders.

Da Gama has his men board the Miri and take all its cargo, including all valuables. He then orders the men, women and children to be frog-marched into the now empty hold and locked in there. He orders the use of artillery, and flaming arrows, and the ship is set alight, and slowly begins to break up and sink under the constant firing of the artillery. All of the three hundred people die in horrific circumstances. Some of them, mainly young boys, escape from the hold into the water. They are speared by Portuguese guards as they reach the water's surface.

Felani is mopping a lower deck. He comes on to the top deck and sees The Miri sinking and the people being speared.

He notices the scrivener Thome Lopes, who has only recently joined the ship, scribbling away in his journal, with tears dropping from his eyes on to the paper. He stays there a moment, observing, curious, and Lopes becomes aware of his presence.

'It was a scene out of Hell,' says Lopes.

'What have you seen?' asks Felani.

'The merchant ship, the Miri, I will never forget it for the rest of my days. A massacre.'

'A massacre of whom?' asks Felani.

'A few hundred Muslim pilgrims, including children, and their mothers. Da Gama acted with great cruelty and without any mercy whatsoever.'

'Why would he do such a thing. Did the Portuguese men offer first their souls to the seagulls, leaving them barren of any normal feelings of the soul as they tortured and killed so many?' asks Felani.

'Well may you think that. I reach into my soul and I cannot find an answer,' says Lopes.

'You, at least, seem a good man,' says Felani. 'I was starting to wonder if I had entered the gates of Hell in coming here.'

Felani, in a state of shock, mops the floor around him unthinkingly, and then slowly moves out of the cabin.

The Zamorin is still more antagonised by Da Gama's latest actions, noting that da Gama has killed several times more Muslims than the Portuguese who were killed by rioters the previous year.

He makes some concessions regarding a treaty with Portugal and a trading post, but insists that Calicut is a free port and has been for centuries and he will not ban the Arab merchants from the port as Da Gama demanded.

Da Gama thinks that force will make the Zamorin change his mind and soon arranges for Calicut to be bombarded with cannon fire for two nights, mainly destroying the homes of poor people who work in the port. He also takes fifty local fishermen hostage.

Da Gama tells the Zamorin that he will only accept full agreement to his King's proposals, and now also demands that the Zamorin pay for the cost of his bullets and his cannon balls.

Da Gama heads for Cochin, where he is able to sign a treaty with the town. While there, the Zamorin plans an ambush when Da Gama returns, the Zamorin now using a private Arab ship to add more firepower.

Da Gama's ships are still too powerful for the Zamorin's fleet, and he then returns to Calicut and orders a further bombardment of the city, causing devastating damage.

The Zamorin still refuses to give in to Da Gama, stating that force will never influence his mind, given the centuries-long tradition of the free port.

Da Gama has the fifty fishermen killed, and their hands and feet cut off. He despatches them, and their body parts, to the Zamorin, suggesting that the severed hands and feet are used for curry.

He then leaves his uncles, the Sodre brothers, to patrol the port and keep Arab ships from trading there, and concentrates on consolidating Portugal's position with smaller ports along the Kerala coast, including Cochin.

When they depart the Kerala coast with the Sodre brothers, Da Gama is clear in his mind that the Zamorin has the wisdom to secure outside support, not only from Arab privateers, but also Venetian gun specialists. He realises that Portugal's superior might will not be sufficient to win over Calicut to the King's demands, given the distance its forces need to travel. He envisages Portugal's focus being Cochin and Goa in future.

After Da Gama's departure, the Zamorin destroys the town of Cochin to punish it for supporting the Portuguese against Calicut.

Vincent Sofre and the Islands

As the armada approaches the Gulf of Aden, Da Gama has a word with his uncles Vincent Sofre and Bras Sofre.

'You will recall that the King wanted to give you free rein in the Gulf of Aden on our return, to block Arab trade at source when it wishes to use the Indian Ocean. My task was to have the Arab merchants booted out of the main Indian cities on the East Coast. We didn't quite accomplish my task. I am hoping to report back to our King that we achieved your part of his orders.'

'I get the King's gist, Vasco,' says Vincent. 'We will patrol the waters in the area of the Indian Ocean closest to the Gulf of Aden and Saudi Arabia, and we will wreak havoc with the Arab merchant ships.'

'Like pirates,' says his brother. 'Like pirates for the sake of good.'

'Pirates for good or bad, we will destroy the Arab trade at this top end and grab all their merchandise for us.'

'For Portugal,' corrects Da Gama.

'Of course, for Portugal.'

'The next armada will come in about six months, and you could link up with it at Mogadishu then.'

'That's a deal, nephew,' says Vincent.

And they part.

The Sofres terrorise merchant shipping heading out of the Gulf of Aden, often from Jeddah, for the next few months. They attack and destroy every Arab merchant ship that they see, using their extra speed and mobility and their more powerful cannons.

They take a large proportion of the merchandise for themselves personally, alienating their own crews and captains in the process.

Once the merchant ships have been stripped of merchandise the Sofres have them burnt, with the crew still on board. The crew are left with the choice of swimming tens of miles without knowing where the nearest land is or being burned to death.

A mutiny follows, with their captains at the forefront, and the Sofre brothers end up anchoring by an island just off Oman. Their attacks are put on hold.

The Sofre brothers become caught up in an unusually violent storm while they are stationary, and their ships are destroyed. They both die, along with much of their crew.

The Arab trade in the Indian Ocean is affected for some time by Portugal's reign of terror.

Felani and Mai

When Felani and Kotani are dropped back at Mozambique Island, they walk with weary faces back to their homes.

Many angry islanders come out on to the beach and protest at the attack launched at the end of the previous visit. The town is still reeling.

Felani heads up to the township to comfort Mai and his children and show that he is back and still in one piece.

They first celebrate his homecoming, but when Felani hears about those who were killed by the previous Portuguese attack, he is deeply saddened for a while. Felani then spends some time with his children, holding them tight. He is pleased that they don't press him for details of his journey.

When the children are settled and in bed, Felani goes out to the veranda, where palm fronds provide cover, so they can enjoy the evening air to the full. He explains to Mai what he saw on his last trip, and above all the attack on the Miri.

'These Portuguese are bad people, as though crows flew down and took their hearts and put in their place the black feathers of the crow,' he says. 'They have already caused much damage here and forced a treaty on this island. I see only further bloodshed if we stay around here.'

'I am glad you are thinking this way,' says Mai. 'There is much talk of the danger of staying at Mozambique Island. I am thinking we could head further inland. The Portuguese seem to focus on the coast. If we head back towards the area south of Zimbabwe city, where many of our friends went, we may find that safer.'

'Maybe, although I would prefer Mombasa. I am not hopeful of finding work south of Zimbabwe. In Mombasa, which has been attacked, there is known to be plenty of work repairing the façades of historic buildings in the centre of town. If we live a little inland from the town, we will be less vulnerable if the Portuguese decide to release their heartless aggression on the town, ignorant as they are of its beauty.'

'Well, as long as we are a good way inland. I know you have spent a lot of time with those Odj, Bodj, Sodj speakers, and you don't trust them either, but I don't ever want to have anything to do with them again, if I can help it.'

'I hear you, Mai, and I'm with you. I just want to work on old buildings, and repair the coral-based lime carvings, where they have been damaged. Mombasa has plenty of these carvings, more than here, and I can earn well. If a ship appears on the horizon, I will leave town sharpish and come to you. There is no way I want to travel again with the black-hearted pink skins.'

'That sounds a plan, for now,' says Mai. 'Let's tell the children.'

'Sure, and I'll tell Kotani, and see if he and his family will come with.'

'And I will tell Aneni. I suspect her family will want to come with us too.'

Moving to Mombasa

A moon later, the two families move to a compound inland from Mombasa. Kotani joins them also.

They settle in quickly. It is like their previous compound, with rose-pink mud and straw packed hard for the walls of each hut, and timber slanting to form a conical roof with dried grass to keep out rain. There is straw on the floor where they sleep. Each hut holds four to eight depending on the number of children. Four huts form a semi-circle, and there is a straw and mud wall nearly two metres high around the compound, with a gap of about three metres for entrance and exit. The earth in-between the huts has the same rose-pink colour and is packed down.

Felani and Kotani set off to find work. They soon find they are much in demand, as many historic buildings remain badly damaged from bombardments by Portugal.

Felani and Kotani

'Remember that game we played on the ships before they gave us all that shit-cleaning work?' Felani is finalising repairs to the coral dust lime lattice work on a merchant's house.

'You mean the stone, gazelle horn and leaf? Yea, that was fun.'

'Real fun.' And he returns to carefully teasing away a blemish on an earlobe with his fine chisel to improve the ears on a lime-sculpted giraffe.

'We had some mad times on those ships. Remember sword-fighting with mops?'

'And we sure got whipped for that.'

'And stinking swill thrown over us. Shit. They sure could punish!'

'They punish everyone except themselves.'

'Yea, Muslims.'

'Hindus.'

'Jews.'

'Us.'

'They don't discriminate, they just hate them all.'

'But you know I can't get this town at all,' says Felani.

'We can't get caught up in their troubles. We just need food on the table, brother.'

'But, that business up north, with this town taking troops to Malindi, and giving the people there a right beating. They are just inviting those black-hearted big moustachioed guys with their big ships to come and hurt Mombasa.'

'Well, the bearded guys have killed much of the business in Mombasa, so I guess they needed to fight back.'

'Next time we see those big ships, we need to head home fast as cheetahs. Can't face that cannon fire.'

'Well, I'm not sure about you, dear friend, but I can't face doing that ship journey to India again either.'

'Ship journey to evil, massacre of innocents. I agree, no more of that, no never.'

'Family, and chisel work, and friends, that's the life for me from now. I also want to try my hand at poetry.'

'Well, get your head out of the clouds and concentrate on your chiselling – you've just chopped off its ears.'

'You are precious about this work, old friend, but I confess that you are quite right to be.'

'It's beautiful to me, the artistry in the coral lime. The sea creatures form the coral over a timeless time; we collect and dry the coral, and grind it to dust, mix it with water, to coat these fine houses.'

'And the whole pieces of living coral? What about them?'

'Of course, porites, as builders call it, or chunks of living coral, are used a great deal for window decorations, niches, doorways. They are also very malleable for artists to work on. Either way, this coral lime is still millions of sea creatures in a different form, that dance to the tune of our fine chisels, and we create creatures of the land, and creatures of the imagination, and these cover the houses and come to life and perform to the people who pass by, stimulating their imagination.'

'You sure talk some stuff, friend. I will pay more attention.'

Seventh Armada, Tristao da Cunha

When Portugal does not have an armada present in the Indian Ocean, it experiences setbacks.

Its main ally on the East Coast of Africa, Malindi, was attacked by troops from Mombasa in 1503, and Lisbon becomes concerned that it will soon lose control of the gold-trading ports of Sofala and Kilwa.

In India, Calicut is able to bring in Arab allies, and seeks to reassert its position as the main trading port on India's west coast.

King Manuel I remains determined to reassert Portugal's power, and in 1505 sends twenty-one ships, holding one thousand five hundred soldiers and one thousand crew as the Seventh Armada, under Francisco de Almeida, to the Indian Ocean.

The King's orders are, on the one hand, to secure the dominance of the Portuguese navy over the Indian Ocean by establishing fortresses at key points, including Sofala and Kilwa on the African coast, and Anjediva and Cannenore in India. And on the other hand, to reduce (i.e. destroy) those cities and towns seen to be a threat to this dominance.

Almeida has received word that Mombasa has attacked Malindi, and he also hears that there has been a coup d'etat in

Sofala, with a new Emir usurping power who is not interested in supporting Portugal. As his armada starts heading up the east coast of Africa after rounding the Cape of Good Hope, he has two main tasks: to restore the fortress , the trading post and a pro-Portuguese ruler to Sofala; and to punish Mombasa.

He sends the captain Pero de Anaia to Sofala, with clear instructions. Sofala is bombarded until the town surrenders. The Emir flees inland, the Portuguese force moves in, and Portuguese troops set to work creating a fortress and a garrison for five hundred Portuguese soldiers.

Almeida, for his part, heads to Mombasa.

The lime-coating of Mombasa houses reflects the sun, and as ships approach from the sea, the whole city shines brightly as though to welcome those arriving.

In 1505, it is the cannon-filled ships commanded by Admiral de Almeida that are approaching, and the brightness of the town in the sunlight acts more as a magnet.

There is an attempt by many in Mombasa to flee as the ship masts are seen on the horizon, as the populace is generally aware of the dire consequences for them of Mombasa having attacked Malindi.

Amongst the most fleet of foot getting off the island and up the hillside from the shoreline are Felani and Kotani.

Aneni, for her part, remains in the town where she is working as a maid, and is not made aware of the ships arriving.

Mombasa has prepared to some extent for the Portuguese attack. They have a few cannons removed with gratitude from shipwrecked Portuguese ships, and they have brought in five hundred Bantu archers.

The firing of the Mombasa cannons is not wholly successful, as the cannonballs do not reach the Portuguese ships. The archers appear merely as Lilliputians to the armada Gulliver, as the arrows fall into the sea. But the attack is at least slightly delayed by these Mombasa defences, and this gives more time for residents to flee.

However, many thousands of people are unable to get boats off the island in time.

The Portuguese bombardment soon commences. Felani feels every blast of cannon as a personal attack on his fine artistic work on historic buildings. Kotani feels every blast of cannon as an attack on the people there, and imagines severed limbs lying bleeding in the gutters, and corpses at every corner.

The town is barely recognisable when the bombardment is finished. Even the hospital is damaged. Almeida's soldiers then sack the town, taking some of the much-prized Chinese ceramic work from merchants' houses, and most of the specialist cloth, silk, ivory and well-crafted furniture. But they do not appreciate the Islamic tapestries and leave these.

Almeida's men capture seventy to eighty women from Mombasa, for the crew to treat as sex slaves.

Almeida leaves the surviving Mombasa residents to their fate, sets sail, and takes his armada to Malindi, to restore the treaty with Portugal there.

De Almeida's voyage to India

The armada has barely left Malimba when Aneni has her first confrontation with one of Almeida's officers, whose first name is Francesco. By now, after working as a maid in town, she had learnt some Arabic, and some words of Portuguese.

Francesco drags her out of the cabin, where twenty of the women are sardined together in a two-berth cabin. 'I am not your wife,' she says, in her heavily accented Arabic.

'Just shut your trap with that gibberish. Just follow me!' he barks in Portuguese, while he tries to pull on her hand.

'I'm a married woman,' she says, and digs in her heels, trying to resist his persistent tugging.

Francesco stops, walks round to the back of Aneni, and grabs her round the waist.

A crew member passes them, asks, 'Not willing?'

Francesco scowls, and lifts Aneni round to his cabin, with her legs kicking against his shins, her fists pummelling his wrists, and her throat roaring anger. 'I will not! I will not!' she roars. And the women back in the cabin cheer in support.

Francesco throws her on the bed and reaches for a long piece of rope that hangs by the door. Before he can reach for her with the rope, she has rolled off the bed and under it. She screams 'I will not break my rituals!' But he understands not a word and tries to grab an ankle or a wrist that he can pull her out with.

She takes one wart-lumped hand in her mouth and bites on his smelly fingers, causing him to let out a whelp. He now grabs a whip from the opposite wall and starts lashing any part of her body he can reach with a sideways whip. She screams and tries to move further under the bed to escape the whiplash action.

The Portuguese thinks fast. Realising that her hair is within reach on the other side, he drops the whip and leaps around the bed to grab her hair. Her response is too slow, and she quickly finds herself being dragged by her hair from under the bed, and no scraping of fingernails, or holding on to the bed leg, is going to help her.

Francesco now has her in his grip, for all her flailing legs, and he uses the rope to tie first her hands and then her legs. She is trussed up. He places her on the bed and takes the whip in his hand.

He rips her simple wraparound dress off her, and starts whipping, methodically. She screams before and after each whip and screams more in between. Welts appear on her skin very quickly. Soon after, blood starts to weep slowly from one particularly severe wound.

He stops. Aneni has now fainted. He lays her on the bed on her back. She groans momentarily but remains unable to comprehend what is happening. Francesco parts her legs and rapes her.

Francesco puts his codpiece back on a little clumsily, grabs Aneni's torn dress, throws her over his shoulder, and carries her back to her cabin, where he dumps her down on the floor like a sack of potatoes.

'Let that be a lesson to the rest of you,' he shouts in Portuguese, and leaves the cabin.

This voyage to India is not a great success. The situation in Calicut is much as before, with Portugal despised for its past massacres of Muslims and Hindi.

The fortress at Quilon is lost after an error by Almeida, and another has to be built in a hurry at Anjediva, where trade is very modest.

While in India, and after crowing at his success in building a fortress at Kilwa and bombarding Mombasa, Almeida declares himself Viceroy of the Indes.

Consequently, after the great expense of sending a mighty fleet, the armada leaves India with three fortresses, just the same number as when it started, and the main trading port, Calicut, remains out of Portugal's reach.

In addition, the attempts to weaken Arab trading on the West Coast of India are no more successful than hitherto.

The Kilwa fortress is abandoned by Portugal in 1512, and the five hundred soldiers are withdrawn.

Mogadishu and Tristao da Cunha

'It brings back memories for my grandmother,' says Halma.

'The threat of an attack on our city?' asks her best friend Sarayu.

'Less the threat, more the involvement of the whole city. She had such fond memories of the whole population coming to the main square, the great excitement, the strange clothes of the Chinese ...'

'The Chinese?'

'Yes, a great explorer came by ship from China, and brought extraordinary gifts of gold, jade, and ceramic vases to the Sultan, as my grandmother loved to tell me.'

'And did they threaten us then?'

'No, I don't think so. There were animals lined up two by two to go on the Chinese ships. Giraffes, gazelles and hippos, as the Chinese had not seen anything like them. It was a joyous time, and the sad thing is it contrasts so much with what is happening now."

'Do you think they may invade, these Portuguese? They plundered and burnt the poor town of Barawa just along the coast.'

'So I understand, truly seriously horrible actions, but my mother says that they were unable to occupy it as the resistance was so fierce.'

'But at a heavy price.'

'Of course, so I am told, a terrible price.'

'What I object to is that these Portuguese have no tradition here. Arab traders have been coming for centuries, have kith and kin and friends all the way down the coast.'

'And Swahili was developed with part-Arabic, part-Bantu to give people a language to communicate with.'

'And the Portuguese come along with a big stick, like a playground bully.'

'Exactly. Let's just hope that the extensive defences of Mogadishu, and all the help we can call upon from our Arab friends across the Straight, and from the Ottoman Empire, will seem too much of an obstacle for them.'

'Insha Allah.'

'Insha Allah.'

* * * * *

'You will be biting off more than you can chew,' says the captain-major under Tristao da Cunha.

'You will have the wrath of the whole Ottoman Empire upon us!' says a captain.

'I will not let any Muslim city escape our actions,' says Tristao da Cunha, commander of the Eighth Armada.

'You cannot jeopardise all our forces, by taking on a foe whose strength you cannot gauge, and by setting in place consequences which are impossible to foresee, and by seeking gains that have never been defined.'

'The gain is defeating our number one enemy in his most important citadel in East Africa; it will raise me to the status of the greatest of Portugal's admirals.'

'You cannot do it sire. You do not have one captain, one captain-major, one pilot, nor one chief adviser who supports this enterprise.'

'This is a fact I am aware of.'

'This is a campaign of unprecedented risk,' says the captain-major. 'You would only have the remotest chance of avoiding a great defeat if you have the whole armada working in unison, but you do not have this unity. You have all of us against you, and this is because your ambitious enterprise lacks your usual wisdom.'

'I will back down, but only because you are right on one point. The armada would need to act as one body, with no commander failing to follow orders to the letter. Your treachery means that I cannot rely on this. I will desist. But his Majesty will receive a full report on this, of that you can be sure. And you will have to suffer the consequences of this decision.'

Aneni and other women on the Armada

The women are cramped together in a cabin faced with a dilemma. One, Carmina, says:

'We cannot all be beaten and abused like Aneni. We have to find a way of surviving our time on the ship.'

'I say we just let them fuck us,' shouts Isabella.

'But we will just be whores, and they will still abuse us,' counters Maria.

'We will just have to have a plan. A way of getting our own back,' suggests Imelda.

'Just go in there, open our legs, and get out quick, is what I say,' says Isabella.

'We could get hold of sharp things, like razors, knives,' says Imelda.

'Yea, how the fuck do we do that, on this bloody ship!?' exclaims Charo.

'We gain their confidence by playing along. Get a chance to be in their cabin when they are asleep, or drunk.'

'Yea, and when they catch us, they kill us.'

'I am just saying, we look out for that moment, when we can check where his razor is, or a knife for cutting rope,' says Imelda.

'It's not daft, not completely. But where do we hide razors and knives?'

'In our camisoles, or – better still – we use the cracks in the floorboards here. There are gaps we can use, look,' and Imelda uses a fingernail to show a typical gap.

'But once they see a razor in my hand, they will kill me,' says Maria.

'We will use our undergarments, hide the razor there, and when we know we are near home, we can find the time to strike,' says Imelda.

'We may get some revenge,' says Charo.

'I'm not doing it,' moans Isabella, under her breath. 'I would rather live.'

'There is nobody forced to,' suggests Charo. 'It's up to you. But we need to be as one, like a Portuguese man of war. Nobody spills the beans.'

'Portuguese man of war? I hate those,' says Carmina

'Well, yes,' concedes Charo, 'they awake fear in most. But they are a model for us. It is lots of organisms working as one, for the good of all.'

'Yuk, horrible thing,' says Isabella.

'But the idea of us acting together makes sense,' says Maria.

'I am with Charo,' says Carmina.

'I won't dob on any of you,' says Isabella.

'I will go for his penis,' says Imelda brazenly. 'You can go for any bit of him you want.'

'But he will just kill you if you go for his prick,' warns Aneni.

'I will disable him, don't worry.'

'So we fuck for now?'

'Yes, we fuck them. But we plan for the final day,' responds Imelda.

* * * * *

Seven weeks later, the ship is leaving the harbour at Malindi.

Imelda tells the other women, 'Tomorrow we reach Mombasa. I suggest we attack in the morning.'

The white seafront of Mombasa is visible on the horizon when the first screams are heard.

From one cabin, a man comes running out with nothing on but a chemise, and blood dripping from his groin. He is yelling at the top of his voice.

Almost simultaneously, another peers out from his cabin, screaming in agony, with blood dripping from his nose and mouth. Inside his cabin, screams are coming from a woman.

As men emerge shouting, cussing, and yelling with pain from several cabins, the captain issues an order for the women to be thrown overboard.

Imelda is trying to loosen the ropes holding a long boat when she is grabbed from behind by two crew members and thrown overboard.

One by one, all the women are thrown into the sea.

Three of the women flap madly in the water and scream hysterically that they cannot swim, and in each case a woman comes to their aid. They head for a small island a little way off from the shore and scramble on to the rocks there to catch their breath.

Three of the women are holding their faces and nursing wounds, after having been thumped before being thrown overboard.

The ship drops anchor in the harbour.

The women spend some time gathering the strength to swim the last stretch to the harbour. They also gather together fallen branches that the non-swimmers can use as floats. They agree that each swimmer will assist a non-swimmer. Then, when they feel up to it, they get back in the water, keeping close together, and using the floats.

It is well into the evening before Aneni is able to wend her way back to the village where her family lives with the family of Mai and Felani.

Battle of Diu, 1509-10

In the following year's Armada, in 1509, Almeida commands a better prepared and also more powerful Portuguese naval force. In the Battle of Diu, in the Indian Ocean, they defeat the Sultan of Gujarat, the Mamluk Burji Sultanate of Egypt, and the Zamorin of Calicut, who also have support from the republic of Venice.

The Portuguese hang, burn alive, tear to pieces, or tie to the mouths of cannon, almost all the Mamluk captives they hold, as retribution for the death of the Admiral's son in an earlier battle.

After this victory, Portugal is able to dominate the spice trade for around a century using its Cape of Good Hope route, and Portugal quickly captures Goa, Sri Lanka, Malacca and Ormuz. The Muslim trade is set back heavily with this defeat.

The armada departs with the Mamluk leader Hussain and twenty-two Mamluk soldiers as prisoners.

But soon Almeida is to miscalculate badly, and underestimate to his cost a less powerful foe.

7.

De Almeida: A Cock May Crow too Loud

It starts with a skirmish on the beach on 28th February 1710. Almeida has dropped anchor and takes long boats to the shore on Table Bay Beach near the Cape of Good Hope, on his return journey to Lisbon after the Battle of Diu.

About one hundred and fifty to two hundred Portuguese soldiers come ashore, including twenty-two Mamluk prisoners and their leader Hussain.

Some Khoikhoi are at the other end of the beach hoping to catch the next whale that beaches. Others are further back from the beach, and there is a strong smell of roasting flesh. One of Almeida's men, Goncalo Homen, asks to follow the Khoikhoi to where the cooking is going on. He mimics drinking water and two of the whale-watching Khoikhoi agree to go back to their village with him.

There is a cluster of improvised huts. Just in front of the huts is a large fire, with what seems a good-sized seal cooking on top. It gives the impression of being well cooked.

Homen shouts to the Khoikhoi, 'Water, water,' and he again mimics taking a drink from a bottle. A Khoikhoi man, Akasu, goes off to fetch water.

As Akasu walks away, Homen grabs at the seal's flesh, and rips off as big a chunk as he can lift and starts carrying it towards his crew mates and Dias.

A crowd of Khoikhoi is on top of Goncalo Homen before he knows it. Akasu's brother Zan shouts, "You will not come here and humiliate us, treat us worse than animals. We are here cooking and trying to catch a whale, you are guests, yet you think we are animals that you can trick us like this.' As he shouts, the others beat Goncalo with sticks.

The Khoikhoi retreat back to their homesteads, which are a short distance away, at the head of a small valley. These are simple homes of sticks and long grass that are easy to construct, to permit their nomadic lifestyle.

Homen finds his way back to his ship, covered with bruises. He has no seal meat.

The next day, the Portuguese find the kraal, abduct most of the women and children and try to steal cattle, in retaliation for the previous day's beating.

One captain, Fernao Soares, asks Almeida, 'Are you not underestimating these people as you did with Mogadishu? We do not know them at all.'

'Don't insult me again, sire. These are nothing people, wearing blankets round their waists, or no clothing. They are barely better than animals. I am starting to feel I have a bunch of lily-livered cowards as my captains!'

Fernao Soares nods, and they continue.

As the Portuguese start to head back with their abductees and the cattle, the Khoikhoi move into battle mode to take them on and rescue their women, children and cattle. They see the Portuguese action as an act of war against them.

The location is called Gorinhaiqua, and the Khoikhoi's battle technique has become legendary.

To make his one hundred men seem a more numerous force, and to look far more imposing, the tribal leader adds armour to the Khoi oxen, and has them lead the charge. The Khoikhoi, coming up behind, and from the sides, are armed with spears and bows and arrows.

The overconfident Portuguese have no idea what is about to hit them. They are emerging from a small valley, with a slope on each side, on the path between.

The oxen are charging at them from behind in full armour, their horns tipped to gouge into any person they encounter. From each side, men with masks and penises flapping are charging down the slopes throwing spears at them with accuracy and force.

The Portuguese have nothing with which to defend themselves from spears.

Before they can even raise their arquebuses to cock and fire them the spears are flying at their heads and chests and the oxen are gouging or stamping down those at the back.

As they come on to the beach, at the end of the kraal, there is a pile of Portuguese bodies bleeding profusely, or already dead. The Khoi women have run back to their men, and the cattle are chewing on grass.

The Mamluk prisoners, who were at the front of the Portuguese group, are already at the end of the beach running for their lives. A few Portuguese, but none a captain and no de Almeida, are in a long boat doing their best to get back to the ship.

The Khoikhoi concentrate on ensuring that the speared and gouged Portuguese are dead, and they then start preparing a large grave for them there. They note that the leader, with his special hat and all his fine clothes, is among the dead.

The twenty-two Mamluks and their leader Hussain escape on horseback. Hussain reaches as far as Cairo, Egypt. He finds few who are prepared to believe his story.

Several Khoikhoi blow ox horns in celebration of their victory.

The Portuguese ships head off the same day for the journey back to Lisbon.

The bones of forty-nine of the dead Portuguese, including Almeida, are only found in around 2010 by staff of the university of Cairo.

Poet Luis de Camoes wrote in his Os Lusiads poem: '*the stormy cape which keeps his memory, along with his bones, in dispatching from the world a soul, neither Egypt nor all India could control.*'

* * * * *

Aneni spends many days in her room inside her compound after her return, either curled up in a ball on her own, or, where possible, curled up hugging her daughter Tia Tia with her son Wotambo close to her. She finds it difficult to be close to her husband Mufaso.

After a fairly long time in self-imposed Purdah, she ventures out, and finds herself in Mai's part of their compound.

'It was a living hell on that ship,' Aneni tells Mai, in hushed tones.

'There is no rush to tell me. Wait until you are ready,' says Mai.

'These ugly stinking white men just beat me and beat me until I was senseless, and then raped me. I tried so hard to protect myself but could not.'

'I am sure you fought bravely, but those Portuguese men are very strong.'

'He could not have had me if I was still conscious. I battled and fought until then, and my knuckles became so raw they bled.'

'But they made you suffer for it?'

'They did. We decided to play ball during the voyage, as otherwise they would not have hesitated to kill us. But we took our revenge on the last day.'

'Tell me what happened.'

'I stole a razor from the man's cabin when he fell asleep after raping me. On the last day, I hid the razor in my petticoat, held in place with pins, and when he wished to enter me against my will, I whipped out the razor and slashed his stiff willy.'

'No! You are as brave as a lioness, Aneni. You may have died.'

'The top bit of his dongle was dangling off, but did not fall, and the man was shouting and screaming.'

Mai struggles not to laugh. In the next room, Niambi is finding it hard not to laugh also, and she comes through.

'I tried to run back to the cabin we were sleeping in, but I was grabbed by two men from behind and thrown from the deck into the sea. It was only by a stroke of luck that I was helped by one of the other women, who swam towards me when she saw me panicking. I was at that moment struggling to hold on to a piece of wood in the ship's wake, and I thought I was a goner.'

'My dear Aneni, what an extraordinary ordeal! I really feel for you.'

'Me too,' says Niambi. 'Hard to believe what you went through.'

'Thank you. It will take many moons and a thousand prayers to the sun for me to get over it.'

'You should allow it to take the time it takes. I can help with the children, if ever you need that. They and my two became very good friends during your long abduction.'

'You are as sweet as a ripe mango and have been too kind. But I don't think I can stay here. It is too associated with what happened, with being abducted by these Ozh Bozh speakers.'

'That is sad. Where might you go to?'

'That is a long discussion still to be had,' she says.

'Take your time,' replies Mai.

8.
Khoikhoi: Coming of Age

'If we stay here, we will not come near to a dik-dik,' says father, as he surveys the flat red savannah ahead, with just a small hill to the right, which appears to have a gulley through it.

'Why is that?' asks Tsawe Tika.

'Because the wind is heading eastwards and will carry our scent to the nasal glands of the deer,' says dad, Akasu. 'So we head upwind. We then need to think about outwitting the dik-dik.'

'Because they are faster than us?'

'Yes, well done. As with the springbok, they have speed on their side. But if we ambush them we may catch a small one, which will give us a good supper for a couple of nights, and bones for soup.'

'So shall I be looking for a narrow channel, where we can perhaps hide behind rocks as they come through?'

'That will help, but we must also provide them with a reason to enter the channel, as they would normally stay on the open savannah where they can look out for danger all around them.'

'They are not carnivores. Would they be tempted by tasty berries, perhaps?'

'Perhaps, but what we do is split up. I will go one way, and mimic the female's alarm call, with its distinctive dik-dik sound. You will hide with your bow and arrow behind rocks at the side of the thin valley there, and you will use your archery skills to try to lame one that comes through.'

They divide up. Akasu uses a leafy branch to camouflage himself as he moves into position in a copse of trees. He notes that Tsawe Tika seems now to be in position.

He makes the alarm call. The small herd of dik-dik immediately react, their ears pricking up, one or two standing tall for a moment on their legs, and they then split up, two heading into the gulley, and the rest heading across the savannah to the north.

Tsawe Tika prepares to shoot, his bow fully drawn. As the two deer come racing through the small valley below him, he fires his arrow at the rear of one. It barely glances it and falls to the ground.

Crestfallen, Tsawe Tika goes down to collect his arrow, and heads back to where his father is.

'No joy?' asks his father, as they approach each other.

'Not a clean hit, the arrow bounced off,' says Tsawe Tika.

'A good lesson', says his father. 'Where will you aim next time?'

'At the neck.'

'That is correct. And how much time do you have to reach when they come within range?'

'No time, father.'

'Very good. So you are ready to fire in the split second they are within sight.'

'And my bow must be strung very tightly, for speed.'

'Also true, yes. You will not have a true aim without an extremely tight bow, as tight as a boa constrictor's grip on a goat.'

'Yes, father.'

'So, what is tomorrow's test?'

'I race a cheetah tomorrow. They say they have not done this before, except perhaps generations before.'

'Very good, so we will need to get you home to eat, and you will need to sleep well under the stars tonight.'

'Yes, father. But no dik-dik.'

Mai and Aneni

'Let us move much further inland. What do you think?' Mai asks.

'Absolutely. After my abduction even more so. We both think so. It is not easy leaving what you know. But you and Felani and your children are very dear to us, and if you come with us, it can work.'

'That is sweet of you. You are very important to us too.'

Niambi comes

'I have something wriggling in my ear.' And she points at her right ear.

'Let me have a look,' says Mai, walking round to her right side. 'It's a bit dark. Come more into the sun.'

She looks again. 'Looks like an insect, probably a beetle. We need something to get it out.'

'I try heat,' says Aneni. 'when the fire is lit, I will light a stick and try that.'

'There is a fire in the next compound,' says Matimba. 'I will bring you a burning stick.'

Matimba returns with a red hot stick. Mai sweeps back Niambi's frizzy hair, to free her ear.

Aneni holds the flame by Niambi's ear.

'It's too hot,' says Niambi.

'It needs to be hot to make the beetle want to leave. Wait, it is coming, Matimba get ready to grab it.'

Matimba grabs the beetle as it pokes out and squeezes it between his fingers.

'Ouch,' says Niambi. 'Not a pleasant experience, but thanks, it has gone now.'

'Sorry it was so hot,' says Aneni.

The KhoiKhoi Puberty Race with Cheetah (Puberty 2)

'Are you ready?' asks Granny Krotoa, as she enters the family hut shortly before dawn. There is only a full moon and the first weak orange glow of the sun providing any light.

'I think so,' replies Tsawe Tika. 'I am just waiting for my running guardian, Tsoko. I have not eaten this morning, as told.'

'The course is all mapped out, with posts every thousand strides. Fifteen posts in all, heading due north from our huts, and finishing near a welcome waterhole. Make sure you carry your bow and arrow, won't you?'

'Seems unnecessary. I can fight.'

'You never know. Besides, the cheetah might be in a bad mood and may turn on you.'

'The cheetah has just eaten most of a dik-dik. He is sat there purring like the cheetah that's got the cream. He should be fine for the duration of the race. Besides, there is deer scent at each of the marker posts to keep the cheetah on the course, isn't there?'

'Yes, that's true.'

'Besides, no cheetah has attacked the runner in this race in past times, have they?'

'No, you are right. The main thing is that life is about thinking ahead, and on the savannah there are many dangers, as you know. Tsoko is running near to you, to look out for possible predators, and will be able to deal with most dangers. But there could be two predators, and you would be unwise to have no bow with you.'

'Of course, granny, you are quite right. No lion leaves her pride without first sharpening her teeth, as we say.'

'Ok, I will tell Tsoko you are ready for your next rite of passage test.'

The race starts at dawn.

The cheetah is let loose as Tsawe Tika starts, and the cheetah races ahead and reaches the first deer scent long before the boy; the same for the next eight marker posts.

But the cheetah's weakness is that it cannot sweat. The boy can. From eight kilometres, the cheetah tires and the boy gains ground on it steadily.

By twelve kilometres the boy is tiring too, but the cheetah is simply ambling at walking pace towards the next scent, so the boy overtakes, at a gentle jog.

The boy has severe cramp for the last two kilometres, but limps to the end, the cheetah having stopped at thirteen, and heads for the waterhole.

'Get out of the waterhole now and get up a tree! Grab your bow!' shouts Tsoko.

Tsawe Tika sees the lioness from the corner of his eye, as he grabs at branches and hauls himself up a few before turning round, panting hard. The lioness is at the base of the tree.

Tsoko is beckoning her, in the hope of persuading her against climbing the tree. He has a bow and arrow but it would only work, he surmises, if he strikes the right spot first time.

A few impala wading in the water give Tsoko an idea. He moves into the water behind the impala and splashes the water vigorously. It seems to work. The lioness is now focussed on the impala rather than Tsawe Tika.

The lioness crouches, then charges and leaps for the smallest of the impala as they start to splash out of the waterhole. She manages to bite into a leg. The young impala fawn then momentarily breaks free, and hobbles on three legs a bit further, before the lioness is able to bite at its neck and bring it down.

Tsoko signals to Tsawe Tika to climb down, and they start running back to their tribal village.

Tsawe Tika is still exhausted, so they barely jog, but it is not until the first marker post on the return journey that they stop for a breather.

'I think we are safe from the lioness now,' says Tsoko, 'and there is no indication of the rest of her pride coming this way. We have fairly good vision all round. Let us walk on.'

They reach the village mid-afternoon and there are cheers for Tsawe Tika.

He has passed the rite of passage.

But all are concerned when Tsoko tells them about the lioness.

Puberty Dances held – KhoiKhoi Tsoko! (Puberty 3)

The clearing is surrounded on its perimeter by large trees. All bushes and their roots have been removed to make a space for celebration. The earth is red.

A crowd is beginning to form in the clearing and the flute-players and drummers have already started a pulsating rhythm, with delightful melodies.

The pubescent boys, with red and orange decoration on their chest, back and legs, and grass skirts, begin to line up rather sheepishly at the side of the clearing.

Girls stand at the side with colourful grass skirts, multicoloured beads decorating a headband, and beads on necklaces cascading over their sky-facing breasts. They goad Tsawe Tika.

'Come on Tsawe Tika, your turn now. Everyone has to dance.'

'No, I will wait for my friends Zan and Tsama. I am just gearing myself up for it.'

The boys perform a dance together, and then begin to dance individually.

It is soon Tsawe Tika's turn, and he now tries hard to impress, with a flamboyant flamingo impersonation followed by a swooping vulture, complete with vulture feathers attached to his arms, and a vulture head attached on top of his head.

Tsawe Tika gets his choice of girl, who is tall, with large brown eyes and a broad smile.

'I am called Malaika,' she says. 'I know your name, Tsawe Tika. All the girls know you.'

Tsawe Tika laughs an embarrassed laugh, and says, 'Are you from my family, Malaika? You know that I cannot marry you if we are related.'

'My grandfather and his father came here from a big city to the north, Mapungubwe.'

'I thought that Mapungubwe was just a legend, the so-called town with the golden rhinoceros.'

'No, it was all very true, many thousands of Khoi people lived there, trading gold and ivory like my own family. But the gold trade moved more and more to Zimbabwe or Kilwa, and it declined, so my folk came here.'

'One hears in the legend of a golden rhino?'

'Yes, the town was famous for it, but I don't know what happened to it.'

'A sad story for your family, having to leave Mapungubwe, but it's also great news for us, as it means we can marry.'

'Yes, Tsawe Tika. I am the luckiest girl. Come, let us dance to celebrate, then we can talk to our parents.'

9.

East Africa and Brazil: Upheaval as Portugal Arrives

As three ships arrive at the same bay as before in Brazil, the Tupis from the village arrive with the two criminals who had been left with them.

The two tell the Portuguese ship captain, Oriego, of the Tupi lifestyle. Diogo explains how they hunt and live off the jungle in part, but also farm sweet potato, cassava, beans, a bland vegetable called potato and other foodstuffs.

They all act as one, each looking after the interests of the others.

There are fireflies all around the encampment in the evenings to give light for a short time.

He also explains how when he suffered a bad cut when he tripped on a rock, he was healed by Tupi herbs.

'Do they worship God?' asks captain Oriego.

'They worship the moon, and the creatures of the forest.'

'As I thought, they are ungodly and sub-human.'

'We were each given a girl,' says Diogo, 'who was a 'sister' of the men they were staying with.'

Oriego then speaks to the Tupi in Portuguese, with Diogo interpreting, and insists that they will want to take fifteen young women on the ship with them, and they want to take twenty pau-brazil trunk with them.

The Tupi agree to the pau brasil tree trunk, and Oriego despatches his first mate and some crew with saws to cut down the trees.

The request for Tupi women leads to an argument among the Tupi.

'They are not having my sister,' says Ubijara

'But that is what we do,' says Jaci

'They are not having my sister.'

'You must give a little, 'adds Jaci. 'When you battle with an alligator in the river, you know that the alligator will get his way if there is no give and take. You feed the alligator a small pig, and you and the alligator both live.'

'My sister is not a pig,' replies Ubijara.

'Listen, we make peace with another tribe, and our sisters marry their men, and we have a good relationship with the tribe. No more war.'

'But these are not another tribe. They come on a strange craft that appears to have come from nowhere. They have blotchy pink faces with skin peeling off like a snake. They look like they want to copy a parrot's clothing but get it all wrong; they put far too much on their bodies for our humidity and so they sweat with a smell worse than a jatoba fruit. We can laugh at these people, but we cannot trust them.'

'Some of us don't agree. We are willing to give these clowns with beards and firesticks a chance. They have been peaceful so far. If our sisters join them, and some become brothers-in-law we get two advantages. We have sisters learning their off-the-wall language and we get some idea if they are up to no good.'

'It is too early and too dangerous. What if these people plan to kill us all and take our land? Your plan will enable them to have their own guinea pig ferreting round us. And our sisters will tell them things about our culture that will open us up to their tricks and traps.'

'You see it one way, we see it another. I think either way we have the wellbeing of our tribe at heart. We will compromise. They may have ten of our women. No more.'

'We will pay for it,' quips Ubijara.

'If you are proven right, we will apologise,' says Jaci.

* * * * *

Soon, the Portuguese ships depart. Ten of the Tupi women go with them. The Portuguese also take with them a large number of branches of the pau brasil tree for its red dye.

One of the parrot-like-clothes-wearing people stays behind with one of the criminals who speaks Portuguese, but they have no firestick with them. They again stay with the tribe.

The other criminal travels back in one of the ships, to translate for the women where he can.

It is not long before a number of the Tupis who have had contact with the Portuguese become very ill.

When measles and influenza strikes, the Tupis have no internal defences. The sick ones are confined to their hammocks. The witch doctor prepares elaborate concoctions but nothing seems to work. One by one, the sick ones die, with very few recovering from the illness.

Some leave the village in the hope that they will escape the disease, believing that its timing can only mean that it is the white man's witchcraft. A number survive, and later return to their village to help restore it to health.

Mai and Aneni and their families move again, 1510

Mai, Felani, Niambi and Itepi start the trip inland to Bunyoro province.

On their backs, Mai and Felani carry bedding and clothing. Their feet are bare. Aneni and Mufaso and daughter Tia-Tia and son Wotambo are immediately behind, with Wotambo holding the tethers of the two cattle, and Itepi holding the tether of the two goats.

The journey is hard, with one hill after another, and Niambi and Mai, in particular, find it tough.

As they come over the brow of a hill they see a herd of elephants in the distance, walking in line, with each trunk holding on to the tail of the elephant in front.

Mai asks Niambi, Itepi, Tia Tia and Wotambo to walk with her while she tells them a story. They happily agree.

'The story is called, "why elephants don't hiccough,"' says Mai.

'Is it a true story?' asks Niambi.

'No, it's a story that has come through the family, through generations. It's an invented story, that becomes embellished, I suspect, in each generation.'

'OK, fire away.'

'Hellooo! Hello there!'

Elephant does not hear. He just continues to chomp on his banana leaf and looks ahead.

'Hello, Mr elephant! How are you today?'

Elephant still does not react, and continues to chomp on his leaf, his mouth gurning each chomp.

'Hey fatty, what's up? Got wax in your great flappy ears or what?' shouts grasshopper.

Elephant hears the word 'fatty' and looks down. At last he notices the grasshopper leaping up and down, and, deeply hurt, he states, 'Don't ever call me fatty. Do that once more and I will crush you with one stamp of my excessively large foot.'

Grasshopper is of a cheeky disposition and thinks he can outwit the mighty elephant.

'I have a message for you, fatty. Do you want to hear it?'

'I want to hear it without any of your insults,' replies Elephant. 'This is your last warning not to call me fatty.'

'The message is that you are a great fat hephalump,' says Grasshopper, now acting so cheekily that he does not deliver the true message.

Stamp! Down comes Elephant's huge foot. As it did so, Grasshopper simply hopped to one side, and sat there making his clicking sound by rubbing his back knees together.

'Missed me, missed me, silly hephalump. Not exactly twinkle-toes, are you, hephalump?' chirrups Grasshopper.

Elephant is now getting madder and madder. Stupid Grasshopper, he muses, does not realise that he is normal for an elephant, and only fat compared to a grasshopper. Which stands to reason.

But to stomp like this is to come across as a buffoon, as Grasshopper can always hop faster than he can stomp.

So when Grasshopper shouts one more time 'Clumsy old fatty, ha ha ha!' Elephant comes up with a plan.

While Grasshopper sits gazing cockily at Elephant and clicking his back knees, Elephant's ears flap right back, his eyes stare deep into Grasshopper's, and he makes his trunk rigid, all in one move. Then, a sudden mighty suck on his trunk sees Grasshopper shoot up inside, through his voluminous mouth, down his throat and into his cavernous stomach.

'Got you,' he chuckles. 'Your days of insulting me are over, my little friend.'

Grasshopper gets up and shakes himself. Some hurricane that, he thinks. Short and sharp. Now, what do we have here? A big pink sack going in, out, in, out. And me inside it! And no obvious way out of it!

Doesn't look too rosy for me, he thinks.

Grasshopper starts leaping round and round, searching for a way out. With each hop, he says to himself, 'I'll never call an elephant fatty, I'll never call an elephant fatty. So, please pretty please, great green grasshopper in the sky, please let me out of this horrible pulsating pink sack.' Hop, hop hop.

Meanwhile, his host, Elephant, is getting this funny tickly feeling in his tummy. It is as though – poing – someone is using – poing – the inside of his tummy – poing – as a trampoline. 'It's that pesky damned grasshopper,' he thinks to himself. 'Methinks a good drink of water is called for.' And off he lumbers to a nearby pool.

What's happening now? Grasshopper asks himself after one unusually high hop. He suddenly finds himself not in the pink sack, but in a much thinner tube heading upwards. This, he thinks, must be the way out. And he starts scrambling up the long tube, even as it squeezes in and out, in and out.

Elephant stops in his tracks. Now his throat feels distinctively ticklish, a grating, irritating tickling that makes him want to hiccough.

But, he thinks, 'I have never wanted to hiccough before. How do I do it now?

The tickling worsens, as Grasshopper climbs up his throat and slides back down again. And suddenly there is a great jolt, a trembling, a dramatic leap in the air such as a heavy elephant rarely manages. Elephant hiccoughs.

Over and over he rolls in the grubby dirt. Over rolls Grasshopper, as he finds himself back in the pink sack of Elephant's tummy.

Elephant is shaken.

Grasshopper is shaken, and now wet from the dampness of the throat.

First a hurricane, now a typhoon, he thinks. What strange weather today.

'Time for a break. We will sleep now,' says Felani, 'after having a bite to eat. We will continue the tale tomorrow.'

'Thanks mum,' says Niambi, squeezing Mai's hand. She nods and squeezes his.

Tupi women on the ship

The women are all put in one cabin. They argue with the first crewmember who comes in.

Diogo, the criminal, helps with translation.

'We are not going to have sex with you,' says Aroi, a Tupi woman

'I agree', adds Wai.

'You don't get to decide,' says the Portuguese sailor, Manolo. 'I get to decide.'

Diogo, the criminal, intervenes.

''Manolo, the women need time, they need to get to know a man before they have sex.

Manolo is not happy. 'How can I get to know a woman who has no Portuguese? I will wait a day and then I want sex.'

In the cabin, the women speak among themselves. They all agree that they don't want to have sex with the Portuguese. They also agree that they don't want to die on this strange boat; they want to return home. Idoi suggests compromise. They agree to compromise.

'We know,' Tupilaroma says, 'that if a chameleon falls into a den of snakes, it does not want to be eaten. It will take on the look of the snakes and play along until it can escape. We know these odd men have balls for brains, but we are in agreement that we will have to consent to sexual relations, but we as one woman want to be treated well.' They all agree.

Tupilaroma explains to Diogo that, if they are treated well, they will agree to sexual relations, within reason.

Oriego tells his chief mate that the next voyage to Brazil is likely to involve taking land from the local tribes people and beginning to farm the pau brasil tree for the Portuguese dye market.

'It has the potential to become a major producer of red dye for us,' he says.

The chief mate, Firminho, agrees.

Diogo intervenes: 'The slave women want to be treated well. Then they will consent. This is what the women are saying.

'We will pretend to agree,' says the chief mate. 'Tell the women we agree. That will shut them up until we have had our way.'

Mia's Tale (Part Two)

The next day, Mai continues her tale.

'I will continue with the Elephant and the Grasshopper where I left off,' she says.

Having at last hiccoughed, Elephant hopes his tickle may have gone. Not so lucky. Again and again he hiccoughs, each time shaking the ground under him. And each time shaking Grasshopper, who bounces around all over the pink sack of his stomach on each hiccough.

A giraffe walks past. 'What's up with you?' she asks Elephant.

'It's a hic-hic-hic-hiccough,' replies Elephant.

'Oh, is that all? I thought there was an earthquake.'

'What's up with you?' asks a lion, wandering past, head lowered.

'It's a hic-hic-hic-hiccough,' replies Elephant.

'Oh, that's a pity. I was hoping a stampede of antelopes might be on its way.'

'Boo!' goes the rhino, trying to shock Elephant.

'What's that for?' asks Elephant, with a deep frown over his eyes.

'It's to stop you hiccoughing,' replies Rhino.

'Oh, th-th-thank you,' says Elephant, hiccoughing regardless.

'Come down to the water,' says Hippo, and Elephant follows her past a copse of trees to a large pool of water.

All this time, Grasshopper is still shaking with each hiccough, and moaning, 'Can someone please get me off this pink trampoline?'

'Right, Elephant,' says Hippo abruptly, 'this is how you rid yourself of hiccoughs. You need to lie down on your back, and drink water through your trunk while upside down.'

As Elephant with his great bulk steps gingerly into the water, all the water buffalo and hippos walk out. With each hiccough, there are waves in the pond, and each laps the pool's shoreline.

Elephant flops down and tries to roll over on to his back. Then tries again, and again. But somehow he cannot get right on his back.

'Curiouser and curiouser,' says Grasshopper to himself, as he rocks and rolls.

The waves lapping the shoreline grow bigger and bigger, forcing little lion cubs and small springbok calves to rush back from the side of the pool.

With a shove from Hippo, a shove from Rhino, and with encouragement from onlookers, the great trunked beast is finally forced on his back.

'At last,' says Hippo, 'now get drinking. Twenty hippo-gollops at least.'

So Elephant sucks and sucks, and sucks and sucks, wondering what on earth twenty hippo-gollops may be. Inside his tummy, grasshopper watches the water rise around him and he prepares to meet his maker.

Outside the pool, the animals watch the pool's water level sink ever lower and wonder where they might find their next drink.

Finally, the pool is empty. Grasshopper, breathing heavily, is squeezed into a tiny pocket of air high in Elephant's tummy. The animals look on in anticipation to see if Elephant will either hiccough or, perhaps, explode.

And boy does he hiccough.

Not once, not twice, but a rapid succession of hiccoughs that made the empty pool shake and the animals rattle and the alligators roll.

And Grasshopper becomes grumpier and grumpier, and in a soft gentle whisper says, 'Help me.'

'I've got it,' says a little hummingbird, as it hovers near Rhino, and observes perplexed expressions on the faces of the assembled creatures.

Resplendent in bright green and purple, the hummingbird buzzes over to Elephant's right ear and says, 'Elephant, you can end all these hiccoughs if you do this one thing: hold your breath until we have all counted to a hundred.'

Elephant, deeply unhappy at his body shaking massively with each hiccough, decides to give this new idea a try. He hopes beyond hope it will work.

So Elephant takes a deep gulp of air, holds his breath, and the animals start counting.

'One, two, three, four ...' they count rhythmically, slowly and loudly.

'Twenty-one, twenty-two, twenty-three ...' and grey Elephant is becoming redder and redder.

'Forty-one, forty-two, forty-three ...' and his face is red, his tummy is red, and even his trunk is going red.

'Sixty-one, sixty-two, sixty-three ...' and his face is now going purple, his tummy is now going purple, and Grasshopper inside is absolutely sure he is about to meet his maker.

'Eighty-one, eighty-two, eighty-three ...' and as they all look on in anticipation, counting steadily, the unexpected happens.

In one mighty burst, and with a power that shakes the ground for miles around, Elephant explodes.

Water bursts out from his trunk in one magnificent, stupefying fountain. It gushes over all the animals, soaking them to the skin, the alligators excepted.

It gushes over the copse of trees, and it gushes into the basin that Elephant had emptied. Slowly but surely, the pool is restored.

'You didn't reach a hundred, Elephant,' says the hummingbird, flapping its wings so fast they are soon dry.

'Thanks, dear Hummingbird, that is all I need to know,' replies Elephant.

'But the best news, my friend,' says the hummingbird chirpily, 'is that your hiccough has gone, it seems.'

And indeed it has! And all the animals and reptiles and birds around, each of them still dripping wet from Elephant's wondrous fountain, say in unison: 'It's gone. Elephant's hiccough has gone.'

And Grasshopper, sitting on top of the highest tree having been carried aloft by the first burst of Elephant's fountain spray, sighs to himself. 'It's gone for him. What about me, stuck up here in this silly old tree?'

And he clicks the backs of his knees to try to gain attention.

But all eyes are on Elephant as he turns himself over and stands right up in one surprisingly graceful movement.

He is a very contended elephant now, and he beams and waves his trunk at the animals watching from the side.

Grasshopper, meanwhile, high up in the tree, has a thought. 'The message,' he says to himself, 'I forgot to give Elephant the message. What's worse, I've forgotten what it was. Oh dear, oh dear.' And forgetting his apprehension, he hops down the branch, down the tree trunk and hotfoots it in the direction of the lion's den, to ask for the message again.

But elephants do not forget. And since that day, no elephant has ever hiccoughed.

Because, since that day, no elephant has swallowed a grasshopper.

Which has all been easier, because no grasshopper has since been asked to give an elephant a message.

'I am sure all this is true, my darlings. After all, have you ever heard an elephant hiccough?'

'That's lovely mum,' says Niambi. 'I love the cheeky grasshopper.'

'I want more,' says Itepi. 'I love it.'

'Me too,' says Felani, 'but probably we should strike camp soon.'

Tupi women return from being on ship

'Who is this?' asks Jaci.

'They are our women,' replies Ubijara.

'But they have strange cloths on them, and odd colours on their face.'

'The blotched face men have firesticks. We need to stand back and wait.' And they retreat a little to the bushes at the back of the beach, as the women and a few Portuguese men arrive.

The Portuguese crew members send the women towards Jaci and the others. They scuttle up the beach.

The two criminals run at the same time from the Tupis to the Portuguese.

The Portuguese gather in a huddle.

The Tupis greet each other.

'It has been a nightmare!' screams Aroi, to Jaci, as they reach the men.

'A horror,' says another, Wai.

The other women nod in agreement, some of them shedding tears. They all turn to head back to the village, leaving the Portuguese in conversation on the beach.

'Tell me more,' says Jaci, gently.

'Every day, they rape us. They don't care, just throw me on a bed and jump on me and stick their thing in.'

'A bed? It all sounds terrifying.'

'They sleep about hip height from the ground. There is a wooden platform and on that a softer platform they call 'mattress'. They call the whole thing a 'bed'.'

'Sometimes the man would come and spurt in his own face as soon as he had thrown me on the bed, and he would hit me, and take me back to our women's cabin. Later, he would take me again and do the same.'

'Did you try to fight back?'

'Early on, young Idoi kneed a man in the groin when he tried to mount her on the bed,' says Wai. 'And he beat her so hard with a stick we had to nurse her for two days before she could stand again.'

'We decided after that,' adds Aroi, 'that we would simply go along with it. We didn't show any pleasure, just lie there still. And wait until we could get home.'

'I understand that. You had to stay alive somehow,' says Jaci.

'Idoi got pregnant,' adds Wai. 'She lost a lot of blood when it popped out, but with a lot of water, and cloths everywhere to stem the flow of blood, she got through it. They keep the little girl after it was born but made her nurse her.'

'It was a terrible time. They still fucking poor Idoi until the day before the baby was born.'

'They have no shame,' says Jaci, 'no shame.'

'One woman is staying with them, Udoi. She wouldn't listen to us. Just pouted her lips and said that was her decision. She is with child also.'

'What did you eat?'

'Mostly watery gruel, with little flavour, and hard things they called 'biscuits,' which they couldn't get enough of,' replies Aroi.

'They had these birds in little huts, with bars on to stop them getting out,' adds Wai.

'I have seen them. They make this funny sound,' and he makes a clucking sound, and Wai and Aroi join in, with others following.

'Sometimes they killed one of these cluck-clucking birds,' says Wai 'and we would have a bit of bird meat in our gruel. We relished this, as some of us became weak with the food being so bad, but now and again the boat would stop for more provisions, and it got better for a few days. We would sing with joy then. We had to find some way of laughing amidst the misery.'

'Indeed. Even the fly will try to enjoy the occasional flutter of its wings when caught in the spider's web.'

'We learnt some of their Ozh Dozh language.'

'Yes, we know a bit what they are saying now.'

'That could be very helpful,' says Jaci. 'What were they saying when they handed you back to us?'

'One say: "Have your bad women. We don't want them."'

'Ungrateful. Do you know what they plan to do while they are here?'

'They did say. It is the pau brasil they want,' replies Aroi. 'They are going to fell some more trees for the red dye, like last time, and take them back on the ship.'

'But I think they plan to take a lot more this time. They keep talking about this word 'money,' which we don't understand,' adds Wai.

'You still have your cloths on, in this heat and humidity. Will you not take them off now you are with us?'

'We had to wear the cloth all the time except when they fucked us. We sort of got used to it,' says Aroi, taking her simple hemp dress off. The others take theirs off.

'So Udoi will stay with them,' says Jaci. 'Have any other women talked about going to live with the Portuguese?'

'Some like the stuff they give us to put round our eyes, and on our lips,' says Aroi.

'Black above the eyes, and red on the lips,' adds Wai.

'But our Tupi dyes are so much more beautiful.'

'Too true,' says Wai, 'but a parrot that lives with hummingbirds may learn to hover.'

'You know, we stopped a short while at their land.'

'What was that like?'

'We didn't see much,' says Aroi,'as we were taken off to go into a big house with water in, and after a good and proper wash together we were taken back.'

'Do they have jungle where they live?'

'No jungle, no. All big houses, not like our food huts. They have animals I did not recognise, like beautiful big deer, pulling people along in carts on a path between the houses. There were rats everywhere, eating bad food in the streets, and a terrible stink of shit and piss and mouldy food. There were small cats, not big like ours. I saw a cat running after a rat, but the cat was still too big to get into the small hole the rat scuttled into.'

'People wearing dirty, torn clothes would sit outside houses with frowns weighing their head down. Houses looked grubby, with little inside. Children ran around the streets and when they saw a passer-by with strongly coloured clothes, they held their hands out like they wanted something. If given food they would break into a smile and run off, with other children chasing after them.'

'Perhaps they come here for our fine jungle and plentiful food, if their conditions are so bad.'

'We only saw one or two streets,' says Wai. 'But it was not a happy experience.'

'Despite that, one of our pregnant women, Udoi, is staying with them,' adds Aroi, 'I think we may lose more women if these strange people keep coming.'

'Maybe we should not offer women as sisters to the Ozh Dozh speakers anymore,' says Jaci.

'Now you say, after the fly has left the web', says Ubijara.

Felani's poem

'I hope you agree,' says Felani, 'before we finish this journey, that I can perform a little poem, inspired by a recent event.'

'Of course,' says Mai. 'It is your turn.'

'Thank you. My poem...'

I know a woman
I have known her
my life long long
A friend so dear
to my wife
it never needed said

when something happened
as though an evil spirit
entered her
took her goodness
and put it into a meat grinder
dragged it through depravity
confronted it with Portuguese thuggery
nine moons long long
it
ground her good spirit
sought to destroy her
but the iron, the rock, the gold
that surrounds her goodness
preserved her
rescued her
and brought her back whole
her goodness restored
her Aneni

'That is beautiful,' says Mai.

'I am very touched,' adds Aneni, wiping a tear.

10.

Resistance Builds

The pattern established by Portugal's early armadas is continued unabashed from 1509-10, regardless of setbacks.

There is some rearranging of priorities in East Africa, with the garrison at Kilwa abandoned by Portugal in 1512, and Sofala deprioritised for lack of gold.

Later that century, they venture inland for gold, establishing trading posts at Sena and Tete.

In 1528, Nuno de Cunha lays waste to Mombasa, and in 1541 they destroy the shipping at Mogadishu. In each case punishment seemed to provide the rationale for this aggression.

In India, there is a further concerted attempt by Portugal in 1509 to gain a monopoly position over the spice trade. Afonso de Albuquerque is appointed second Governor of Portugal's eastern possessions that year, and Marshal Fernao Coutinho leads the armada. A fearsome attack is launched on Calicut, and the Zamorin's palace there is captured and destroyed. The Zamorin fights back, and Coutinho is killed and Albuquerque injured. A truce is arranged, and by a new treaty between Portugal and Calicut the interests of Portugal in Malabar are to be protected.

But the Portuguese continue to try to assassinate the Zamorin between 1515 and 1518.

The upshot is that Portugal negotiates a permanent settlement in Goa, and this becomes the headquarters of Portuguese India and the seat of the Viceroy. The Portuguese are subsequently able to acquire other possessions in Gujarat and near Bombay.

The pattern remains, as before, of using brute force to seek to establish significant trade advantages, and to gain territory from indigenous peoples where this territory is seen likely to be advantageous in trade, or (in Africa) to gain access to valuable minerals such as gold.

Brazil

In Brazil, the felling of pau brasil trees for red dye for the Portuguese textile industry grows rapidly in the years from 1505. With very few Portuguese on the continent, the Portuguese try to use the Tupis to fell and chop up the trees.

In a few cases, the Tupis agree to do this in return for cloth, iron nails and other practical items, but for the most part the Portuguese force the Tupis to work for them, often at gunpoint.

Coupled with this, the Portuguese can only fell pau brasil trees using land that belongs to the Tupis, and which the Tupis rely on for their homes, their food, their medicines etc. The forest is their lives.

Conflicts between the Portuguese and the Tupis grow as the Portuguese demand for the red-dye from the pau brasil grows.

Brazil: Tupis start to resist, 1510s -1520s

'They are taking more and more of our land, these overdressed sweaty ones,' says Caua.

'They show a lack of respect for our right to land and to our traditions. They are even taking land we farm for cassava and manioc,' replies Jaci.

'They have no respect for us women,' says Ulara. 'Before, we agreed women could marry a sweaty one to be sister-in-law to our men, but now they take who they feel they want. They were even going to take my eldest daughter until I fired an arrow at the one that grabbed her.'

Caua laughs. 'They are taking some of us to work in cutting down trees, offering us only beads or cloth in return, or useless metal. They do not understand that our men have a hundred tasks every day, between farming, hunting, teaching youngsters, fixing broken hammocks, sourcing herbs and so on.'

'The work is deadly,' says Ubirata. 'They come to the village with their firesticks and make us march or face bullets for two days. They have us up before dawn and working until after dusk to cut up pau brasil trees. They give us a bit of water to drink at dawn and at dusk, and if we are lucky a banana to eat. It goes on until we are about to drop, and then they march us back and get more men.'

'And they have no respect for trees which have been part of our family since the beginning of time,' says Caua.

'I don't mind them like you do', says Potira, with a red face.

'How can you say that? After all they have done against our men and women! How can you possibly say that?' says Ubirata. 'Is it the jewellery your man has given you?'

'Why shouldn't I like jewellery? Silver and jade are lovely. And he is quite kind to me. I don't mind their life. They are not so bad when they are on their own. But I have to cook that strange bird that they have, which is difficult. They cluck and cackle and run around until you catch them, and then you cut off their heads. They still run around for a bit, and then they die, and you pluck the feathers off them before you cook them. In the end, it is a bit like the birds we eat, but with slightly stronger flavour. It is the same with their eggs.'

'But their food is little better than flavoured piss water without the spices and herbs we use.'

'The food is ok with meat and vegetables, a bit like ours. I secretly add a bit of spicy berry I take from here. But I do have to wear cloth over my body all day, which is hard, as I sweat all day.'

'I don't know how you can bear that, when here you are as free as a bird.'

'I put up with it. Besides, Portuguese men are so grabby, not like us. If I don't wear a cloth over me, they want to grab at my breasts all the time like a baby.'

'What about this silver sign they have around their necks? And this woman they are supposed to idolise?'

'I just play along with it. It is all I can do. I would be sent back here if I said anything against it. I might even be badly hurt, as they don't like criticism of their religion.'

'What does the silver sign mean?'

'They believe in a God, some being in their minds that created us and created the world all around us.'

'Very odd.'

'They believe that this God had a son who became a man for a short time, and who told people how they should live.'

'What, a guide as to what people should do and what they shouldn't?'

'I don't know that bit, but I guess it is a bit like that.'

'It doesn't stop them acting like animals in the way they treat us Tupi?'

'No, perhaps not. But the symbol they wear is a cross, and they believe that the son of God gave his life for the benefit of mankind, by being killed on a cross.'

'But their cross is so small. How do you die on it? None of it makes sense.'

'From what I was told, two trunks of trees were bound together in that cross shape, and he was nailed to it with iron nails so that he would die.'

'Quite barbaric these people, like I said.'

'Perhaps, but I am not sure this son of their God was so bad.'

'It's all a load of nonsense to me. Our beliefs rely on knowledge of the jungle, and all the beasts that share it with us. We look to mystical beings for rain, as we would die without rain, and the mystical beings give us some hope when there are many moons without rain. It is practical and common sense. You need to give your mind a reason to be hopeful when we are running out of water.'

'Well, perhaps their son of God is not so different. It gives them reason to be hopeful in hard times.'

'It's no reason for them to act so superior, either way,' says Ubirata. 'The only reason they can force us to work cutting trees is because of their fire sticks that can kill a man instantly.

Without these, we would be far superior because we are expert jungle dwellers.'

'I am going to refuse to work from now,' says Caua, boldly.

'They will come with their guns,' replies Potira.

'We can hide in places they don't know, the bits of dark jungle that we use when escaping after a tribal battle. There is water there, and animals we can eat. They won't dare come there,' retorts Caua.

'I'm with Caua,' says Ubirata.

'But what if Potira tells the Portuguese where we are?'

'My loyalty is to the Tupi, not the Portuguese,' blurts out Potira, defensively.

'But it will be easier for you if you don't know where we are. We can tell you eventually, when we have been safe for a number of moons. Then we can visit you and see if you want to join us.'

'I suppose so. I may even join you now, except my husband will come to find me, and threaten you all with his firestick.'

'Best to play along for now. Be a cockatoo, acting nonchalantly amongst the parrots, as though it is just the same as them, so that they don't suspect anything.'

'I am not sure a cockatoo is the best example to follow, they may be more likely to think I am up to something if that is how I act.'

'Well, you get my drift anyhow. Be a baby swan among ducklings.'

'Worse.'

'Or a baby guinea pig among pigs.'

'That may work. I would be so small I would be invisible.'

Tupi's story of Tapir and how his nose became long

'I have been having nightmares lately, dad. Can you tell me a story to help me sleep?' pleads young Cauasan.

Ubirata nods. 'I will tell you about the tapir. As you know, the tapir looks a little like a pig, but it has an unusually long nose.'

'A really big hooter, like a tail out of its mouth. Is it a really ancient tale?'

'It is as old as our people, from when we travelled here from a white land, full of ice and snow, to this warm land, where food is all around us.'

'Tell me, tell me.'

'And the tale also tells how the tapir eats nightmares, so perhaps it will eat yours.'

'Oh wow! I am all ears.'

'It was a time when the moon was bigger and the days were shorter, and mighty waves crashed on the beaches and made the rivers flow backwards.

'And every day the toddler cries and cries, and mother can't sleep and father can't sleep and brother and sister can't sleep. And still the toddler cries and cries, until from the corner of its eye…'

'What?'

'It espies something strange. "A pig!" she shouts. "A funny pig!" And it points at a reddish-brown creature sniffing beneath the hammocks where they lie. And as the tapir comes nearer to the toddler's hammock, the toddler's cries turn to muffled snuffles. And as it gets nearer, the toddler's muffled snuffles turn to little sniffs.

'And father leaps from the hammock and says, "Come near to the ear, tapi-ire,

hear the baby cry, tapi-ire

take the baby's pain, tapi-ire

take the baby's nightmare, tapi-ire

'to ease her pain, tapi-ire."

'And the tapir now places its nose by the toddler's body, and it places its ear by the toddler's head.

And it listens and listens and listens to the toddler, and as it listens it places its nose by the toddler's head. And the tapir sucks and sucks and sucks, and sucks and sucks and sucks, until all the nightmare has gone, until the wrinkles on the toddler's brow have gone and its brow is as smooth as a butterfly's new-born larvae.

'And as twelve moons pass, and as the tapir sucks up the nightmares of hundreds of children, slowly its nose begins to grow. And as another twelve moons pass, and as the tapir sucks up the nightmares now of hundreds of parents as well as the children, slowly its nose grows and grows. And as another twelve moons pass, and as the tapir sucks up the nightmares now of hundreds of grandparents as well as the parents and the children, so its nose grows longer and longer, until at last the tapir's nose is as long as it is today.

'And still today, the tapir can devour nightmares by sucking them up, but its nose has at last stopped growing.'

'I love that story,' says Causan, who now drifts off to sleep.

1512-1520: Felani and Mufaso working

'I don't mind being a farmer,' says Felani, 'I mean, I became an expert artist in fixing the facades of Mombasa buildings, but the Portuguese were determined to ruin our lives there. Farming is a good alternative.'

'We have been pushed from pillar to post by the Pink Skins, though,' says Mufaso. 'For me, this life is closer to where I started, with my family outside the city of Zimbabwe. Land is good, it is in touch with nature, with the seasons. But the past few years we have had our lives dictated by the Portuguese, first here, then there. This is not good.'

'It is about finding the small things that matter most and knowing the truth of these small things. This way, we do not allow the badness of the Pink Skin people to hurt or damage us.'

'What do you mean, Felani?'

'In a piece of land, we pull up plants that have no use to us, but have use to the birds, the bees, the ants, and because we carefully replant these plants away from our land, the bees give us some of their honey, the ants show us their genius, and the birds entertain us with their song.'

'Nicely put.'

'Then, when we plant a seed, something magical happens. The sun, and water, and the goodness in the soil, help the seed to grow into a plant. This plant will give us food, and also produce seeds for many more plants.'

'There is a beauty in this, in being close to nature. I do not disagree that we have been done wrong.'

'Aneni, your wife, was done a terrible wrong, of that there is no doubt. I was taken twice on the ships that took me into a world of darkness, a world where all the good things that human beings have done until now seem to have been cast away with the human heart cast with it. When the Portuguese soldier was ordered by his superior officer to throw a spear from the Portuguese ship at the young boy in the sea off India, he showed to me that the Portuguese and those who share their view of the world have no rightful place as human beings.

'That spear was thrown to kill a young boy who happened to have been born into a Muslim family. He had his life before him. He had just escaped from the hold of a ship that the Portuguese captain had made to sink because of hatred of Muslims.

' Very true, my friend.'

'This young child was not to be given a chance to live his life. He was struck down by a self-appointed God. No person can claim to share attributes with other humans if they can take a life of a young boy like this. This is what these Pink Skins mean to the world.

'You know, the physical world that we love, the people, the animals, the birds, the insects, the flowers, they have no relevance for these Pink Skins except as a means to gain wealth.'

'Evil men', adds Mufaso

The African Sage and Old Africa
Mai talks to Old Sage

It is a month since Mai, Felani, Itepi and Niambi, along with Aneni, Mufaso, Tia Tia and Wotambo, arrived with their animals at a village in land where they believe some families from Zimbabwe may be present. They meet up with Mr Ojo.

His granddaughter has told Niambi that he is a fine narrator of stories of old times.

'I hear you are the bearer of extraordinary tales, Mr Ojo,' ventures Mai, as the two families gather round.

'If you can bear with me, perhaps. I was old before I was young, and am older than that now, and all the while my memory stays alive, even if my body slowly withers.'

'It is kind of you to talk to us all,' adds Mai. 'But do say if you become tired.'

'That is fine. As you know, we people go back to the beginning of time, to when deserts were forests and forests were deserts, when seas were once savannah and savannah was once sea. We are a constant in this land. Our young have travelled to other worlds, and there become softer in colour and weaker in muscle and shorter of memory. But always the people of other worlds trace back to our peoples.

'Here, we were present on this land when lions were so big that their teeth were as long as my arm and their head was as big as an elephant's bottom. Fortunately, we were nimble and their legs were long so we could run between their legs and hide. Strange to say, the lions are more dangerous for us now they are smaller, as they are more agile, but their jaw is no less ferocious.'

'So don't be caught lying down when a lion comes,' says Niambi.

'That's right,' says Mr Ojo. 'For many generations, before Egypt's pyramids and the great empire of Nubia, we were pastoral people and ancestors of the Khoikhoi who now live much further to the south. We hunted game, and ate seeds and herbs, and bit by bit we learnt to herd sheep and use the sheep's wool and milk and eat some of their young. We also tamed cattle, which were once twice or three times their current size, but declined in size after years of drought. Their milk became our favourite drink, and we use their hides for our huts, and to ward off cold at night-time. The Khoikhoi became expert at locating sources of water so that our sheep and cattle could survive, and the cattle and sheep learnt to trust man. We had simple huts of sticks and long grass as we were constantly on the move. This worked fine for a very long time.

'But many generations ago, before the civilisation in Zimbabwe and after Egypt's decline, larger, stronger men, the Bantu, came from further north, searching for better supplies of water. The sand of the Sahara desert, much of which was once a mighty forest, expanded like flies on a fresh cowpat, and many people who had lived there when it sustained life moved south, and pushed the people they encountered further south. For East Africa, these were the Bantu, mostly Tsonga.

'The Bantu were better farmers than the Khoikhoi, able to grow sorghum, yams and beans. They lived in compounds that were grouped in a village, and their huts were made of mud interwoven with sticks and twigs that would form a semi-permanent structure. They also worked iron and copper to make tools and weapons and made fine pottery. Above all, they were stronger than the Khoikhoi, and they were better able to make use of the land for the life they led. The Khoikhoi couldn't stand up to them and moved further south.

'The Bantu have lived here since that time, mostly managing cattle and goats, living off the land, and hunting for game on the savannah or in the forests when it suited. During this time, demand for copper grew, for cooking and for jewellery, and some were involved in copper mining a little way from here. Coupled with this was a growing demand for ivory, and elephants we had in abundance. With this and the copper, there was more trade with other villages. The Bantu swapped their ivory and copper for cotton fabrics, to decorate their homes and sometimes to wear.

'A little further from here, where two great rivers join together for their long and winding dance, there was until recently a far larger settlement, perhaps the largest in this region. They called it Sleeping Cow, or in Tsonga, Ing'ombe-Ilede, as this is what its ancient baobab tree resembled. There, they traded with the coast, via the great river, and had textiles from India, ceramics from Arabia and gold, which was mostly from the city of Zimbabwe. This town was very large compared to our villages here, so life was varied, with more dance, poetry, singing and a wide variety of goods. But the town Sleeping Cow had started to give up the ghost by the time of my great grandparents, and not much is to be found there now. When the great civilisation of Zimbabwe collapsed quite recently, after years of drought, some of its inhabitants found their way here.'

'That is how we came here, via Mombasa,' says Mia. 'I am hoping we may find here some old friends.'

'Yes, well you will find a few families here, although most went further south, I believe. In a more dramatic way than Sleeping Cow city, the city of Zimbabwe showed that the Bantu people are capable of being great and courageous architects and able engineers, adept at working stone to very precise measurements, and also making fine sculptures like soapstone birds. As with the earlier great city of Magungupwe further south, and also the fine city of Thulamela, close to the mighty Levuku river, the knowledge of astronomy and the cosmos was profound. The magnificent stone buildings in each case were located in alignment with the sun at the summer solstice and also those stars of most significance to cosmologists. As such, the architects and engineers in these cities were true descendants of the Egyptians, even if they were unable to match all their extraordinary achievements. It seems man does not forget great skills and expertise, the memory passes on, even if there are passages of time in history where the memory is weakened. There are other examples of this.'

'What do you mean?' asks Mai. 'Are you saying that there are other great towns and cities of the past, like great Zimbabwe and Sleeping Cow city?'

'That, dear Mia, is a small question with a big answer, and it will need to wait until the morrow,' says Mr Ojo.

'That will be something to look forward to, thank you,' she replies.

Wedding of Niambi and Katchani

'Mum, Dad, I have news. I have here a young man, Katchani, who I want you to meet.'

'I am pleased to meet you, Katchani.'

'Me too,' says Mai.

'I wish to tell you that I am a young man with feeling for this land and joy in my heart, and I love your daughter Niambi and would like to ask her hand in marriage.'

Felani looks at Niambi, who is gazing at Katchani admiringly, and then at Mai, who nods at him.

'Yes, of course you may marry my daughter.

'Thank you, sir,' Katchani bows. 'Thank you, Mai.' He bows again.

Niambi hugs them both with an especially warm hug.

'Please invite your parents to visit us tomorrow, after the sun begins its descent. I will have returned from the fields by then.'

'I will,' says Katchani, 'they are only at the foot of the next hill.'

'And a date?' asks Mai. 'Do you have a date?'

'In seven days, if that is agreeable,' says Niambi.

First signs of Tupi going to war

Moacir is angry. He addresses a large crowd of Tupi, who have agreed to join him in fighting the Portuguese. They are in a clearing in the forest, and the cackling calls of parrots and macaws accompany Moacir's tirade.

'They come with their gifts of beads and their cloth and their pieces of metal. They pretend they want water and seek to understand where our red dye is from. Just as their skin peels off like a snake, so their tongue is forked like a snake.'

'Like a snake!' shouts the throng.

'Before they have grown baby teeth on our land, they are taking our sisters. When our sisters return, they tell of men with a penis for a brain, and a peashooter for a penis. They beat and maltreat our women away on distant seas, and we have to nurse them when they eventually return.'

'Penis for a brain, peashooter for a penis!' shouts the throng.

'They come to admire our fine tree that produces red-dye, the tree they call brazil, and when these people are but tiny saplings with their short time on our land, they are taking territory from our people and telling us it will be theirs forever.'

'Tiny saplings!' cry the throng.

'And when they have barely spent a day on our land, while we have been here for hundreds of generations of our people, they are saying that they are Master and we are slave. They drag us from our home, our family and our way of life in the jungle, and place us in wooden cages, and use their firesticks and whips to force us to cut down brazil trees from before dawn to after dusk. This is no life for an ant or a beetle. It is certainly no life for our people.'

'No life for our people!' sing the throng, repeating the phrase over and over.

'They kill our friend the pau brasil tree in large numbers, this beautiful tree which gives us shelter, food, branches for our homes, dye for our skins and our cloth, and food for so many creatures we love. They kill them like they are just fleas or mosquitoes. This is no different from killing us, or killing our land, as we are all part of the same living world, mutually dependent, loving. These people are savages.'

'Savages, savages.'

'They are not welcome here,

They are dangerous here,

They have no respect for the land here,

They have no respect for our friends, the creatures of the forest here,

They have no right to be here.'

'They have no right to be here,' cries the throng

Baby for Niambi and Katchani

A year or so after their wedding, Niambi gives birth to baby Matimba.

Within a few weeks of this, Aneni's daughter Tia Tia gives birth to Vimbo.

Matimba and Vimbo grow up in the same compound, and are best friends.

Mai and Old Sage (2)

It is the next evening.

'You offered to talk of other empires in Africa,' suggests Mai to her elderly and wise friend, as Felani joins them.

'I did. My grandfather explored far and wide, and found many cities and towns across this continent that left him very proud of the African tradition. I followed in his footsteps. When you travel from here, you find many peoples, as this is such a large continent, and man has always lived here, since we came down from the trees.

'There are many villages en route. The people in these villages have their own traditions, often going back to the beginning of time. They may have their own language, or a dialect of the language in the district. They may well have their own distinctive body markings. One village may traditionally place rings around their neck, more and more, until their necks become longer. Some of the Masai north of here also have this tradition.

'Some may burn markings into their back to resemble the skin of a crocodile, or perhaps make masks for evening dances where they represent animals or birds or perhaps spirits they revere. I respect every village that I visit, and they respect me back. If there is danger, perhaps a pride of lions in the vicinity, they will tell me. If there is a war between two tribes to the west, they will encourage me to go to the north.'

'You pat my back and I will pat yours?'

'Something like that. Tonight, I wish to speak more of one of the oldest civilisations in Africa, the Ethiopian, which is a few moons walk to the north of here. Ethiopia goes back a long way.

'When much of this continent, outside the Upper Nile areas of Egypt and Sudan, took the form of contented pastoral societies tending sheep, goats and cows, Ethiopia had a more urban society, and was famous for its large ornate thin towers, called obelisks.

'Back in the days that Egypt was fading as a great civilisation, Ethiopia was known as Aksum. It was seen as one of four major powers alongside Rome, Persia and China. It was on the Roman route to India and was then a major trading centre.

'The legend is that the modern Ethiopian Empire started some fourteen generations ago because of a rooster. The rooster was heard to prophesy that whoever ate his head would be king of Ethiopia. The King killed the rooster and gave it to the chef to cook.

'The chef, Yekuno Amlak, discarded the rooster's head, and gave the king the body to eat. Yekuno Amlak ate the rooster's head and became king.

'As king he led the army to take over lands previously lost to empire and re-established the Ethiopian Empire, which still survives. It was through the connection with Rome that I mentioned that a sect not seen before in Africa found its way to Aksum. It was a sect that believed in one God, and that God's son had come to earth to save mankind. Outside Aksum, this strange sect did not feature in Africa, to my knowledge, until the recent arrival of men with Pink Faces and firesticks.

'Christianity seems to us a bad spirit, as it speaks to Africa with cannon balls and firesticks. It seems to fear that its tongue has no persuasion in the face of our long traditions and our deep culture. It prefers to bully, like the elephant that happens upon a small group of antelope.

'It has also developed a side to it that is even more troubling, the capture and theft of our young men as slaves. This is a further blight on this strange and unpleasant sect.

'Ahmad Gragn recently conquered Ethiopia. Those men from Portugal caused fear in the Muslim world that they would weaken the Muslim position along the so-called Red Sea. The Muslims sent arms to Ahmad Gragn, enabling him to take power in the Ethiopian Empire. They have held out against most foes. I sense that Ethiopia may hold out against the Portuguese.'

'Sounds unbelievable,' says Mai. 'When the children have children they can travel. We must travel there, however long it takes.'

'I agree,' says Felani. 'Thank you, Mr Ojo.'

'Thank you for your interest,' says Mr Ojo graciously

Matinda and Vimbo's wedding

'I think your wedding was very special, Matinda,' says Mai. 'It was in some ways the perfect wedding, as we were all so close.'

'I loved it being family and us all being close,' replies Matinda, 'it was just a bit unusual. We were in a new village, and didn't know people, so none were invited for the main event.

There was no need for me to be in a secret hut as Vimbo and I have known each other since we were tiny. We didn't do the main things beforehand.'

'Well it didn't make sense. It was about you and Vimbo being in love.'

'And it was that. Like no other Bantu wedding before it, our wedding was about us, with our two very close families very intimately together. I was so emotional I was in tears, and so was Vimbo.'

'But I get the sense that, as much as you found it emotional, you felt that something was missing.'

Vimbo and Aneni join them at this point.

'I loved it,' continues Matinda. 'I completely loved it. It was just unlike all the weddings I have been to.'

'But, Matinda,' counters Vimbo, 'I haven't missed all the conversation with strangers. Our wedding was a perfect ball of happiness, small enough to be held in your hand, to hold inside your mind forever, as it was tiny but perfect.'

'Nicely put, Vimbo,' says Aneni.

'Well, I agree with all that totally,' says Matinda. 'I was only remarking on the mismatch in my mind between all the traditional weddings I have known, and our tiny ball of perfection, as you call it.'

'But it was the perfect solution to have the big wedding stuff the next day,' says Vimbo. 'Your dad was a genius suggesting that, as it is a chance to get to know all our neighbours, but with us all able to let our hair hang out in a gorgeously silly way.'

'And it turns out that our neighbours are good Bantu people, like everywhere,' adds Matinda.

'And serious good dancers,' adds Aneni.

'And seriously good drinkers,' laughs Mai.

'And why not?' asks Aneni.

Khoikhoi catch a whale

'We have one, a whale, trapped. A small one, probably three man lengths, but fat!'

The boy Muko is running round the village shouting.

The women run out, grabbing four cow hides; the men run out, grabbing spears, wooden knives and strips of cow hide cut as leather straps. Five also bring drums. A dozen children follow.

The men run down to the beach with Muko. They know that a whale will be trapped by the coral and will be thrashing around. It happens barely once a year, but it means meat for weeks and is a special occasion.

They reach the beach, move as close as they can to the angry whale, beached as it is in the calm water between coral and sand, and throw spears into its blubbery flesh as forcefully as they can muster. They know from experience that it will take time. They flatten an area of sand. They tie together the strips of leather with tight knots, to make several long strips.

A few of the women appear at the top of the beach with dried grass, kindling and firewood. They rub sticks and start a fire. It is far enough up for the high tide not to reach it. Soon the flames are strong, and they fetch bigger logs to place on it.

The whale starts to scream, an otherworldly out-of-body scream. The water around it becomes redder and redder.

The men with drums start drumming. The other five men start to hum, with the children following suit.

They believe the whale's scream is the pain of its spirit leaving it. Their humming and drumming create a seductive sound, curdled by the winds that swirl in from the ever-big-bad-wolf sea. They hope through this to soften the journey of the whale's spirit and make the flesh of the whale sweeter.

Eventually, the whale's thrashing weakens, the volume of its screaming lessens, the men stop drumming and humming. The men start to approach.

Akasu, the eldest, touches the whale. It responds as if to say 'I am not dead yet,' but the force of its movement is not strong. After a few more minutes, the whale does not respond to touch. Eight men first remove the spears, then move to the other side of it, up to their chests in the blood-infused water. The two other men throw leather straps over the whale at the head and tail ends, which the others pass over and under. The women leave the fire and join them.

Bit by bit, they try to roll the whale, eight pushing and two pulling. A sudden shudder by the whale causes them to hesitate, but soon they start again.

A large wave comes over the coral and lifts the whale nearer the beach, and they use all their strength to try to stop the whale sliding back as the wave ebbs.

Another large wave brings the pullers on to the sand. Bit by bit they edge a little further on to the beach.

Four women come to the beach carrying a few cowhides that they have sewn together. They lay this cow hide sheet as close as they can to the whale's great mass.

More of the village come down now, three with axes long ago obtained from the Bantu, and other with knives.

Akasu leads the team, shouting 'Heave,' every few moments, as the whale is moved, inch by inch, on to the cowhide sheet.

Those with knives and axes now start to attack the head and tail. Blood pours out, and some of the men cup their hands to catch and sup it. The children follow suit. The bits of head and tail that are chopped off are taken up to the fire to start roasting.

The whole party now try to pull the cow hide sheet with the rest of the whale on it. Many push, many pull, the seams of the cowhide sheet start to give. Slowly, they bring it nearer the fire.

When they are within twelve or fifteen feet of the fire, they stop, and a number of the men start chopping the whale up as best they can, starting with each end, where the head and tail have been removed. The smell of the roasting meat now acts as a strong incentive to keep going.

During the chopping, a few of the men and women head back to the reddened water between the coral and the beach. Part of this was walled off to make a pool when the last whale was caught, and they start using flat stones and large boulders to build the wall up again.

Much of the whale meat that cannot be used now will be kept cool here. It will attract other predators, but it is just for a day or two until all the meat can be smoked.

Some women have made a second fire, and as this settles some of the chopped meat is put on there.

The baleen, the filter for tiny sea creatures like krill, is taken out and put on rocks to dry. When dry it will be unravelled and used as a line for hanging out the skin and some organs to dry. The skin is a delicacy.

There are some flat rocks near the village. Bits of blubber are placed there until they can be heated to make candles.

There are a few holes dug to the side of the village, with rims made from cowhide, and a cover of turf. Once the whale meat has been smoked for a long time on the ashes of the fires, and has cooled, it is stored in the holes and can be brought out over the coming weeks when needed.

The whole village is involved in the whale catching, chopping and cooking exercise all day.

There are wild celebrations in the evening. The drummers start up again and all join in the party.

At the high point of the party, Muko is lifted up by two men and carried round the other villagers for each to pat him and thank him for finding the whale. The women all join in a long ululation.

Baby for Matimba and Vimbo

'It's coming now, the crown is clearly visible!' exclaims Aneni excitedly, squatting in her hut with a clear view of her daughter's vulva.

Cloths are spread over the floor. There is a bowl of cold water and a basin of warm water, next to which is a freshly cleaned knife and some rags.

'Please let it be,' cries an exhausted Vimbo, bathed in sweat and on all fours.

Aneni reaches forward and dabs her forehead with a damp cloth.

'One more mighty push, puuuuuussssh!' exhorts Mai, squatting next to Aneni.

'I have no energy left,' sighs Vimbo, as she nevertheless tries to push.

'Head's coming now, so so near, try and push one more time.' And Aneni holds the head, and gently eases it towards her as Vimbo pushes again.

'We have him, we have him!' shouts Mai excitedly, taking hold of the knife.

'A boy! A boy!' shouts Aneni, as the baby slides and slithers its way out, and she takes a clean towel from her shoulder. 'Stay there a moment, sweetheart, while the afterbirth comes.'

She wraps the baby in the towel, leaving his head free, and she holds him caressingly by both body and head and takes him round for Vimbo to look.

Vimbo now turns on to her back, and holds the baby on her chest, admiring him lovingly.

'He's purple,' she says, as a frown forms.

'That's normal at first', says Aneni. 'From ugly to beautiful before you know it, is the usual.'

'He's not breathing,' says Vimbo, with a deeper frown.

'Will you let me take him for a tiny second?' asks Mai. 'I can help start his breathing.'

'Ok, but be very gentle,' and Vimbo hands him to Mai.

Mai takes him to her left shoulder, held gently with left hand, and touches either side of the baby's spine with the softness of a feather with her right. She touches a second time.

The baby makes a spluttering sound, then bursts into a cry.

Mai hands the baby back to a smiling Vimbo as the baby exercises his lungs to the full.

'Thank you,' says Vimbo. 'And thank you from Barawa. We are calling him Barawa.'

As Aneni mops up the afterbirth with the dampened rags, Mai calls in her son Matimba.

'Heh, Matimba, come on in, you have a son!'

Matimba comes in with a smile as wide as a new moon, and kisses Vimbo while admiring the baby, his crying notwithstanding.

'My beautiful Barawa,' he says, his smile still unwavering.

'Our beautiful Barawa,' says Vimbo, now ecstatic, even while he continues to cry and despite her exhaustion.

'Two boys in the space of a week,' says Mai. 'First Itepi's Mabvuto has Masiye, and now you have Barawa. How perfect.'

'How perfect,' agrees Vimbo.

And Niambi comes in with Masiye cradled in the crook of her left arm, and admires the new baby, while hugging her brother and kissing Vimbo.

'I am complete,' says Mai.

Tupi Tale: Chameleon and the Tarantula. The story of why chameleons do not play chess with tarantulas

Mato offers a story in the evening moonlight, with the glow from the fireflies starting to fade, and the villagers sitting cross-legged in a circle round a fire whose embers offer a gentle glow.

'What kind of story? One of your funny ones?' asks Idoi.

'I think it's funny. I hope you find it funny too.'

'Ok, we are all listening. Fire away'

Pawn takes queen. Checkmate. Sad little caiman. He had not played chess before and he so hoped his first game against the chameleon would be successful; it was not.

The chameleon was rapidly becoming the chess champion of the jungle, so the caiman was just the latest in a long line of conquests. But caiman was mighty upset and decided to have a snack. He leapt on a red brocket in the audience and ate it.

Chameleon's chess trick is simple. During the game she gradually turns herself into the creature she is playing. The opponent becomes very confused. Are they playing themselves? Is chameleon cheating? They lose their concentration. Without their concentration, the opponent cannot compete, and they soon lose. All over the country, Chameleon is known as queen of the chequered board.

A long way away, Chameleon's fame spreads to a spider community where there lives a large hairy tarantula. The tarantula thinks of herself more as a dancer than a chess player and has perfected the finest eight-legged Kick dance ever seen.

However, when she does the Backward Kick Dance, she loses all concentration and falls flat on the floor, hence her nickname Terrible.

The idea of challenging Chameleon appeals to Terrible. It occurs to her that she could shake off this negative name if she could just defeat the Chameleon at chess. They might at last stop laughing at her, and act more normally towards a tarantula, like being scared out of their minds.

So Terrible ventured off across the plains, skittered across rivers spider-style, swung on Virginia creepers through the bush, and ended up on the edge of the jungle.

After weeks of travelling, with numerous baby birds and animals consumed on the way, and at least one hunter stung on the bottom, Terrible arrives at her destination.

She is shown to a clearing, and she is suddenly aware of the extraordinary sight before her. The chessboard is made from matting, some squares pale, some dark. The pawns are snails, all standing in line waiting to be moved slowly forward. The rooks are termites, who build a little mound in each corner while they wait and sit on top.

The knights are grasshoppers, which sit there clicking their knees, waiting to hop over other pieces. Praying mantises play the part of bishops, while cockatiels play the part of queens. The king, finally, is played by a small sloth, who enjoys the fact that he does not have to move very much.

Terrible admires this collection of edible creatures, thinking to herself what a fine feast may lie in wait if she is lucky enough to win. 'But where,' she wonders, 'is my opponent, the famed chameleon?'

With the game due to start, dozens of animals are gathered round the chess board. There are panthers, eagles and hummingbirds, geckos with babies, a maned wolf and even a small tapir. Birds flutter in the trees, and insects swarm above the throng. Not for some time has there been such a buzz in the air about a game, especially among chameleon's chess opponents. Many of these former victims of chameleon have come along, hoping chameleon will at last be defeated.

Suddenly, a baby brown gecko becomes green and climbs on to the chess board as Chameleon.

She eyes up the large hairy spider across the board from her. 'Ey, up,' she thinks. Terrible stares back, without blinking. 'Toast,' she says to herself.

Terrible is black.

The game starts slowly, almost like a waltz. And Terrible wastes not a minute in trying her devilish trick.

Terrible quite ostentatiously moves one piece, a pawn, with her eyes focussed on Chameleon, who remains focussed on the pawn as it moves. Chameleon is not aware of Terrible's other legs moving a black knight at the same time.

The crowd remain silent, as they are determined for Chameleon to lose. Chameleon looks at the pieces. Two have moved after only one go. So she goes over to the black knight, and moves it back to its original position with her long and flexible tongue. Terrible's ugly mouth turns into a smile so aggressive Chameleon wants to pee on the spot. Chameleon turns to the referee, a puma, and nods her head. The puma reciprocates.

Chameleon controls her nerves and makes her move.

This stop-and-start waltz through the opening moves continues, pieces moving forward, then back, and somehow Chameleon keeps control of the game despite Terrible's appalling tactics. Soon, the hyena starts to laugh, and the lions and cheetahs laugh, and the birds giggle. This is affecting Chameleon's concentration.

Sensing a plan on Terrible's part, Chameleon starts to turn into a tarantula, with furry legs, but initially only four.

Terrible again moves two pieces, both a rook and a bishop.

Chameleon shouts 'Got you, false move! I want the game awarded to me for cheating.'

She looks at the Puma, who looks at Terrible's furry legs, and looks at Chameleon's furry legs, and says, 'I cannot distinguish between your hairy legs. I will have to ask you to continue, but please desist from false moves.'

Chameleon moves.

Terrible again does a double move with pawn and knight, and Chameleon reaches a furry leg across and shouts, 'Got you, yet again, cheat!" But the moment her tongue is reaching right across for the moved knight, Terrible grabs the tongue, and passes it from one of her sticky legs to another. Chameleon's tongue is now attached to Terrible's sticky legs, and as Terrible starts a Kick dance, so she finds her tongue being thrown up and down and around, outside of her control. She is shell-shocked.

Now, Terrible switches to the Backward Kick Dance, her high-kicking legs tossing Chameleon's tongue up with her legs, and then down. The crowd claps the beat. Monkeys, who arrived late, play castanets with coconuts. Terrible has finally mastered the Backward Kick Dance and beams an ugly smile.

Now Chameleon is up in the air, being swept up by the high kicking legs of Terrible. The birds are chanting da-da-dada, di-di-dada, da-da-da ...

Terrible goes ever faster, turning in a circle as she does so. Chameleon , its tongue attached to Terrible's legs, is flying in a circle. And hating it.

At last, Terrible lets go of Chameleon, who flies up into the sky on pure momentum, her face glum with the impossibility of resistance. She flies over and beyond the whole throng.

She passes a flying bat. 'Who are you, flying here?' asks the bat.

'I am a chameleon out of control,' she responds, trying as she does so to become a bat, so as to glide.

'The best advice I can give you,' says the bat, 'is that when you go down there, don't come up again.'

'Thanks for nothing,' says Chameleon, now heading rapidly earthwards.

She nose-dives headfirst into a pool, the splash being so big that most of the water departs the pool.

She is a deeply unhappy Chameleon.

Since that time, chameleons have never played chess with tarantulas. I am sure that is correct, says Mato with a smile. Have you ever seen a chameleon playing chess with a tarantula?

Sage on Kitara Kingdom

'May I begin?' asks Old Sage.

'You may,' says Mai.

'Yes please,' says Vimbo, cradling Barawa.

'Africa is a long-lived continent. It had so many empires in this time, rising with fertility, declining with aridity. The emergence of a large desert in the Sahara regions has affected the course of many empires, not least Egypt.

'Africa's empires sometimes leave magnificent symbols, such as pyramids in Egypt and miraculous sculpture in Benin. Sometimes an empire does not leave a legacy in fine monuments or sculptures but leaves people that are content in their lives and leaves special natural phenomena. The Bunyoro-Kinyara Empire just to the north of us here but covering a very wide area almost to the great Sahara desert is the latter kind.

'Its most famous symbol is a tree, the ancient Nakayima tree, whose root system is so immense that there are four rooms within. The origin of the tree's myth lies in a smallpox plague that killed most of the people in the village. King Ndahura settled by the Nakayima tree at Mubende. A sorceress, Kamanenge, gave the tree magical powers, and Ndahura's princess daughter, who survived the plague, was thought to have these powers when the smallpox ended. People flocked to her to be healed. Now people still visit to draw the benefit of these magical powers.

'Many moons ago, a prophesy stated: when the sacred cow dies, the empire will end. People started to think that the end was coming, and started leaving the empire, which covered several of the big lakes on the Nile river. Now, the special tree still stands, but the empire is weak. If you visit the tree now, there are witches that smoke special pipes and help visitors to communicate with the spirit world.'

Felani chips in: 'It seems to me, when the sacred cow of money dies it will mark the end of today's empire.'

'The empire of the Hausa, a few moons to the west of here, was very different to Bunyoro-Kinyara. This is much further up the Niger river from Benin. For me, the most astonishing experience in the Hausa Empire was the enormous market-place in Kano, a market that stretches so far in all directions and which is so full of people it is almost impossible to see the other side.

'Anything imaginable could be bought in that market. The finest cloths in Africa, exquisite ivory carvings, tastefully carved chairs and tables, rich velvet tapestries, gold and silver jewellery, animals and birds of every description, and so much else besides.

'The Hausa Empire is mostly Muslim. The towns, many of them walled, have many big houses and some small, many of them with rugs and carpets on the floors, in between rooms and sometimes on the walls. Each market is full of an extraordinary range of rugs and carpets.

'Currently, there is a sign that change may be afoot in the Hausa Empire. There are seven sub-kingdoms of Hausa, and some are restless, I was told. In Zazzau, in particular, there is a king, Turunku, with a very ambitious Queen, and there may be change soon.'

'Well, I think you are tired Mr Ojo,' says Mai.

'I am.'

'Good. Thank you so much. Let us rest now for this evening. That is enough for today, I feel.'

'Thank you,' says Vimbo. Barawa is fast asleep in her lap.

Tupi divisions

'Potira, please stay. This is where you belong,' pleads Piata.

'I am going,' she replies. 'They have my child, my child needs me. In the end, I feel I can live with them.'

'They are heartless people, who steal our friends the trees, who eat our friends the pumas, the ocelots. And who take our women, who we love so much.'

'This land is big enough for them and for us. If we show a willingness to share, it can work. For now, I must be with my son.'

'But we have lost too many of our sisters already. Too often, they have a baby, the Portuguese take the baby, and our sisters, you included, want to be with the baby. We cannot lose more sisters like this. Please stay,' pleads Piata.

'I have decided. I have tried living with my brothers. This is my true home. But every day my heart cries out for baby. The pain is too great. I must go to baby.'

'Let her go, my brother,' says Ubirrata. 'We have to stop this fight. The Portuguese are here, we must find a way. They have firesticks, we have bows and arrows. We are mice against their jaguars.'

'Don't ever say that, brother. These people are blind jaguars, with claws that rely on us being stupid. We are at once caimans and monkeys. Like a caiman we can hide from our enemies with extraordinary guile, and like monkeys we know our friends the trees intimately, and can travel between trees, hide in the trees, eat from the trees, as the need arises.'

'But they have fire, and can burn our friends the trees, and when we are exposed, they can hit us with their firesticks.'

'The Portuguese walk deaf and blind into the jungle. As long as this is our battleground, we can defeat them. Their fire is only a weapon if they know where we are. It is up to us to ensure that they cannot find us.'

'What if too many of us are frightened of the Portuguese and won't fight? A leader is no leader if his people are unwilling.'

'This is our land, this is our jungle. These outsiders do not want to look after this land and keep it for future generations for ever, like we do. They want to take, take, take, and then when they have taken everything and there is nothing left, they will leave. We will have to make friends with all the other tribes, as we all have a common interest. Together we can defeat these Ozh Dozh pink faced people.'

'I wish you luck talking to those other tribes that we have never talked to before.'

'We all face the same threat. Our lives are at risk, our home in the jungle, our land, everything is under threat. Our village is barely six hundred. The next village is nine hundred. The Portuguese are bigger than this. We will need a lot of tribes, working together.'

'I think you need to start soon. I don't think I will be helping you.'

'So you will share our way of life, but you will not share the protection of our way of life.'

'You make it sound worse than it is. I am shit scared of those firesticks,' says Ubirrata.

'So, it is our job to make those firesticks as useless as a legless ocelot.'

'A legless ocelot?'

'Yes, why not?'

'Well, if you can make their firesticks as useless as a legless ocelot, you may win me back.'

'Brother, when we shinned up trees as children to get the best fruit at the top and looked down to see the people, so little, far below us, I never thought of you as a frightened frog. But I think, perhaps, you are back with us. The beautiful land against the blotchy-faced pink-skinned impostors.'

'I am nearly there. Let me just think a bit.'

'I am not with you,' says Potira. 'I am with your blotchy-faced pink-skinned impostors.'

Potira and Ubirata

'Can I speak to you?'

'Yes, Potira, any time,' replies Ubirata.

'I don't like the idea of being an outcast among my own people because I want to be with my son.'

'No, and it's not right if we cannot raise our concerns about putting our lives at risk in the event we fight the blotched face ones. What are you thinking?'

'I want to go to talk to the Ozh Bozh people, or the Portuguese, as they like to be called. I have learnt enough to talk with my man. And though he can run rings round me, taking advantage of my limited Portuguese, I think he will listen. We know the jungle, the herbs that heal, the plants that poison, the animals that are friends, and those to be wary of. We have much to teach them, if they make peace with us.'

'We can try. Anything is better than to fight and die. Their firesticks are so deadly.'

'Arquebuses, they call them.'

'Arsqebuckets or firesticks, it is the same. Let us speak to them. Do you know who we can speak to among these people?'

'My man is good friends with the talking man. I think the talking man is called Federico Dias. I will ask my man if we can speak to him.'

'We need to talk about how they treat us as well. The people they take as slaves, the ones they kill when they do not do what they are told.'

'I don't know. We can try to talk peace for now, try to get more respect for our way of life. If we can do this, then the next stage may be to try to deal with the big issue that faces our people, the brutality of slavery.'

'Ok, I will try to set up the meeting with Dias. But please don't say a cockatiel to Piata.'

'Of course not. More than my life is worth.'

* * * * *

'What do you want, woman? I do not have time for you. Speak now, or go!' barks Dias.

Potira's husband Alfredo is by his side. They are sat at a table holding four beakers of water, by a brick house built in Portuguese style, next to a tree-felling area, where pau brasil trees are being felled.

Potira is small, has a full figure, black hair, chestnut skin and dark brown eyes. She feels herself about to retch from the foul smell coming from Dias, but she manages to control herself. She takes a sip of water from a beaker and speaks.

'Listen me, listen my friend. We talk peace with Tupi.'

'We don't need peace. We do what we want. What are you offering?'

Potira explains to Ubirata. He addresses Dias. Potira translates as best she can.

'We know plants in the jungle. We know what heals sickness. We know poison. We know what gives a man a smile.'

'I don't need that. We have doctors. We don't need your plants.'

'We know how to catch caimans. We know how to avoid being killed in water by piranha fish. We know water snakes, and other dangerous river creatures. We can teach you all this.'

'So you may help us in the water. Our men are dying in the water. We don't know your creatures.'

'So we can talk?'

'Just bloody talk, I may listen. What are you putting on the table?'

'I don't understand this table,' says Potira.

'Tell me what you are offering, and what you want.'

'We want you to cease attacking our people and enslaving us. We will tell you about our plants and how to avoid dangers in our rivers in return, and try to persuade our people to agree peace,' says Ubirata.

'We need workers to cut trees, and you are the people who live here. You listen when an arquebus speaks,' says Dias.

'These trees are living beings, they give us our homes, they give us food and clothing, they give us red dye. We worship these trees. Killing them is killing us.'

'Stop this crap!' shouts Dias. 'First you want no more slavery. Now you want us to stop cutting down trees. We are only on this godforsaken land to take wood from your tree home. So fuck off.'

'There may be war,' says Potira.

'War! What, with your arrows? We can kill a hundred of you before you kill one of us. Just go away.'

'There are very many tribes. The tribes are angry,' says Ubirata, as he and Potira stand up.

'I don't care if there are a hundred tribes, all angry. We can beat your tribes.'

'We know the jungle like we know our lover's body,' says Ubirata. 'We know all its secrets. How will you find us in the deep jungle?'

'I think we have ways. Your people should think hard before you try to take on our arquebuses. You may find your arrows are just too weak to help you.'

'So nothing changes?'

'Hell no! Nothing changes. We will make Potira teach us about the water and its dangers. That is all we need. She will resist but we can persuade her.'

Potira walks Ubirata to the edge of the settlement. She bids him goodbye, and he soon reaches the jungle.

He knows now whose side he is on.

Felani as Poet visits Mombasa, 1535

Felani, as a silver-haired touring poet, tours with Niambi as his helper with travel and sleeping arrangements. They are now in Mombasa.

She introduces Felani. He addresses the crowd in the shaded marketplace, seagulls accompanying.

Felani begins:

What is this spectre that is haunting our continent?
life in Mombasa sweet as mango and coconut.
Arab and Bantu living like the crocodile
lives with its friendly plover,
respect mutual, help at hand .
beauty on the facades of so many buildings.

A well-dressed woman, our Mombasa.
the exquisite ancient wooden mosque.
our woman's altar.
the benign sublime climate.
the waterfront houses whose shining beacon
offers a welcome
as visitors arrive on the waves
the azure wonderment of the ocean.

But a beast arrives to fire metal balls.
why? To force out Arabs
who may compete
to gain some penis-size advantage
No 'hello, how do you do,

can I make you an offer?'
No laying out its goods to the buyer
nor the prices it offers.
Just bang bang fire the cannon.
destruction of years
of fine chiselling
of the beautiful face
of a handsome woman,
our Mombasa.

I have seen this Portuguese beast close up.
I have seen a beast with no soul.
I also believe, that
were I to cut into its chest,
I would find no beating heart.
but a dark tunnel leading
to the bowels of the earth

This beast is not satisfied with
dropping its violent excreta
all up the coast of Africa.
It visits the ancient land of India
repeats its bad toilet habits there.
I have witnessed this beast at work.
When the local Indian ruler rejects
rule by Portuguese mandate,
the lizard-like beast wraps its
vile sticky tongue around
a ship full of Muslim pilgrims,
takes their worldly goods,
ends the life of women, children and men,
and prepares to go on its way.

In our homeland we have done bad things.
We have battled over land,
we have brothers
who both want to be king,

and fight to the death for kinghood.
This has been the case since man began.
but we have a heart,
we have a soul.
We love our people, our cattle, our homeland
we respect other human beings.
Other species

When our women are dragged
at gunpoint
on to a Portuguese ship,
the Portuguese act like
our women are subhuman.
Beaten, raped, beaten again

In our history, we treat
all other people as people.
There are slaves,
but we treat slaves as humans too.
We don't see this with Pink Face.
They bestride our world
with their big ships
like they are Gods.
they delude themselves
they are soulless and heartless ghouls,
who blacken and turn to dust
wherever their spectre haunts.

The applause rings out for many minutes. Many onlookers walk up to Felani and embrace him. He is embarrassed. Niambi embraces and steadies him, as his legs are now not as strong.

Puberty for Masiye and Barawa

'It is near time for Barawa,' says Niambi.

'Also for Masiye,' replies Aneni. 'They are both ripening and waiting to be plucked for manhood.'

'We will have to tell all the village and prepare well.'

'We can start painting them in the next few days. The paint will take a day or two to fully harden on the skin.'

'Do you have a particular design in mind?' asks Niambi.

'I will need to involve Vimbo and Matimba regarding Barawa, but I imagine blue eyes on his upper chest, to help him see into the future, and white hands lower on his chest, to guide his technical ability. I can make an elaborate bead headdress and find beautiful ostrich feathers to attach round his waist. What are you thinking?'

'I think that the beads and feathers sound perfect. I would prefer ears and eyes on his chest, so that he remains alert to the faintest sound when out in the bush. But we can discuss it with their parents, of course.'

'The men will need to arrange a week-long stay in a special hut, where they learn all that a lion, a cheetah, an elephant and a man know of how to live as a man.'

'During mine, in Zimbabwe,' says Niambi, 'we were told it was the journey of the sprit from child to woman. I liked that idea. We called it the unumela.'

'I have heard that said too, but we called it the Thomba. You know, the men may already be doing their rituals at a special hut, getting it ready, for all I know. Maybe that is where they are now.'

'The worst thing was the large piece of smelly ox fat which you had to wear while you danced in front of everyone. I tried to put the fat down, but I was told off for fear our ancestors would not protect me in later life. I had to dance with it until a boy danced with me, but of course the boys didn't like the foul smell either. Eventually, a boy took pity on me, and I could put the fat down.'

'Sounds horrid. You know, we will need to kill an ox soon for the gourd of blood the boys need to drink. The village won't be keen, as there's only currently two oxen, and there are more children reaching puberty a few moons from now.'

'Interesting dilemma. But we must kill the ox today, and find more oxen when the village needs them.

The wedding of Barawa and Miri, 1537

'I am so pleased for you,' says Vimbo

'And me too, if I am allowed a say in things, with Mai and Aneni always doubling up.'

'Don't say that, Matimba. Of course you have a say.'

'Well I have no reason to object. Miri is a young woman from the next village. We know her parents. The family are a good farming family, like us, with a good heart. So, this is fine. We don't need to instruct a kindly relative to investigate young Miri's background.'

'This is your final comment on the matter?'

'I just need to know two things. First, the proposed dowry.'

'Four cattle, a dozen chickens, I understand. And the second thing?'

'Well that seems reasonable. And the date?'

'Four days' time.'

'Ok, I will organise Barawa's preparation right away. Miri's family will organise the big get together of the families in the next day or two. They can sort the cock for the brother that does all the hosting.'

'Surely, we don't still do that with the cock, dress it up for the brother?'

'Oh yes, nothing has changed there as far as I know.'

'Aneni and I will help Matimba and Vimbo prepare a great feast for the wedding day,' says Mai.

Matimba thanks them all. 'I am sure it will all be fine,' he says.

Aneni and Mai also delight in preparing a boozy but also tasty brew to take to his intended's family.

Mai quietly gives thanks to the ancestors at her own private shrine.

A baby for Barawa and Miri

Barawa and Miri have a baby girl, Atwooki, in 1538. Two years later, in 1540, they have a baby boy they call Otapo.

The Bantu seek Khoikhoi land

'Fathers, there are men on that hill over there. They are large ebony men, with spears.'

One of the elders, Akasu, nods, and says, 'You are right to point them out. It is a sizeable group, heading this way. We have seen these people before. Bantu. Their skin is blacker than ours, with a sense of purple. Their posture is not warlike. Do you agree, Baruka?'

'Yes, I agree. I think we can walk slowly in their direction. We will take spears with us also, but held low.'

They head towards the hill.

The new arrivals stop at the bottom of the hill. They hold their spears by their sides to show peaceful intent.

One of the Bantu walks forward towards Baruka, Akasu and their brothers.

As he approaches them he holds up one hand and says, 'My name is Maphatusama. They call me Phat. I speak some Khoisan as one of my wives is Khoikhoi. We wish to talk about sharing some of your land.'

'We use our land for our way of life,' answers Baruka. 'Where there is water and we suffer drought, we move to the water. Where there is game, we move to the game. There are many families who do the same. We do not wish to share our land.'

'We have suffered many moons of drought to the north of here. We abandoned our city when there was no more water. We found water further south and children were born and also their children, but again the water dried up and the rains did not come. Here, you have water to share.'

'Our ancestors came here because Bantu wanted our land to the north,' explains Baruka. 'They said we could have this land and we would be left in peace. Now, you wish to interrupt our peace.'

'Our gods have not been kind. The rain chooses to stay away, not for twenty moons, not for thirty moons, but more. Too many of us have died. If you share your land with us, we will leave you in peace.'

'Are you holding a hand of peace with one tongue, and holding up a spear with the other tongue?'

'Our people are dying. We will fight to have land where we can live. But we wish to do this peacefully. We do not wish you to suffer bloodshed, to see children without their fathers, women without their husbands. To the north of here, over five more hills, some of our people fought Khoikhoi people who chose to fight and not share. Too many of your men died. There is another way.'

'I understand what you say. I ask you to make camp here. As you have seen, there is a river here for fresh water. We will talk with our family. We will talk with other Khoikhoi families. We will give you an answer when we have spoken to our people.'

'We will wait one moon. We will bring our people here. You will see there are many.'

'Very good. There was a full moon last night. We will talk when the moon is again full.'

The Bantu behind Phat, their Khoisan speaker, have a drum, and its holder starts beating out a steady but insistent beat. Before long, hundreds of Bantu men, women and children start appearing at the top of the hill. An hour or so later, Akasu realises that Phat was not lying about there being many Bantu.

Further settlement by the Portuguese in Brazil, 1541

'Our very first sugar canes on this land,' says Federico, whose African porters are carrying the canes for him.

'When the Spanish who travelled with that Genovese Columbus planted sugar cane on one of the first islands they discovered, Hispaniola, it grew almost before their eyes. That is their story, anyhow. In Europe, any sugar that goes for sale now disappears from the stalls immediately, whatever the price. The price per quintal is now higher than that of gold.'

'So we need to find the land to grow it here, and we can soon be rich. As easy as that.'

'We have to force the Indians off the land first, this is the first objective. They seem to think they have some rights here.'

'They are just savages. They don't realise that the King of Portugal, in his wisdom, divided their country into fifteen captaincy colonies. It is now five years since 1536, when that occurred.'

'We will just need to bring some soldiers from the ship to make the savages aware that they cannot stand in our way.'

They say the place to try to grow sugar is called Pernambuco. They are starting to clear the jungle, but the jungle is like a dog with a bone, it just keeps coming back to land it loves and, when it does so, it grows voraciously.'

'Well, if we start experimenting there, and employ people to fight off the jungle, we may be able to produce sugar commercially in one or two years.'

'It may take a little longer. Also, we will need to employ soldiers to fight off the Indians, as they won't give up the land so easily. If we employ some of the Indians, the money may make them like us more.'

'We have not found a way of satisfying the men with payment so far. Take the pau brasil loggers – some will exchange their labour for goods in return, but this relationship soon breaks down. They seem to like their backward and pagan way of life. Only the women have been amenable so far, especially if they have a baby with one of our men.'

'Well, we can get the soldiers, and we can find women Tupis who may talk to the men in the jungle about working for us. But if our sugar scheme is to be really successful, we will have to think about using African slaves, like we have started to do in Africa. The Spanish are already heading down this route with their sugar production. Portugal has a slave port in Loango, Kongo and in Guinea on Africa's west coast, and we can take advantage of these if the need arises.'

'I can start imagining the piles of gold, the grand houses, a glamorous wife and a few mistresses.'

'My friend, the chicks have not yet hatched and can't be counted, so let's first see how well this sugar grows before we spend too much on outgoings.'

'You are wise, you are wise.'

Sage on Ghana

The Sage offers to tell Mai and family a further tale of empires of Africa.

There is now Mai, Felani, Aneni, Mufaso, Niambi, Katchani, plus Matimba, Vimbo, Aneni's son Wotambo, and Barawa, Miri and Masiye and Eneco. Also baby Otapo.

'Please, please,' says Niambi.

The others signal their agreement.

'The camel is not originally from Africa. As the Roman Empire started to decline, the camel came to the Western Sahara from the Nile Delta area for the first time. Before time began, it came to the Nile Delta from Arabia.

'The camel's two humped arrival in the western Sahara laid the basis for a trade network from Morocco to the Niger river. This reliable trade route replaced irregular and unpredictable routes, so that such essentials as salt and such riches as gold ornaments could trade freely.

Ghana, which then covered the western Sahara and the area between the Senegal river and the Niger river, became an empire by dominating this valuable trade, and then expanded as it took over other valuable trade routes.

'The original rulers were most likely berbers, nomads of the desert, from Sanhaja. The empire was successful for many centuries, with ivory, horses, swords, spices and silks, as well as books, being mainstays of its economy. It developed a system of laws and rules over this region over six to eight centuries. Koumbi Saleh, its capital, had an impressive Royal Palace, surrounded by domed buildings and a large stone wall. Burial mounds were inside the wall, unusually. The capital was situated at the edge of the Sahara desert when it was built. The desert has had a rather voracious appetite for fertile land since then, sadly, and it was sadly no longer there when I visited. The sand won. The empire ceased about fourteen or fifteen generations ago.

'Two huge dogs had an important place in the Royal Palace. They guarded the entrance to the king's chamber and sat in place for hours on end in their gold and silver collars, studded with gold and silver balls. They knew there would be a large lamb bone when the day came to an end. Inside the palace, there was also a sacred grove of trees where the priests lived, with birds accompanying their praying.

'Education was central to Ghana's success, as it was to ancient Egypt, and it was a vital centre of learning when Africa otherwise lacked this. Alexandria's Egyptian traditions were continued in Ghana, as in the Byzantine Empire.

'As Islam spread through the western Sahara, Ghana adapted to this, and many of its towns and cities became major Islamic centres, including Timbuktu. Ghana is now part of the Mali Empire. Timbuktu is a major city in this empire.'

'I like the idea of the huge dogs guarding the entrance,' says Niambi.

'The dogs must have been very impressive,' says Mai.

They thank the Sage, who departs to take a rest.

Background to the Tupi-Portugal war, 1551-1567

King John III of Portugal declares Brazil to be a formal part of empire in 1550.

A senior Jesuit priest says to King of Portugal in 1550 re Brazil:

'Your highness will draw much profit because there will be many strict farms and there will be many plantations, even if there be not much gold and silver.'

Jesuits try to justify murder and enslavement of Tupis in the context of Christianity replacing paganism. They also accuse Tupis of cannibalism, for which there is no hard evidence, only adventurers giving their fantasy-filled stories for personal gain.

Jesuits try in addition to settle Tupis into artificial Portuguese villages, denying their nomadic hunting and gathering and their relationship with the forest.

For a period, some Tupis are encouraged to live in these villages, and receive items they value in return for felling pau brasil trees for the Portuguese.

But more and more Tupis become disillusioned with life away from the jungle. They know they will have to fight for their way of life.

1551

An elderly Piata wants to rally Tupi villagers for the coming battle, but his voice is now weak. He asks Moacir to take his place.

Moacir, also now elderly, is angry. He addresses a large crowd of Tupi, who have agreed to join him in fighting the Portuguese. They are in a clearing in the forest, and the cackling calls of parrots and macaws accompany Moacir's tirade.

'They do not change these parrot-clothed people from far away. As I have told you previously, but it remains the truth.

Just as their skin peels off like a snake, so their tongue is forked like a snake.'

'Like a snake!' shouts the throng.

'They come to steal our fine tree that produces red-dye. They are taking land from our people and telling us it will be theirs forever.'

'Taking our land!' cry the throng.

'This is no life for an ant or a beetle. It is certainly no life for our people.'

'No life for our people!' sing the throng, repeating the phrase over and over.

'They kill our friend the pau brasil tree in large numbers. This is no different from killing us, or killing our land, as we are all part of the same living world, mutually dependent, loving. These people know this not. These people are savages.'

'Savages, savages.'

'They are not welcome here. They are dangerous here. They have no respect for the land here. They have no respect for our friends, the creatures of the forest here. They have no right to be here,' shouts Moacir.

The crowd repeats each phrase enthusiastically.

* * * * *

Piata examines the traps. On every path into the village there are traps at several points along the path, to ensnare any invader and keep them dangling from ropes made from strong lianas.

'We have ropes to tie them and enable us to keep them as captives for negotiations, and spears to kill them if we are forced to,' he says to Caua. 'There are twenty-three Tupi high in trees as lookouts. They cover all directions. Further down each path, tarantulas and poisonous snakes are encouraged with their favourite food to set up home by the path. We ourselves know where the traps and creatures are, and have our own routes to follow, on a camouflaged platform higher up.'

Caua replies, 'We have many villages fighting with us, but not enough. We need to use the jungle as our friend like you have set out, to confuse the enemy and give us an advantage.'

'I have also taken to our caiman killer, Iandara,' adds Piatra, 'who is very intimate with the lives of caimans. He knows how to tempt a number of them to swim down the river. He will lay scent by the Portuguese huts, and the scent will attract the caimans towards the Portuguese.'

'Very good. We also have our specialist rope bridge builder, Iuna . There are a few rivers between us and the Blotchy Faces, some in gullies with high rope bridges. Iuna will set up the bridges so that they will collapse as soon as someone steps on the bridge. For us, there are at each river three canoes that he has buried in the ground and covered with forest debris. For each one, there is a mark with our village symbol on the tree by the buried canoes. We will cross the rivers with these. There will be piranhas, caimans and water snake in the rivers. I think they will enjoy feeding on any Pink and Blotchy Faces that fall in.'

'This is very good news, brother,' responds Caua. 'I think all this helps us, as we are using the jungle to our advantage. As long as the jungle is our terrain of battle, we have an advantage. On the open ground where the blotched skins have killed our forest, they have their firesticks and we have no defence.'

'This is true. We also have extra defences if needed. As you know, we have a small village ready to move into, much deeper into the jungle, if we have to leave here. We have traps set to protect that village. Beyond that village, we have another village even deeper into the jungle where we can go, if the need arises. The people there will welcome us in, and join the battle, if need be.'

'Excellent,' says Caua.

Otapo and Atwooki

'Have you seen Wooki?'

'She was playing with sticks and a mud ball just here.'

'Wooki, where are you?' calls Miri. 'Can you help me find her, Otapo?'

'I will look in Aneni's hut, she is often in there.'

Each of the huts is similar, with smooth mud, grass and stick walls, in the brick red colour of the soil, with a dried grass conical roof.

Miri looks in Mai and Felani's hut. 'You looking for your little rascal Wooki?' asks Mai, who is now very elderly, and barely ventures past the entrance to her hut.

Otapo draws a blank in Aneni's hut and tries the neighbouring compound.

There is a distinctive mop of dusty tousled hair by the wall near a friend's hut. The friend, Calani, notices Miri, spots Wooki, and smiles. She says, 'Sorry, I should have noticed her creep in here.'

'No, my apologies. Wooki, what have you got in your mouth? Yuk, is that snails? These are not the snails we eat, sweetie pie. Come here now.'

And she lifts Atwooki, who is promptly sick on her shoulder.

'We are going to have to get you clean, and me clean, you naughty rascal. Let's go down to the stream.'

'Can I come?' asks Otapo.

'You may, we can get you clean too.'

The Portuguese troubled by jungle fighting

'Ribeiro! Come here now!' barks Dias.

Ribeiro leaves the dozen or so soldiers squatting outside and walks into the simple log hut where Dias is staying during the war, with a wooden table, four chairs, and a plank for a bed in a room with bare log walls, except for the charcoal drawing of King John III that is hanging by a nail on one wall.

'Report to me on our latest battle with these heathens in the jungle. Why are we losing men?'

'There are three obstacles we face sir. The cunning of the Indian, with their traps; the creatures of the jungle; and our unfamiliarity with fighting in the jungle.'

'Explain, man! I will not accept that these godless Indians have any advantage over us!'

'They lay traps in every direction, sir. You may spot one part of a path where the leaves have been disturbed, and step to the side, but before you can shout 'yelp!' a liana has wrapped around your feet and your body is held upside down by vines and your hands cannot reach the ground. The binding round your feet is just too high for our men to reach and cut with a sword, and all the while monkeys are throwing coconuts down on you. You are now prey to the next Indian that comes with a spear or bow and arrow.'

'You just have to use the eyes that God gave you, man!'

'They have platforms from tree to tree that enable them to move faster than us through the trees. By the time we can get our arquebuses primed, their arrows are raining down on us. Then there are the tarantulas that keep appearing on the path, often at head height, as though they have been placed there. A few of us have been poisoned. I don't know what we do about tarantulas, it's new to me.'

'Be a man. Grab one of its legs, throw it down, and stamp on it! I am not impressed, Ribeiro. These Indians are playing with us.'

'We have also found that bridges over rivers have been weakened, so that the bridge collapses as soon as we step on it. They have fish here with teeth and if you are bleeding in any way from thorns or bites, they attack you, your feet, your knees, even your private parts, sir. And if it's not fish with teeth, it is caimans, which are huge and deadly here. A few of us have been mauled to death by caimans. I have not seen anything like it.'

'Ribeiro, are we but blind mice in the cat's palace, with the cat licking his lips when we arrive?'

'No sir.'

'Sir! Sir! Caimans! Here! Outside!' It is a soldier, his face white with fear, at the entrance to the hut.

Dias rushes to the entrance with Ribeiro to see perhaps two dozen caimans just a few strides away.

'Shoot!' he screams. 'Shoot at their heads now!' A volley of shots ring out as one or two caimans are within feet of the soldiers.

One caiman, not yet hit, moves towards the leg of one soldier, who trips as he tries to leap out of the way. The caiman grabs his foot between its teeth as a shot rings out by him and stops the caiman in its tracks. It rolls its eyes, and slowly releases its grip as it struggles to breathe.

But the soldier realises that there is only a bit of muscle still holding his foot on to his leg. He faints.

Further shots ring out as a few caimans keep moving forward. Soon, they all appear dead.

'Ribeiro, come back inside!' Dias is now beetroot-faced.

'Yes, sir!' Ribeiro follows him in.

'These Indians are making fools of us. We have to show them who is boss, really show them.'

'Yes, sir.'

'You have been involved in forest-burning before, clearing land for pau brasil growing. How did you deal with the greenness of the trees, and the water retention in the upper part of the trees?'

'It's necessary to start with a large pile of dry logs, cut a year before, and generate intense heat. With sufficient heat, the moisture in the trees will be burnt off, and the trees will start to burn. It then progresses from there. Once the fire in the forest is strong enough, the heat intensity tends to rise, and the fire will gather force. After that, we just need wind to keep it going.'

'So, you are not just a complete imbecile, Ribeiro?'

'Sir, I am here to serve our king in whatever way necessary.'

'Well, to serve our king you will source the dry logs we need. By yesterday. Take those men outside and come back within twenty four hours. We are going to see how these Indians deal with a new enemy, an enemy with hot flames.'

'Yes sir.'

'There is one more thing, Ribeiro. Have you seen any evidence of cannibalism in the jungle, any evidence at all of cannibalism?'

'No sir, not skulls.'

'You are instructed to report any signs of cannibalism, Ribeiro. If necessary, invent it. We need to show that we are superior to these godless creatures. Cannibalism will be a perfect story for those at home. None will question the deaths of Indians if we can show that they eat us when they kill us.

'Yes sir, I will tell the men, sir.'

The tale of the Cuckoo and the Magpie

A very elderly Aneni offers to tell her tale, which she says came to her after her experiences on the ship many years ago. 'I am old now,' she says, 'I may not have many tales left in me.'

'I would like to hear it,' says Niambi. The others all agree.

Well, the pretty hamerkop bird labours for two long moons. It carries in its beak thousands and thousands of twigs, making an exquisite nest insulated by additional mud and small sticks for greater warmth for its eggs.

Meanwhile, a little while away, a magpie has in its nest two rings, some coloured beads, a silver bangle, a gold brooch, a silver buckle and a necklace, and it is just flying back from a trip with more coloured beads.

A cuckoo flies from nest to nest, searching for an empty one. It notices the hamerkop is absent, and so it occupies its nest, oblivious to how much work has gone into this masterpiece. When the hamerkop returns with food, the cuckoo beats its wings vigorously and pecks aggressively with its beak, and forces the sad hamerhop away. The hamerkop then has to find another location and start the laborious eight-week process again.

The cuckoo gets bored of the hamerkop nest. It flies around from nest to nest, and spies the finely woven and beautifully hung, deliciously snug nest of the weaverbird, balanced over water to make it particularly attractive to a mate. The cuckoo takes the nest while its owner is away finding food. When the weaverbird returns it is no match for the cuckoo, and it flies off to find a place to weave a new nest.

In time, the cuckoo gets bored of the weaverbird's nest. It flies from nest to nest and spies the magnificent nest of the coot, made from dozens of pebbles lifted one by one with much effort and great care, to make a snug nest capable of withstanding the strong water current. The cuckoo takes the nest while its owner is away. When the coot returns, there is a mighty flurry of feathers, a battle between beaks, much scratching with claws. But the cuckoo wins, and the coot flies off to find another place to build a nest.

In time, the cuckoo gets bored of the coot's nest. It flies from nest to nest and spies the sparkling nest of the magpie, full of stolen jewels. The cuckoo takes the nest while the magpie is away finding food. When the magpie returns, she flies into a blind rage, and dives at the nest to grab a ring. She flies to another nest with the ring, and then flies back.

Other magpies are now alerted to the magpie's haul being in the possession of a cuckoo, and the word gets around. One by one, several magpies start attacking the cuckoo so that the usurper flies up to fight, while other magpies go for the jewellery. The weight of all these birds, the flutter of fighting wings, and the battling with beaks, causes the nest to fall with most of its haul. The jewellery lies scattered on the ground.

The other birds hear that the cuckoo is under attack, so the hamerkop and the coot and the weaverbird come and attack the cuckoo too. They peck it so much that it falls to the ground, specked with blood. They also frighten off the thieving magpie. The greedy magpie flies away with its tail between its legs, with no jewels and no nest, and its pride hurt.

The cuckoo hobbles away with cuts and bruises and no nest.

Let today's cuckoos learn that, if it chooses a particularly large nest, it must do so with particularly greater wisdom. Otherwise, the large nest will be its undoing.

Let this be a lesson to those from foreign lands who ride roughshod over our traditions and take what is not theirs from our land, whether gold, or our precious homes, or our women.

'Wonderful!' shouts Niambi. And the others shout in agreement.

Niambi's great-grandson goes missing, 1558

They go hunting okapi. Part of a herd has been seen by neighbours, and Mai's son in law Katchani, Aneni's son Wotambo, Niambi's son Matimba and grandson Barawa go with Barawa's teenage son Otapo. They carry spears and a couple of gourds of water.

Niambi, Mufaro, Miri, and Otapo's sister Atwooki come part of the way with their gourds, and to see them off. Atwooki is in a sulk, as she wants to go on the hunt. They see off the men some ten minutes away from the village.

They walk for what seems like hours, across savannah, past waterholes full of hippos and a few ibis. A small group of giraffes stand wondering what to do with their sky-reaching necks as they wait for the hippos to finish their overlong bath and drink.

They see the tails and backsides of the okapi across the savannah, as they head into a cluster of trees, mostly baobab.

They break into a run in the direction of the okapi. They know that they probably have more stamina than the okapi, but they may have to travel a long way.

They reach gentle hills, and head over and into the valley on the other side. The woodland is thicker here. On the next hill, Barawa's son Otapo lags behind as they climb, and the others are well ahead when he reaches the valley.

Otapo is aware of a rapid movement nearby, and is turning when he feels a blunt object on the back of his head. Everything goes dark, and he realises he is hooded. But his head feels another thud and he feels no more. His gourd slips from his grip.

He is thrown onto the back of a simple wooden cart, with big wheels and a flat base, along with two other prone bodies that lie across half the base. An ox pulls them along. Men with clubs and guns walk alongside.

Matimba, Katchani and Wotambo come back over the hill a little while after. They look around them, look behind trees. Barawa runs up the previous hill that Otapo would have climbed but returns to warn that there is no sign of him.

Wotambo shouts, 'His gourd!' and picks it up. Matimba takes it from him, his ebony face as grey as a black face can be. He falls to his knees, and tears form. Katchani joins him, now unable to hold back the tears himself.

'There are no big cat prints around here,' says Wotambo, who is crestfallen. 'But there are wheel tracks nearby.'

'It must be slave catchers,' says Matimba, wiping his tears. 'It's the only way he could have gone like that.'

'We could track them, and see if there is some way of getting Otapo back,' says Barawa. He is distraught and seeks the hand of his father, who embraces him.

'Perhaps for a while,' says Katchani. 'But slave catchers are said always to have weapons, usually guns. Even if we find them, we would be defenceless against the weapons.'

'Where is the port?' asks Matimba.

'The slave port is Loango, Kongo,' says Wotambo. 'I think it is a dangerous place to go for an African. A friend in Mombasa told me about these places, as he has lived in one. He said he would never go back, it was so brutal.'

'I need to go. I need to find my son,' splutters a deeply upset Barawa.

'I need my grandson also. But you are most likely to end up a slave yourself, if you go there,' replies Matimba.

'Why not, if I can be with my son?'

'But you have an obligation to your wife, Miri, and your parents. It is bad enough that Otapo has been taken, but to lose you as well would be too much.'

'Well, I will go back and ask Miri's consent to me going,' says Barawa.

'You can try.'

'Are we going back?' asks Wotambo.

'Yes, let's go,' says Matimba, wiping away his tears.

In the jungle as fire rages

'The heat becomes ever fiercer, the orange lick of flames looms ever nearer. We must go now,' shouts Moacir.

'I have sent the children ahead. Most of the birds and beasts went before them. Do we have everything?' asks Caua.

'We have hammocks, pots, spears, bows and arrows – we must forget the food and run.'

'Let us go. I fear though that the great bird of fire flies higher through the tops of trees than we can run at the base.' They run.

'We must go quickly to the river and see if the water there can protect us.'

'We will need to persuade the caimans that we are not tonight's supper.'

'We will. Let us go there. I will use my usual bird voice for the caimans. We have two boats there as well, which should help.'

'I feel the heat.'

'It is bad, very bad. The blotchy faces hate our land so much they would destroy its bountiful forests, and they love it so much they would destroy our right to live here, to take the land from us. They are true monsters.'

'My hair is burning, Moacir. And I keep passing dead toucans, parrots, hummingbirds, iguanas, rats, even a puma.'

'My hair is burning too. The river is near. Yes, so many dead creatures. Let us go on our hands and knees these last one hundred strides.'

'I am, but my bottom is burning, the earth is hot for my hands. We must run as though carried by the wind. Drop our pans, weapons, everything.'

'Yes, let's go.'

As foul-smelling flames curl up from the hair and feathers around the top of Moacir's and Caua's heads, they dive into the river for brief respite.

The flames lick and spit far above them, reaching out for more branches to enwrap with their heat. Across the river, which is about eight or nine body lengths away, there is jungle as dense as the jungle that has been destroyed by fire behind them.

Moacir and Caua look around for caiman eyes. Caua feels sharp nibbling at his feet.

'Piranha!' he says. 'We don't have the armadillo meat we always take with us when visiting a river.'

'Grab reeds!' shouts Moacir. 'Remember when we were children. Wrapping reeds round and round our feet, and tucking them under. It won't last long but it will give us a few minutes to think.'

'Bloody hurts,' moans Caua.

'The fire will hurt a great deal more. Just get the reeds wrapped round quick. That's it.' Moacir sees a charred branch coming down the river and breaks it in two. He gives Caua one piece. 'In case of caimans' he quips.

The fire is still very close, and the heat is intense. They sense their chest hair being singed. For the moment, the fire is not able to reach the branches on the other side of the river. But they are still only a few feet from the bank they started from.

'Our last backup village is about half a day from here, once we get over the river.'

'That's right. I am hoping the others are on their way.'

'The boat is just up there.' He points a little way up the river, where the flames are high above the riverbank. Shall we go for it?'

'I think we should swim. Keep your stick. It's risky but I think the way to the boat is further.' They both start swimming, paddling with their hands and kicking their legs.

'I see caimans.'

'So do I. I think they are weighing up which one of us they think is tastier. Just paddle.'

'No, they want to get the weaker one first, kill him, and then go for the other. We are not yet halfway.'

'One caiman is heading towards me.'

'Right, I will try and grab its tail. As it turns it should be angry and open its mouth. Try at that moment to get your charred stick into its mouth to jam it open. If that fails, I will try to ride it, you try to swim.'

The caiman gets nearer. The bank is still a few full strides away, a lot of swimming strokes.

'I'm getting its tail now,' shouts Moacir, grabbing fiercely with all his strength.

'I can't. I can't...' screams Caua, trying to reach out to its open mouth.

Moacir fights and fights to get on top of the caiman, which now rolls over and over to try to shake him off. Gradually, imperceptibly, they are moving nearer the riverbank.

Caua has given up trying to get the stick into the caiman's mouth. He tries to head towards the bank, but quickly realises another caiman has been creeping up on him all this time, and is nearly upon him.

He reaches desperately for the bank, but the caiman grabs him round his thighs and starts taking him down under the water.

Moacir is still being rolled, but thinks he is just a few strokes from the bank if he can jump free. He senses he must get to the bank before this caiman realises where he is.

Caua is hurting badly round his groin and is very short of breath under water but realises his only chance is to get his stick into the caiman's jaws and try to find a way to get free before he drowns. He tries to push the stick in with one hand, but the caiman's grip does not weaken. As the caiman comes up for air, Caua gets a lungful himself, but between the pain and the lack of breath he is weakening.

With the bank almost reachable, Moacir releases his thighs' grip on the caiman, and thrashes in the water as he reaches for a root to grab. He yanks himself half out of the water as the caiman tries to snatch his left leg, and he is fully out and scrambling away from the bank before the caiman's jaws come for him again.

Moacir looks around him. There is no sign of Caua.

There is suddenly a big splash in the river nearby. A large caiman rises up with Caua between its jaws and dives down again. The water is red with – Moacir concludes – Caua's blood. There is no indication that Caua is still alive.

Moacir feels powerless either way. He looks on disconsolately, his head in his hands. He has no weapons now, having left them on the other side when running to the river.

He also senses he has no time to wait. He has to make a decision. As the caiman comes up with Caua again, and still no sign of life in Caua, he calls up to the spirits, kisses the ground, and heads for the village.

He knows that a strong wind could bring the fire across the river any time. He runs steadily, knowing he must preserve his energy for a long journey.

There are still birds in this part of a jungle, which gives him hope. The caws and the birdsong that accompany him even more so.

He comes to a gentle hill and slows a little to climb it.

He also sees an armadillo, which also gives him hope, although these creatures would struggle to run fast if the fire were to come. They would try to survive underground.

At last, he sees the smoke of a campfire. He calls with a toucan's cry, and one of his friends responds in kind and comes out of the village to embrace him.

'Where is Caua?'

'A caiman took him. I was preoccupied with my own caiman, so I couldn't help him. I have addressed the spirits. They have taken him. What is the position here?'

'Very bad news of other villages. Several were killed almost outright by the fire. Only one or two got away in time to pass on the word. Many of us have got here from our village, fortunately, but we are short of allies.'

'How many are we?'

'We have about four hundred and fifty. We have had word that there is another village a day away with another few hundred. But two or three thousand have died.'

'For all the years since the Gods brought us to this land, all the many generations, we have fought with spear and bow and arrow, and we have been equals. These blotchy Pink Face people use the tricks of someone who has no eye for beauty, no heart, and who only have a head for doing evil.'

'You speak the truth.'

'We will need to rest a few days, but all the while listen for wind and the risk of fire coming this way. When we have rested, we can think about what we may do next.'

The killing of the Bishop in war

Tupi Caete leader Cauocau speaks:
We treasure this land as we do our children. The cuckoo invaders do not. Our jungle is our home, the place where our children are born and grow. Our refuge, the source of our food. We worship it every day, and the sun and rain that feed it.

The cuckoo invaders come, destroy our forest in the coastal areas where we live. They kill the god we worship, and when we fight to protect our home, our livelihood, our spirit, they use their firesticks and kill us. They have no respect, no respect.

These cuckoo invaders come with a cross, and talk as though this cross guides them. What do we see from these worshippers of the cross?

We see murder and destruction. We see people who act as though they have no heart.

Take the burning of our forest. What do I see after this callous and brutal action?

I see parrots, their bright red and green feathers now charred and ghost like, their body gone, their cheerful chatter but a tear-filled memory.

I see an armadillo, its fine shell black and holed, its body just a skeleton, its busy furrowing no more.

I see a great pau brasil, felled like a giant and prostrated on the ground, its branches reaching out in pain, its nuts screeching.

I see a tarantula, now but a skeletal black star, except that its eyes still appear to look up at me, unblinkingly.

So this cross only means bad for us, only death for us, only loss of home and livelihood for us.

I see a flock of mynah birds, now laid out in a diamond shape on the ground, nothing left but their bones, their fine song lost to the jungle.

So, when a man comes in a cuckoo invader ship and this man wears a purple robe and a cross, and claims to lead and guide the cuckoo invaders, we can only see that this man brings more death and destruction for us.

Like any invaded people, our response is to protect ourselves.

When this man of purple was vulnerable, we took his life.

If he does have a God, like the invaders claim, then he will go to his God.

We must protect our God, our people.

The Tupi war with the Portuguese reaches a new height with the 1556 killing by the Caete tribe of Bishop Sardinha, the first bishop in Brazil. This is after he was shipwrecked on arrival.

The Tupi see this as just, as thousands of them have been killed since 1554, with the Portuguese destroying several villages by setting fire to the jungle all around where they lived. The dead include medicine men who they revere.

The Portuguese see the bishop's killing as giving them the excuse to continue their campaign of destroying Tupi villages by burning the forest. This is even more difficult for the Tupi, as their whole lives were inextricably bound up with the forest, and they were being forced to go deeper and deeper to their back-up villages.

The Portuguese fight ruthlessly after the killing of the bishop.

Large numbers of Tupis are rounded up and corralled into Jesuit-run aldeias, or settlements. There are thirty-four thousand in the Bahia area alone. Others are killed by fire.

But the biggest number, at least sixty thousand, die from the smallpox, influenza and measles the Portuguese brought and to which the Tupis have no resistance.

The Tupis are able to attack some towns, none of which are of great size in the 1550s. They come close to taking Sao Paolo at one point, but their chief is persuaded to withdraw.

The Tupis know that they cannot force the Portuguese out of Brazil. But they wish to be sure that their jungle home will remain theirs.

War goes badly for Tupis, 1566

'Reports are coming from so many tribes,' says Moacir gloomily. 'The wasting disease brought by the Blotchy Face people is spreading everywhere.'

'What can we do? So many of us are dying.'

'It is troubling. If it is not the wasting disease, then it is the spots and blotches disease that kills us. We have no medicines for any of it. Our healer has no solution and he is now ill as well. His replacement as healer is also unwell.'

'Moacir, it is the enemy's invisible poisonous viper that climbs inside us and turns our guts inside out, while weakening our heart,' says Piata. 'Tens of thousands of us have died.'

'It is a miracle you and I have not succumbed.'

'We have done well. For a hundred moons we have kept the Portuguese out of most of the jungle.'

'But they have destroyed so many beautiful parts of our jungle home with their twin dragon of flames and hateful spite.'

'Too much. But the question is, if we stop now, are we conceding defeat? Can we still hold our heads up?'

'When the puma, the python and the ocelot take three of our people, and we seek peace by making offerings to them, we are not giving in, we are protecting those who survive and recognising that other dwellers of the forest have their needs also. The Blotched Skins are not forest dwellers, but they have earned a right to live on our land by their fearsome weapons.'

'And their inhumanity.'

'Yes, there is that too. But we still need to protect those of us that remain. Even with this terrible illness, we still have many who live, and more live than have sadly died. It is time to talk peace.'

'It is with great sorrow, but it is wise. I agree. Let us send word to the Blotched Skins with their hairy faces.'

'I will.'

The Peace Talks, 1567

Moacir:
You Portuguese speak with forked fire
You feign to speak peace then you burn our forest home
You must stop burning our jungle,
Stop capturing Tupi and making us into slaves
Stop taking our women.

Leave us with our lives in the jungle.
Help us with medicine for these diseases,

We will then leave you in peace while you grow pau brasil and your sugar cane and practice your religion. We will no longer question your right to be in this land.

Dias:
No. No and No.

Dias holds out. He will not negotiate.

11.

Otapo

Otapo cannot feel his hands or feet. He can feel pain all over his body, but he cannot place it. His vision is blurred. He shakes his head to try to clear it, as he has just come round. He realises he is in chains, both his hands and his feet. They are also bound together.

Around him are more men chained just the same. The sun is beginning to rise, casting a vermilion glow across the unfamiliar scene.

The gulls cawing and circling around and the salty freshness of the early morning air remind him of the sea coast sensations his dad talked about.

Otapo becomes aware of groans around him, and similar but faded groans further away. He senses that there are people in chains like him over a wide area. His nose is aware of high levels of sweat, urine, shit, mingled with the salty air of sea, which combine together to make him feel slightly nauseous. He tries to raise himself from a curled prostrate position. Aches cry silently from too many parts. He needs to face more pain to sit up, but he raises his head and torso a little against a small back wall behind him.

'Ow, yuk!' is his reaction as a bucket of water is thrown over him. The same happens to his neighbour and so on down. He immediately smells what he believes is the sea, and realises it must be saltwater. But the effect is also to lend more vivacity to the smell of urine.

He tries talking in Tsonga. His neighbour on his left side responds in a tongue he does not recognise. He tries the limited Swahili that he learnt when in Mombasa. 'Anyone speak Swahili?'

'Yes,' responds the man to his right, and a disembodied voice further away.

'Where the Hell are we?' he asks.

'Luango,' wherever that is.'

'Somewhere in Kongo,' says disembodied voice.

'We are going in a slave ship, if we don't die first,' says his neighbour.

'Do we ever get food?'

'That was it.'

'What, that bilge?'

'That is about it. They will throw some very thin soup at you later.'

'And the heat of the sun?'

'Think of it as health-giving, when not burning you to a frazzle.'

'When do the ships come?'

'When they feel like it. We may wait for ages.'

'Stop talking there!' someone barks in broken Swahili.

'That is us, I guess.'

'Yes, you can't even breathe here, and some give up doing even that.'

And they are silent a while.

There is the sound of a loud thwack, followed by an anguished scream. He catches the lash of a whip in the corner of his eye. There is a second thwack, followed by a third. The scream is thinner with each lash.

As the sun starts its downward path, seeming to gather pace as it does, there is the gentle sound of splashing.

Soon, the ladle reaches Otapo. Barely half the gruel gets into his mouth. Much of the rest is on him, already sticky. As a few globules seek to escape his mouth, he reaches round with his tongue to tease them back in.

* * * * *

Three weeks on, his limbs now numbed beyond aching, there is commotion. A ship is coming into the harbour. Indeed, it soon emerges that not one, but two ships are coming. Beyond Otapo's line of sight, barrels of wine, crates of food and crates of toiletries are unloaded by muscled Black men, who, unusually in this town, are not chained, except possibly in their minds.

Pink men with moustaches and sticks then walk along the rows of chained men for sale, with tall bald burly Black men behind them. They nod as they pass particular men, and these are pulled up roughly by the burly men. They are freed from their ankle chains and made to stand in line, ready to be walked, in chains, down a gangway, before being taken by rowing boat to the slave ship.

Otapo is chosen for the second ship and finds himself standing in line, and then having to inch forward with his chains down the gangway, with no chance of freeing his arms from their chains to keep his balance. It is no surprise that men in front of him tumble, only to be whipped for doing so.

* * * * *

The conditions in the ship only differ in so far as the relentless sun is replaced by relentless darkness. This is only leavened by tiny chinks in the upper part of the wooden hull, through which wafer thin slivers of daylight can penetrate.

The chains are much the same, and the gruel likewise. The smells are more intense, unbearably so. It is as though an overseer grabs in his fist a pool of mixed urine, shit and sweat, and squeezes it through his fingers into Otapo's nostrils. He is only not sick as his throat is so parched.

If anybody is heard speaking, they are whipped. If they complain, they are whipped more soundly.

Many of the slaves die. When this is discovered, which might only happen because of the wretched smell, the chains are loosened, and the corpses are thrown overboard unceremoniously. Otapo and his companions grieve inside.

A storm compounds the problem. The ship is tossed and turned in the mountainous waves like a toy boat in a park fountain. Water pours into the hold, which is initially refreshing, but soon combines with urine and shit to make the stench far more noxious. This, combined with the tossing and turning, makes many of Otapo's companions sick. Gruel and bile find their way up and out, somehow, through parched throats.

Even the sailors cannot abide this noxious soup, and almost all crew are set to work emptying the hold as far as possible of this sewage, and tipping it into the open sea.

There is momentary relief for Otapo when the ship docks in Brazil, around twenty days after leaving Luango.

He would be out of the frying pan, at least.

The notice on a wall at the side of the slave market-place in Bahia, one of dozens of such notices that day, reads:

An 18 year old African slave boy from Angola, thought to be originally from Bunyoro in Central Africa. Strong and in good health with good figure. No vices or bad habits. Farmer by trade. Price 30 reis. Contact Joao Reyes, Travessa de Manuel I, upstairs, Bahia.

A buyer comes to buy Otapo soon after, with three other male slaves. They are taken away chained by their hands and feet to a simple horse-drawn cart, with the slaveowner's servant sat on a seat at the front.

Life as a slave on a sugar plantation, 1558

The plantation hut is not large, but twenty-four men are crushed inside. When sleeping you cannot turn over. You are tight against your neighbour on either side. Each neighbour's fart reverberates through your body, each snore, each groan of pain, each laboured breath. If one weren't so desperately tired, the smell would make one retch.

The day starts at four am with a loud ringing of the plantation bell. The tired men fall over each other as they stagger out in the moonlit gloom.

The cane fields are adjacent to the huts. Otapo is given a cutlass when he starts, and cutting is continuous until nine am. Otapo is then allowed thirty minutes for breakfast and milking cows. The cutlasses are again handed out and he cuts until noon. He now has two hours in the suffocating heat of the midday sun to feed the cows and horses, give them fresh hay and grass, make lunch, catch a nap. From two he works until sunset at six pm, and then he needs to fetch more hay and grass for the cattle and feed them, as well as locate dry cow dung and brushwood kindling for a fire to cook tea, and make breakfast for the next morning.

The men all need to go to bed at the same time, as there is no space for latecomers to bed down, and they tend to finish all their chores as midnight approaches and get to sleep at twelve.

After a week or two, Otapo gets to know a few of his hut mates, and they share the sourcing of grass for the cattle, the cooking, the sourcing of dry cow dung, the making of fires. They also share the milking of the cows at the breakfast break.

Otapo finds a couple of men who speak Tsonga and they become good friends, apart from one, who is a loner. A few others speak Swahili, and Otapo is able to make friends with them.

For those from north west Africa who speak Arabic, the Swahili speakers find a way of speaking a sort of pidgin mixture of Arabic and Swahili for everyday conversation, using the many common words between Arabic and Swahili. Gradually, a majority of those in the hut can communicate. With others, they use sign language until all have a few words of the common pidgin language for everyday communication.

Food is typically manioc, or what the Tupi call potato. They cook in a similar way to yams back home, except the potato cooks more quickly. Once a month they are given a leg of a calf to share, and they make a large pot together.

Mobuka, a fellow Tsonga speaker, says to Otapo, 'They are driving us to an early grave. It is hard not to think it is deliberate.'

'It is desperate. They expect us to do the work of three people, with no rest,' says Otapo.

'We cannot continue this every day, every week, every moon.'

'We must think. We are twenty-four. We must find a way to do this and live. Use African cunning.'

'Like if we are trying to catch a cheetah. Stealth, stamina, staying alert, perseverance.'

'Exactly, we have those skills. We need to pool them.'

'Let us talk each day, when we can.'

* * * * *

It is lunch, they finally get a few moments.

'Hi Otapo.'

'Hi Mobuka.'

'I have an idea, Otapo. Too many of us die young. The work is so punishing.'

'It's true. So what do you have in mind?'

'How about we do half days hard, half days less hard? We try that way to stay alive.'

'So how does it work? If you and I work less hard, they will count less sugar cane at the end of the day.'

'We split our hut in two when it comes to how we work. One half does a hard shift in the morning. The other half work within themselves, keep their energy. In the afternoon, we swap round. The morning half that worked less now works extra hard, and the other half the other way around.'

'This may be clever, Mobuka. None of is dead on our feet at the end of the day, and we still produce well.'

'The hard shifts will be hard, but it will be worth it to have a lighter shift.'

'You are indeed clever, my friend. Let's give it a try at least.'

'Let's tell the others.'

1583

'There are places where slaves go when they escape. They are called mocambos,' says Mobuka.

'What do you know of them?' asks Otapo.

'Manuel in a hut along the way was in one, until he was found and brought back. He says there were about a hundred and fifty escaped slaves there. They built huts and they farmed land, and sometimes they hunted birds or animals. He says the life was much better than here.'

'Can he say how we get to one?'

'He thinks that the mocambo that he was at has been ripped apart now by the conquerors.'

'I suggest we talk to all newcomers, to see if any has word.'

'I think we need to have a language that only we understand.'

'What do you mean?'

'I mean this plantation owner will give Hell to any slave who he hears is trying to escape. At best, he will be whipped soundly and maybe have a foot chopped off. At worst, he will be hanged from the nearest tree. So we have a language that only those we trust will know.'

'Are you thinking an African language?'

'Not exactly. A lot of us understand Swahili, and it is easy to learn.'

'Right.'

'I propose that we move one letter along. So with our greeting "hujambo," we say "ivkbncp."'

'Sounds complicated. And it needs brothers knowing the alphabet and being able to spell.'

'Well, it's a matter of life and death, so I think that our brothers will make an effort. But think about it. If I want to say to you, "new plan, mpango mpya," I say "nqbohp nrzb." I write it with stones outside the hut. The brothers who need to know will be told where to look for the stones. It just needs one brother in each hut to understand for them to get it.'

'Ok, that sounds a bit better. Shall we have a place where we meet?'

'Sure, there is that large tree that is so bent it looks like the shape of an elephant. I can show it to you. We can meet there.'

'The elephant-like one? Yes, I know it. I can tell the brothers.'

'Yes, do so. That would be good.'

'And perhaps soon we need to dig some secret pits a little way from the camp. If a nail is put there every now and then, nobody should miss it. The same with strong twine. We will need these for building our huts. These things will keep. We can start a supply.'

'You are wise. I agree. This is all good. I will think about your language.'

'Good, enough for today. We need to get grass for the horses and cows.'

'We can make friends with the horses, you know,' says Otapo. 'We feed them. They know who keeps them well fed.'

'It is true. Let us be extra kind to them. It is better to run like a gazelle when we escape than run like a human.'

'I agree, and the owner will come after us with horses.'

'Yes, horses and guns and big thugs, like our overseer.'

'Let us go.'

1600

'The stones give the important news,' says Otapo, whose hair is now white. It is seventeen years since their discussion, and there have during this time been a few false alarms.

'We need to meet after dusk at our tree,' replies Mobuka.

'I will tell the brothers this way,' (he points left). 'Will you tell them the other way?'

'I will. I will see you at dusk.'

* * * * *

When they meet, there is a bald African, his skin more pau brasil than purple-black. He is medium height, muscular, with thin legs. They do not recognise him.

'I am new here,' he says, 'my name is Haram.'

'Hello Haram,' they say.

'I can tell you a special secret. It is good that you keep secrets here. Talking openly kills more slaves than fever.'

'I agree,' says Otapo.

'There is a new country for us. A mocambo for ex-slaves, run by slaves. It does not have a name yet. It is just starting. But this time it's here to stay.'

'Why is this mocambo different to the others?' asks Otapo.

'There are hundreds of escaped slaves, with room for many times this. The reasons that you have for being by this tree are felt by Africans everywhere. Like you now, they are responding to the call.'

'Sounds great. When do you want us to be ready to leave?' asks another slave, Matummo.

'The day after the next full moon. Just after dusk. Try to put away as much food as you can for the next few days. It will take time to grow new food in the mocambo. And game is quite limited.'

'And keep it a secret.'

'Yes, until we are actually leaving, keep it a secret. I will on that night show you the way out of here.'

'Do we fetch horses? There are horses that will come with us.'

'No, no need.'

'Why will the plantation owner not follow us and shoot us all dead?' asks Otapo.

'On that, you will need to trust me. I have done this many times. Some things are best unsaid.'

That night, Otapo and Mobuka dig fresh pits, camouflaged by giant rhubarb leaves. The following day they keep by a few beans and pieces of yam, and put them in the pit. They do this over the next three weeks. By then, there is enough for four or five gourds. Otapo has been sourcing gourds in the meantime, so has enough.

The work in the fields seems lighter as the night approaches. Otapo can barely control his excitement. When other Africans ask him about his new demeanour, he says his bad foot is now finally better. People say, 'I never noticed your foot was bad.' He then says, 'It felt far worse than it looked.'

* * * * *

On the night after the full moon, there are fifty-five Africans at the elephant-shaped tree, each carrying gourds. As Haram beckons them to follow him, two dozen other Africans can be seen running towards them. When one shouts 'Wait for us,' this man is thumped round the head and told to shush.

About eighty head off down a mysterious track through forest with Haram in front. He passes the word down the line for each to hold the hand of the man in front. Haram seems to know the way in the darkness.

After about an hour they reach a river, deep but not too wide. There is a bank on the other side, just visible by moonlight. Haram undoes ropes that are attached to the trunk of a pau brasil tree by the river. Each rope is attached to a strong overhanging branch of this ancient tree, and one by one each of the escapees follows Haram's example and swings across to the other side on the rope, gripping their gourds by their waist with their elbows as they do so. With the more nervous escapees, fellow escapees push them vigorously and they swing over, with one of the Africans helping as they land.

Most take the opportunity to get a drink, but this becomes less popular when a caiman is seen lurking near the water's surface nearby, its eyes glinting in the moonlight.

When the last African swings over, Haram swings back and cuts each rope except one, throwing the cut ones into the river. He swings across with the last rope, and then cuts it as high as he can and wraps the cut rope around him, tying a knot.

At Haram's silent signal, they follow him through some dense undergrowth, but soon they are on a path again, heading steeply uphill. The moment they start heading uphill, they hear dogs barking. Otapo shivers uncontrollably at the sound of the dogs. Many other escapees do likewise.

Many struggle up the steep path, and some need to be encouraged by companions to keep going. The sound of the dogs in the distance is an incentive.

Eventually the jungle thins out, and they reach a rocky area that starts to flatten out. They come to what initially seems a cliff top, with a view across a canyon to the other side. It seems to be a dead end.

Haram points to three of the strongest escapees, and beckons them to join him by a large boulder. They follow his lead by pushing this boulder and it begins, very slowly, to roll.

Otapo, who is standing with a few escapees nearby, can now see a gap. Haram stops pushing and he encourages Otapo and others to go into the gap. Otapo catches a whiff of Haram's intensive smell of sweat as he passes, and there he sees a path that passes down with a gentle slope adjacent to the cliff's side. The path is about a metre wide, but the drop at the side is steep.

Each of the Africans goes down the path except the three strong ones who first help Haram to roll the boulder back enough to make it difficult to get through. This proves harder on the cliff side of the boulder, but once they are satisfied Haram places a stone wedge under the bottom of the boulder and kicks it with his heel, so that it is snug. Then they head down the path.

It is a long path down, that winds backwards and forwards down the cliff edge. Eventually, they reach the bottom. They are still carrying their gourds.

Otapo sees a dog barking at the thin gap by the boulder, and two of the plantation men fire muskets at them to little effect at such a distance, but the pursuers appear unable to follow.

* * * * *

The escapees walk for another hour or so, mostly in jungle. No dogs can be heard barking anymore. They put one man on watch and kip down for a few hours. Otapo hears monkeys calling, owls to-wit-to-wooing, crickets knee-rubbing, and numerous other insects, but he gets to sleep in time. The next two days, they are mainly walking through jungle. The third night, they sleep on a hillside, in the entrance to a large cave. All around are bits of bones of animals that have died there. They brush these aside before they sleep.

Before dawn, Haram calls them to wake. He leads them once again through jungle, but as the dawn light arrives, they are on open ground. There is a fairly rudimentary fence of upright pointed stakes ahead, tight with one another. Where there is a gap between the pointed stakes, large fallen frees, with trunks as thick as elephant legs, bar their way. Haram approaches the trees, beckoning the others to follow, and he puts two hands to his mouth and makes a bird call. Otapo recognises it as a parakeet.

Two Black men wearing grass skirts start moving the trunks of the trees to create a gap for them to come through.

Haram turns to the escapees, who are gazing in wonder.

'This, my friends, is Palmares. This is the first country of free slaves. Soon we will be inside, and you will find many other Africans wrongly captured and brought to this land, but now tilling their own fields.'

As Haram greets the two Africans at the gate, who welcome him, the escapees walk through the entrance, barely able to conceal their excitement.

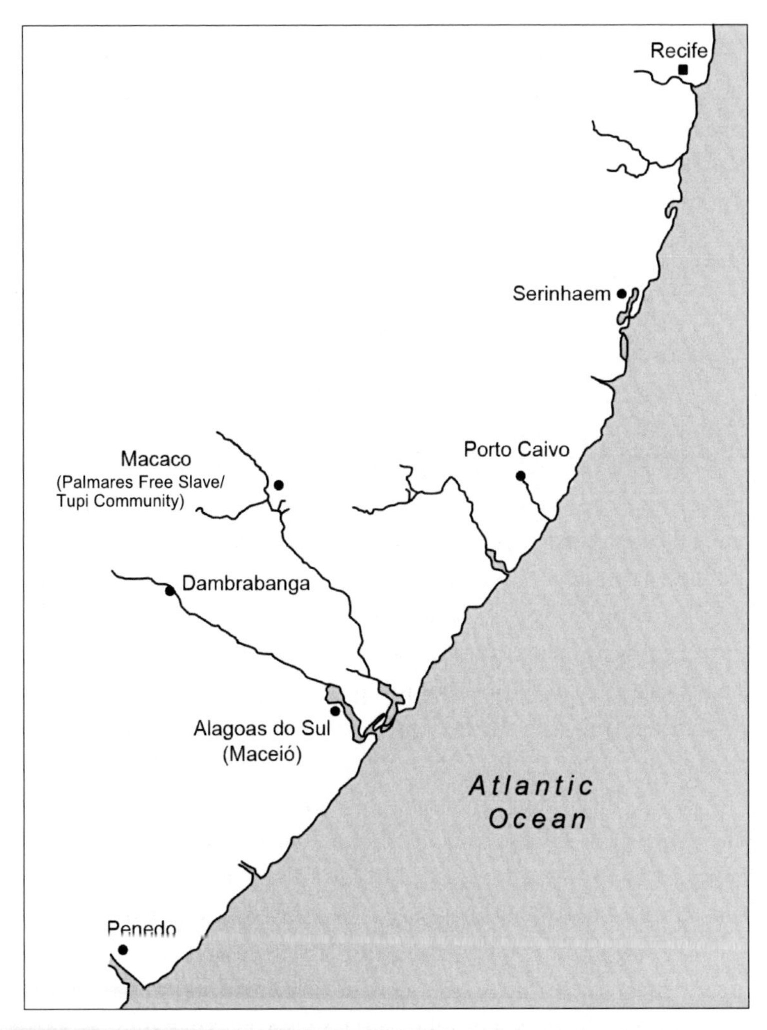

Palmares free slave/Tupi community as shown on 19th century map of Portugal's Brazilian colony, adapted

Haram points out to the two men on the gate the eighty escapee Africans and the guards tell them in broken Swahili that they are welcome.

The new arrivals start hollering and shouting and then break into a dance. A number of them go up to Haram and thank him personally.

An African man, also wearing a grass skirt, arrives from a log hut with palm leaf roof inside Palmares.

'You must be Haram,' he says in Swahili. 'Welcome. I am Mo. You have done a great job bringing so many more brothers here. I hear that you have bought many others before these. You are indeed a good man.'

He turns to the escapees: 'If you all follow me, I can show you where you will all be living.'

'Not me,' says Haram.

'No?' asks Mo, quizzically.

'I am a slave liberator,' says Haram. 'I want to go and find some more, and bring them here.'

'Very good,' says Mo, 'but rest a few days, and just help these men adjust. It's all very new for them here.'

Mo shows them to an open area, with a number of logs laid in a circle. 'This is where we meet to dance, to celebrate, to bring back African traditions. One day, we will build a large communal house by this area. Come here at dusk, you can have a dance like you probably haven't enjoyed in years.'

'Brilliant,' says Otapo, remembering back to his teenage years. All the men have beaming smiles.

Mo points to another open area perhaps seventy strides away.

'Just over there,' he says, 'we plan to build a church, at the request of some of our brethren. Those small wooden huts next to the cleared space are smithies. We have two iron smithies already, making nails, hammers and axes. We plan to build two more, for bronze and tin, and possibly steel. We have men here who are skilled from their days in our homeland. There is a much-used carpentry workshop next to the smithy.'

'I have worked iron,' shouts Mbeki, one of the older new arrivals. 'I have also worked bronze.'

'Very good,' says Mo. 'The territory goes on forever, by the way, which is why we sometimes call it our country. You can walk for five days and not reach the end of it. There are scattered settlements, but slowly we will no doubt fill the gaps in between. When the Portuguese came to attack us, they took one little village and then went away. They thought they had destroyed Palmares but it was just a few dozen people, who sadly died.'

'Do the Portuguese attack often?' asks Otapo.

'In our short time, there was that one attack,' replies Mo. 'But we know they will come back to try to hurt us again, as we threaten the lynchpin of their economy, which is slaves.'

'Stands to reason,' says Mobuka. 'So will the smithy also make weapons?'

'Sure, plenty of weapons in time, but we need tools for growing crops first.'

'Makes sense,' says Mbeki.

'Your days will be easier here than when you were on the plantation. You can wake after daylight. Part of the day you can join fellow Palmarians tilling the fields. We will soon be harvesting corn, potatoes and cassava, which will be a time to celebrate.'

'I can't wait,' shouts Otapo.

'We like each of you to help for two days a week with the building work. We are building huts for the ever-greater number of Africans...'

A woman walks past, heading for her hut. The escapees, most of whom have not seen a woman for decades, gawp at her, and Mo laughs.

'There are a few women here. It is important you respect the women. Most are married. More women will come, do not worry.

'We are also starting soon on the communal house, so you will also be asked to work on that. The other days you can divide between working the fields and getting to know each other as free men, not as slaves.'

They all laugh, and some slap their thighs in excitement.

Mo takes them a bit further, a minute or two on from the communal space, and they notice a row of huts each oblong and wooden with palm fronds for a roof, and Mo points.

'You will sleep here,' says Mo. 'The fields for growing grain and vegetables are a little way away. I will show you tomorrow, but you can rest for now, after a hard journey. We also have livestock here, mainly cows and sheep, you may prefer to work with livestock. We hope we may soon get some goats.'

As soon as they reach the huts they will be staying in, they celebrate again, and embrace each other. They put down their gourds.

'It's like paradise, compared to what we had,' says Mobuka.

'It is amazing,' says Otapo. 'I have not felt so good since I was captured in Africa.'

'Me neither,' says Mobuka.

'Listen all of you,' shouts Mo. 'We are cooking a big meal this evening to welcome you all. You are welcome to come and help cut up the vegetables if you wish. The more the merrier. There will also be meat.'

'Meat is fantastic,' shouts one escapee, Arai.

'There is a place near the communal area, where we hope to open a shop or two. We are still very new here. We have men who find supplies of beans, potatoes, cassava etc., and they leave full sacks in that space every two or three days. Each hut may take their gourds and collect a few gourds-full for their own meals.'

'The palms give us coconuts, and from the milk we make butter as well as having a refreshing drink. As I am sure you are familiar with, the palm fronds are woven into mats and baskets, and we make bowls and cups from the coconut shells.

'We made string from the fibres,' says Mobuka. 'And also stretched it thinner to make shirts and dresses.'

'At night time,' adds Mo, 'you will see lamps lit with palm oil, and we also use the oil for cooking. The heart of young palm trees is also good.'

'So Palmares is the ideal name for a place where palms give us so much,' says Mobuka.

'One note of warning,' adds Mo. 'You may have noticed through the trees the mountain tops. There is a mountain range through the middle of Palmares, the Serra de Barriga. It is dangerous to try to climb these mountains. Men have died falling from icy rocks, and men have died of cold. It is best to stay away.

'That is all for now. Many of you will want to rest after your long journey.'

'Many of us just want to dance,' shouts Mobuka.

* * * * *

Otapo finds his groin is only now calming down after seeing the young African woman. But tiredness suddenly overwhelms him and he heads into the hut. He is pleased to see there are wooden boards for each of them to sleep on, twenty in total. There are open windows at head height to allow air in. Following a faint malodorous smell, Otapo heads out the back door and sees a simple path leading to four pits. There are gourds of water by the pits.

A few head off in a direction pointed out by Mo to help with food. The others mainly rest.

Otapo and Maira

It is two years before Otapo is able to talk to a woman without blushing with embarrassment and heading back to his hut in shame.

He is working at the smithy, making nails.

A girl walks over from the neighbouring smithy, speaking in faltering Swahili and a bit of Portuguese with a soft voice. She is petite, with long black hair, a smooth face, and dark brown eyes.

Otapo realises that the hammerhead is not set right on the hammer she is making, and this girl wants help to get it right. They go back to the other smithy together.

Otapo is working to remove the errant head when he realises to his embarrassment that this ironsmith colleague has small breasts under the cowhide protective breastplate. She is not just a girl.

His face goes red as he asks the workmate if she is a woman.

She laughs and says in Swahili: 'Yes. Tupi woman,' she adds.

Otapo manages to laugh also, realising that it was a daft question, but she has forgiven him.

'My name is Otapo,' he says. 'I am from another land. What is your name?'

'I am Maira,' and she blushes.

When Otapo has repaired the hammer he hands it to Maira, who bows and says thanks.

He asks her to come and share coconut milk with him by his hut. She agrees.

As they return, his friend Mobuka laughs when he sees Otapo with a woman. Otapo smiles back.

For some time, Otapo and Maira sit sipping their drink and looking at each other. Otapo then points at his cup and gives its name in Swahili. Maira repeats this and gives its name in Tupi.

They continue this until Otapo points to his mouth. Maira does not reply in Tupi, but says in Swahili, 'Kiss.'

They kiss awkwardly. As his lips tingle in a highly memorable but unfamiliar way, Otapo tries to remember if he has kissed before. He thinks he has not. He sheds a tear.

Maira raises her left hand and gently wipes his tear, and kisses him where the tear was. She tastes salt and smells more strongly his sweat.

Otapo takes her face in his hands and gently kisses her on her lips again. He feels that he may be about to come, and lets her go, his face both black and bright red, like burning coal. The build-up of a long buried feeling subsides, and he takes her hand in his. He kisses her fingers, even though they taste of iron.

She points to his fingers, and hers, and points in the direction of a stream, which is a about fifty strides away.

They head to the stream and take off their loin cloths and bathe in the stream, keeping their eyes out for piranha. They spot an iguana on the other side, half asleep, but with one eye on them.

Otapo laughs and helps rub water over Maira's hands, face and torso and she does the same to him. They scoop up some mud from under the shallower water by the riverbank and rub this on their hands before rinsing them again.

Maira then asks Otapo to lie down, and he consents. It is a bit muddy, and there are tree roots, but he lies back all the same, his head resting on one of the roots. She scoops up more water and washes his penis. Otapo comes very quickly and blushes again.

Meanwhile a bright vermilion and cerise hummingbird hovers above them, its soft humming accompanying them.

Maira looks at him and points at her breast, then signals one with her finger and points at him with a questioning look. She says in Tupi, 'Your first woman?' And then in Swahili, 'One?'

'You are my first woman,' he replies, signalling with one finger and pointing at her and nodding.

The hummingbird flits across a few feet, still at the same height, and then returns to its stationery humming position.

Maira now arouses his penis again with her right hand. He again goes red when it happens again. She laughs. He laughs, and they embrace.

Soon, they are trying again, and Otapo now finds he can stay hard for far longer. He finds he has feelings stirring inside himself that he has never known. His mind feels cloudy, mesmerised by Maira.

In the months that follow, they often go to the stream to wash after they have been working with a smithy. They agree at the outset that Swahili will be their main language, as Maira realises that she needs it in Palmares. But Otapo agrees to start learning Tupi also, so as to reduce Maira's burden and to be able to speak to her kin.

A few moons after their first meeting, Otapo asks Maira for a quiet word. They head for their spot by the stream.

'I am innocent at my advanced age. I know little about matters of the heart,' he says, holding her hands.

A richly coloured male toucan looks down on them from a branch just above. Birdsong rings around from larks and thrushes.

'I let my heart guide me,' she says, 'I have known beatin's, rape, anger. I have not known tenderness since I became a woman.'

'I think we share a black past. But I see a white future. Can we be together? This is the question my heart asks.'

'You mean marriage?'

He embraces her. 'Yes, I think that is what people do when they love each other.'

'Do you love me?'

The toucan is joined by a female toucan. The male starts a mating dance, while the female stands there, nonchalant.

'I don't know what to call this feeling if not love. When I beat the molten iron into the shape of a hammer head, my heart senses the same red hot heat, and the picture it holds is of you.'

'I feel the same. I love you.' And they kiss, a long deep kiss.

'Shall we marry?' Big smile.

'Yes, let's marry!' She smiles an even bigger smile. They kiss passionately.

She then pulls away a little, but still holding his hand.

'But they is more good new I wish to gi' you.'

'What? Tell me.' He pecks her on her lips.

She takes his right hand and places it on her belly. 'I am wi' chile.'

'Oh my. What good spirit flew over us last night to bring this joy?'

They embrace for many minutes, laugh, and collapse to the floor, and laugh again.

The male toucan finishes its mating display and flies off. Another male toucan arrives and starts its display.

This one strikes lucky.

* * * * *

Mo is overjoyed with the news.

'In celebration, Otapo and Maira, you shall have your own space for a small hut, where you can be together and start a family. Do you want someone to help you build it?'

'Thank you, Mo, but I think we can manage. Maira is very practical and has many skills. But could we have a plot a bit nearer the river than my current hut?'

'You may Otapo. I will source it for you myself and get back to you.

Soon Otapo and Maira are collecting reeds, sticks and dried grass to make their hut. The first time for each that they will not have lived communally.

Otapo is sixty-two.

Wedding

They discuss the wedding.

'Shall we have two days of celebration, one a Tupi celebration, and one a Bantu one?' asks Otapo.

'I think tree. For us it is usually tree days. The third day can tek in parts of Aftica that others here are fro', which is nice, and can involve all the peeps we know.'

'Ok, why not? We have plenty to celebrate, and masses of friends. Can we have the Jinongonongo?

'The Jinon ... I can't say it. Tell me more.'

'The Jinongonongo is from my homeland. Some here will know it. It's a fun dance that builds around symbols, and the audience is invited to guess the symbols. So I may choose the symbol of the fire. The drums are tuned from this dance, full of strong rhythms and high energy. The drums themselves are a symbol, symbolising the spirits of our ancestors.'

'That bit sounds familiar,' says Maira.

'The circle form of one dance, with the couple in the middle, is a symbol of fertility. We could be the couple. The drums drive the rhythm, and we have flutes and the unucungo, a wooden instrument. I can make this, I think. Then we have dancers in extravagant masks, the jongeiros, with their mysterious dances drawn from the dawn of time, on themes of animals, spirits, in a circle. Men take it in turns to do their own dance.'

'I like it, but what about the women?'

'Some women like to clap to the drums. Others perform their dances of the belly strike, with their intense physicality.'

'The belly strike?' asks Maira

'It is a way of dancing where the belly almost seems independent of the rest of the body, very sensual, but very hard to do. But it is joyous to watch and has almost magical qualities.'

'It sounds great for the Bantu feast. Does it go all night?'

'It can go through the night, dancing to the light of the moon. We will make a fire, too.'

'We must have our wedding at the time of the full moon.'

'I agree. But what of your Tupi feast? What do you have in mind?'

'We wear body masks and paint in lots colours, to be spirits of the forest, or just be funny or scary.'

'I would like to do a body mask also.'

'Yes, of course. Also I love our drum dance

'Sounds fun. How does that work?'

'We start by carve tall post from a tree in the forest and the drum captain, mebbe my father, makes the post pretty with big headdress. He captain asks the music band to follow him, and goes from hut to hut inviting everyone to dance round the post. The women prepare coaba, a drink of fermented cassava which I think I gave you try.

'Mm, yes, an acquired taste, I think.'

'The men play drums and the cassaca, which is a hollowed out bamboo, with dents.'

'Notches?'

'Mebbe. Carved into it.'

'Yes, I have seen your family playing it. There is a wooden wand, which is rubbed across it to produce a rhythmic sound.'

'Yes, and we also have drum, made of hollow wood covered with leather, stretched hard.'

'Stretched tight, perhaps?'

'Yes, tight. We made the best masks.'

'I think we made better masks.'

'Ours covered the whole body. we painted spirits to frighten enemies, or to make you laugh. We used soot for black paint, arrato for red, clay for orange and yellow, and limestone for white.'

'We used limestone for white. Our masks covered the top half of the body.'

'We used the inside of tree bark.'

'So did we.'

'I think I can make the best masks for our wedding.'

'I think I can. We can challenge each other.'

'We can.'

"This dance is used for several occasions, but will be a lovely way to invite all peeps.'

'It will.'

'And we have tobacco at wedding.'

'Tobacco? Some men in another hut at the slave planation chewed this. Some kind of plant? They were hard to talk to when they chewed it, but they said it made them forget they were slaves for a day.'

'We use it to reach spirits, and it can tek you into a trance. Some Tupi use it wrongly, use it too much, but we use it at wedding to better talk to spirits.'

'Maybe one day, but not at our wedding?'

'I like it for feast days.'

'Ok. This once if you wish. You know, we have another dance I love. We called it Kipura back home.'

'Can you show me?'

And Otapo gets up and starts moving his head like a chicken darting back and forth and then to the side, with his neck almost like rubber beneath it.

Maira laughs.

'We have two dancers acting like roosters and provoking each other, one going forward and the other going back, and then the other going back, and then going forward, so they pass. Then one gives way, and another rooster comes in, then the other first one gives way, and so on. Each being a rooster, pecking. And all the while, the drums keep up a strong rhythm, and the chicken dancers make their head movements in line with the drums.'

'Fantastic. I like that too, especially the way you do the rooster,' says Maira.

Maira on her time in the forest

'What memories do you have of forest life?' asks Otapo.

Maira's Swahili is now much improved.

'We were happy in the jungle, such a good life, big family, and other families, maybe three hundred of us in our village. You didn't have a worry, but that changed. We had oval-shaped communal huts where we usually slept, each had the name of a bird, mine was macaw, my best friend's was toucan.

'We had dances all the time, and joyous music with drums and flute that often went on all week when there was a wedding, a birth of a child, or even when the harvest was collected in.

'We had our way of stopping any family becoming wealthier than others. We had an evil drink called Bad Kawi, which could make you violently sick. The wealthier people who had more gold or had fine beads would not drink it. If poor man drank Bad Kawi, then he would be paid by the wealthier men.

'We ate well, but sometimes food was disrupted. One year, a plague of ants destroyed our cassava and our potato plots, which gave us food for months.'

'Yuk. I am not that keen on ants.'

'No, well we had to forage for food in the jungle for more the year after that.'

'I can imagine. We had bad harvests at times, too.'

'You know, when Tupi women pregnant, then other men sleep with her as their semen is thought makes baby stronger.'

'Ah, is that why some of the Tupi men look at you that way when you told them of your pregnancy? I don't think I want that to happen with you.'

'Don't worry, it won't happen with me. I have told them.'

'Thanks.'

'We had tough times, after the spotty achey disease arrive when the Pink Faces come to this land. I lost a grandparent, two uncles, three aunts, cousins. It was hard.

'They burn part of our forest, the Pink faces, so we had less forest, but we survive. One time, after a fire, and we are looking for a new home, a strange thing happen. We hear music, gentle music, they – about twenty-five or thirty of them – get near, we see them through trees. They are dress strange, and act mournful, with sad clothes. Seems maybe mystical, hard to tell.'

'As they approach us, the men throw off their outer garments, they have guns and swords. Some are half Tupi and speak to us in Tupi. Say we will be killed if we resist capture. Life will be better if we go with them. When Jaci objects, they kill him. The others then no not resist.

'We taken to place where we are made to be slaves. The men cut sugar. The women sometimes too, but also help in the home of the Portuguese.

'They rape me. Portuguese. Three men, and one young one, not yet a man.'

'They are so evil, the Pink Skins.'

'We were there many moons, perhaps thirty or forty moons. My children were taken away from me. Haram, my hero, come and rescued some of us, about fifteen escaped and came here.'

Trying to return to Africa, Spring, 1610

'Maira, I love you. I love our children Mande, Tucan and Caua, but I have a deep ache in my heart that won't go away.'

'Your family?'

'Yes. As you know, I was taken from my family when very young. My heart longs for them. I never thought I would ever see them again but Palmares has given me hope.'

'But how you see them?'

'I want to try. If former slaves find a ship to cross the ocean, then I want to go. Only to see them, and then I come back.'

'It would be very hard if you go. I have found happiness for first time since being kid in jungle. But I understand your pain in heart. I have a pain in mine, and I may one day want to return to jungle.'

'I am sorry. It is very hard to talk about.'

'Very hard. I love you.'

'I will go and see Mo and see if he knows of any way of getting to Africa. I will tell you if anything is happening.'

'Tell me everything, my darling.'

'Will you hate me if I go?'

'I will hate you. You abandon me. But I will love you too. Because you love your family back home so much.'

* * * * *

'Mo, I like it here. The people here are amazing,'

'So I get the impression you want to ask me something, Otapo,' says Mo, 'and you are worried I won't agree.'

'We have built the communal hall together. The smithies are all built and working well, and I've learnt how to smelt iron and make tables and chairs. I have a wonderful wife and gorgeous young children. But I am free now, the plantation owners haven't come to kill us all, and I want something bigger than this place, as good as this place is.'

'You are talking about going home?'

'I am. Is it at all possible?'

'There is a brave and determined African man who brought you here. Do you remember?'

'Haram? How could I forget him? He saved our lives.'

'He has been looking for a ship, a ship big enough to cross to Africa. He heard of one shipwrecked on the coast. He found it. It is perhaps four or five days walking from here, by Haram's reckoning. But it needs a lot of work to fix it.'

'Amazing. I will help fix it,' says Otapo, excitedly.

'If former slaves go there, they could be caught, and they would be hanged, or if they are lucky just shot. Haram is trying to find free men who are not ex-slaves to help him. It is not easy. The last time I saw him, he had two men, but he needs at least three more. And one or two need to be skilled carpenters.'

'Well, I want to help, whatever the risk. Can you get me some extra carpentry training here?'

'Yes, Edmundo is an excellent carpenter. I will ask him to train you in some of the skills you will need on the ship. But you must know you are taking a huge risk with your life doing this.'

'You have been very good to me, but I am getting old. If I am very lucky, and get home in the next year, I may just see my mother and brother alive. That would bring me great joy. If not, I would love to see my brother's children. I would love to be under the African sky again. I would love to feel whole again.'

'Your mother?'

'Well, perhaps not my mother. But I have not felt her die inside of me, like my father.'

'I see. Well, let us get you trained. I will tell Haram you are interested. It is possible you will be ready in four or five moons, or even three moons if you are a very good learner.'

'You are a good man, thanks. Please tell me when you have spoken to Haram.'

Summer, 1610

'Otapo, there is someone at the gate to meet you,' says Mbeki.

'Who can that be?' asks Otapo, as he half runs half jogs to the gate.

'Haram! So good to see you!' he exclaims, as he reaches the gate.

'Otapo! I have news.'

'You are keeping me in suspense.'

'Well, it is news but not all good. There is a shipwreck on the coast.'

'Abandoned?'

'It seems so. It has beached in a cove where nobody lives, though there are signs that Tupi fish there. The hull has a big hole, the sails are ripped, and much work is needed to make it float again on the water.'

'But we can try?' asks Otapo eagerly, but also a bit anxiously.

'We will need skilled carpenters, ironmongers, and seamstresses. We will need to work for several moons, I fear.'

'Let us do it. I am an ironmonger, and I have learnt carpentry.'

'But you will not be safe if you leave here. You can be caught and returned to slavery.'

'Do you have anything to suggest? Can I perhaps sleep in the ship?'

'I have some land in mind, mostly jungle, for a small mocambo. It will take a little time to be sure I can claim it and make it safe. The land is near to the cove where the ship is.'

'I can wait.'

'I have a few men sourcing logs, some for our hut, some for the ship. I have another one checking with the nearest Tupi village to see what they know, and to ask if they will object to it. As I am known for my help to enslaved Tupis, they usually trust me.'

'Well, I am happy to build a hut for me and others. Get word to me when you think it may be safe to go there'

'I will. I also need to make sure there is a safe jungle route for you to get there. We cannot risk using any open tracks.'

'Very good. I will tell my wife Maira and my children Mande, Tucan and Caua.'

Haram raises his eyebrows.

'Yes, I have a wife and three children. But I need for my soul to make this journey and be whole again. I can then return to them.'

'I understand. But you know the whole journey is full of danger. The storms attack in the Atlantic like angry dragons. There are slave catchers in Africa who may try to take you again. The journey across Africa will be long and full of risk.'

'What the heart desires, the heart must have.'

'So be it. I will contact you when it is time for you to join me. We have around six others, God willing.'

'Thank you. Thank you so much.'

Otapo and Maira

'The time has nearly come. You know how my heart is torn, but I will never be whole until I have made this journey to my homeland. There is a ship. It is broken, but we will work to fix it.'

'But you may never come back. Right now, our love is so perfect. Our children grow, and become little people, learning carpentry, helping to farm, helping to make new houses. How can you not want to see them become men and woman?'

'I do want to see them become men and woman. I hope to be back in twelve moons, or eighteen. And you know I love you.

I simply cannot miss an opportunity to resolve the deep hurt in me. I am old. It is my last chance.'

'I do understand. I know that hurt too. It is just too painful to see you disappear, not knowing if you will return. I hate you because I hate this hurt. This not knowing.'

'Soon, Haram will come and invite me to a mocambo he is creating. He is planning a route for me to reach the new mocambo safely. I don't know if you want to come there while we are working on the ship, or whether you wish to stay with family and friends here.'

'It is difficult. The children are now eight, seven and six, and get a full education in life now. I have all my family and friends here. It is difficult leave all this behind.'

'I will come and visit you when I can, and when it seems safe to travel. We will try to make this work.'

'With love, everything is possible.'

* * * * *

The moon has moved but a quarter when Haram returns to collect Otapo. The two of them head through semi-dense jungle to a headland, where the land opens a little. Haram points to a log wall a few hundred yards away. The sea is visible some way beyond this.

They walk towards the log wall. As they approach, Haram makes a call like a toucan, and one part of the wall opens just enough for them to squeeze through.

Haram introduces his five companions and then points to a half-built hut.

'A day's work should do it, to have the hut liveable,' he says.

'I don't mind starting work now,' says Otapo.

'Just sit down for a little while,' says Mwesu in Swahili, who hands him a coconut with the top sliced off. He is tall, with broad shoulders, purple-black. 'Enjoy some coconut milk to refresh you. Is your heart dragging you to Africa too?'

'Desperately,' responds Otapo. 'I had barely become a man when I was taken. Most of my life I have been treated as not a man. Not an animal even, a sub-species.'

'We all feel the same. Where are you from?'

'It was a Bantu village. I need to find the source of the Congo River. A huge lake there, then another. I can find the village from there, I think. We hunted in that area.'

'I am from near Boma,' says Tyere, short, thick set, his Afro hair cropped short like the others. 'Also on the Congo River, but the river there is as wide as a thousand crocodiles. Like a small sea.'

'Similar area, me,' chips in Nyasa, tall, angular face, thin.

'Guinea,' says Ayala, less dark, open round face, winning smile.

'Ouidah in Benin, on coast,' pipes up another, Efe. 'And Mwesu is from the south of Kongo.'

'Good to meet you all,' says Otapo. 'Where are you at with our hut there? Do you need a hand to finish the walls and get a roof on?'

'We can finish the walls today,' replies Haram. 'It's mainly the last wall. The roof can wait until tomorrow. Thanks. Can you help line up some logs, and bang some nails in?'

'Sure, not a problem. Heh, Haram, what is the plan with the ship? When do you plan to start?'

'We have started, Otapo, but only clearing out the damaged bits, and seeing how big the problem is.'

'And, how big is it?'

'Very big.'

'Too big for us?'

'No, with you here, we can do it. But we will need a lot more nails, and planes and hammers. You say you can work iron?'

'Yeah, of course, if need be. I will need to make a forge, though, and that will need some iron, and some powerful fuel. Might be easier to go back to Palmares to do the ironwork, as I'm not sure how we would do it here. Can we finish the walls with what we have?'

'Yes, I would say so. Let's get on with the last wall then.'

They finish the wall that day, and head to the ship the next day.

Back at Palmares

Maira holds a white dove. She places a pau brasil leaf in its beak and releases it. It heads off in the direction of her people. She turns with a start.

'Heh, Maira, come to me.' And he gives her a big hug.

'I am so pleased to see you!' she exclaims. 'You have only been gone two days.'

'This ship needs a lot of work,' he says. 'I need to make a lot of nails here, planes, and two more hammers, plus a saw. I will also make an axe, to help with the wood chopping.'

'Stay a week or two, won't you? Play with the kids a bit.'

'Yea, of course. We can have fun while I am here. But this ship is exciting you know. I think that in a moon or two we could be leaving for Africa.'

After a week back at Palmares, Otapo takes the jungle route back to the new mocambo carrying a sack full of nails, planes, the hammers, a saw, and the axe over his shoulder.

A Tupi whispers from behind a pau brasil, 'Wait here. Pink skins near!'

Otapo has learnt a fair bit of Tupi from Maira over the years, so he does as instructed, first brushing away a cobweb he has just walked into.

'How come you here?' he whispers back.

'Message from Maira. We come to watch for you,' says the Tupi.

Otapo notices through the undergrowth a flash of clothing, distinctly Portuguese. They are walking on a track parallel with his in the opposite direction to him. He waits until they are well past, and then nods a thank you and continues.

The work on the ship proves harder than Otapo imagined. The precision required in repairing or replacing the planks in the hull tests Otapo and his work mates to the full. Many planks need to be re-planed a few times to make them fit precisely, and in a couple of cases new planks need to be cut due to splitting.

When the hull planks are all fixed, Haram brings tree resin he has obtained from the Tupis, and they rub the resin over all the joins in the wood, and then repeat the process a day later once dried. They then manage with some difficulty to turn the ship over to the side, and they apply two coats to the other side of the hull.

Before working on the deck they make sure the ship's anchor is still secure, as it was when they first looked at the ship, and they then manhandle the ship into the water.

Otapo looks on anxiously as the ship sits in the water. 'Some water is seeping through down there,' he says, when they have heaved the ship back on to the beach. 'We need more resin, once it has dried. I think we need something else too.'

'If we apply mud in any of the cracks between planks,' says Mwesu 'the wood will expand when in the water and will move in on the mud, compressing it, and ensuring that there is no gap left. This should make it extra waterproof.'

'How do you know that stuff?' asks Efe.

'I just watch the guys by the water back home, how they use mud like that.'

Within two days, the hull is waterproof to their satisfaction.

They now keep the ship in the water, close to the shore, and most of them work on the damaged areas of the deck and the lower deck.

Haram, for his part, has obtained needle and thread from the nearby Tupi, and is working on one of the sails.

A week later, they are all relaxing after a day's hard effort. The ship is starting to look like a ship again.

And suddenly Mwesu shouts, 'Hey, we have company!'

Otapo turns and shouts, 'Maira! Kids! How brilliant! And Mobuka too!'

'We have big news! We are coming too!'

'You are coming? To Africa? How come?'

'We need to be with you. That is all there is to it. Me, the children. And Mobuka feels the same.'

'Well, it is lovely, really lovely. But you know, it is very dangerous on the ship, with storms like dragons. And there is a lot of work all the time. And it will be dangerous all the time.'

'Don't worry, being together is everything. And look what the Tupis got me.' She unwraps a giant mallow leaf and shows them two muskets, which the Tupis had got from two Portuguese soldiers.

'Excellent. Muskets. They may well come in handy,' says Haram, having a look. 'I will get some shot for them.'

'You have come after all the hard work,' says Ayala.

'We will work our passage, don't you worry,' says Maira.

Seven more Africans arrive the next day, and Haram introduces them as Aftab, Takana, Rufaso, Sembene, Nguni, Wakuu and Fey. All, except Aftab, are from villages north of Boma, Kongo; Aftab is from north of Benin, River Niger.

They are carrying various foodstuffs with them, including plenty of beans, cassava and potatoes, a sack of coconuts, and another sack of bananas.

'I have located a quadrant in the captain's cabin,' says Haram. 'We can find east with this and adjust as necessary as we travel. We can also follow the middle belt of the star constellation Orion, which is always bright in the sky. I am no more than self-trained sailing, from when we stole a ship on the south east coast of Brazil to get some escaped slaves to the north more safely. A sailor on the ship showed me how to adjust the sails to different wind currents, and how to steer. I am happy to show anyone who wants to learn.'

'I will learn to sail,' says Nyasa.

'Me too,' says Tyere.

'I will learn, too,' says Maira, 'and teach our children, who will be keen to learn.'

'Excellent,' says Haram cheerily. 'We need a few, not least for night-time, when I sleep, but also for illness. It is also tiring.

'We are in your hands, Haram and the hands of fate,' says Efe, 'but perhaps I can learn from you how to use the quadrant.'

'Of course, Efe,' says Haram.

'I will learn the quadrant also,' says Otapo. 'And help to steer.'

'Me too,' says Tucan, not wanting to be outdone by the adults.

'It seems that fate has taken us to this land,' says Ayala, mournfully. 'We can only hope that fate will help us home again, as we have no skilled sailors.'

'Very good. So be it.' says Haram. 'We will leave tomorrow. It may take one moon or more to reach Africa, maybe a little less with good winds. I want each of you to take your gourds to the stream at the edge of this Quilombo to fill up and take to the ship. You may get wet, but the water only goes up to your armpits.

'Sembene, there are two large barrels on the ship with a simple cover with a cork in it. You be on the ship, to collect and empty the gourds into the barrels. Just check the barrels first for rats. It is a tedious task but without this you could go for days without water.'

They all nod and collect up their gourds, ready to head to the nearby stream.

'Just one last thing before you go – we will not have much to eat each day, so the local Tupis are doing a feast for us before we leave, and are giving us some manioc and cassava to take.'

'Great, but might we starve before we get to Africa?'

'I don't think so. We will make the food last, but there will only be a little each day. We can make up for it when we get to Africa.'

12

The Return Passage

The following day, they negotiate around the partly hidden rocks that had caused the ship to get holed, and head out towards the ocean.

The children become expert at pouring slop on the decks and wiping it all down every day, to keep the planks wet.

They also help cook and serve the food.

They are heading past the North East tip of Brazil, and starting to head East, when a ship appears to the starboard side. They do not recognise the flag. Haram watches it nervously, fearing a slave trader. Fortunately, it then changes tack and heads towards the stretch of coast they have left.

Haram hopes they will locate Ascension en route, to top up on water and on food. The plan is then to find Benin, as Haram has contacts there who will help the escapees on the next part of their journey. But Ascension is further south than the direct route, and Haram is not sure he has the skill or the equipment to find the island. He mentions this to Bufaso, Mobuka and Sembene.

Sembene stops for a moment, before saying: 'There are birds that will want to find Ascension also. The journey by sea is long, and they will also need fresh water, I believe.'

'You may be right, Sembene. Let us look to see if any flocks of birds may be flying over us.'

Bufaso and Sembene keep their eyes peeled on the sky.

Meanwhile, Otapo comes to Haram and says: 'You may have noticed. A storm is brewing. The wind is getting up, and to the north west there are storm clouds heading our way.'

'You are right, Otapo. I should bring the sails down. Bring your boys to help. Is there anything that should be tied down that is not already?'

'I think all except the pilot should be in their cabins,' says Otapo. 'And if you are to be the pilot, perhaps I should tie you to the wheel before I go into our cabin. Any man, however strong, is capable of being swept off the ship by the storm. We experienced one when we came over as slaves. We in the hold were thrown all around, only held from floating away by our chains. It feels like the whole ship will be turned upside down, it is that bad.'

Mande and Caua skittle up the mast to loosen the sails from the top and Otapo and Tyere roll up the sails as best they can. Tyere places them in the hold.

The temperature drops as the storm approaches, the wind gets stronger, and the sudden darkening adds an air of foreboding. All except Haram are now in the cabins, holding on to something.

Rain starts lashing the ship. The waves start tossing it one way and then the other. The waves are soon as high as the ship, and it is almost horizontal.

Mande, Tucan and Caua are struggling to hold on. Maira starts to hold Mande as best she can, while holding on to a handle herself.

Otapo is trying to hold Tucan and Caua but does not have a firm grip on Caua. As the ship is again thrown horizontal, Caua goes flying across the cabin and bangs his head. He is thrown back with the next lurch of the waves and Otapo can see from his eyes and his pallor that he is probably concussed. He leaves Tucan for a moment to grab Caua and sits back down with Caua on his lap and Tucan's arms around his right arm.

Caua's breathing is uneven. Otapo holds him to keep him warm, and preys to his spirits for help.

The next minutes of the storm seem like hours, as the ship is tossed around. Bufaso is thrown around the cabin like Caua, and crawls back to his seat the best he can. It seems he is still conscious.

As the waves finally subside, Otapo and Maira look at Caua. Maira takes Caua and hugs him close to her.

Slowly, he starts to breathe more easily again. The ship is able to move forward again, under Haram's guidance. Tyere fetches the sails and Tucan and Mande re-hook the sails to the mast.

They are again proceeding at a steady pace.

Caua is in the cabin with Maira and is regaining consciousness, but is still confused.

'A flock of geese!' shouts Sembene, on the deck. 'Let's follow the geese.'

Haram notes the direction of the geese is a little south of east. This is where he expects Ascension to be. He sets the ship on a path following the geese.

Eight days later, a bruised Bufaso cries: 'Land ahoy,' like he has sailed all his life.

Haram sails along the coast, with Bufaso at his side looking for a cove. They spot one, and move closer, dropping anchor. Sembene and Otapo fetch the long boats, and they take the men ashore, each gripping their gourds. Maira is at the back, still holding Caua, who is now on his feet, but unsteadily so.

Takana and Nguni head off looking for fruit. The others soon find a stream flowing near the cove, and get their fill. After a brief rest, they start filling their gourds again, and Otapo takes them back to the ship. He calls Haram, who takes the gourds two at a time to re-fill the barrels. He slakes his thirst from one gourd in the process.

While they are filling the barrels, Takana is running back with pineapples. 'Nguni has been bitten by a snake, he is bad.'

Haram grabs his knife and a cotton kerchief and jumps out of the ship, swimming until he can touch the seabed and can walk. On reaching the shore, he runs with Takana to where Nguni lies, looking a deathly grey.

Haram identifies the bite just above Nguni's ankle, and gives the scarf to Takana, ordering him to tie it tight around the lower thigh while he cuts around the bite, taking out as much flesh as he can, with blood flowing freely. Haram then gives the kerchief ends an extra tug to make the tourniquet that much tighter.

'Did you see the snake?' asks Haram.

'Not clearly. I got a sense of black with yellow markings as it slithered under a bush.'

'Hard to tell which one,' responds Haram, as he lifts Nguni and places him over his shoulder.

They walk back to the rest of the crew, who are happily eating pineapples.

'How bad is he?' asks Otapo.

'It's touch and go. All depends on how much poison got into his bloodstream before I cut it out. We will take him back on the ship shortly. Someone will need to stay with him constantly and keep giving him water. I will loosen the kerchief when back on the ship.'

'You are a lifesaver,' says Takana.

'Not yet, he might not survive yet.'

The barrels are full, they have extra pineapples, and they are back on board.

* * * * *

They are about to set sail when Otapo comes to Haram.

'It seems he has not made it,' he says.

'Very sad. A good man. Can you bring Takana to me?'

Takana is distraught when he comes out of the cabin to Haram.

'I think we will have to bury him at sea,' says Haram, 'as sad as it is to say. We cannot be sure we can bury him on the mainland.'

'I fear you are correct,' says Takana.

On Otapo's request, all the crew come out as Nguni is carried through.

The kerchief is placed over his head.

They all lower their heads with the exception of Otapo and Haram, who lift up the prone Nguni and drop him over the side of the ship. Ayala preys to Allah, and the others express thoughts privately.

The ship then sets sail, heading north-east.

In a week, they see the coast of Africa.

There is euphoria on the ship, but Haram calls them all to come on deck.

'Listen, some of the ports on this coast are used for transporting slaves. You have come a long way to escape slavery and to try to find your way home. We need to go along the coast until we find somewhere that should be fairly safe. In particular, I am hoping that Efe will be able to help me identify his coastal town of Ouidah when we reach there. I know Benin a little, from one visit, but Efe should know Ouidah really well, which is a bit before Benin itself.'

'I think so,' says Efe.

The ship inches along the coast, just far enough offshore that any slave traders they pass will not be able to see who is on board.

As they begin to approach Ouidah, Efe recognises the hills and the mouth of the river, and tells Haram, 'This is Ouidah now.'

'Thanks Efe. We now just need to keep our eye out for a cove a little way past Ouidah, just in case there are slave traders in the port there.'

They soon find a cove. There is much excitement amongst the whole of the crew as Haram orders for the anchor to be dropped. They start dancing, and Sembene and Bufaso start a song.

Haram calls Otapo and Maira to him. 'Can you see any persons here that may be slave traders? Any sign of life at all?'

'Can't see any people at all. Or any signs they have been there.'

'Ok. Ask Efe and Takana to start releasing the longboat, or maybe both of the boats if need be, and we will head for the beach.'

They grab their gourds and head for their first sensation of African sand and soil for many years. They sing and dance on the beach for a few minutes until Haram advises they calm down until they know it is safe.

'A stream!' shouts Caua, from behind some bushes.

They all rush there, some just putting their face in the stream to drink and feel the coolness, and others using their hands to scoop up water.

They then fill their gourds.

Haram calls them back to the beach. 'I want you to wait here for a while. The sun will be a little higher in the sky. There are real dangers here – very real dangers from slave-hunters. My contacts will help. For some of you, there will be boats to take you nearer to your homes. For Efe, there will be safe passage here. One or two will be coming with me soon to find the best route for you here. Africa is now full of slave hunters, so please listen to the advice that I and others give you.'

'Great,' says Otapo.

'Very good,' says Efe.

All except Maira nod to imply acknowledgement and agreement.

Maira enquires, 'And food? Our children have barely eaten in weeks.'

'And we stink,' shouts Mande, and several chuckle.

'I will source food for you by this evening,' replies Haram. 'Efe and Aftab will help you know which leaves around us here are edible. As we came in, I saw the tops of a banana tree just a little way back from the coast a short way back. As I have said, you put your life in danger if you venture from here before I return. But the banana tree is near. If three of you go there to fetch a gorilla's hand each of bananas, it should be OK. As for washing yourselves, use the sea here for now. Within a day or two you will have freshwater.

He holds up a hand to wave and leaves through the back of the beach.

In no time, Sembene and Bufaso head off for the banana tree, while Aftab pounces upon the bushes around them, tearing off leaves. He shouts in turn 'Na'a naa... Bitter Leaf... Okuzi... Ugu.'

Efe nods agreement and starts chewing on the Okuzi, saying 'Spinach, is good.' He hands some to Maira to check for

Caua, Tucan and Mande. She nods, and grabs a bundle to share between the children.

Otapo tries the Na'a naa. 'It's mint!' he exclaims. 'Lovely,' and again shares some between the children.

'And some for me,' asks Mobuka.

'Of course, my friend,' replies Otapo, offering him mint. 'This is nearly the end of our epic time together. You have been a very good friend.'

'We have this last leg of the journey, and then I will find my family in Congo. I hope you find yours.'

'I will, dear Mobuka, I will,' says Otapo.

Takana tries the Ugu, and says, 'It seems like pumpkin leaves to me. Quite tasty.'

They start decimating the bushes almost like a cloud of locusts as they gobble down the leaves, helping them down with water from the stream.

'Papaya, bananas!' shouts Sembene, and puts down a huge bunch of green bananas in their midst, while Bufaso releases his armful of ripe papaya.

They gorge themselves with relish, after many days on the ship with a humdrum starvation diet of a few beans and half a cup of water.

With the worst of their pangs of hunger satiated, calmness returns to the group.

Efe offers to tell them all about Benin.

'Yes please!' pipes up Caua. They all agree.

'Very well,' says Efe.

The Benin Empire

'Far to the north, and quite a bit west of here, is my home, the empire of Benin. It is three moons's walk from here, but a very rewarding walk.

'In Benin, one is immediately awestruck. There is a stone wall around the city, with nine magnificent gates to enter through, and fine roads within. Then, as you walk into the city, there are towering walls, which even block out the intense midday sun. Inside these imposing walls is the finest palace, amongst the most opulent of its time in Africa, with magnificent sculptures and plaques in the Benin tradition, intricately formed in bronze and brass.

'The sculptures include figures of Benin soldiers in battle, with their features and armour in intimate detail. Other sculptures, equally consummate, are made from ivory, wood and ceramics, some from a time before my grandparents, and before their grandparents. There are long galleries, resting on wooden pillars and covered from top to bottom in copper, engraved with images of past battles.

'Within the palace complex is a smaller palace, I am told, for the king himself; there are quarters for courtiers, and all the hangers on. A courtier I once knew told me of the elaborate life in the court, which involved no end of foreign dignitaries, courtiers, soldiers, mercenaries and so on in a well-rehearsed pantomime. The king's palace is surrounded by a dry moat. It was built by King Oba Ewuare, who was still alive when I lived here, but I suspect he has now died.

'Near the King's palace are the houses for craftsmen and other dignitaries. These are not craftsmen like dear Otapo here. They are some of Africa's finest workers in bronze and brass, and formed the guild of bronze-smiths. These craftsmen are behind the intricate sculptures that captivate all visitors to Benin. Other craftsmen work in silver and textiles, one or two in gold and ivory, even ceramics.

'A fisherman from near here who I used to know told me how he and dozens of others would be collected off the streets without warning, washed, and put in a simple skirt and sandals to act out scenarios for the King in the great court.'

'Just picked up? Just like that?' asks Sembene.

'Indeed. So as an example, for a farming scenario these amateurs off the street would be given a hoe or a pitchfork, and some would be given a woollen coat and horns and asked to walk on all fours as sheep. There was a large cowhide that went over two men together to be a cow.

'For a fishing scenario, said the fisherman, they would give everyone rods and lines, and the cowhide would double up as a dolphin hide, which we would pretend to catch with great difficulty. The musicians would make a sound like a powerful wind, and we had to stand like we were trying to ward off the force of the wind. Bit crazy. But you did exactly as told. My fisherman friend had his back whipped viciously when he made fun of the farming scenario. Took him days to get back on his feet.'

'Another time, a couple of little huts were built. The musicians struck up a cacophony of noise to represent thunder, and all would cower in a corner by the little huts covering their face with their hands as though a storm were raging.

'I recall once meeting a wizened old man, who was bald on top but had a white beard to his chest, and he said how King Ewuare inherited a very old empire, and that he expanded it to more than double its size in his time. It is still an important empire now, but everyone here thinks that it is most important as an inspiration to all of Africa with the quality of its art.

'The old man also told me a surprising thing; he said that copper and zinc were smelted in Benin back at the time of the later Egyptian pharaohs, such as Ramses II. It is a very long tradition here.

These Europeans coming here to buy slaves from this region know none of this past. They were still living in caves when we were making copper sculptures.'

'Too true,' says Otapo.

'Just one last thing, in case any of you visit here. Naked is not the way to dress here, unlike much of Africa south of here, I am told. Many women wear brightly coloured skirts and dresses, and often multi-coloured scarves wrapped around and above their hair, and colourful beads around the neck. Some wear coral necklaces instead of beads if they are attached to the court, to complement their fine dresses. Only young women just have beads over their breasts. Men will often wear a shirt and a skirt, or loose bottoms.'

'Sounds amazing,' exclaims Caua.

'Can we visit it?' asks Tucan.

'It sounds an altogether extraordinary place to visit,' says Maira, 'but we must move on now. We must put safety first. Maybe one day we can come back.'

'Thanks so much Efe,' says Sembene, and the others nod agreement.

* * * * *

The sun has only moved on a little, and many have drifted off into a post-prandial nap, when Takana has a vision of a beautiful young woman, with a grass skirt and beads over her breasts, holding a pot of food. Two more delightful young women follow. He slaps his face to be sure this is real.

'Have I died and gone to meet our spirits?' he asks.

'No, my friend.' Haram comes on to the beach, a small bald man next to him. 'This is my friend Femi, and his three daughters have brought the feast I promised you. Please eat.'

There are banana leaves, and each takes one and folds within it a selection of the spiced meats, aubergine, pumpkin and grilled fish laid out, alongside yam and bananas.

'I have never known such flavours!' exclaims Otapo, with a beaming smile, as Maira helps Caua, Tucan and Mande with their food, until they each protest that they can manage on their own.

'The toucan and the macaw are looking down kindly on me today,' says Maira. 'I forgive the long delay.'

'My gods look favourably on me at last,' says Takana.

'If they joined all our smiles together, they would form a bridge to the ship,' says Mwesu.

'It is the ship to which we owe eternal thanks,' says Wakuu

'The ship and Haram. He has been a giant,' adds Efe.

'Well, this is very kind of you, but Otapo and others also helped rebuild the ship so that we could sail it,' says Haram.

'Thanks to Otapo and the boat builders!' shouts Wakuu, and others cheer.

'Listen everyone,' shouts Haram. 'Soon I will be leaving some of you. My friend Femi will explain what he has in mind for Efe, Aftab, and Ayala. You guys will be in his safe hands. But you others – and you Bufaso – will be coming in the ship with me.'

Bufaso is not listening. He is holding the hand of one of Femi's daughters, Ekhorose, as they head – with Bufaso leading – into the bushes.

'This will be a much shorter journey,' continues Haram, 'but will bring you to the Congo River, and the town Boma, from where you will be able to start the next stage of your journeys.'

'So, listen please Aftab, Efe and Ayala,' says Femi, in Swahili. 'I have a safe house for you this evening, and you can view the great palace of Benin tomorrow, but then we must move deep into the countryside.

'Efe, you do not have far to go. For Aftab and Ayala, I will advise each of you where you may go to live more safely. I can take you to your families, but I am not confident you will be safe there. This we can discuss as we walk.'

They all thank Femi and his daughters for the food.

Bufaso returns with a broad smile. He gives Ekhorose a parting kiss.

The departees bid farewell with great fondness, after their long voyage together.

Haram calls together all the crew who are coming with him.

'We will leave at dusk and sail by moonlight. It is almost a full moon tonight. We should arrive at our destination by the morning, but make sure you have enough water, and at least a couple of bananas. I cannot be sure that you will soon find food after we land in Kongo.'

* * * * *

They climb in the longboat in good time, with their gourds full of water.

The ship sets sail, always in sight of the coast, but at the same time well clear of it.

Haram has obtained in Benin a chart showing islands and rocks, including hidden rocks, in the waters off the coast of Africa. In the moonlight he looks at it with Mande and Tucan, who helped with piloting on the route from Ascension Island to

Benin. Tucan with her keener eyes in this weak light, points at a symbol indicating rocks just south east of Benin.

'Good job Tucan! We'll steer south for a while. Here, give me a hand.'

'I love holding the wheel,' says Tucan.

As dawn breaks, casting a soft orange glow over the tropical coast they are passing, they all start to wake. Haram tells everyone to look out for the wide mouth of the Congo River. It arrives earlier than he expects.

Soon, the crew are cheering as they enter between the river's lips and start heading upstream.

For a few hours they are coasting up the river, which is here as wide as a large lake.

Eventually, Haram feels it is probably far enough up the river and asks Mande and Caua to look out for a good cove or beach to use in the next few miles.

He says to the others, 'When we find a beach, I will leave you there to continue your journey. For much of your onward journeys many of you will need to find a boat, as it is too dangerous on the land. There are plenty of traders with boats who will help you for short distances.

'But beware, there are more slave-hunters here than in Benin. Bufaso and Tyere, you only have a short way to go, so this will soon lighten the boat. Mwesu, you will want to go due south from where I leave you, so you will need a boat across the river.'

'I could come with you a little further,' says Mwesu. 'You could leave me at the next port.'

'I have a better idea, but it is a big thing to ask, so do think about it. Why not help me in my work, rescuing more slaves? I could take you to your family first, and then you could return with me.'

'I don't need to think about it. I agree, it would be an honour,' says Mwesu.

'Very well, Mwesu. That is excellent news. You stay with me. We need to find some food. For Otapo, Maira, and your great crew members Mande, Tucan and Caua, you can take one of the ship's longboats further upstream. But you will be best advised to make a raft once you find enough twine and driftwood. The boat will be far too heavy. There are dangerous rapids and great waterfalls to negotiate, and it is only with a raft that you will be able to carry your craft upstream. You have the carpentry skills to do it, so it should not be a problem.'

The children's smiles are as wide as the river.

'Very good' says Maira, as Otapo nods. 'But we will take all our Congo friends for the first part of their journey, and drop them where they feel safe.'

As they glide further up the river, the Congolese crew members see banana trees and fields of yam. People work in the fields. It is at last more reminiscent of the Africa they knew, and they look out at it nostalgically, but also admiringly.

'A beach,' shouts Mande, 'a big one.'

Haram slows the ship down. 'There are trees on the sides as shelter,' he says. 'This should do.' And he asks Otapo and Maira to drop anchor.

'Take a longboat for all of you then for the next stage of your journey,' adds Haram. 'Please bid farewell to me here, and then you can continue.'

There are long hugs from all concerned.

'I and my family will be eternally grateful to you,' says Otapo, with tears in his eyes.

Maira is also tearful, and plants a kiss on his cheek.

The children all hug him at the waist, and he puts his hand on their heads.

They also bid farewell to Mwesu.

They take a longboat to the shore, and fill their gourds from the river before continuing. They take turns rowing with the four oars, the children helping too. For now, the river is placid.

Behind them, the ship turns a full semi-circle, and crosses to the other side. The ship then continues on its way. In a few weeks, it will be back on the coast of Brazil.

The river is so wide, they feel like a tiny minnow. The sun is still strong, but on a downward descent.

As the number of the boats on the river grows, it becomes clear to the Congolese that they are nearing Boma.

At certain points where they hope to disembark, it is too marshy to walk. They decide to pull in at the riverbank at the next opportunity where there is beach or some solid bank.

The opportunity comes, and they pull in at a riverbank with a suitable height, at the level of the boat's rim. Otapo holds the bank at the front end to try to steady the boat as Sembene and Mobuka hop out, almost slipping back into the water as they do so.

Sembene and Mobuka then hold the boat at the back end as the other Congolese clamber clumsily on to the riverbank.

Caua and Mande take the opportunity to fill up their gourds with water while they are stationary.

They bid a fond farewell, wishing each well on their onward journey, knowing it will be hard and full of risk.

Mobuka and Otapo have an especially long embrace, after all their years on a plantation together, and then at Palmares. They exchange a wish to meet again, knowing they probably will not.

Sembene, Mobuka and Bufaso help to push the longboat away from the bank. Maira and Otapo manipulate the oars, and they are soon on their way again.

They pass the main port, which is full of boats large and small, some crossing the river, others coming and going. Some are slave ships, and Otapo has a sinking feeling in his stomach.

After this, the first two days are steady with the river in a gentle mood, and the sun beating down.

'We need fish today,' says Maira. 'We have not had fish yet. I will show you all how to catch fish with your hands.'

'With our hands?' asks Caua.

'Indeed. Now, watch me! But keep very, very quiet.'

She reaches over the side and puts her face close to the water, then holds her right hand just above the surface of the water, by her face. All is still except for the ripple of the water with the oars, and bird song.

She strikes. A fish comes flying into the boat and wriggles furiously, expressing its disquiet at proceedings. Otapo hits its head with his oar, to express disquiet at its wriggling.

Another two follow soon after and Otapo obliges again with the coup de grace.

'Well done mum,' says Tucan. 'You've caught our supper for tonight.' Caua and Mande touch her back to thank her.

Storks fly above them in arrowhead formation. Mande asks Otapo why they fly like that.

'I can only think of running behind someone. If you run behind me, then the air will be kinder on you, and you will find it easier to run. With birds, their wings make them wider than us, so I would imagine that the arrowhead formation lightens the air for the two birds behind the bird in front. As storks fly great distances, I would think that the rest they get every now and then as a bird behind a wing allows them to fly that much further.'

'Father, you are so wise.'

'No, I think it is the stork that is wise. I simply seek to understand its wisdom.'

'Good driftwood over there!' calls Maira, 'help me.' They steer the boat towards the driftwood that is kissing the river bank and pull it on board, to place it alongside the other driftwood she has in the boat, drying in the baking sun.

'You know, Otapo, I think we could use the base of this boat for the raft and make it wider with the driftwood,' says Maira. 'We could then separate off the sides of this boat and use them for arrows, a bow and a few spears.'

'I like that idea. Very good. What about a cutting tool and twine?'

'I picked up a flintstone when we last stopped,' says Maira, 'We can splinter this by smashing it on a larger rock, and fashion flint tools from that.'

'Mum, how do you know all this?' asks Mande.

' I was shown how to do this when I was little, as we used flint when we were out on a hunt and needed an extra cutting tool on game that we caught.'

'You are very multi-skilled, dear Maira. You are also lovable. The baobab tree, always our tree of life when I was little, will give us twine.'

'I like twine,' chips in Caua.

'When we next see one, we can stop,' adds Otapo. 'The bark has a consistency that allows it to be torn into strips and plaited to give it the strength of rope.'

'I like plaiting,' says Tucan. 'I will teach Caua and Mande.'

'Maybe,' say Caua and Mande together.

It doesn't take long for a large baobab tree to appear, a little back from the riverbank. They pull into the bank, and Mande and Caua hold on to the riverbank at each end while Otapo climbs out, an oar in hand.

He casts around for anyone who may be in sight, and in particular for anyone who may wish to do him harm.

He runs to the baobab tree, a great beast of a tree, with branches sticking out like flailing arms, and which is beautiful to all comers in offering shelter, nutritious leaves, and tasty fruit. Otapo, showing little respect, smashes one part of its reddish-brown bark, at the height of his forehead, with the oar. After a few hits, he tests the bark and it starts to come away in his hand. He bashes a little lower down. Now he is able to obtain a larger piece of bark by peeling it away from the trunk. He repeats the trick a little further around the mighty trunk, which is at least twice the width of an elephant's thigh. Again, he peels off the bark.

He collects up his spoils and runs back to the boat.

'I think the tree cried with pain,' he says. 'I suspect my bashing felt to the baobab what a torn fingernail feels to me.'

'Otapo, stop that now!' Maira berates him. 'Just thank the tree for the bark and we will get on with making twine and rope.'

'Dad, hop back in and let's get going!' pipes Mande, and he does.

They use the oar to push away from the bank and set off again.

'Time to work on our twine,' says Maira. 'It's different from the twine back home, but I have plaited enough twine in my time and I'm sure I can make this work.'

She takes a bit of bark, pulls a bit down, and sees quickly that the twine comes away easily, even more so than with the bark back home. She pulls off several strips. With twelve pieces of twine, she hands three each to Tucan, Mande and Caua and offers to demonstrate her plaiting method.

'I will tell them. It's just like at home,' says Tucan, as she merrily plaits her three lengths.

Mande seems to pick it up fairly well. 'Just make it a bit tighter,' Tucan says, 'and I think you have it.'

Caua has not yet got the knack, and Tucan helps him take one length, entwine with the second, and bring in the third. He tries it again, very gingerly. 'Almost', she says, encouragingly. 'Just a bit tighter, and have a bit more confidence. You nearly have it.'

Caua tries again and starts to get the swing of it.

After a couple of hours, they have four pieces of rope. Not perfect, but usable. With Otapo happy to keep rowing, they make four more.

Eventually, Otapo says: 'I think I need a break and a drink, and I sense that now would be a good time to make our raft, while we have two or three hours until the sun bids us farewell for the day. There is a patch of flat riverbank coming up, and it looks like there is a bit of space there to work. With luck, we can sleep here, and finish it off in the morning.'

Caua works from one end, grabbing a bit of riverbank, and Tucan the other, as they pull the boat level towards the bank. Tucan is able to grab a root, which fortunately doesn't come loose as he pulls on it.

They tie the boat to the root with a piece of the new rope. 'Heh, my rope works,' says Mande.

'No, sorry, that one's mine, as it has my personal end bit,' says Tucan.

Maira grabs the two fish and goes off to a tree a little further along. She pulls off two big banana leaves and wraps each fish in one, putting them down by her.

'We have a big job now,' says Maira, 'we need to use the base of the boat to make a raft, as the boat will be too heavy to carry when we reach the rapids and waterfalls that we are told lie ahead.'

'There is another job,' adds Otapo, 'which is to make arrows and spears from bits of boat, and you may focus your energy on these if you wish. We will guide you when needed.'

'Won't we need a bow to go with the arrows?' asks Tucan, knowing the answer.

'Sure we will,' says Maira. 'But the bending of a bow is a special art, and is the secret of its success, so we will supervise the bow-making when we get to that bit. But you can certainly help.'

'We need to break up mum's piece of flint for cutting. Mum will guide us all how to make best use of that,' says Mande.

Maira smashes the flint on a granite rock at the back of their piece of land. She picks out pieces of sharp flint to use.

She collects the driftwood from the boat, and uses a piece of flint to break into the top. She pulls on the cut area and a strip of wood peels away like a banana skin, so dry is the wood.

She asks Otapo and the children to watch. She takes a piece of rope, and with intricate, interweaving moves with her nimble fingers, she has a small axe. To show its worth, she takes the same piece of driftwood, brings the axe down on it vertically, and a whole strip comes away.

Tucan picks this up and says, 'Wow mum!'

'I think I can do it,' says Mande. He takes another strip of wood, a flint piece and a rope, and starts winding as he understood it.

At a certain point, Maira intervenes. 'A good start,' she says, 'but you took a wrong turn then. When you are here, you whip it round the back a couple of times to hold the flint in place, and then carry on. But you have picked it up well.'

'What about mine?' asks Tucan, glowing with pride.

'Wow, perhaps you have your mother's blood. Well done.'

I want to make arrows and a spear,' says Caua.

'Ok, well you can have my first axe. Tucan and Mande, you watch too. You use the axe like this for delicate work.' And she shows how to chip away gently on a piece of wood to form the point of an arrow. 'When you do a job like this, you want to be as gentle as when you are removing sleep dust from your eyelash and as firm as when you squeeze on a snail shell when eating boiled snails.'

'I will try that,' says Caua, feeling his eyelash.

'Me too,' butts in Tucan, feeling hers.

Otapo heads down to the boat. 'Great that we now have axes and willing arrow makers. Who will help me lift the boat out to start work on it?'

'I will,' says Mande.

'I will come when I've done this last axe,' responds Maira.

Otapo slips into the water by the boat, slipping in the process on the slimy riverbed. But he senses that the bottom at this point is not too deep.

He leaves the bit of root tied on to the front of the boat, and pushes up from under the front of the boat to the point where it is ready to go on to the bank.

'Are you there Mande?' he asks, with only the boat's bottom and a bit of bank visible to him.

'I am here dad.'

'Can you untie the rope from the root? Use the rope to pull the boat as far as you can on to the bank, while I ease it forward from my end.'

'Ok, but it's a bit much for just me.'

'Maira, are you there now?'

'I'm coming now.'

'Can you help Mande by pulling the front of the boat on to the riverbank while I ease it over the bank's edge from here?'

'Ok, got it. Mande, let's just give it one more pull and then ease it down, and we are just about there.'

Otapo scrabbles back on to the bank, with mud on his tummy and very muddy feet. The boat sits proudly on the bank.

'Shall I turn it over?' he asks.

'No, I think we can separate the sides from here, most likely. Part brawn, part flint axes I suspect. Let's start.' And he uses an axe to start weakening the joints at one end of the starboard side, while Maira attacks it at the other end.

Bit by bit they see the boat's grip on its starboard side ease. They start to attack more vigorously with their axes, always being careful to leave the boat's bottom untouched, and at last the side comes off. They repeat the exercise on the port side with gusto.

With the boat bottom now looking a trifle lonely, they ask Mande, Caua and Tucan to join them on the new raft's core piece.

'Bit tight,' says Tucan.

'I would fall off,' says Caua.

'I think another two feet lengths here,' suggests Maira. She puts the removed port side two feet away, and suggests they imagine the raft with the grass area and the boat's base. The children move a little to fill the extra space.

'That's better,' says Tucan.

'I might avoid falling off with that extra bit,' adds Caua, 'but it's still a bit tight.'

'Ok,' says Otapo, 'let's add a bit more, and relax on our raft. We have probably two more moons of travelling to get to my home, so it needs to be right.'

'Two more moons? Asks Tucan, with eyebrows up, 'but haven't we done about one moon?'

'We will have done a moon, tomorrow night, you are right, but this river is longer than a crocodile's greediness multiplied by a python's anger, multiplied by the beats a hummingbird makes in an hour. I was told to expect to travel for three or four moons.'

'I think this Congo River wants to reach the moon,' quips Mande.

'Reach the moon and back again,' laughs Caua.

'Time for supper,' says Maira. 'Who can fetch me some dry grass, some shavings from our hard work on the arrows, some small dry sticks, and some bigger sticks?' She reaches over to collect up two reasonably sized bits of flint.

Caua brings the shavings, Mande the dry grass, Tucan the small sticks, and Otapo the larger ones. The fire is lit in no time, and she puts on the smaller sticks, and soon after the bigger sticks.

'More bigger sticks please, and soon we can start cooking.'

She fetches some bananas from the banana tree, unpeels each and wraps them in banana leaves. She puts these by the fire. Otapo returns with some good-sized sticks, which burn giddily, and as soon as the flames have given way to a steady red smile she adds the fish, and then the banana.

'How do you like your fish?' she jokes.

'Maira-style' says Tucan.

They laugh, and tuck in to half a grilled fish each, with grilled banana.

* * * * *

In the morning, all are ready to start work again at first light.

'Ok, we will get to work on the raft, mum and I,' quips Otapo. 'Are you three happy to work on the arrows?'

'I want to make a spear,' says Tucan.

'Ok, make a couple of small spears, for catching fish, and I will show you how to spear them,' says Maira.

'Great mum, I would love that!'

With the raft mostly ready, Maira leaves Otapo to finish it off while she makes a bow. She invites the children to watch. She stresses that they don't have the right kind of wood, with the ability to bend right back and despatch the arrow at great speed. But the wood from the side of the boat has some flexibility, so she is using this. She carefully shaves the wood to the right slimness for the bow, and then explains how to bend the wood right back on itself and attach the string at that point, to make the string particularly taut.

When ready, she tests it out by trying to fire an arrow at the banana tree. The arrow maintains a fairly horizontal path, but barely penetrates the banana tree. But Tucan, Mande and Caua cheer her effort, and Caua collects the arrow, while also grabbing some bananas for the next leg of their journey.

Soon after, the raft is complete. Maira decides to test the strength of the twines, and the knots, at each part of the join. She is satisfied.

Otapo takes it on a test run, and they are provisionally happy that it floats.

Maira adds two ropes to the front, for pulling it along past the rapids. They then test it with all five of them, somewhat nervously. Their homemade ropes work on the new extension, and they consider it a success.

Soon, they load up with their spears, bow, and arrows, and axes, plus some bananas, and set sail.

A bit further upstream, Maira delights in displaying her skills in catching fish with a mini spear from a raft.

First, she attaches a rope to one end of the spear.

Then, with her keen eyesight, she identifies a fish, and they float along at the same pace as their prey. Then, Maira gets in position on her knees, to be stable; draws back the spear, throws with considerable force; the fish is caught.

Maira then pulls with her rope and hauls the fish (and most importantly the spear) on to the raft.

The children cheer.

Mande vows to have a go himself.

'Watch out, a rock,' shouts Caua. And Maira and Otapo try to steer with the oars away from this grey structure.

But the grey rock rises up and tips the raft almost on its side, with Otapo falling off, and everybody getting a soaking.

It is a baby hippo, basking. Mande and Tucan admire it in the brief moment they have before it goes under again.

13.

Mande

They take a break. The rapids seem to go on forever, and the raft gets heavy when carried. To drag it with their ropes weakens the bindings on the raft, as the ground is very uneven, so they mostly carry it. Now is the time to rest.

They drink fresh water from the raging river. Otapo has a nap. Caua too. Maira is braiding Tucan's hair.

'When we find your father's family,' says Maira, 'we need to look at organising your puberty ceremony, Tucan. And Mande's ceremony is barely a year away, with all this travelling.'

'I would love that, mum,' replies Tucan.

Mande, who is whittling a stick, sees a baby bonobo nearby, which seems to be separated from its mother. Intrigued, he follows it away from the stream, past some bushes, and into a glade, where the bonobo finds its mother by a baobab tree. It is soon in her embrace.

He is just turning to head back when he feels a mighty crack on his head. He loses consciousness and drops his stick.

The next thing he knows, he is in a cart next to two other teenage boys. His hands and feet are bound, and also bound to each other. He feels powerless to do anything. His heart sinks like the fly, caught up in a web, when it realises that to struggle is only going to make it worse.

* * * * *

Otapo stirs, looks around. 'Time to move on,' he says. 'Has anyone seen Mande?'

'He was right here,' says Maira, 'whittling a stick.'

'He went after a baby bonobo,' says Tucan, 'that way.' And she points to the gap in the bushes.

Otapo and Maira run through, with Tucan and Caua following.

'His stick!' shouts Maira, picking it up as tears start to well up.

Otapo casts around. 'Could it have been a lion, or some other big cat?' he asks, not wanting to believe the worst possibility. He shouts 'Mande!' as loud as he can, and makes the toucan bird call they have learnt from Maira.

Maira also tries to make the family toucan call, but her tears are now in full flow, and she is struggling to stay on her feet.

'If it was a lion, there would be blood, and there would be signs of him being dragged. I can't see that,' ponders Otapo aloud.

'There are footprints that are wide, so aren't ours,' says Caua, looking closely, with Tupi forest-cunning. 'The footprints go through here.' And as he goes through the bushes, and it opens up, there are ruts like wheels make ...

'Caua! Come back here now! Tucan come to mum.'

And Otapo runs, as fast as his sixty-five year old legs allow, then faster, along the ruts in the dirt. He runs beyond tiredness, but when he finally sees the cart and the three men wheeling it, brandishing muskets, it is far in the distance. He collapses in despair, holds his head in his hands, panting hard. Then he realises it is beyond him, and there are two others to protect.

He pulls himself back up on his feet, and trudges back.

'Let's sit together and hug,' he says, in a husky voice.

And as they join him, Otapo lets out a guttural howl from deep inside him that echoes around the nearby hills. Maira starts to ululate, Tucan following suit. Caua just blubbers uncontrollably.

Otapo cannot howl any more, out of emotional exhaustion. He lets out powerful intermittent sobs.

Maira's ululation now subsides, Tucan's too. Their sobs, and Otapo's, and Caua's crying continue through the remaining hours of daylight.

As the sun sets, they check the raft is safe and will not get swept away in the night. They douse themselves with fresh water from the river before settling down.

Violent emotions and slumber, as ever, are unhappy companions.

A dark cloud hovers over them as they embark on their journey the next morning. A large aching hole, invisible to the outsider, accompanies them. It weighs heavily on their tongues and they say very little.

Otapo thinks of his great grandfather, Felani, and what he may say. He nurdles around his mind for words, which trickle out in spite of him:

A chasm claimed me
Thought man could suffer
no greater agony

Imagined escape would elude me
Feared every new morning
Dreamt of sweet death for release
The weight on my soul too great

Through noble men and noble deeds
A dream was kindled, and became a fire
I found love, and we created three more
Loving beautiful and young
A hole in my heart needed healing
Our love brought us here.

The chasm has returned
Far deeper than before
As I knew how to elude
Knew the evil that awaited
And yet failed
I failed Mande
I failed my family
I failed my soul

Which now knows pain
Still deeper
Than even the capture
That ended my innocence
I cry for Mande
I cry for his pain
I cry for a humanity
That could allow its opposite
In such abundance

It takes many more days to pass the rapids, and it is a great relief when at last they can climb on the raft, and simply row along with their oars.

There remains a deep air of mourning through these days.

There is a surprise for them when they follow a fairly tight horseshoe bend in the river and hit more rapids, leading them to quickly shift to a rough and ready path to the side.

What is more surprising is the unfamiliar low growling roar. The reason is soon apparent as they emerge at the end of the horseshoe.

It is like a mountain of water before them.

'Just look at that!' shouts Otapo.

'A thunderclap of water,' adds Maira.

'A wizard's playground,' says Tucan.

The spray from the gushing water is lit by a bright rainbow, the full width of the magnificent falls, and this casts its indigo, violet, yellow, orange and blue, with hints of green and red, on to the glistening backcloth of white and silvery rocks, bursting with baby bubbles as gushes of water trampoline in triple saltos.

They try to freeze this magical image in their memory, then turn back to the track, and gawp open-mouthed at the wondrous sight for as long as it is in view.

They carry the raft between them, climbing up by jagged awkward rocks that tumble by the side of the waterfall as though thrown there by a giant.

At the top, the path flattens out. They take a breather. For quite a while.

'The river is heading too fast over the waterfall at this point,' says Maira, who is used to waterfalls from her childhood in Brazil. 'We can enter the river further up when the river becomes more placid.'

They top up with water and set off again, re-floating the raft about ten minutes further on. For a couple of days all is calm again, although there are plenty of crocodile eyes peeking slyly out of the water to keep them edgy. They know that one day they will come upon a very hungry crocodile, and that they will then need to react very quickly with their weapons.

They come to a point where the river appears to disappear into jungle, and all they can see is little rivulets, barely wide enough for the raft.

Little bitterns fly between the reeds, booming in an unearthly way. There are also Egyptian ducks, with a line of ducklings obediently following.

It seems impossible to know what rivulet to take. They keep rowing. Up above, the sun beats down at around nine o'clock to them, in their current position.

Otapo resolves to keep rowing in a direction where the sun is where his instinct takes him. He relates his thoughts to Tucan, Caua and Maira, and they agree.

The foliage all around, dragging tentacles through the water, is dense. But they make slow, steady progress.

Maira realises the water in the jungle here is teeming with fish. She holds her face close to the water, as usual when in fish-catching mood, and scoops first one fish on to the raft and then another. They wriggle angrily until Caua kills each with an arrow, and puts them by his feet, now still.

Maira grabs some foot-sized leaves from an overhanging tree, and passes them to Caua as wrapping.

'We will eat well again this evening,' says Otapo.

After what seems an age they emerge out of the jungle, and the rivulets open out to proper river.

Until the next waterfall.

This time the waterfall is a bit less of a surprise, and this one is not quite as magnificent. There is also no rainbow here, as the sun is not so high as last time.

Otapo almost thinks that it would be worth skirting completely round, away from the river, where it may be less rocky and less steep, but he is wary of slave hunters.

'I think we will look for a place to sleep when we reach the top,' he suggests. 'These climbs are so tiring.'

'I agree,' says Maira.

There is a flock of flamingos in the river just beyond the top of the waterfall, catching fish as they turn to avoid cascading down.

A little further along, crocodiles again float past at regular intervals, their ever-watchful eyes looking greedily at them. Plovers sit atop of many of them, plucking fleas off their snouts, and flies.

Well past the crocodiles, they find a spot to stay the night, and settle down.

After two months of this marathon journey, the river is thinner than ever before, now just four or five widths of the raft.

There is one more waterfall, and a climb as before, and then the river is more serene for a few days until they start climbing up the foothills of a range of mountains that is apparent some way up in the distance.

They struggle with the raft for a little while in the tumbling water, but Otapo then looks at Maira and says: 'Let's take the raft to the side, and have a chat.'

'I think it's too hard rowing here,' says Tucan.

'I tend to agree' adds Caua.

'Come and chat,' says Otapo. 'The question is whether we now abandon the raft. There is a good bit of climbing now, if you look at the hills before us.'

'So a lot of carrying,' says Maira.

'We will only need the raft when we reach the big lake, which could be days away, for all I know.'

'I think we keep the ropes, and tools and the weapons,' suggests Maira. 'We can find new wood if we need it.'

'It is a good idea, between us we can carry the weapons and hammers, as well as our gourds. I agree with mum,' suggests Otapo.

'Let us do it,' says Caua, and Tucan nods.

They set to work disentangling the ropes from the lengths of wood.

Eventually, they set off again. It is difficult, with long hours of climbing, but they stop earlier in the day to eat and sleep, to allow for the extra exertion.

At last they reach a big lake. It is more than three moons since they had set off.

'I know this lake,' says Otapo, with a beaming smile. 'We came here once when we were hunting okapi. I was not yet a man then.'

'Are we making a raft?' asks Tucan.

'I think we are,' replies Otapo. 'Are you up for it?'

They each nod.

The next day, they set off on their new raft across the lake. It takes more than a day.

Otapo struggles to find a place to land on the other side, but he sees some farmers, and steers the raft their way.

He hears his people's language for the first time since he was captured as a slave. They all embrace.

He introduces Maira, Tucan and Caua, using his language first, for the farmers, then Swahili, for his family.

'Khoi?' asks one, pointing at Maira.

'No, from Brazil' says Maira. And they look at her nonplussed.

'Across a great ocean, that way,' says Otapo in their language, pointing west.

They look impressed.

'You have travelled a lifetime,' says one, Felamani. 'We will take you to your village.'

'You are very kind.'

'It is three days,' says Felamani. 'We have another lake to cross before we reach the area you are from. We have boats. But we should eat soon before it is dark.'

'I like that idea,' says Caua.

'Me too,' says Tucan.

14.

The Reunion

Felamani's son had run ahead to the village, so that when Otapo, Maira, Caua and Tucan are about ten minutes away, a host of family members, dressed in bright local colours, are on the path heading towards them, with a drummer drumming and trumpets blaring.

Otapo collapses on his knees and breaks down in tears, overcome with a torrent of emotion.

Caua, Maira and Tucan sit down by him to console him.

His sister Atwooki sees Otapo and runs towards him, falling on to him as she reaches him and shouting, 'Otapo, Otapo, Otapo, we thought we had lost you forever.'

Otapo is barely able to speak but manages to hold her face in his hands, and say: 'Wooki, dear Wooki! Here, these are my wife and my children, Caua and Tucan. Our son Mande was taken by slave hunters on our way here.'

Atwooki greets them all.

Atwooki says, 'Mum is not at all well. You will see her in her hut. She is well into her eighties now.'

Otapo looks at her with sad eyes, and says, 'I understand. I was unable to leave the slave plantation.'

'Mai and Felani died many years ago, along with Aneni and Wotambo. I will show you their graves. We must talk soon about your terrible loss.'

'Of course,' says Otapo.

Your grandad Matimba died many years ago also, and your father just four years ago.'

'I felt dad's death, I felt it quite strongly. I didn't feel mum's death, so I held out hope.'

'These are my children, Felani junior and Aneni, named in honour of lovely ancestors.'

'Great to meet you. I fear you have lived much of your lives – puberty, marriage, children – while I was a slave in a faraway land.'

'Mum always told us about what a great brother you were, and she always believed that you would return one day.'

And they embrace.

'I did always believe,' says Atwooki.

'I know. I always felt your spirit. But forgive me. I must come in the hut and see mother. It has been a lifetime.'

He enters the compound to find his mother Miri in her hut. She is squatting on a mat on the floor. Her deeply wrinkled face lights up as she embraces Otapo, and welcomes Maira, Caua and Tucan.

Miri and Otapo hold each other until Miri's arms fall away. Miri smells of essence of rose; Otapo of days of sweat, and grime. She does not mind.

Atwooki now squats by the side of her mother, and Maira, Tucan and Caua sit just behind Otapo.

'No words,' says his mother. 'I feel your love, I feel your pain. I have felt your pain since you were taken all these many years ago.'

'I know, mother.'

'Let me also hold your son and daughter. And also your wife.' And she hugs each in turn, but her arms soon tire.

'I feel in your wife what I feel in you darling son.'

'Mother? You know?

'You have both felt more great pain on your journey, but not a death in the family, something worse.'

'My son Mande was abducted by slave hunters, just like I was abducted. It was the most painful thing imaginable.'

'Let us think of Mande,' whispers Miri

Maira confirms, 'Yes, let us think of Mande.'

Tucan and Caua hold their mother more tightly.

Otapo pulls away from his mother and stands up.

'Tomorrow,' he says, 'we can have all the embraces we have missed these long years, but now we must celebrate a joyous occasion, our reunion.'

'Of course, my son,' says Miri.

'But I want you to dance too,' says Otapo, laughing.

'I am long past that,' she replies. 'But I will stand while you dance.'

'Let's have music, drink, food,' he says, ebulliently.

'Give us time to get some food on,' says Atwooki. 'You all need a wash, and probably a change of clothes. A pig would turn up its nose at your smell right now, dear brother, after your long journey. Let me show you all where you can clean up.'

The other family members thank the farmers who brought them here, and offer them refreshments in the compound, which they accept.

A little later, there is a huge party in the compound, overspilling into the neighbouring compound. All the village is invited, and two neighbouring villages.

This goes on all night, and all the next day and into the following night, and three cattle are sacrificed for the special occasion.

15.

Like Father Like Son Under Unrelenting Sun

Mande is still angry about his abduction when he arrives at Pernambuco in Brazil.

He hears with dread the language that has signified the enemy all his brief life, Portuguese.

But the leg irons are much as his father spoke about with deep hatred.

When he reaches the plantation, there are also the same excessively long hours of work in the sugar cane fields as his father experienced for so long. Even the hut seems little different from what his father described, with twenty men cramped together, a nauseating smell, and a latrine pit in the ground at the back.

What did his father say? He survived because of the close friendships of fellow slaves, the tactics they used to survive, and the certainty that he would eventually escape.

'How are you all doing?' he asks his hut mates in Swahili, in the brief break for cattle and horse feeding, and their own food around midday. Most look at him nonplussed, but one says, in broken Swahili, 'We are Congolese here. I am only one with bit of Swahili. I am Sando.'

He recalls the bits of Kicongo he learned from his Congolese shipmates. 'I am Mande,' he says. 'I will try learn Kicongo.'

They all give their names and embrace him. They then get on with their tasks.

Before they head back to the fields, Mande says to Sando, 'You teach me Kicongo?'

Sando nods. 'We talk later.'

* * * * *

Mande finds Sando when they finish work for the evening, after their fifteen hours of work. 'How long have you been here?'

'About four years now.'

'Has there been any talk of escape while you have been here?'

'Only guys saying that they hate it and would love to get away. No plans.'

'Have you heard of a mocambo?'

'No what is that?'

'It is a home for free slaves, where we live and farm as we wish. I was born in a big one called Palmares.'

'How did you end up here if you were a free slave?'

'My mum and dad took us back to Africa to see my grandparents. I was caught near the Congo River, in Kongo.'

'Terrible. I was caught in Kongo too.'

'I will try and find out about a mocambo we can escape to,' says Mande.

'It would be great if you could. But be careful. There are Africans here who may not speak truth to you.'

'Not truthful? How?'

'You may think they on your side, but they may talk to the plantation owner. Be careful.'

'Thanks, I will,' says Mande.

The Dutch arrive on the north coast of Brazil, 1630-31

'Others come here now, same pink faces, different garments,' says Boacir, son of Moacir. 'They set firestick against firestick, all for the sweet canes they have brought to this paradise.'

'One wonders what magical quality lies within the sweet canes that they are willing to die for the right to the canefields.'

'Who knows the ways of the pink faces? They have destroyed so much of what was most precious to us, our jungle home, and the creatures that shared it with us, to grow this cane?'

'And they dragged our people to work their fields for no benefit to us, making us use their iron knives shaped like the young moon.'

'I fear the heart has long since fled from the pink faces, and they only see gain and gold in these fields. Why otherwise such bloodshed?'

'The simple life knows less strife,' says Boacir. 'Living the jungle life, allowing life's circle to complete.'

'It is true. But the new pink faces have sent an emissary to us, who seems to have troubled to learn our language. He says they will spare us from fires in our jungle, and no longer force us to cut the sweet cane.'

'How do they call themselves, the new pink faces?'

'They say Datch, or Dutch, or Dotch, I am not sure. They speak in an odd way, more guttural than the Ozh Dozh people.'

'I will never get used to these languages.'

'No, nor me. I think I don't trust these pink faces when they promise they are better than the other pink faces. Why have they come here with their firesticks if it is not to gain something for themselves?'

'I agree, but when you first go in a river, and the caiman does not attack you the first time, because he is sizing you up, looking if you have enough fat on you to justify all the effort, you do appreciate the brief respite, even if you know not to trust the caiman next time.'

'So, we give these newcomers a try?'

'I think it is more that we do not panic, and we prepare. We cannot simply take them at their word, but if we have to choose between types of Pink Face, we can test their offer. If our young ones can perhaps reach manhood without being taken at the point of a gun to their fields that would be a plus.'

'I fear it may not end well.'

'We are up against forces that our people have not encountered before. Our way of life is threatened like never before. We have to think on our feet a little and face each new obstacle as it arises.'

'Well, either way, we will need to talk to these Dutch or Dotch or Datch and see what they are made of.'

1635

'Are you Mande, Otapo and Maira's son?'

Mande turns to see Haram, now quite a bit older and greyer.

'Haram! Great to see you!'

'Be quiet, Mande. We cannot talk here. There is a tall pau brasil tree about fifty paces from the hut, down the hill. We can meet there shortly before midnight.'

'Ok, is there anyone else who wants to leave?'

'Sando?'

'Wait until we have met before you speak to him.'

* * * * *

As his hut mates head into the hut for sleep, Mande slopes off to the pau brasil. He is not aware of the eyes on him in the subdued moonlight.

'Good to see you again, Mande,' says Haram, as he reaches the tree, 'but sad to see you on a plantation. What news on Otapo and Maira and your sister and brother?'

'When I was taken on the Congo River, we were heading for my father's home village. I think my father said we were then about two moons away. I was the only one taken.'

'God willing, they will have got home. Both your parents are wise people, and very capable of overcoming most difficulties. Did you get separated from them?'

'I stupidly followed a Bonobo baby.'

'I want to help you leave. It will not be easy. Mwesu has become a good worker for me. He will come here in four nights. I am leaving tonight. Meet Mwesu here on the fourth night. He will inform you of the plan. He will also talk to Sando. Please say nothing to him in the meantime.'

'I will keep quiet. It is good to see you again. I will come here in four nights to meet Mwesu.'

'Very good. Hope to see you in Palmares. Good night.'

And they part.

* * * * *

'Mwesu! Good to see you,' whispers Mande, by the pau brasil tree around midnight.

'Very good to see you, Mande! A young man now.'

'What is the plan? Is there a mocambo I can reach?'

'The quilombo is about two days hard walking, in the direction of the dawn sun. Your knowledge of Tupi language will help you, as there is a bit of a battle between Tupi and Portuguese in the jungle, on the way there. It would be difficult for you without speaking Tupi.'

'Ok, and do you have an idea when?'

'Listen, we must finish now. It is dangerous here. You will need to wait for a signal ...'

'Stop there!' comes an officious voice, in Dutch.

A plantation foreman, Ugglay, and three of his team, have muskets. They also hold chains. Mwesu and Mande cast around for an escape route but feel powerless. There is nowhere to run and it is too dark to risk the forest below them.

They are chained up and manhandled for several hundred yards to a makeshift jail, with bare stone walls, a mat floor, and rats, to the side of the plantation owner's house.

* * * * *

The next morning, they are brought out in chains. All the slaves are there to see.

A morning off cane-cutting for a vital lesson, from the owner's point of view.

The viewers' heads are bowed, except Sando, who looks awkwardly at Mande.

The foreman says in Dutch: 'Let this be a lesson to you all.' His number two repeats this in Kikongo.

The plantation's foreman, Ugglay, is a brute of a man, half Tupi, half African, with broad shoulders and bulging muscles.

Mwesu is brought forward. He can only shuffle awkwardly. His hands and legs are shackled. His afro hair has been shaved off. His face reveals sheer terror. The sturdy block of wood for his head is in front of him.

'Kneel! Put your head on the block!'

Mwesu obliges, his body visibly shaking.

Mande looks on with horror, as pale as a Black man can look, wondering if the same fate awaits him.

Ugglay lifts his broad sword and brings it down with great force on Mwesu's neck. His head falls to the ground, blood spurting out from his neck. Ugglay's helpers pull his body away and put this in a sack. Ugglay picks up his head, places it in a bag, and then holds the bag up to the crowd.

'Let that be a lesson to all of you,' he bellows.

He turns to Mande.

'You, Mande, cost the plantation money. You will not be beheaded. You are here to cut cane, to repay the plantation its investment. But you will never escape again. Step forward to the block.'

Mande shuffles forward in his chains.

'Daewu! Take the chains off the prisoner's legs.'

He does so, clumsily.

'Mande, put your left foot on the block!' shouts Ugglay.

Very gingerly, with his teeth biting his tongue, his heart beating at a hundred miles an hour, and his soul silently screaming, Mande lifts his foot on to the block.

'Stay still!'

And he brings the sword down.

Mande lets out a gut-wrenching scream.

'The front half of the foot is not quite off, Sir,' says Daewu.

Mande totters, in a faint.

'Hold him! Hold the bastard!' screams Ugglay, angry that his first blow was misdirected, but blaming it on Mande. 'And shut the fuck up, you!' he shouts at the screaming Mande, whose face is ashen and awash with tears.

As Daewu holds the miserable Mande up, Ugglay brings the sword down again, and the front half of Mande's foot falls off the block.

Mande faints, and Daewu lets him fall to the ground. 'Get a tourniquet on the blackguard's thigh this minute. Our life won't be worth living if the bastard dies.'

He barks at an underling: 'Keita, pour some of your alcohol on his stump quick, and wrap it all up with the bandage. Sharpish. Somehow, we executioners have to keep these slaves alive when bleeding to death. Not worth the effort in my book, but who am I to know?'

They keep Mande until the time comes to remove his tourniquet, and then carry him to his hut, where they drop him on the floor and leave him.

Potira and the new Dutch rulers

'This land is ours,' says Van Hydeck. 'The women and children come with us.'

'I don't understand,' says Potira, in Portuguese. The other women say: 'We don't understand either.'

A Dutch soldier says in Portuguese, 'Women with us, not with Portuguese.'

'I am not going with you!' screams Potira.

Two other women embrace Potira and shout, 'Nor us!'

Three soldiers grab Potira and the other two protesting women and drag them away with those women who are not seeking to resist. All the women are Tupis.

The Dutch have arrested the Portuguese soldiers based at the town, including Potira's husband. Van Hydeck orders that the Portuguese soldiers, all bound by hand and foot, be stood against the wall at the back of the main house. He then orders six Dutch soldiers to shoot them dead.

Once this instruction is carried out, the soldiers bury the men in shallow graves a little way from the house.

They then take the women and children inside the house and squeeze them into one bedroom, where they are locked in together.

The following day, Potira tries to escape to her village with her children, but she is caught. She is whipped and locked in a room with her children for three days, with only bread and water.

Mande back at work

After two days with a fever in his hut, and still running a temperature and in great pain, Mande is made to head back to the field to cut cane.

'I can barely walk,' he says to his hut mate, Farka, as he hobbles along. 'The pain of every step sears up my spine.'

'I will work harder, and cover for you,' says Farka, drawing Mande nearer to him.

'But we have to do 350 bundles a day.'

'Yes, a dozen canes a bundle.

'It's too much. How can you do more?'

'Here, don't worry. Lean on my shoulder.'

'Thank you.' They move forward again.

I am furious with Sando that he reported you.'

'You are very kind. It is my mistake with Sando. I thought as a slave he would want to escape. Naïve of me. He will get privileges now.'

'He will, but none of us will ever trust him, and mostly that means not talking to him, as who knows what he will report? He will have a very lonely existence here.'

'Owww, will you just stop a second, friend? I need a breather. I am close to fainting with the agony.'

'Sure, it's not much further now. Just to give the appearance of you being here, even if you cannot work. I will then get cracking on the cane. Mtatu will help you too, cutting extra cane. You are not alone you know.'

Mande tries to thank Farka but faints from sheer pain. Farka lets him lie for a minute, but places a rock under his head and rests it on one side, to avoid him choking on sick or saliva.

* * * * *

Eight days later, thanks to Farka, Mande has a makeshift crutch, and a piece of wood attached to the stump at the bottom of his left leg to enable him to walk, or at least hobble more evenly.

'Is it a bit easier now?' asks Farka, who has just re-attached the piece of wood with strong twine.

'It's better than the total agony I experienced before, yea. I can get around thanks. It will never be like having two feet, though.'

'You are a brave man, though, Mande. You've battled on with it and you are now a cane-cutter again, just a bit on the slow side. Well, very slow side. This has probably saved your life.'

'You and Mtatu have been great,' says Mande. 'You have kept that Ugglay bastard off my back.'

16.

The Rise of the Dutch Empire

'Out everyone, we are under attack!' It's the son of Ganga Zumba, Zumbazari, drum in hand, frizzy black hair, thin bony body, going around each hut in the town of Macaco.

'My uncle is on his way from Surupira township' shouts Zumbazari. 'He is bringing more warriors.'

The freemen run out by their hundreds, guns and spears in hand and head for the front gate. Zumbazari too.

The front gate remains locked. The double palisade all round is secure.

Shots ring out, and the huge logs at the front gate rattle. Then there is an explosion and a hole appears in the front gate. As a couple of soldiers come through, two freemen throw spears at them, killing them instantly.

They rush to remove the spears from the dead while other freemen bring logs to patch up the damaged gate. They notice one more soldier trying to force his way through the remaining gap, but they cut his throat with a knife.

A freeman high up a pau brasil inside Palmares shouts: 'More explosives coming.'

Ganga Zumba originally built steps from half logs, and two of these steps are placed by the log stockade. Two climb up with muskets, two with bows and arrows.

The archers raise their heads and fire quickly at the soldier who is handling the explosives, ducking quickly as a volley comes from a pair of muskets.

The musket-armed freemen now fire their muskets at the explosives man, who is injured but still apparently alive. They then try to duck, but one is hit before he can get down and he falls to the ground. Zumbazari runs to him and drags him away from the wall.

The Dutch soldiers have bound logs together to charge the front gate as a battering ram. Archers climb the steps in turn to fire at the soldiers holding the battering ram, but one archer is hit. The musket men then rise in turn, and some of the enemy fall, before two of the musket men are hit by a further volley of shots.

The charge by the Dutch battering ram weakens the front gate, but they draw back with the twin attack by arrow and musket.

The Dutch withdraw. After two hours, a Palmares scout reports that the Dutch soldiers are far away and heading back to a town.

There are celebrations in Palmares that night.

But the next day, they bury three men that died in the attack.

The Dutch first arrive in South Africa, 1647

'Sounds like we have a sea lion,' says Doman. 'Let's go on down.'

And he leads the village down to where his son Itoi has been calling out.

As the son beckons them to follow him they see the sea lion on the beach, pools of blood nearby and a spear right through its neck.

'Well done Itoi,' says Doman. 'Let's cut this poor creature up into manageable pieces to carry him back to the village.'

They attack its flippers, its neck and its head with knives, and gradually work their way through.

Four men carry the body back, and others take the smaller bits. One has been collecting blood in gourds to the best of her ability, and she brings two blood-filled gourds up to the village as a special treat for the sea lion killers.

A little later, the fire is hot and the sea lion is being cooked for a big feast. It is near dusk.

'There is a ship coming close,' shouts Itoi, from a mound just above where the others are cooking.

'That is not like the Portuguese ships,' says Doman, as he joins him. 'They have different sails and a different flag.'

'It is being eaten by a whale, I think.'

'Perhaps not a whale,' says Doman, 'perhaps the ship is injured. It is falling to its side unnaturally.'

'Some men are climbing into a small boat. And a second boat, with more climbing in.'

'And a third one. More and more are getting out, perhaps the ship is no longer working.'

'I think we should stay away. We don't want them to take some of our sea lion, it is not as if we have such fine food very often.'

'I agree. They seem to have firesticks like the blotched skin ones have. We don't want to risk making them angry or even scared.'

'Ok,' says Doman, 'let's keep out of the way. I will keep one of us in position on top of the hill, to warn us if they start coming our way. We will enjoy our feast of sea lion and only then prepare to move a little way away and see what we are up against.'

The Dutchmen cast their eyes around as they stand on the beach next to their longboats, all now pulled clear of the water.

'There is plenty of wet sand here,' says Jan, chief mate. 'There is driftwood. We have to allow for locals, as the Portuguese have lost at least one admiral on this coast. We could be here for a while before we are rescued. I think we need a fort for protection.'

'I agree with Jan,' says the captain, Dirk. 'Let us gather up some of those pebbles that lie further up from the sand. We can mix wet sand and pebbles to make walls and shore up with driftwood. For a roof over us we can fetch a sail from the ship and find some longer pieces of driftwood along the coast here as beams for support. It will be a simple construction, but it will do for a few months if we have to wait that long to be rescued.'

'We have our muskets for protection,' says another, Piet. 'We will need to keep them bone dry, of course, if they are going to work when needed.'

'Yes, we will bring some chests from the ship to make sure that any inclement weather is kept off the muskets,' says the captain. 'We will certainly need them if the locals come calling. Make sure you bring some bedding and some wicker lamps too.'

'Ok,' says Jan, addressing crew members. 'Three of you row back for some chests and the rest. Four chests should do. The rest of us can start on this fort. We can start first off collecting pebbles, as the captain says.'

* * * * *

One year later, Doman and his son Itoi watch from the hill above as four ships arrive. They are similar to the one that capsized in the harbour.

Five longboats head to the shore with only two men in each boat.

The men on the beach stand together and cheer as the longboats come near.

They abandon their fort, and collect up their chests full of muskets, their bedding, some wicker lamps and various other items collected from their ship. As the longboats reach the beach, they are pulled just far enough to clear the water. The shipwrecked crew climb into the longboats and head for the ships.

On one of the ships is one Captain Jan Van Riebeeck.

As they look on from high above, Doman says to Itoi: 'We can go back to grazing the cattle by the beach like we do, when the sun sails its boat across the sky a little shallower than before.'

'And when the colour has finally gone from our handsome bushes with red and bluegreen cone-shaped heads and lilac tubular flowers,' replies Itoi.

* * * * *

Four years later, Doman and his son Itoi are on the hill above the bay, tending cattle, when they see more ships, very similar to the ones that briefly visited to collect the shipwrecked sailors. They count five of them.

'It is the come-and-go-ones,' says Itoi. 'They could not make up their mind last time. They stayed on the beach for twelve moons, and then went. I wonder what they will do now.'

'They came before for one reason, I think, to collect the people whose ship had died. If they have now returned, does this mean they like our bay, and want to stay? I suspect that this is why they are here. We may have to announce ourselves soon, if this is the case.

'You know, the old man who has been in the hut all his life has a right to that hut. The crow that flies down to look, because he likes the roof, has no right to it. We must be wary of these crows trying to take our hut.'

'I agree father. But I fear that they may have more to them than the crow has to him.'

'If so, it is for us to show that we are superior.'

* * * * *

The Dutch are captained by Jan Van Riebeeck. He arrives with a copy of the contract he had signed before departure with the Dutch East India Company to establish a refreshment station by the Cape of Good Hope, to supply ships en route to India.

He says to his number two: 'This is key to challenging the Portuguese position in India. We will obtain for Holland a share of all that wealth the Portuguese have had to themselves. But for me it is also a very pleasant land. I liked it last time I came.

'We will call this bay Tafelbaii, and the river here Salt River.'

* * * * *

They build a wooden fort with four wooden bastions on the left bank of the river.

With them are ninety Dutch people who have in mind to live there, but at this juncture, they know nothing about the land.

When they see cattle on a nearby hill, they think that their God is on their side. They use sticks to encourage the cattle to come to their beach. The cattle lumber slowly along, unsure but not resisting.

It is possible that these Calvinist settlers misread their God.

* * * * *

'I think that these new blotched face people are a bit unclear about who owns the hut,' says Doman to his son.

'You mean the missing cattle?' asks Itoi.

'I do. They have simply taken our cattle as though the beasts are wild animals on the savannah. As you know, and I know, cattle are our family. They represent our wealth. The cattle cannot be taken like that.'

'Shall we go at first light?'

'I think we will go in the dark. We will take their favourite grass and feed them as we walk back. They should be nice and quiet. I don't want any firesticks up my backside if I can help it.'

They go into the hut and beckon two more of the family to join them, two of Doman's brothers, and they head to the grass by the beach where the stolen cattle are grazing.

Not a word is spoken as they walk down to where the cattle are resting. The cattle do not utter a sound. A few are lying down, but they soon rise when they smell the grass held close by their noses, and soon each is chomping happily on the grass as they accompany Doman and his family back to their village, or kraal.

Doman leaves the cattle on the edge of their village. He asks Itoi to go to the top of the hill overlooking the beach at first light, and to warn him if there is any sign of the newcomers coming to fight for the cattle.

* * * * *

Inside the fort, Van Riebeeck listens to Kies Van Steen, who says that he represents the settlers.

'They have stolen our cattle. I want to go after them, whoever they are. They cannot be far away.'

'We have to be a bit careful, Kies. Yes, we want to assert our right to be here. But on the other hand, we don't know how many people we may be up against. Nor do we know their military capacity.'

'So what do you suggest, Jan? How do we get the information we need?'

'I will send out two men with muskets as scouts. They will try to get a sense of where the cattle have been taken, and how many people are on their farm. They will also try to find out if they have weapons.'

'That is good. And then we will get the cattle back?'

'Well, that will depend on what my scouts say. You are only ninety people. I cannot take actions that put you at risk of shrinking to many less than ninety.'

'I see. I will wait to hear from you.'

'You will not have to wait too long.'

* * * * *

When the scouts report back, they report that the cattle can be found about a twenty-five to thirty minute walk away, over the hill above the fort and a little way further. They say that there is a small village, with perhaps twenty to twenty-five men, and a similar number of women. One or two spears could be seen at the front of one hut, which suggests that they use spears. They suspect that they may use a bow and arrow too. There was no sign of any muskets or similar.

* * * * *

'There were two men on the hill, blotchy faced men,' says Itoi.

'They will be looking at where we are, and where the cattle are,' says Doman. 'We will retreat one more hill and one more valley, and then try to hit them when they come.'

They retreat. Doman places sentries on each hill. They report when the Dutch start coming, and the Khoikhoi retreat one more hill.

This works with the first Dutch raid. But eventually, in a night-time raid, the Dutch are able to take some of the cattle, and the Khoikhoi only realise when they wake.

* * * * *

There follows an unplanned random game of cat and mouse.

The Dutch take the cattle, the Khoikhoi take them back. Resentment builds.

As more Dutch arrive, and they take more of the Khoikhoi land, and more of the cattle, the tensions rise.

The Khoikhoi become more resentful about the taking of their land and of their cattle. They are also still upset about losing their seasonal grazing land on the beach, which the Dutch took without asking for permission.

Doman decides to ask to stay with the settlers, in their fort by the Salt River. He wants to understand their thinking better, so he can plan his tactics.

Van Riebeeck agrees that Doman can stay at the fort, on the understanding that Doman will learn a few words of Dutch, and he, Van Riebeeck, can learn some Khoisan which would ease communication.

Doman wears a skirt for his visit, out of respect for these people's evident dislike of nakedness.

Doman notices that most of the Dutch are not armed, and that only a handful are.

He is also struck by the strange way that these oddly coloured people even wear cloths inside their house. Worse than that, the stink of stale sweat inside all the buildings, and the stench of sewage outside the building, make his visit highly unpleasant, even nauseous.

One day during his five day visit, it rains incessantly. Doman notices one of the armed Dutchmen trying to show two of the settlers out in the courtyard how to use a musket, but it won't function in the rain. There is just a pathetic splutter from the musket. They give up the lesson.

After the visit, the Dutch stop taking cattle for a while, and Doman decides to leave the Dutch with the cattle they have.

However, when two more ships arrive, the tensions return, and this time it leads to a war between the Dutch and the Khoikhoi.

Portugal's net closes in on the Dutch in Brazil, 1653-54

The Dutch control provinces in the north east of Brazil, and numerous sugar cane plantations in those provinces, for several years.

But they do not commit a sizeable fleet to protect their imperial ambitions.

When Portugal sends a substantial fleet to regain the provinces they have lost to Holland, they begin to regain the upper hand.

Holland have won over a number of Tupi tribes to assist them against the Portuguese.

For their part, the Portuguese have many mixed race (Portuguese-Tupi) soldiers and are allied with some of the Tupi tribes. Hundreds of Tupi tribes remain independent.

The Dutch begin to lose ground militarily. As they do so, the Portuguese plantation owners seek to regain control of the cane fields.

With so much profit in the fields, there are many pitched battles.

One such battle occurs at the plantation where Mande is a slave, with the murder of the plantation owner and his family creating an opening where for a brief time nobody is fully in charge.

Mande escapes to a Quilongo

'Nobody in charge! Foreman gone!' shouts Farka.

'Are our African friends leaving?' asks Mande.

Sando runs over to them. He is panting.

'I've been up to the house. Ugglay is dead – his fellow thugs too. The owner has gone. We are all trying to leave before anyone comes.'

'No thanks, Sando,' says Mande.

Sando heads to the next hut.

'Lots are heading towards the house,' says Farka

'There are two ways to escape if we go that way, and both of them are bad,' says Mande. 'Let Sando go there. You will have no reason to be sorry if you come with me.'

Sando comes back and shakes Mande's hand. 'I was very bad, but you forgave me. You are a good man.'

'We all had our ways to survive in the kingdom of evil.'

'You could kill me, but instead you shake my hand. I must learn from you.'

'Go now before I change my mind. Farewell.'

Sando leaves.

'What do you have in mind?' asks Farka.

'If we follow the route I have been given, I can find a mocambo.'

'A mocambo?'

'Yes, where Africans can be free, and mixed race like me too.'

'A place that we run ourselves? How do the people live?'

'We farm and make things with carpentry and by working iron, like back in Africa.'

'Very good, I am with you.'

'Try to find a few others who want to come with us. But tell them, the route out by our hut is full of danger. At the same time, any other route on trodden paths could well see them falling into the hands of the Pink Faces.'

'Fine, we will meet soon by the hut.'

'Good. Don't be late.'

* * * * *

They meet shortly at the hut. Mande has burnished in his mind the direction of the sun at dawn. He has his crutch, and a gourd. 'Grab your gourds, machetes, let us go.'

A dozen go with Mande, past the pau brasil tree where he was caught, and down the hill, heading deep into the forest. They soon meet their first Tupi, who Mande embraces like a long-lost brother, and the Tupi takes them to get some food.

'Is this your village?' asks Mande.

'No, it's a Portuguese ship,' replies Tecaua, who is medium height, with a bald pate but hair round the rim, like many Tupi, and a thong, with green and yellow parrot feathers protruding from it at his rear. He has white geometric patterns on his otherwise red chest. He smells of fresh sweat.

'What?' asks Mande.

'Of course it's my village, Mande, what does it look like? These are my folk. Hey, Lazybones, say hello to former slave, one-footed brother Mande, son of Maira, who was with the Tupirama but was enslaved.'

Lazybones says: 'Hi Mande,' in Tupi language.

Tecaua puts together beans and herbs, with roasted wing of parrot and mangos, wrapped in banana leaves.

'Best food I've had since before I was caught and sold as a slave,' says Farka.

'Hey,' shouts Lazybones, 'are you using up all my roasted parrot? I wanted that.'

'These men are freshly escaped from slavery,' says Tecaua. 'They need food for a long journey, whereas you can fire an arrow any time for a bird.'

'You owe me.'

'If you say so.'

'Shall I give him some of my food?' asks Mande, who is halfway through his, and licking his lips.

'No, not at all. He's just winding me up. Now, you need to think about your journey from here. I am going to take you up a small mountain near here, which takes you away from the Pink Faces. From the mountain I can direct you where you need to go.'

Farka is trying unsuccessfully to break off the top of a coconut.

'Hey, let me help you,' says Tecaua, whipping out a knife and slicing through the top of the coconut. 'Here.'

He also prepares three other coconuts, and hands them around for a refreshing drink.

'We should get going,' says Tecaua. 'We have three or four hours of daylight.'

'See you,' says Lazybones, in a disinterested way.

'Does your village smell a bit of sewage?' asks Mande, as they leave.

'It's Lazybones not cleaning out the latrines, as usual,' replies Tecaua. 'I will sort it when I return, otherwise it will stink.'

'What's with Lazybones? He is not a typical Tupi,' says Mande.

'Lovesick.'

'Because?'

'Because he smells.'

'Say no more.'

They soon start heading up the mountain.

* * * * *

'Here,' says Tecaua, as they reach a promontory about half-way up a mountain. He points roughly north west. 'If you go in that direction for about a day, you will first cross a river, cross more jungle, and then reach the hill that you can see in the distance. The hill has a bobble on the top that is quite unmistakable.'

Mande calls Farka over, and points in the direction that Tecaua had shown him. 'Can you see the hill in that direction with the bobble on top?'

'Yes, that seems fairly clear.'

'We are heading across a river, then through jungle to reach it. Tell everyone to stay very close to me. The river may have poisonous snakes that bite you, or caiman that eat you alive or dead. The jungle has any number of dangers, if you don't know them. My mother taught me a fair bit about the jungle, and how to survive in it, but I will need to have my wits about me to get through in one piece.'

Farka explains to everyone in Kicongo. Some visibly whiten when he mentions poisonous snakes. Then they say farewell to Tecaua and set off for the hill with the bobble.

On Mande's directions they all pick up fallen logs on the way to the river, while Mande finds good twine.

They make a raft which takes half of them, and they make two oars of sorts from branches. Mande goes on each trip over the river, as he can see the caiman's eyes in the water. The river is not wide, about four man-lengths. As Mande drops off the first few, he notices the bank has slightly stepped access to the grassland on top, which makes it easier to disembark.

On the second run, the caiman makes a move for them. Farka and a friend are rowing. Mande realises that he cannot fend off the caiman from the raft, while being rolled over by the caiman, while holding a machete does not appeal. Instinctively, he dives into the river to divert the caiman from the raft and starts swimming towards the bank. He knows the caiman is much faster than him, but he is relying on the stepped bank to allow him to climb out smartly.

He has misjudged the distance. Or perhaps the caiman's speed. The bank is three or four strokes away, but the caiman is right on him.

He realises his feet can touch the riverbed. In a flash, as the caiman prepares to pounce, he waves the machete across the caiman's eyes, catching some of its ageless but ancient skin as he does so. The caiman starts, and in that moment he can make two quick strokes, and start climbing up the bank, just as the caiman lunges. The caiman grazes his calves, causing nasty burns, but he is out.

The raft arrived immediately before Mande, so the crew were all safe on the bank.

The jungle proves a little less full of adventure. Mande introduces them to an armadillo, the glorious birdlife and some of the spiders that have made this jungle their home. Farka and his friends are not keen on the spiders, so Mande delights in putting one on his skin, then feigning a bite, feigning death throes and finally death, before getting up from the 'death' much to their surprise.

Mande finds a space to spend the night. They gather up firewood and dry grass and tap the machete on a stone to generate a spark. Mande makes sure that they are all close together, and that nobody is bleeding; he warns about the bats, which are just starting to appear as the evening light quickly fades.

Mande stands guard while they sleep, but drifts off. He is suddenly woken by a loud purring right next to him. It is a puma.

He calls 'Farka!'

Farka leaps up with machete in hand and shouts at the puma, which slopes rather disconsolately off.

They arrive at midday at the mocambo, which like Palmares has enormous logs to block its entrance.

Mande tries a toucan call and is pleased that they are let in.

The gatekeeper is friendly and speaks Swahili.

'Welcome, it is good to see you all. Do you speak Swahili?'

'I do,' replies Mande, 'and Farka here gets by. The others speak Kicongo but Farka can explain things to them.'

'We are quite a small mocambo, and still fairly new. We have about a thousand here. My name is Manu, by the way.'

'That sounds fine, Manu. When I was younger, I grew up in Palmares.'

'Well that is the granddaddy of us all, and we are much newer and much smaller. Look, I will ask some freemen to help with your hut. They know where the logs, nails, hammers and saws can be found. I will show you where you will be putting it up.'

They all start walking.

'What about communal space, carpentry workshop and the like?' asks Mande.

'Well, we have the beginnings of a communal space, which we will pass by soon. You can create a carpentry workshop if you like. Do you have carpentry skills?'

'My parents were both carpenters and ironmongers at Palmares, so I learnt quite a bit from them.'

'Great! Where are they now – by the way?'

'Back at my father's village in Africa, I hope. I was captured when we were travelling up the Congo River to get home.'

'Shit, that's extremely bad luck. Here, this is your spot. Do you want to wait here while I get some men to bring your materials?'

'Sure, we will.'

By nightfall they have a hut, as well as some mats made with coconut fibre to sleep on.

Farka looks Mande straight in the eyes. 'This, my friend, is the finest moment since that day I was happily fishing, and I was caught by the slave hunters.'

'I agree,' says Mande. 'By a long way the happiest moment since the hunters stole me.'

The others nod agreement and burst into song. The singing goes on long into the night.

Tucan and Maira in East Africa

'I fear I am now far too old to go back to Brazil,' says Maira, 'and I feel bad for you as you are still cut off from your people too.'

'I understand,' says Tucan. 'It was too hard to go back in the first year or two, like we planned, as we had no idea where Mande was, or even whether he was alive. If he was on his way here, we did not want to be in Brazil looking for him, so we became trapped. The tortoise of time has travelled all this while, instead of going into hibernation as we may have wished.'

'Well put, Tucan. Would you like to go back, with Caua?'

'Not without you, and you are now in your forties. It is such a long journey, too, fraught with danger.'

'There is something else too.'

'What is that?'

'My people were always under attack. It was like a three-pronged assault on us, and whatever we did, we couldn't escape it. These terrible illnesses that the cuckoos brought.'

'The cuckoos?'

'You know, the Portuguese, or Pink Faces as we often said. So many of us died. We had no defence. Then those costumes they used to wear to trick us with, to leave the protection of our family and get us into slavery, as happened to me. Whole villages were taken.

'Then the third thing, the utter brutality of burning the trees, the birds, the insects, the wonderful animals and the life that we had in that magical place. Even in my short life there, we lost so much, forcing us to retreat deeper and deeper into the forest.

'The cuckoos to the south of here are just the same. Here it's gold they want. They don't care about the people who live here. Their minds are simple. Gold and greed are all that drives them.'

'So all this helps you see better what happened back home?' asks Tucan.

'It does. It is like the chameleon and the iguana. The chameleon uses disguise to catch its prey. It's not obvious at first. This is the Portuguese in Brazil. The iguana is very direct, like the Portuguese around Sofala and Zimbabwe here. But they both want the same thing. The cuckoos in Brazil have set about killing off and enslaving the Tupis for gold also. Their gold is the sugar cane.'

'When you put it like that, it makes sense. But then the capture of our dear Mande is part of it all, not to mention all the slaves that have been taken from here to Brazil, of which we saw so many in Palmares.'

'So much anguish and destruction to satiate the Portuguese and Dutch appetite for gold.'

'Should we try to help Mande return? Grandpa Otapo's sister says they used magic to bring him back.'

'So I understand. But the price the sorceress demanded to help Otapo was a terrible one – to punish Mande with enslavement. It was a horrible price to pay.'

'Maybe we could ask the sorceress to reverse her curse and free Mande. He has paid the penalty for his father's freedom.'

'It couldn't hurt to try. The sorceress may refuse, but perhaps we should at least try.'

'Sure, I will go tomorrow,' says Tucan. 'I will take Caua.'

Mande and Farka in Flores Rosas

'I like it here in Flores Rosas, Farka, and I am very pleased not to be a slave. But I need to try to get home to Africa, to see my family.'

'I feel the same, but how would we do it? When we came to this land of disappointment in the bottom of a ship, it seemed to take forever. Surely, we need a ship to cross all that water?'

'When I was little, a man called Haram, who was a slave rescuer, found a damaged ship, and he and my mum and dad fixed it up. It took us back to Africa.'

'How amazing is that!'

'When we left him, Haram was sailing back to Brazil to rescue more slaves. I am hoping this ship is still taking freemen back to Africa. It is a long time since I last did it, so the ship may no longer be doing the trip, but I would like to find out.'

'Where would we get information?'

'I want to get to Palmares. In Flores Rosas, the men who try to guard the entrance and look after us do not know about any slave rescuers. But Palmares is enormous, with thousands of freemen and women. I would like to go there.'

'Well, I will come with you.'

'I will keep asking freed slaves that come here. Hopefully, one will know of Palmares. The alternative is to find the bit of coast where we found the shipwreck, I can find Palmares from there. But the coast is so long, like a mighty python that never stopped growing. I think that finding the bit of coast may be too hard.'

'Ok, Mande, but I will ask about Palmares too. There are lots of people to ask. Together we will find it.'

Aftermath of the Dutch defeat in Brazil in 1654

The Portuguese took out their vengeance on Tupis who had fought with the Dutch against them.

When they took over the town where Potira lived, they killed the Dutch soldiers, and took the women inside and raped them repeatedly. As the women protested vehemently that the Dutch had forced them to live with them, and even though Potira stated over and over that she had tried to escape many times, and had the whip scars to show for it, they were taken to the back wall of the main house and shot. Their children were taken to be placed with Portuguese families.

The women's corpses were placed in shallow graves near to the house. The decayed bodies of the Portuguese soldiers buried there some years before had long ago been dragged away by large cats, probably pumas.

The Portuguese lost no time in torching the forest area of those Tupis known to have sided with the Dutch, killing thousands and forcing others far from their homes.

They enslaved tens of thousands of the Tupis that were forced out by the fires, as they looked to take the opportunity to rapidly boost sugar exports, with the European market growing fast and proving highly profitable. The more so with slaves. This was a particularly difficult time for the Tupi, as tens of thousands were also dying from measles, smallpox and influenza.

Mande and Farka

'I have news!' shouts Farka excitedly.

Mande has been tending crops and has just returned, sweat dripping.

'Hi Farka. Sounds good, tell me,' he says, as he drinks from a coconut.

'A new freeman has said that there is a bigger mocambo a half a day from here, if we follow the midday sun. I am hoping we will find Palmares from there.'

'Ok, well I fear we are just treading water here, much as it has offered a safe haven while we try to start a new life. So let's go. When do you have in mind?'

'I think we could go tomorrow.'

'Ok. I will tell Manu. The other guys will come with us too.'

'Let's do it!' exclaims Farka.

* * * * *

As they enter the jungle Mande realises how much he loves it, in his bones, as though he was born there. The toucan that brightens the leaves of a tree; the hummingbird that hovers in front of your face while it sups nectar from a bright pink flower; the dappling of leaves that are now gold, then amber then rose; the armadillo that appears at the side of the path then shuffles back; the spider that dangles from a web attached high up in a tree, and that scuttles up at breakneck speed once prey is caught; the delightfully unpredictable sounds and vibrant colours of the multitude of birds, the calls of animals from far and near; the constant change in hues of the trees as the sun rises and falls through the day, the rich variety of colour in the undergrowth.

'I am not doing another river!' shouts Mkelu, one of Farka's friends.

It is the third one, and the last two have contained caimans and piranhas.

Mande and Farka lift the rudimentary raft they have created, and Farka holds the mooring twine that dangles from it, as they lower it into the river.

'Well, I will take four of you first,' says Farka, who is now more confident with the raft compared to the last trip.

Mande tries to calm Mkelu. He looks at the width of the river, which is not excessive. He looks around at the trees that grow by them. He grabs the trunk of a tall thin one and pulls it down until it snaps at the base.

He pulls some of the branches off, and then tests it out in terms of feel. He then moves a little downstream of the raft, hops and hobbles in a poor imitation of running with his pole horizontal and mostly to the fore and stabs the riverbed with the end of the pole. His momentum lifts him half-way across the river, but no more. He looks down. Pole stuck in mud. He looks at the caiman eyeing the raft.

'Wait there, Mr Caiman', he says to himself. He leaps into the water. The bank is tantalisingly near. The caiman reacts to the splash, heads his way, salivating.

Mande paddles ferociously and he grabs roots on the bank. He can smell the foul stench of rotting teeth as the caiman opens his huge jaw. Using the root, he yanks himself up on to the bank and out of harm's way just in the nick of time, leaving the caiman snapping pure air.

Straight after, the raft reaches the other side.

Mande shouts to Mkelu, 'Will you try doing that?'

Mkelu shouts in Kicongo, 'No way, I will go on the raft!'

Mande laughs. Then realises he has wetted himself.

Farka now takes the raft back across and collects the other three before rowing back.

Caiman eyes are following them the whole way, but the caiman seems to think better of it. There is no attack.

* * * * *

They soon reach the mocambo, which immediately gives the impression it is a bit older than Flores Rosas, and more established.

Mande gives his usual signal. There is no response. He tries again, and this time a gap opens in the main gate for them to get through.

'Hi,' says the woman at the entrance, 'welcome to Pau-Pau. My name is Rosa.'

She is large, Black, with braided hair curled up on her head, and a bandanna partly wrapped around. She has a grass skirt, and simple beads hanging down over pendulous breasts.

'Hi,' says Mande. 'We have been free for a few weeks. We have been staying at a small mocambo about a half day to the north. We needed somewhere bigger.'

'It is good to have you here. You have come at the right time. One hut just came free in the last few days, so you can use that one. I will fetch you a few mats. I will show you one or two places you will need to know about on the way to the hut. Follow me.'

Soon they are resting in the new hut.

'Women here!' exclaims Farka. 'I have not seen a woman for a very long time.'

'I think most of the men will say the same,' says Mande with a smile, as he fantasises about Rosa.

Rosa comes to check if they are OK. They nod.

'Tomorrow, I will show you the field where we grow our food for Pau-Pau. You will work a bit most days, but not tomorrow. You can have time to adjust. For now, there is some good food in the communal area this evening. We do a communal meal once a week, but also when new guests arrive. Come on over.'

They willingly follow.

The next morning

'Looks like you had a run in with a plantation owner,' Rosa says, pointing at Mande's foot. 'What's your story?'

It is the morning, outside Mande's hut.

He tells her about his parents, Palmares, and the journey by ship, his capture and his time as a slave, before finally getting away. He avoids talking about his foot.

'So that's why I don't want to start life in a mocambo and end life in a mocambo, much as I love and admire what you and others are doing to help free slaves.'

'So you really want a ship?' she asks.

'As you may imagine, I would dearly love to see my parents, if they are still alive, as well as my sister Tucan and my brother Caua. And that means finding a ship.'

'I did hear about a ship for freed slaves to go home. And the man Haram who helped you was seen as a legendary figure, navigating great oceans to help our people. But then word came that Haram has been killed, and I didn't hear about the ship anymore.'

'That is too bad,' says Mande. 'I will need to keep searching.'

'But, Mande, you are here now, and you are very welcome to stay until you have further news.'

'That is true, and I should be extremely grateful to you for welcoming us here.

'It is the least I can do.'

'Do you have carpentry and iron work here, Rosa?'

'We have carpentry, but not yet iron work. I am having problems getting hold of a forge. Why do you ask?'

'My parents were carpenters and ironworkers. I learnt some skills from them, but I would like to become a skilled carpenter like they were. Also, a skilled ironworker, if you are ever able to secure a forge.'

'Well, a good carpenter would be useful to me. I need a good carpenter for the new huts we are building.'

'I'm your man for the huts.'

'Wonderful!'

It is good here, Rosa. There are good people. But I do need to see my family again.'

'Do you think that can ever happen?'

'I was able to get to Africa before. I will not give up, while there is a chance of going there again and being with my family again.'

'I do understand. I would love to see my homeland too. I just never had hope that I would, and that remains the case. I dare not hope.'

'Where are you from in Congo?'

'It is not so far from the Kwanza river. After Luanda, it is around three days to the south.'

'If I find a ship, will you come with me?'

'I will have to think hard.'

'And your children?'

'I would need to ask them. I think, like me, they do not see it as possible, so have not thought about it.'

Further meeting of Mande and Rosa

A little later, Rosa sees Mande on the street near the carpentry workshop.

'Come to my hut,' she says.

'That is kind of you. Do you have a hut to yourself?'

'I share it with my children, but they are out tending crops at the moment.'

'How many children do you have?'

'Three, two girls and one boy.'

'And their father is not here?'

'He died escaping slavery. Shot in back.'

'I am sorry to hear that.'

'It looks like you nearly succumbed to the same fate. But perhaps you prefer not to talk about it.' She points with her forefinger at his missing front of foot.

'Haram's assistant, Mwesu, was trying to help me escape. A friend betrayed us, and Mwesu was killed. Beheaded. I lost half my foot, but they spared my life because they wanted me to work.'

'I guessed something like that. Will you let me hold your stump?'

Mande starts a little. Nobody has touched this, except Farka when fixing his stump. But after initial hesitancy, he lets her lift it. She deftly removes the piece of wood that helps to balance him.

'I know how you have suffered,' she says, as she strokes his stump. 'I suffered long after my husband Femi's death. I see in you the same spirit as Femi. I see a man with a true desire for freedom, a desire so strong that nothing must be allowed to stand in the way.'

She caresses the ugly stump, a blotchy purple, with gnarled knots of skin and gristle; she kisses it affectionately.

Tears seep from Mande's eyes.

She feels up from his stump and around his ankles, which she strokes. She then caresses his calf.

'I think my parents gave me that desire,' he says, wiping away his tears. 'They were determined that slavery should not destroy or direct their lives.'

She continues to caress his calf, and then moves to his thigh, and squeezes it on the inside while hooking inside his thong and pulling it down a little. He is now erect.

'You are a special man. You have a handsome face, moulding Tupi gentleness in your eyes and the strong brow of Bantu, with a warm wide smile. You have a broad chest, and muscular arms and shoulders, but your legs are quite slender, like a deer in the jungle.'

'Nobody has ever said such things,' he says, his eyes still moist. 'All I ever heard was, "work harder you bastard cripple."'

'You are a beautiful spirit. You are not a cripple.'

'You are an angel, with deep brown eyes that shine like gold.'

'I would like us to spend time together, Mande. Could we do that?'

And she moves her hand to his penis. He shudders, and a distinctive whiteness appears on his cheek.

'Oh no! I have never done this before, never been with a woman.'

'I understand. Life of a slave. At first, it's as quick as a tarantula shooting out of its trap to catch a grasshopper. But, if we do this together more, you will adjust. You will become slow and steady like a sloth trying to reach the end of the branch. Will you stay with me a little longer?'

'Can you hold me?'

'Sure.' She hugs him tight. She does not let go.

He hugs her too, his mind going back to hugging his mother when little. Tears flow again. His arms grip a little tighter on her large warm body. They stay in a deep embrace for a long time.

'I have not seen my mother since I was just attaining puberty. I have never been with a woman before you. I feel like a new-born baby.'

Tears are trickling down his cheek.

'Mande, just stay still. Let's just hug. Your pores ooze pain. Unabashedly.'

'I don't know what you mean. I don't understand.'

'Just stay still.'

'Mmm.'

'We can hug whenever you want you know, Mande.'

'I will want. Thanks,' says Mande. 'I like our regular meetings. I love being with you. I have experienced feelings that I never knew existed. But it is not fair to you. If I can leave for Africa, I will. You will be alone again.'

'Don't think I don't know this. I knew from the first day. But my heart has been content all this time with you. With my children, it is full of mango. With you, it is full of mango but with coconut cream on top. I love that coconut cream, but I could live without it.

'Have you thought about returning to Africa?'

'I have, but it is far from a straightforward issue for me. My children Kanda, Tsepo and Rosalina were born here, so for three of us it would be a return to the land of our ancestors but would not be going home. Then there are the reports of my homeland. According to many slaves that have come here, my part of the Kongo may be a centre for the slave trade.'

'This is also what Farka and his friends say, I fear. And both I and my father were transported through a port in the Kongo.'

'For me, my heart would be more complete if I returned home. There is also the deepest longing in my heart, after not seeing my homeland all this time. The pull to the Kongo is strong. The counter pull is strong. So, you can see, just like two deer rutting, their antlers entangled, I have competing feelings.'

'Well, dear Rosa, I have no wish to overcomplicate your feelings. But you can be sure that, if I do find a ship, then the person I will most want to come with me, along with Kanda, Tsepo and Rosalina, is you.'

'Today, dear Mande, I would have to stay with Kanda, Tsepo and Rosalina here. I cannot say what my answer will be in years to come.'

Mande meets with Tupi who knew his mother

'Can I have a word?' asks an elderly woman in Tupi.

Mande is taken aback, but replies in Tupi, 'You are Tupi! Where are you from?'

'Well I think you are only half son of Tupi, as a true Tupi is not from anywhere. We belong to a tribe. But all this land is our land.'

'I am sorry. Of course. It is a pleasure to meet you. I am Mande.'

'Yes, I heard your name being called. I am Tulapu. I think your mother is called Maira.'

'That is true. How do you know?'

'In your eyes I see the eyes of Maira. I felt you must be her son. I knew your mother quite well many years ago, before she became a slave.'

'Are you part of our tribe?'

'No, but we were in a tribe near to Maira's. And when the Pink Faces started burning our special and magical forest, and we retreated, we came together in one of the reserve villages we had. I took to your mother immediately. She is such a special person.'

'That is lovely to hear. Was she captured by the Pink Faces before you?'

'She was. But, you know, we became great friends when we lived together, and we cooked together and talked about men, and about the horrible Pink Faces and how we would fight if we became slaves. She had a great spirit, and I can see that spirit in you. Where is your mother now?'

'We were all travelling back to my father's village, which is on the eastern side of Africa. My mother married my father Otapo, and I have a sister Tucan and a brother Caua. I was captured near the Congo River by slave hunters and brought to Brazil, and I only hope that my family reached our ancestors' village.'

'So your father was brought here first as a slave?'

'Yes, he met my mother Maira at Palmares mocambo after finally escaping from his plantation. All three of us were born at Palmares. We were fortunate that the man Haram who rescued us found a ship. My parents repaired it to sail to Africa.'

'An amazing story. Do you hope to find another ship now?'

'I hope to, but it sometimes feels like a hummingbird hoping to mate with a toucan. My hopes are not high. But you never know.'

'Well you should come over to my family and share some Tupi food this evening. I am sure your mother cooked lovely Tupi food for you.'

'She did. She also did amazing things when we were travelling, catching fish with her bare hands.'

'She learnt that as a child, and I am sure she taught you?'

'She did yes, although I could never do it as well as her.'

'I was captured when fishing.'

'What happened?'

'Stupidly, a friend and I got separated from the main group when we were hunting one day, and we stopped to catch fish, to make up for us not getting any meat. Some Portuguese just happened to be in that part of the jungle, and although we ran and got monkeys to throw coconuts at them, they had guns and we became too frightened to run further. I escaped from the plantation a few moons ago.'

'A big relief for you.'

'Unbelievable.'

'I will be very happy to eat with you. We can talk more then.'

'Let's go.'

17.
Hope Wrestles with Fear

'Who are you?' asks Rosa.

'Mtatu. I am a freedom fighter.'

'Let me look at you.' She looks him in the eyes. 'Good, come in.'

Mtatu squeezes through the entrance. He is medium height, stocky, has a thick head with very short hair, no beard, big smile, ebony, wide chest. Rosa greets him.

'I was a friend of Haram's. Maybe you know Haram.'

'I have heard of him.'

'He was killed. I found his ship where he hid it. It needs some work. It is about two days away. I want to talk to your freemen here. To see if any want to come to Africa.'

'We have some certainly, possibly quite a few.'

'Very good. I also want help with the ship. Mainly carpenters.'

'Well, Mande is your man. Mande and Farka. They will certainly come. Mande is a good carpenter, Farka too. I will ask around and see if there are others. Obviously, we have some Tupi here, who would not wish to come. But there are Africans too. Plenty of Africans.'

'That sounds good. Where can I find Mande?'

'At the carpentry workshop. Farka may well be there too. I will get them soon. Why don't you have some food first?' or at least something to drink?

'I'll have some coconut milk.'

* * * * *

Mtatu is just resting for a few moments with his open-topped coconut when Mande comes over. They speak in Swahili.

'My name is Mande. I believe you may have a ship.'

'Well, it is good to meet you. I have a ship, Haram's ship, and I need a crew.'

'You knew Haram?'

'I did, very well. Did you hear what happened?'

'No, tell me please.'

'He had come back with his ship and was playing his usual swashbuckling role rescuing slaves so he could then recruit them for his freedom voyage.'

'How did you meet him?'

'I was at a plantation he came to. He rescued us and took us to a mocambo about two days away from our plantation. Somehow, we shook off our pursuers. En route, he told us where his ship was, in case anything happened to him.

'The mocambo, or quilombo if you like, was maybe similar to Pau-Pau in size. Somehow, whether he was tracked there or whatever, the Portuguese sent some fearsome and ugly soldiers to the quilombo. They only wanted Haram. The other men in the quilombo tried to hide Haram and to find a secret way out of there, but the soldiers found him, killed him and took his body away.'

'That is terrible, the worst news possible. Haram was a great man, and my friend.'

'It was very hard for all of us. Fortunately, the soldiers didn't capture me or the other men, so I was able to stay at the quilombo. When I had got a few men interested in the ship, I came along here to get the extra crew we need, especially a couple of skilled men, as the ship needs work.'

'Well, Farka and I are carpenters, and we would come. I don't know yet about others. Where is the ship?'

'It is near a small quilombo named Candiru. It is partly hidden by trees as you approach.'

'And does the ship need lots of work to repair it?'

'Just some repairs to the woodwork, which is where you come in.'

'Have you mentioned to Rosa that you are looking for others to come?'

'Yes, Rosa says she will ask around,' says Mtatu.

'She is probably doing it now.'

Mande says thanks to Mtatu and goes off to bed. But as he lies in bed, unable to sleep, he remembers Sando, the treachery, and losing half his foot, and realises he will need to talk to Tulapu in the morning.

Tulapu and Mande talk

'Hi Tulapu,' says Mande, 'I need to talk to you.'

'I am here, we can talk,' replies Tulapu, who is wearing a yellow and orange skirt and smells of lilac perfume. They speak in Tupi.

'I may be able to go on a ship soon,' says Mande. 'But I am worried that the man Mtatu, who is taking us to the ship, is not a good man.'

'You do not trust this man, Mtatu?'

'There was a very good man, who was also my friend, who was called Haram. When Haram was killed by the Portuguese, Mtatu was present, but the Portuguese did not capture Mtatu, even though he was, he tells me, an escaped slave. It is not like the Portuguese to be kind to escaped slaves, as you know and as I know.'

'You think the Mtatu man is a cuckoo in our nest, wearing inside his skin the dark soul of the Portuguese?'

'This is what I fear. I can see us going to the ship, many of us, all freemen, and being arrested by Portuguese soldiers. They would then either kill us or, more likely, return us to slavery.'

'I am not sure which is worse.'

'Exactly. So, there is something I want you to do to help.'

'I would do anything to help the son of Maira, however old I am. What can I do for you?'

'We may leave in the next day or two to go the quilombo by the ship. It is called Candiru.'

'A little fish.'

'A fish?'

'In Tupi, candiru is a little fish.'

'Ok, well it seems a very small quilombo as its name suggests. When we leave, I would like you to go to the Tupi who live nearest to the Candiru quilombo. I don't know how near this will be, but you know better than me how the Tupi network of villages works.'

'That is no problem. I can find my way near Candiru, and find the Tupis there. This is the kind of thing we grew up doing, as I am sure Maira told you.'

'I would like the Tupis to be prepared to come with bows and arrows, spears, blowpipes and poisoned arrows. The best will be if a large number of Tupis is made ready, then one of them, perhaps you Tulapu, come to find me to see if I need your help. I have a fallback plan too.'

'What is that, smoke signals?'

'Well, as a Tupi I should have guessed you would know. Yes, I would gather up flint, wood and dried grass, and damp wood, and make smoke signals if things are fine. If you don't see the smoke signals, I want the Tupis to come.

'Ok, I think I will try to come to Candiru in any event, if at all possible, as I will know for sure then. But the smoke signals can be a fallback.'

'I am very grateful. As you know, when you have been in slavery, the very last thing you can face is to go back to it.'

'I agree. I would sooner jump into the open jaws of a caiman lizard.'

'So, I will watch this Mtatu man like a hawk.'

* * * * *

As Mande heads back to his carpentry workshop and begins to root around for a tool he rarely uses, Mtatu strolls up.

'I have found about twelve or thirteen who will come. I think that will be close to a full complement for the ship, as we may well find seven to ten more men at the quilombo.'

'That's good, so when are you thinking we might leave?'

'I think the day after tomorrow. There are just a few more of the people here that I still want to speak to before we go.'

Mande and Rosa talk

'I still hope you will come, Rosa, we leave tomorrow,' Mande pleads the following morning.

'I just don't know,' she says. 'I want to be with you, but I want my children to be here.'

'If you decide after we've gone, we will be at Candiru quilombo.'

'Ok, I hear you. But stay with me tonight, won't you, before you leave?'

'I will.'

To Candiru Quilombo

They are fourteen strong when they leave. Mande makes sure he collects up hammers, saws, chisels and nails before he leaves. He checks this is OK with Rosa, and she replies by giving him a leather bag to take the bits in. He looks at her askance when he sees the bag.

'I thought the Portuguese soldier who owned it was dead, when he collapsed on the road outside,' she says, 'so I took his saddle bag. He called to me then, which completely shocked me. A little later he did die.'

'How?'

'I put a knife through him, one I found in this bag.'

Mande smiles. He asks Farka and the other men to join him at the front gate, which he does.

It is a three day walk to the quilombo, but they are in good spirits.

On the way, Mande talks to local Tupi on the jungle path. He is able to find a village, and ask for something to eat and a hammock for everyone to sleep in each night.

There are the usual dangers, between a banana spider hiding in its nest right on the path, and snakes and caimans in the rivers, but the worst that happens is a coconut falling on Farka's head, causing him quite a bruise. He shakes his fist at the monkey that threw it.

When they arrive at Candiru quilombo, Mande has some recollection from years ago when he was last there. Now there are ready made huts, and fields being tended. There are around forty to fifty people there, who prove to be mostly from Kongo originally.

The Kongolese say that they are happy for Mande's people to share the huts.

'Do you want to see the ship?' asks Mtatu, the next morning after they arrive.

'Sure do,' says Mande. Farka and a few others follow them down.

'It's floating,' says Mande, as it comes into view a few minutes later. 'That's more than it did last time.'

'Yes, it's looking ok', replies Mtatu. 'Let's take the boat out to it.'

Mtatu lifts up the branches of a willow tree, and is relieved to see a long boat there. They row it out to the ship.

'It will need a lot of work on the woodwork, you were right,' says Mande, who then proceeds to the lower deck.

He recalls much of the ship and is excited to be back. On the lower deck, some of the planks of the deck are soft to touch. When prodding with his fingers, lumps come away.

'We will need to replace some of the decking on the lower deck,' says Mande to Mtatu. 'We may also find more when we remove those planks.'

'So how long?'

'At least a week, probably two. We need to start by cutting down and cutting up a suitable tree. I identified the ideal one when we arrived.'

'Just say if you want a hand,' says Mtatu.

'Have no worry, we will need several hands soon, Mtatu.'

They head back to the shore.

* * * * *

'There is a woman at the gate, says she knows you from Pau-Pau,' says Farka to Mande.

'Thank you so much for coming, Tulapu,' says Mande, as he approaches. 'Let us walk towards the ship.'

And they leave the quilombo and take the rough path towards the sea. Mande kicks a snake that ventures on to the path in front of him. The snake turns and hisses at him but thinks twice about a strike on a human thigh and slithers off.

'You look concerned,' he says, turning to look at her sideways on.

'The Tupi have word that Pink Faces are heading this way,' replies Tulapu.

'Do you know how far away they are, or how long we may have?'

'I think a day, from what my friends say.'

'And can the Tupi mobilise a force to defend us from them?'

'I think the Tupi will prefer to do things their way. They will set traps, blow the odd poisoned arrow, catch the odd soldier in a net dropped from above, and generally weaken them, reduce their numbers, and make them anxious.'

'Perfect. I like that. It reminds me of mum's stories. Do you know how many Portuguese there are?'

'About twenty-five or thirty is what my friends say. If we can reduce them to about fifteen, we can deal with them better with our weapons as they come nearer.'

'Very good. So it seems my suppositions about Mtatu were on the nail, sad to say. It seems to me we will need to separate him from the others, make sure he cannot do us damage when the Portuguese arrive. What do you think?'

'I agree, but what do you have in mind?'

'I'm thinking on my feet, really. But Mtatu has already offered me help this morning, so I can quite genuinely take him back to the ship. I am sure he will agree. Ideally, if you can come too, you can distract him for a moment on the main deck, looking at the work needed on the handrail. There is a fair bit of rope in the hold, and if I have a couple of minutes to go down there, we will have time between us to tie him to the rail at the side of the ship.'

'I am up for that.'

'I might just ask Farka to keep an eye on everyone here, just in case Mtatu has an ally.'

'Why not?' asks Tulapu.

When they return to the quilombo, Mande and Farka chat.

'I need you as a look out here,' suggests Mande. 'The Tupis are dealing with the soldiers.'

'They are coming?' asks Farka.

'Yes, we were right about our traitor. Will you do it?'

'I agree,' says Farka

* * * * *

The Portuguese squadron are marching on. The track through the jungle is not ideal. It disappears every now and then, and they need to plough forward in the hope of finding it again.

It is during one such break in the path when the body of a soldier near the front suddenly disappears down a hole, leaving just a head and waving arms protruding. As he screams for help and the others reach to pull him out, they all draw away in a hurry, and let him go. There are snakes everywhere.

One fires a musket at a snake but misses. Three thrash with their swords, trying to cut off their heads. They manage to kill two, with some effort, but they are thwarted by the constant ducking and diving and swerving by the snakes, and not least the snakes' constant threat to bite the thighs of the Portuguese, above their high boots, or their hands.

The soldier who fell in the trap is dead, and the soldiers bury him. Two others soon die from their snake bites, despite desperate attempts to cut out their venom by colleagues, and they are also buried.

While they are digging the graves for the deceased soldiers, a net comes down over one of the gravediggers. As he struggles to free himself from the net, banana spiders climb out, and test his flesh for flavour. He lasts barely thirty minutes in great agony.

As one of the other gravediggers realises what is happening, a banana spider is on his boot and starting to make an ascent. He thwacks it with the butt of his musket. His first effort injures himself more than the spider, his second strikes home. A tarantula, meanwhile, has run a long web-line from high in the tree, and is on his neck before he can react. He is soon writhing on the floor in agony.

The third gravedigger has by now more spiders on him than he can cope with. He has killed the two on his boots with his musket-butt, but a third one is at his neck, and he is soon in death-throes on the floor.

The captain, Felipe Dias, orders his men to leave all the dead where they are, and to move away from these traps and nests. As they do so, blowpipe-blown poisoned arrows rain upon them.

Four of the soldiers are hit in the neck, and another in the thigh, and three of them soon die. The last of them is in a raging fever for an hour or so, and he eventually succumbs.

Captain Dias orders the surviving shoulders to fire a volley of shots in the direction of the poisoned arrows, but the Tupis have by now melted into the jungle.

The captain orders a quick march, and they are able to make some progress.

All of them constantly look around for arrows or traps, despite the reprimands from the captain.

* * * * *

'There is some work you can do on the ship,' says Mande, addressing Mtatu while they refresh themselves with coconut milk. 'You can work with Tulapu, who has just arrived from Pau-Pau quilombo.'

'That is cool,' says Mtatu.

'We will go there now,' says Mande, 'and I will show you both the job I have in mind. I need to check on a few things myself, too.'

They head off to the ship, each carrying tools. Mtatu exchanges a few words with Tulapu in Portuguese, but she finds it a bit of a strain. It is a little easier in Swahili, but Tulapu again tires, so Mtatu mainly keeps himself to himself.

Farka leaves the quilombo a little while after the threesome, as agreed, and he is still some way back when they reach the ship on the long boat.

'Can you look at the handrails with Tulapu for a moment?' asks Mande as they bring the longboat up by the ship.

'That is fine with me,' says Mtatu, and they open the gate in the rail to walk on deck.

Mande heads down the ladder to the lower deck, while Tulapu goes with Mtatu over to the other side of the ship, and they examine the damaged handrail there.

'Just look at this really bad bit,' says Tulapu in Swahili. 'All this will need to come off.'

'And this bit just along here,' suggests Mtatu.

As they focus on the broken pieces of handrail, Mtatu asks, 'What is Mande up to?'

'I have no idea,' says Tulapu. 'You know, this bit of wood has a deep crack all the way along.'

'That looks serious,' says Mtatu, as he examines the crack along its full length.

Mande now comes up behind Mtatu and throws a rope over him, pulling it tight round his arms and chest with the lasso knot he has just made. Mtatu realises too late what is happening.

Mande tries to wrap the rope around his legs also, but Mtatu is now writhing and kicking, despite Tulapu's best efforts to restrain him.

Mande now leaps and grabs Mtatu tight around the waist, and asks Tulapu in Tupi to take the spare length of rope and wrap it tight around his thighs.

'Use one of our super clever knots,' he suggests. With Mande limiting Mtatu's movement and getting a full whiff of ugly sweat as he does so, she is able to tie his thighs tightly, and she now ties this lower rope to the lasso around his chest.

Mtatu does not give up struggling the whole time, but finally he is trussed like a chicken ready for roasting.

'Why are you doing this?' asks Mtatu. 'I came to help you. I brought you to this ship.'

'Tell me what really happened with Haram,' shouts Mande. 'The Portuguese soldiers spared you after you brought Haram to a different quilombo. You set it up so that Haram was killed, didn't you?'

'I did not. It was like I said. The Portuguese soldiers were headbangers, wanting to kill, kill, kill. Above all, they were out to kill Haram, and not the rest of us.'

'So tell me, Mtatu. My parents had experience of the Portuguese for much of their lives, and I have also had much experience, and they have all been viciously aggressive towards escaped slaves in any situation.

'There are not good Portuguese, bad Portuguese and very bad ones. There are just Portuguese. So your story just does not add up.'

'I promised to go back with the Portuguese, so they did not kill me, but then I escaped from them.'

'So, your story now changes. Very convenient. You know, many escaped slaves in my situation and in Tulapu's situation would kill you. You pose a big risk to us. By this I mean a real risk of us becoming slaves again or being killed. For all I know, you have Portuguese soldiers coming this way for us.' And as he says the last sentence, he finds his voice rising in anger.

Mtatu could not avoid raising his eyebrows at this mention of Portuguese.

'Ah, the eyebrows! Transparent as an exploding toadstool! So, there are soldiers coming! Very interesting. We may need to leave this quilombo before we are ready. Now, as I say, we could kill you, or we could leave you to think about your situation. I think we will do the latter.'

And Mande checks all the knots, makes one extra knot, and makes sure the ropes are tight, and they head for the longboat to go back to the quilombo, linking up with Farka at the shoreline to confirm a successful operation.

* * * * *

'Ah!' exclaims Captain Dias, with his shrunken Portuguese squadron. 'Who do we have here? An escaped slave and her children, heading in the direction of a quilombo. And a quilombo, no less, next to a ship. What possible lessons could I draw?'

'I am from quilombo Pau-Pau,' says Rosa. 'My name is Rosa, and these are my children. We are searching for game for supper.'

Captain Dias takes Rosa's leather bag from her and tips it out.

'A grass skirt, a dress! For hunting animals! Ha! I should whip you for lying to me. But I think you may be useful. Very useful indeed.'

Dias orders his men to tie their hands behind their backs and to tie their legs at their thighs, to limit them to a shuffled walk.

He then slaps Rosa hard in the face.

'If you lie to me one more time, woman, you are dead, and your children will be placed with Portuguese families as servants!'

Rosa is angry, but also hurt. Her face oozes pain. Her ears are still ringing.

But she has the presence of mind to wink to the children, and they know what she has in mind.

Kanda, Tsepo and Rosalina all ask to go to the toilet. Kanda says, 'We can't go with these ropes tied on our legs.'

Dias motions to a soldier to untie their legs, but barks to him to keep his musket on them.

Untied, the children go under a tree. Tsepo extends her foot to a banana spider resting by its trap nearby. The spider climbs up her leg, and nestles in a pouch attached to her thong, at the top of her grass skirt. Rosalina does the same.

They finish their imagined wee, and head back to the path, suitably armed.

They march on.

There are now fifteen soldiers, and Rosa and her three children.

* * * * *

Mande and Tulapu discuss the attack.

'My people will have weakened the Portuguese,' says Tulapu, 'but there will still be some coming here to fight. I will go and talk to the Tupi about their plans.'

'I will warn the people here,' says Mande, 'and we will see if we can fashion some spears and bows and arrows in the little time we have.'

'Good, good, and I will try to bring some back with me,' says Tulapu.

'My worry is that we will have to sail the ship from here before we are ready. I am worried that, even if we see off these Portuguese, there will be others who come to find them, wondering why they have not returned.

'I recall that we pass islands within two or three days of our departure. If we can drop anchor at one of them, and find a bay to row to, we could do the necessary work on the boat there, provided no enemies are living there. We can take our wood and resin and all our tools with us for the repair jobs.'

'It's not ideal,' responds Tulapu, 'but you will find an island I am sure, even if not the first one.'

'Sure.'

'But Mande, there is a conversation we must have. I need to explain to you the twisted branches our peoples now face as they speak to our spirits.'

'Twisted branches?

'You, Mande, as much as anyone, symbolise inside so much of where the Tupi future lies. You have within you a powerful Tupi spirit from your mother Maira. This spirit is in no way subsumed by the spirit you have from your father. It lives alongside.

'This is a very common situation now for our people. The Portuguese have taken so many of our women, our men have given them others as sisters, but less so after the war. The Tupi spirit is not lost by these unions. It continues, in the use by the Pink Skins of some of our language, the maintenance of some of our culture, the continuation of our traditions. The jungle has been weakened physically. But the jungle lived on in the town.'

'I think I understand that in part from my mother and from me,'

'This is not to downplay how much we have lost. Just as the river, when it floods, invades all the jungle around it with nothing except strong trees standing in its way, so the Portuguese diseases ravage our bodies, except the strongest ones. This has killed tens of thousands of us, and still kills.

'This has eaten into the heart of the Tupi way of life. Tupi life is like ant society. Ants all cooperate instinctively for the sake of the whole, and there are no individuals. We all cooperate for the sake of the whole, although for us it is a little different as there is a role for some of us as we have jokers, musicians, story tellers.'

'I'm not sure,' says Mande, 'I have known ants play tricks on me. Perhaps ants have jokers too. Do you find it sad what the Tupi have lost?'

'There is a sadness, but I don't want you to leave here thinking that the Tupi way of life has gone. There are many different tribes, and given the size of the jungle, it is likely that our life will always survive, even if I'm sure it will retreat more and more as time passes.

'The worst thing,' says Mande, 'is that the invaders see the jungle as an obstacle to their wealth, but we see all the wealth of our culture and our lives deriving from the jungle.'

'The two sides are completely at odds. But if we resist, they burn and destroy, and they turn into slaves those of us forced out by fire. They are so ruthless in their willingness to destroy. This is ultimately our undoing. It is for this reason that our future lies better in working with the Portuguese, and by influencing their culture through all our women brides. Like I said, this will ensure that our culture lives on in their towns.'

'We have lost a lot since my mother was born.'

'A great deal, yes, but do convey to your mother, if you find her, that there are reasons to be hopeful for the future of our culture. And do pass on the spirit of my heart, which does not forget her.'

'I will. Do you need to head off?'

'I do. Farewell.'

And Tulapu heads off.

* * * * *

Mande asks a couple of freemen to gather up everybody for important news. He then addresses Farka.

'Any problems?' asks Mande.

'I didn't see anyone acting suspiciously, no.'

'That is good. It is enough to have one rat in the bird's nest.'

'Is the rat now quiet?'

'He is, on the ship, tied up. But let me now address our people here. Much is now happening.'

'Sure.'

'We have a problem,' shouts Mande to the assorted freemen. 'Portuguese soldiers are on their way here. We have discovered that the man Mtatu was not helping us, instead he was working with the Portuguese. If he had had his way, he would have ensured that all of us returned to slavery. Now, he is bound in a special place.

'There are three things I want to say: First, if any of you have suspicions about anybody else not being on our side, come and see me privately. And quickly. Secondly, we are going to have some help from local Tupi Indians. They will try to fight off the Portuguese before they reach us and send some of them away with their tail between their legs. A few of the Portuguese may get through, so we are going to make as many spears and bows and arrows as we can in the short time we have.

'Thirdly, and most importantly, we will probably sail from here quite soon. Even if we defeat the Portuguese this time, they will come back. We will take our tools and our wood and resin, and we will stop at the first island that seems right for us and get fixed up for the long voyage to Africa.'

'That is fine with me,' says Farka. And the others all agree.

'Farka, can you and the others look among the local trees for wood that will suit for bows, arrows and spears? Bows are key. We have until about noon tomorrow, so we have little time with the sun now starting to set.

'So we need to act fast,' says Farka.

'Yes, faster than fast,' replies Mande.

* * * * *

'Are you all ready for the Pink Faces?' asks Tulapu.

'As ready as can be,' replies Moacir junior 'They are now fifteen, and we have forty, so we outnumber them.'

'Have you decided where to attack.'

'We have a good place. The track is quite narrow there, with rock on both sides, so we can incapacitate them better one by one. But there is a problem.'

'What is that?'

'They have taken four people, African, a woman and three children.'

'Hostages?'

'Is that what they call it? They think we won't attack with this woman and her children there?'

'The woman is I think the woman of my good friend Mande. They are her children. We do need to make them safe.'

'I think I can do this. I will seek to ensure they have the opportunity to escape. I hope they realise and respond.'

'Thank you. I will tell Mande.'

'You stay there for when we attack. They may need you.'

'Ok I will.'

* * * * *

The Tupi get in position. The narrow track is in a small gorge. They have some of their number high up on either side of the gorge with bows and arrows.

They also have spear throwers in front of where the Portuguese will come out at the far end of the gorge.

Coming down the side of the gorge at the right time on thick twine will be a small group with blowpipes and poisoned arrows, who will try to pick off the soldiers at the back, and give a chance for the African woman and the children to get away.

But the prisoners will need help with their binding, and one, Moacir junior, has a Portuguese cutlass to help with this, and he is staying at the back of the gorge, out of sight.

They make Toucan calls to confirm they are all in position.

Mande and Tulapu

'I have bad news and good news,' says Tulapu, as she returns to the quilombo.

'Tell me both,' says Mande.

'Rosa and the children were on their way to join you. But the Portuguese soldiers have captured them, and they are using them as hostages.'

'Oh Tulapu! I must go there! Where are they?'

'The Tupi know about them, and they have a plan. They will be attacking in the gorge. They will have men coming from the back, killing the Portuguese one by one, and then giving Rosa and the children the chance to get away.'

'But they may be shot to stop them getting away. This is the Portuguese, after all. I will go!'

'Mande, you must protect your people here. You are their leader. They rely on you. Let me go to the gorge and try to help Rosa and the children. I will go through the jungle and come to the gorge from behind.'

'My spirits are against me. I need to be there and I need to be here. I need to split in two and allow my spirit and my strength to help Rosa and the children, and allow what wit and cunning I have to help the people here.'

'I will take your spirit and your strength. I will call for support and help from the ancestors.'

'Then please go now and bring back Rosa and the children.'

* * * * *

'We are coming to a gorge,' shouts captain Rias.'If we are going to face another attack, this will be here. Be extra wary. Stay close together, and close to the prisoners, as we go through. I want one of you behind each of these prisoners.'

As they enter the gorge, Tsepo has one soldier right by her, and Rosalina has one cheek by jowl with her. They glance at each other, with a look that says, 'It is time.'

Tsepo takes out her banana spider gently and places her on the thigh of the soldier guarding her, just where the flesh is exposed; Rosalina places her banana spider on the exposed thigh flesh of her guard.

There is an almighty scream, followed by a matching scream. Each soldier reaches down to try to kill the banana spider. In each case, the spider has moved out of harm's way on to their back. The two soldiers collapse in pain, writhing on the ground.

A couple of soldiers stop to see if they can help, but Dias barks loudly: 'Don't stop here! It's a trap! Keep marching forwards!'

Rosalina and Tsepo edge backwards. There is now nobody behind them. They edge round the rock at the back of the gorge and find trees there. They sit by a tree to plan their next move and Moacir Junior sits by them. 'Shhh' he says. He touches his heart with his right hand to signal he is good. Rosalina and Tsepo huddle up together, nervously.

A Tupi soon slides down his twine to the gorge at the back of the soldiers. He blows an arrow at the soldier guarding Kanda. The soldier stumbles, and sits, holding his leg.

The Tupi calls Kanda with a macaw call. Kanda turns and sees the Tupi and eases back to him. The fallen soldier shouts, 'Prisoner escaping!'

One soldier turns and cocks his musket at the Tupi, who blows an arrow at him and dives down. From above, another Tupi with blowpipe fires a poisoned arrow at the soldier just as he is pulling the trigger. He is unbalanced and the musket aims high into the sky.

The Tupi gets up following his jump and grabs Kanda.

As they come to the end of the gorge there is a new macaw sound.

'It is Moacir Junior,' says the Tupi and they look round the stone at the end of the gorge and see the two girls. They all hug, but the Tupi, holding one finger up to say 'Stay,' hurries back to the gorge.

Moacir stays with the children.

By coincidence, Tulapu arrives at this time, and she tells the children that she will stay with them until their mother is safe. She thanks Moacir Junior.

Meanwhile, Tupis above the gorge are firing poisoned arrows on the soldiers from above, while ordinary arrows are again being fired from behind the Portuguese.

The two soldiers with Rosa, and the two behind her, fall, either badly wounded or dead.

The two in front of Rosa turn around to see she has no guard, and one steps behind her, to keep urging her forward, only to have an arrow fired at him from behind.

He falls down.

Rosa, seeing no guard with her, stands still, while the soldiers go on ahead. The guard who is now in front of her realises that she is lagging behind but is also aware of the exhortations of Dias to keep moving.

Dias is coming to the front end of the gorge now. A spear is thrown right at him by a Tupi waiting ready in the track beyond the gorge, but he displays great nimbleness to step quickly out of its path. The soldier behind him is not so lucky, and the spear goes into his groin, causing him to double up.

Moacir Junior is now standing at the rear of the gorge and sees Rosa standing alone. He rushes to reach her and take her to her children. Moacir does not see a wounded soldier pull out his knife and stab as he comes past, gashing his leg. He reaches for a knife tucked inside the lip of his thong and turns and stabs the soldier, then hobbles to Rosa, where he slices through the ropes that hold her, and they hurry to the rear of the gorge.

They find the children with Tulapu, and the four of them have a huge group hug, lasting many minutes, before Rosa thanks Tulapu and Moacir Junior for their help.

Dias calls his remaining men, of which there are four fit to run, to follow him into the deep undergrowth. They charge between lianas and around thick bushes until Dias feels he has got a bit of distance from the Tupi.

'Sly bastards,' he mutters.

* * * * *

Moacir junior breaks an aloe vera stem and holds it to his injured stomach. He then brings Rosa and her children through the gorge to where his people are.

The Tupis gather together. They are pleased that none have died, and very pleased that Rosa and the children are safe.

Two of the Tupis take Rosa, Tsepo, Kanda, Rosalina and Tulapu to the quilombo, using the main path. Three other Tupis go through the jungle to the side of the path, slightly ahead, to make sure Dias and his men are not lying in wait.

Another twelve Tupis follow the trail of footprints, broken twigs, and bruised leaves left by Dias and his remaining men and head in pursuit of them. The others head back to the Tupi village to prepare food for everyone.

There is commotion at the quilombo when the Portuguese arrive.

Dias and his four soldiers have breached the pointed log fence at the far perimeter, and have killed two of the African freemen, who were caught unawares.

The Tupis who were tracking Dias and his men have only just caught them up when Dias gets inside the quilombo. They are now using bows to fire arrows at Dias and his men, who are taking cover in a copse of trees.

Mande and the rest of his crew of freemen have erected improvised cover with two fallen logs, and they are sheltering behind these trying to get the chance to throw spears at Dias and his men.

As the other Tupis arrive at the main gate with Rosa, Tulapu and the children, the guard tells them to wait, but Tulapu goes through regardless and rushes to Mande as a shot rings out from Dias. Tulapu is hit.

'Rosa and her children are s…' she says, before she collapses. She is losing a lot of blood from the wound in her stomach and is soon unconscious.

Mande puts his hand on her shoulder and kisses her forehead, raising his hands to the spirits. He asks Farka to nurse her. He agrees.

Mande then rushes to Rosa and they embrace for many long minutes. He then kisses the children.

The newly arrived Tupis blow poisoned arrows at Dias's men. One more succumbs.

As they try to break through the fence again on the seaward side of the quilombo, a Tupi throws a spear, and another soldier dies with a direct hit.

Dias and his lieutenant get through the stockade and make their way towards the long boat. Half a dozen Tupis go after them. Mande leaves Rosa and follows.

The chasing Tupis find their arrows are falling short, so they race to catch up. They do so as Dias and his lieutenant are poised to fire musket shots at the ship. A Tupi spear strikes the lieutenant as he is shooting and his shot lands in the sea. Dias's musket fires a hole in the side of the boat. Moments after, a spear goes through Dias. It is Mande's spear.

Tulapu does not make it through the night.

Mtatu, on the ship, is injured by Dias's musket shot, which hits him after penetrating the side of the ship. But he survives.

* * * * *

Mande is deeply saddened by Tulapu's death, as is Rosa when she realises the role Tulapu played in saving them all.

They and Rosa's children accompany Tulapu's body back to her village and share in celebrating her journey to join with the ancestors.

The Tupis form a circle around her body, sharing a gourd of honey wine, as earth is piled on her body to form a mound. They then sing and dance until long after dark.

Farka, meanwhile, is organising the boat ready for setting sail the next day. He asks for as much resin as possible to be drawn from nearby pau brasil trees to help with plugging the hole left by Dias, but also to be used on the lower deck for when they get a chance to fix it at their new island base.

He also arranges the burial of the two freemen who died.

When Mande, Rosa and family return the following morning, they all meet up at the quilombo.

'We will wait another day, because of Tulapu's death. We will start loading tomorrow, and set sail once loaded. Tonight, we hold a feast for the Tupis who saved our lives and saved our ship.

'How many of the freemen who were resident at this quilombo wish to join us?'

Farka translates into Kicongo for the freemen.

A number of men shout their names. Others come to him, including Mabongo, one of the local freemen.

'I make it about twenty, all from Congo,' says Mabongo, one of the local freemen, in Kicongo.

Mande's knowledge of the language stretches this far.

'We came with fourteen, but two have sadly been killed by the Portuguese, so that leaves twelve. Rosa and her three have joined us, that is four more. That gives us thirty-six altogether. We can accommodate this number, but you will be sleeping on bare boards for three to four weeks.'

'What about the Portuguese dead?' asks Rosa. 'The Portuguese could take it out on the Tupi if they find them.'

'Rosa makes a good point about the Portuguese. But we must also think of ourselves. Farka, please translate for me:

'I need you to find all the dead, in the gorge, near the gorge, and by the longboat, and strip them of uniforms, muskets, cutlasses and knives. We want all these things. When we reach the islands, the uniforms will help protect us if there are Portuguese there. The muskets and swords may well help too. Then I want all the bodies taken to the long boat and tipped in the sea about the same distance out as the ship.'

'I want fifteen of you to come with me to the gorge,' says Farka, 'and five to deal with the ones here. Eight more can collect the ones near the end of the gorge.'

Mande repeats it all in Swahili for certainty.

'Before we go, who will navigate the ship?' asks Rosa.

'Any takers?' asks Mande.

'Nketi and Sousse are our most experienced sailors,' says Farka. Both Nketi and Sousse nod to indicate agreement.

'Great,' says Mande. 'You two can hopefully steer us out of here, and also help us ensure we can keep the ship on course for Congo in Africa. In storms, your expertise may keep us alive. I will use my limited experience to play a part in piloting. I helped Haram a lot with maps and navigation with the astrolabe on my last trip. There are maps with details of islands, of the rocks under water that may sink us, and other maps showing the ocean and Africa.'

'Lakoto will help you when you get to Congo,' says Farka, after translating for Nketi and Sousse. 'He will get you to rivers where you may get far away from the slave hunters.'

'Thank you. I think I could get to like Lakoto.'

Nketi tries to interject, speaking in Kicongo.

'Nketi says he and Sousse will work better without your help, especially early on,' says Farka, addressing Mande.

'Of course,' says Mande, his face reddening a little.

'I will help too,' says Rosalina.

'Excellent. Well you know, I learnt when I was about your age. It will be a pleasure to work with you.'

'And a pleasure to work with you. You know, you are like a father to me, Mande,' she says. He beams and goes even redder.

'Right,' shouts Farka, 'once the Portuguese are disposed of, I think we should prepare the feast.'

'I agree,' says his friend. 'Let everybody help, and make it a special thank you for these people. Not only did they save our lives, they are also giving us a whole load of food for our journey.' Farka translates.

Farka and Mande

During the feast, Farka and Mande get some moments together.

'It's been a fruit-bat few days!' says Farka.

'It was like starting to eat what you think is a roasted mouse and ending up with a porcupine. The problems just grew and grew, no thanks to Mtatu.'

'What shall we do with him?'

'I don't know what you think, but I don't think cutting off a man's hand in retaliation for him cutting off yours gets you anywhere. If everybody retaliates, as my great grandfather Felani said to my father, everybody ends up dead – and he had violent attacks on his family by the Portuguese to contend with.'

'So do we take Mtatu to Africa with us, do you think?'

'I am not sure. We need to stop at an island off Brazil. It would give him the opportunity to have a lot of time to think about what he did to us if we leave him there.'

'He may just die there, for lack of food and water.'

'He may, but in the end he will have the chance to make smoke signals to establish contact with boats, or to make a raft, or to find water and try to survive. Ultimately, he is not our responsibility.'

'You are probably right. I guess leaving him on the island makes sense.'

'I will just punch him in the face a few times first, because of Tulapu,' says Mande.

'I am with you there,' responds Farka.

'You have never told me how you ended up in Brazil, dear friend.'

'I think fate wasn't kind to me that day,' replies Farka. 'We lived a good life in a small Congo village, full of good things to eat. Sun shining, colours and sounds and smells all a delight, with one obvious exception – I had five siblings, all older. I had just had my puberty tests, staying in a hut for a week, learning from an elder, my uncle.

And then the ceremony. It's so embarrassing being in front of everyone at fourteen, while in your mind you are thinking you are a child whose body is changing in a way that you don't understand, and yet you have to play at being a man.'

'Tell me about it!'

'But the family all comes together with a big event like that. And of course, you get to choose your wife, if you are lucky. I wasn't lucky.'

'I guess it's a bit like putting your hand in the beehive; you don't know whether you will come out with honey or loads of bee stings.'

'Well, it was a bit like that. But I had my eye on a beautiful girl. Then of course half the lads had their eyes on her, and I wasn't the prettiest ostrich on the savannah.'

'So what happened?'

'I was asked to go to a village nearly half a day away to buy a cow, as the milk from one of ours was down to a dribble. I had a sack of yams to trade for the cow. The Congo is so full of fine scents, beautiful birds, attractive trees full of blossom and all that you may wish to enjoy on a walk like that.'

'Sounds amazing.'

'I am just on the outskirts of the village when three brutish men assault me from bushes at the side of the track. One holds me from behind, so I drop the sack. Another empties the yams from my sack and places the sack over my head. They tie my hands.

'The sensation I recall is the stink of stale overheated sweat as they manhandle me, and the roughness as they march me. It brings back my worst memories.

'Soon, they are lifting me on to a cart and binding my feet together. I sense at least two other bodies lying there, maybe three. One says, 'Fuck this.' I think that sums it up, and I grunt approval. We start moving. There is the constant bumpity bump of the cart on the track, and the constant fuckity fuck in your mind.'

'Ouch, you could be describing exactly what I felt!'

'From there, it will be much like what you went through. The sacks of slave bodies waiting in the sun with precious little water for the never never of a ship; and then when the never never ends, a new evil starts. The utter grossness, the foul stench of cess, the intense incessant pain, and the overall fuckity-fuckness of the hold of the ship. And after that, when you get to Brazil, it just gets worse.'

'You are almost as poetic as my great grandad is said to have been in describing bad things, except he would avoid the fucks.'

'I don't think about it, friend, that's just how it comes out.'

'Time to say something to the Tupi, I think, and then we might get our heads down, if we are loading up first thing.'

'I agree.'

Mande speaks first In Tupi: 'You responded to our call for help. You came quickly, you came prepared, you came with all the guile and cunning and skill that has kept you alive and strong in all the time you have shared the forest with magnificent animals, extraordinary birds, and the unnecessarily gnashing and chewing fish and caimans.'

A cheer from the Tupi.

He repeats this in Swahili, and Farka translates into Kicongo.

'You showed what good people you are. We are soon to leave for our homeland, while you seek the right to remain in yours. We wish you every success in your quest.'

The Tupi cheer again. Translations follow.

The Congolese all stand up. One takes a block of wood he has fashioned into a percussion instrument of sorts. The drumming starts, they all start dancing, then also singing. The mood becomes merrier.

The Tupi bring out three flutes. They play a melody over the beat. The Tupi start dancing also. Their own very different dance. Slowly the two dancing groups merge, and blend, then copy each other's dancing.

It lasts longer than Mande intended, but it is too good to end, he says to himself.

* * * * *

'We will sail for the first island we can land at,' says Mande, as they pull away first to the north, to skirt the dangerous rocks near the coast.

He does what he planned. He walks up to Mtatu, still tightly bound, and punches him in the right eye.

'What the hell is that for, you?' squeals Mtatu, visibly shaken, and still in pain from his bullet wound.

Mande rubs his right fist. 'For Tulapu,' he says. 'A woman I dearly loved.'

And he punches Mtatu in the left eye.

'And who the hell was that for?'

'That was Tulapu's, on behalf of herself.'

'I hope that is the last.'

'If I hit you a thousand times, it would not be enough,' says Mande. 'But I must attend to my duties.'

Mande and Farka are looking very different in Portuguese soldier's uniforms that are a bit tight on them. Mande is even wearing the codpiece, a little cockeyed in both senses.

The Portuguese soldiers' uniforms seem to do the job in deflecting concerns when they start approaching an island that proves to have houses of Portuguese style. They quickly set sail again, and no shots are fired in their direction.

It is two days before they find an island they can stop at. They spend a week there. The lower deck is the main issue, and many of the crew are involved in taking out the rotten wood, sawing and planing the new wood, and laying it with resin to bind and to fill the cracks. Mande supervises it all, checking every plank, every join, and frequently sending back planks for re-sanding.

They also fix the musket hole properly, and the rail.

They leave Mtatu on this island. Mande has a final word with him before taking the longboat back to the ship: 'This is your chance to live. It is up to make of it what you can. I am leaving now.'

'You leave me with nothing here. You know I will die.'

'If you did not despise my Tupi people so much, you would see in wood an arrow to kill, a part of a hut, a fuel for fire; you would see in flint a tool for working wood, and a tool for making fire. You would know that the fresh water here can keep you alive. You would see the birds, insects and mammals here you can catch, cook and eat. You would see the sea as full of fish you can eat, and as a road which others will travel on. If you watch, you can bring a ship here.'

'Just fuck off then.'

'I think I will. You have had a better chance than anyone else in your situation,' says Mande, and leaves Mtatu nursing his wound in his chest.

* * * * *

For much of the time crossing the wide Atlantic, the trip is agreeably uneventful. There is just one storm that tosses the ship around, but for Mande, it is tame compared to what he remembered from his first trip to Africa. They are even able to enjoy an albatross that flies overhead, and a school of whales that passes by.

With Sousse's guidance, Rosalina is able to do much of the piloting and use the astrolabe, while she, Tsepo and Kanda very readily help lower the sails for a storm, and raise them again afterwards, with a bit of help from Farka.

Nketi and Sousse are able to head directly east, until a change in the wind as the coast of Africa seems beguilingly close.

'We have no wind,' says Nketi. 'None at all.'

Mande licks his finger and puts it in the air, then looks at the sails, porcelain still. 'You are quite correct, dear Nketi. Let us hope the wind starts soon, and we can move again.'

'How much water is there?' asks Lakoto, his brow now furrowed. 'This calm can last several days if we are unlucky,'

'Our water supply will run out in two days if we keep drinking like we have been,' replies Mande. 'I suggest we cut our rations by three quarters, just in case.'

'We can collect dew overnight in cloths hung over the longboats,' says Lakoto. 'The cloths need to be stretched tight, and should be waterproof.'

'A bit of sail?' asks Farka, joining them, and looking up at the sails.

'It is probably the best we can do,' says Lakoto. 'We need to collect the water at first light, as the sun will quickly evaporate the water otherwise. We can use a spatula and a bowl from the kitchen.'

'Great idea!' says Mande, with a beaming smile.

'And food?' asks Rosalina.

'I think this is more worrying than the water,' says Mande. 'Is there a way we can catch fish?'

'There is,' says Lakoto, 'but we need to make lines, probably from tearing shirts into thin strips, and sewing the strips together. We could make a line from each shirt. We can fashion my buckle into a hook for one, use the metal from the captain's cabin's clock hand for another hook perhaps.'

'Have you seen a sewing kit on the ship?' asks Mande.

'I have,' says Rosalina, 'in the steward's cabin.'

'All of us, when not fishing, must stay below deck,' says Lakoto. 'The less we sweat the better, and that means staying out of the sun.'

'I will tell them all,' says Mande.

* * * * *

A week later, the water is running very low, and they have only caught six fish, which has helped but has not been enough. More fish are lost than landed, as the hooks are not sharp enough and the fish are escaping.

'There is still no sign of wind,' says Mande, 'and we are likely to run out of water and food in two or three days.'

'We need to catch more fish,' says Lakoto. 'And we will have to cut the water ration to the tiniest sip.'

'Is that enough to get through the day?' asks Mande.

'Some water is better than no water,' says Lakoto. 'I will ask some of the guys to try to shoot birds down with their bows and arrows. We can drink their blood.'

'Will that help?' asks Rosa, who is now on the deck.

'It will not help much, but it may help keep us alive until the wind blows again,' says Lakoto.

'I will try to fashion a net of sorts from part of a sail, nails and a piece of wood,' says Farka 'We will catch more fish with the net next to the lines.'

'Excellent,' says Mande.

'I will help uncle Farka,' chirps Tsepo, coming onto the deck.

'We also need to drink our piss water,' says Lakoto.

'That's revolting,' says Rosa.

'It is a matter of life and death,' says Mande.

'I will suggest it,' says Lakoto. 'Perhaps, if our friends realise how desperate our situation is, they will agree.'

'That's great, Lakoto,' responds Mande. 'They will listen to you.'

'Mind you, it will only work for a few days,' says Lakoto, 'as we are likely to piss far less when we have a couple of sips of water a day.'

'I will make sure the children get through this,' says Rosa. 'Even if I go without.'

'I agree,' says Mande. 'I will go without for them, too.'

A party of five crew fires arrows at seagulls, and by the end of the day four have been shot down and fallen on the deck. Others fall into the sea, but none of the crew want to jump in and risk swallowing salt water, when there is no fresh water to take the salty thirst away.

They have a good meal of fish and some birds that evening, as well as some blood.

* * * * *

A week later, they have still not moved. Of those who survive, most spend all day hiding from the sun, suffering the deep ache of their fading bodies, imagining a solution that never comes to them, and resenting anyone that has the gall to speak.

The boat lists very gently from side to side in what small waves there are; their bodies follow suit. They are otherwise still.

* * * * *

They are feeling desperate. but there is the first hint of this changing.

'That feels to me like the hint of a breeze,' says Mande. 'We can but hope. I am getting more dizzy by the day.'

'It is a breeze, dad,' replies Rosalina. 'Shall we get up and adjust the sails to pick up any wind that comes?'

'Good idea,' says Mande. 'We are desperate now. Several will die any day without fresh water very soon. Ask Kanda and Tsepo to help you.'

'It is bad,' says Lakoto. 'Very bad. I am using the dew for those who are really bad, but there's really very little. Most are extremely tired and are saying they feel dizzy. A few are a bit disorientated. Nobody has the strength to fire arrows now, and the piss has dried up. I fear even Farka may not have long, he's so weak.'

'I will organise a bit of fishing,' says Rosa. 'A few fish may make all the difference.'

* * * * *

A few days later, they can see the African coast. Nineteen have now died, and each of them is dropped into the sea for burial after a few words said by Lakoto and Mande. Even Mande, Rosa and Lakoto are now weak, but Farka has recovered, after some fresh fish.

'Lakoto, do you want to look at maps with me?' asks Mande, with his slowly improving Kicongo. 'You said that it is important we find our way onto the Kwanza river, south of Luanda. I am with you on that, if it keeps us away from the slave hunters.'

'Well,' replies Lakoto, 'let us continue a little further down the coast, go past Luanda, and we will find the Kwanza river. It is perhaps half a day away.'

'We can dive into the fresh water and finally drink,' says Mande, who now finds every movement a strain.

'I can't wait,' says Rosa, holding her forehead. 'I am really desperate for water now.'

'Will most of those remaining want to disembark on the Kwanza river?' asks Mande.

'They will. They are all from the Congo, and even though they were all captured there, they want to return to the Congo. But I am worried about the possibility of Portuguese soldiers being around near the mouth of the river. We need to go some way up.'

'Is it that bad even here?' asks Rosa.

'Yes,' replies Lakoto. 'This whole coastline is a home for slave hunters, and much of the interior, so all the surviving crew wish to continue up the Kwanza river until we start feeling safer.'

'Very good. That is what we will do. But first a swim and a drink,' says Mande.

'And we all need to wash,' says Rosa, with a big smile. 'We all stink like a skunk.'

'Two more have died, I am afraid,' says Wal, coming out to join them.

They stop very soon after at last reaching fresh water in the mouth of the Kwanza. Most dive or simply flop straight in the water and drink all they can.

Mande catches a few fish with the technique his mother had taught him as a child, after discovering a shoal right by them. He tosses each one into the ship.

For those that survive, there is an enormous sense of collective relief. But they have little time to relax.

Lakoto quickly gets out of the water and climbs up the ropes to the deck. 'We must leave,' he says. 'There are Portuguese soldiers nearby. Fill these gourds and climb up.' He throws six gourds down to them.

'We two need to wear the Portuguese uniforms here,' says Lakoto. 'And keep the others below deck.'

'Will do,' says Mande.

They continue up the Kwanza river, and soon pass a ship full of Portuguese soldiers.

Mande breathes a sigh of relief as it goes past, towards the mouth of the river, while Farka starts preparing the fish.

Mande calls Rosa to come up.

'Rosa, there is a conversation we have never been able to have,' says Mande. 'But I wonder if you may now be able to have it with me. You have never felt able to talk about your home, and what happened to you, have you?'

'No, for good reason, dear Mande. It's a pain I never want to experience again.'

'Can you tell me a little?'

'I grew up on the delta of the Okavango river. We may end up on this river if we continue in this direction. The delta is where the river splinters into little rivulets and marsh land. It was good in many ways. For much of the year, fertile, with lots of fresh fish as well. But for three or four moons of the year it was arid and very tough. We had to move closer to the river proper to get food, and to have enough water to drink and wash.

'I was seventeen and engaged.' She starts shedding tears, and sobbing.

'Take your time.'

'Well, you have experienced the shock of it yourself. You are happily tilling a field, thinking of your wedding just days away, and then, in a flash, your life is changed forever in the most brutal manner.' She sobs again.

'Take a moment.'

'I was beaten, and gang raped. My fiancé tried to fight them to get off me, and then tried to run away to escape slavery, and they shot and killed him. My parents were killed with machetes as they tried to come to my aid. My elder brother was taken alongside me.'

'I can see why you never wished to talk about it.'

'On the ship, the nightmare continued. The captain wanted me to come to his cabin every night to rape me. The voyage lasted about three weeks. I think that is enough. It doesn't get better.'

* * * * *

Twenty-four hours later, the fish all eaten long ago, they again feel they need to think about food. Lakoto and Mande keep their eyes peeled for a place to disembark.

'I think we should stick to the south bank,' says Lakoto. 'I see nothing but trouble on the north bank, where the slave hunters are most active.'

Suddenly an arrow flies towards the ship and hits Lakoto on his shoulder.

'Owwwww!' he screams, pulling the arrow out and crunching his face with the pain. 'Where has that come from?'

'I wonder if it's the uniforms,' says Mande. 'It may be rebels. He calls those below deck to come on deck, and pulls off his uniform.

Spotting a movement by a bush, Lakoto shouts, 'We are freed slaves, returning from Brazil. We stole Portuguese uniforms.'

'Prove it!' comes a shout back.

'I was abducted in the Okavango delta,' shouts Rosa. 'I was raped and raped!'

'I was abducted in my home area near the big lakes, tied to a wagon and taken to Luongo!' shouts Mande.

And each in turn shouts their story of being abducted.

The archer who fired the arrow comes out in the open and shouts, 'Take your ship a few minutes further up river, and you will find there a place to dock. We are all fugitives here.'

Mande goes to see Farka. 'You breathe still, my friend?'

'I dreamed of death,' says Farka. 'I felt I was dead. But the bits of fish kept me alive and then, when we reached the fresh water, it was a life saver. I have no energy, but I will try to join you all.'

'They seem good people,' says Mande.

'If they are not, I will eat them alive,' says Farka, and smiles.

* * * * *

'I am Kamona,' says the archer, as they come on to the shore and head towards him.

'I am Lakoto, and these are Farka, who speaks Kicongo, Rosa, who does a bit, Mande, who speaks it worse than a cheetah, and the children of Rosa and Mande. The others will introduce themselves. Meanwhile, I need something for my shoulder.'

'Take this,' says Kamona, breaking off a plant at the join of a branch, and handing it to Lakoto with juice seeping out.

'Thank you,' says Lakoto, wincing again.

'You may just survive it,' quips Kamona.

'Poison?' asks Lakota, his face grey with shock.

'No, it will just make you drowsy,' says Kamona. 'We use it so we can control our enemies and tie them up until we decide our next move.'

'I understand,' says Lakota, with some relief. 'You need to protect yourselves.'

'Do you see many Portuguese on this side of the river?' asks Farka.

'This is a very dry land, away from the river, and only we know how to find fresh water. The Portuguese don't like it here, partly as we always hit them hard with our spears and arrows, and partly because the land is so arid and they end up with tongues so far out of their mouths they look like chameleons.'

'Sounds good,' says Farka. 'And you say you have fugitives here?'

'Plenty of fugitives. For too many years, the Portuguese and their friends to the north have captured Africans in their villages and taken them to far off lands.'

'Don't we know about it!' says Rosa.

'But for now, just follow me all of you,' says Kamona, as he starts to walk away from the river. 'We mostly keep away from the river. We want those who are able to escape and cross the river to know we can keep them safe, so we move inland quickly.'

'What is this land called?' asks Lakoto. 'It sounds like my kind of land.'

'It is Kisama,' says Kamona.

'I like Kisama,' says Tsepo.

'But we are not staying here,' says Rosa, 'as nice as it is.'

'I think I have to agree, dear Rosa,' says Mande, 'as we need to head to the delta. But let us go to the compound of these good

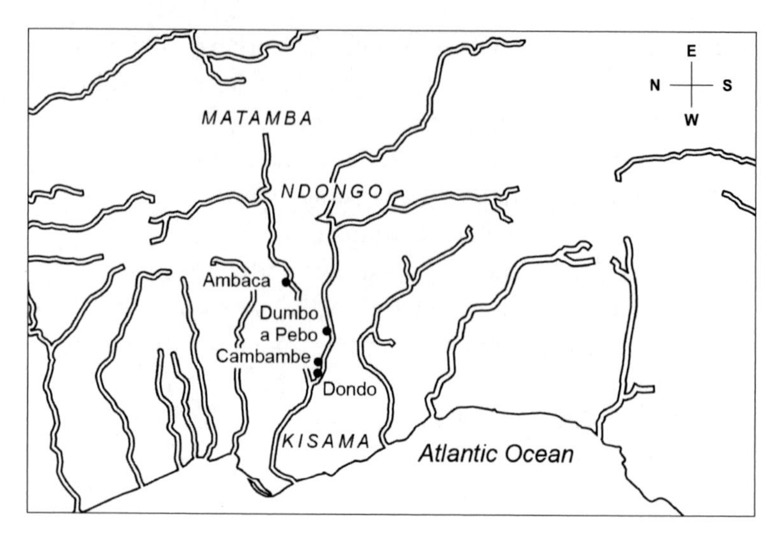

Location of Kisama near Atlantic coast in 17th century map. Kisama is in the south of today's Angola

people, enjoy some morsels for our very empty stomachs, get some sleep if they allow us, and then move on.'

'Yes of course,' says Rosa. 'And I guess any advice these people can give will be of help too, given how active the Portuguese are on the Kwanza river.'

'We can certainly guide you,' says Kamona.

'I will come back with you, Mande,' says Farka, 'as I must find my family, whatever the risk.'

'Of course,' says Mande, as a small herd of deer scuttle away a small distance from them, having picked up their scent.

* * * * *

The compound has a circular wall of grass, mud and straw, much as many of the crew know from home, with huts made with the same materials, and palm fronds for the roofs. Numerous men, women and children are milling round, variously cleaning, preparing food, cooking and chopping wood. Kamona smiles at them broadly as he invites the newcomers in.

'The smell of cooking is beautiful on an empty stomach,' says Farka.

'Let me find you some bread and water,' says Kamona, 'as we will not be eating a meal together for a while yet.'

Children of different ages come and stare at them, and are particularly curious about Mande.

'Why are you not Black?' asks a cheeky, scrawny ebony five-year-old, looking at Mande with a cheeky glint in his eye. Farka translates for Mande.

'I have an African father and a mother from across the great water, who has copper brown skin,' says Mande.

'Did you swim across the great water?' asks an equally ebony six year old with a game leg.

'No,' says Mande, unable to contain a laugh, as Farka translates. 'We had a big boat and sailed here.'

'Why do you have a weird leg like mine?' asks the six year old.

'I had my foot chopped off by a bad white man,' replies Mande.

'I was born with mine,' says the boy. 'It grew up with me.'

And the boy bent down and stroked Mande's foot affectionately.

'I grew down with mine,' says Mande, realising this is the first time he is able to talk about his foot without awkwardness.

* * * * *

Soon after dawn, having fed and slept well, Farka, Mande, Rosa, Rosalina, Kanda and Tsepo ask to be taken back to the ship.

'You should sail until midday,' says Kamona, 'then look for a place to dock where you now have jungle on either side. This will give you cover. Beware hippos in the water round there, though, they may tip you over. If you walk for a day from that point on this side of the river, you should then be away from the Portuguese.'

Mande, Rosa, Kanda, Rosalina, Tsepo and Farka bid farewell to the nine others who are staying.

'Lakoto, I cannot thank you enough,' says Mande. 'Without you we would not have got through the water-less time. We would all have perished so close to the African coast.'

'You are kind, Mande,' replies Lakoto. 'But you were the lion that fought off the Portuguese wolves who sought to sabotage this whole voyage. Without you, I would not again be under my beloved African sun. I would be in Brazil.'

* * * * *

At the ship, Farka asks simply to be taken across to the other bank, and they sail across and briefly anchor again.

Farka and Mande embrace.

I guess this will be the parting of the banana skin from the banana for me and you,' says Farka.

'I will be the banana inside,' quips Mande.

'No, I bags that privilege,' counters Farka.

'Farka, my friend of many years, let us embrace. I am very grateful to have had you by my side all these moons. You have been a wonderful companion, at the Plantation, the quilombo and on this journey. You even fixed my Godforsaken stump, damn it.'

'I couldn't bear it when you were hobbling like a one legged stork on your temporary stump.'

'And you worked so hard when I was too ill to work after that axeman.'

'You would have done the same for me.'

'And remember, you turned into this brave warrior when we were faced with an attack by those soldiers at our last quilombo. I shall never forget you, dear Farka.'

'I shall miss your bravery, too. You were the tower of strength who got us out of the plantation to the quilombo, who took a risk with your life, even after having your foot lopped off,' he says in Kicongo. 'You then found the ship, fixed it, and got us here. I can never thank you enough.'

Mande blushes.

'I do hope you find your family, as you wish,' adds Farka.

'And I hope you find yours,' says Mande.

'We will see. There has been a whirlwind of attacks on our people here, so I don't know what to expect. The same is true for all of us. But I want to find a place to start a farm and live a simple life.'

'Take a soldier's uniform.'

'I will. It may help get me there,' replies Farka. 'Although it may of course backfire when they see my face. I am less than sure. I may try it for a bit and see.'

'I also hope to farm the land, but I will first see what my sister and brother are doing, and their children. I hope beyond wishful hope that my mother is alive. My father's spirit came to me many moons back. It felt like his farewell to me. So I do not expect to see him. But it will bring eternal joy to me to see my mother and sister and brother.'

'And Rosa?'

'I fear that hers is a story a bit like yours. She was born not far from here, but to the south, rather than the north you are heading to. I sense that she does not wish to re-visit that pain. Its intensity burns her soul.'

'I know the feeling well. We ex-slaves all carry within us an elephant of pain, and we bear it on the shoulders of a mouse. It is our lot,' says Farka.

They bid a warm farewell. Rosa, Rosalina, Tsepo and Kanda embrace Farka also.

'Thanks, Rosalina, for your great piloting,' says Farka, with some of the few Swahili words he has learnt. She beams with pride.

'I need to find a way to the Zambezi now,' says Mande.

'Do as Kamona says, and then ask any local you come across. You may need two moons to get there, but if the wind is fair, you may reach there in a few days less than two moons.'

'Excellent. Farewell.'

Mande helps Farka off the ship and into the water. He has a gourd full of water and the Portuguese uniform. They signal to each other one more time.

Around noon, with jungle on either side, Mande draws the ship to the bank at a suitable spot where they can moor the boat on a rock, and use a stretch of beach to prepare the longboat.

Mande, Rosa and the children then pick up the tools, two muskets, knives, and swords, and load up the longboat. They bring the rest of the gourds, and lean over the side of the longboat to fill them up.

Mande then takes one oar, and Mande the other, and they start rowing up the river. They wave goodbye to the ship.

'Your turn next,' says Rosa, looking at the children, and then at the oar.

'It's pretty here', says Rosalina, looking round.

For the first time, Rosa gazes around her at the lush greenery, the playing of sun on leaves, which is then reflected in softer rippling movement in the river; the bright vermillion, cerise, azure and cinnamon of birds and flowers. She is momentarily transfixed.

'Rosalina, you are a wonder. You are absolutely right.' And she turns to Mande. 'You were spot on persuading me to come. I thought I would hate every minute because of what happened to me. But this is beautiful, even more so than Brazil, and reminds of places I visited as a child. I could grow to love it.'

'I'm glad to hear,' says Mande. 'I've only known it for a few moons, before this trip. That was on the Congo River. But it was very special then. And this entrances me now. The more so being with you four.'

They journey by boat for many days.

18.

The Tempting Magnet of Home

As they enjoy the scenery, and with the river now calmer, Rosa asks Mande if he knows the song Ten Green Pebbles.

'Explain,' he pleads, and she explains how in each verse there is one less green pebble after one has accidentally fallen.

'Ah,' says Mande, remembering back. 'We have ten aquamarine chameleons. After each verse one of us gets to choose the colour for the next verse. So, we may have eight lake-water blue chameleons, seven amber chameleons, six emerald green chameleons, and in each case they accidentally leap off, rather than falling. And they enjoy each day singing ten aquamarine chameleons and imagining ever more outlandish colours for them.'

When they come to the rapids, Mande and Rosa look at each other. 'Are we really going to carry this large boat past these long rapids?' They pull in as soon as they reach a beach.

'We built a raft from the longboat when on the Congo,' says Mande, 'and I learnt how to make rope from twine. We tied pieces of driftwood to make the raft big enough. It was easier to carry the raft than the big longboat.'

'I can make rope, too,' says Rosa.

'Shall we make a raft, then?'

She nods. They find a baobab tree not far away and start stripping the bark for twine. Tsepo and Rosalina particularly enjoy this, and soon get the idea of plaiting the twine to make rope.

Kanda and Mande find driftwood for the extension of the raft.

The dismantling of the longboat is eased with the saw and hammer, and by evening they have removed the sides of the boat to leave the basic raft. They add the driftwood to the sides in the morning for greater width, and test its floatability and robustness in the river with great success.

Rosa ties a rope to the front for pulling, and extra ones at the side. They put everything from the longboat on to the raft.

With darkness falling, they settle down for the night. They have their new craft.

* * * * *

'Hippos ahead!' shouts Kanda. It is around noon the following day, and they have made good progress since lugging the raft past the rapids.

'I don't think we argue with hippos,' ponders Rosa.

'I think you are right,' says Mande.

'They seem to want the whole river to themselves,' says Rosa.

'l love them!' pipes up Rosalina, transfixed.

'But their bite can kill in a trice,' says Rosa. 'We are going to beach here and see if we can skirt round them.'

'Ok, one last look,' says Tsepo, also captivated.

But in no time, a hippo takes Mande in its voluminous jaw and tips the others into the water. The raft is left to bobble in the hippo's waves.

Mande scrabbles to find a way out of the fierce grip on him, but the pain is too intense. He is unable to fight any more. He now knows only pain.

It ends, but only because he can no longer feel.

'The hippo's got dad!.' Screams Rosalina.

'Get him out! Get him out! Shouts Rosa. Desperate.

'Dad, dad, are you alive?' bellows Tsepo.

There is a crack, as highly resonant in its meaning as it is quiet in its volume.

The hippo throws his ragged scarecrow-looking body unto the water, which immediately turns crimson.

His head more closely resembles a flattened egg.

Rosa, completely beside herself, runs to him and holds him close to her, with the water rushing by. 'We must get out, now!' shouts Kanda, pointing at another hippo right by them.

They scramble out of the water, with all four of them helping carry Mande, his face now indistinguishable.

They find a patch of grass under a large oak tree, just far enough from the water to put the hippo off following. They huddle together, Mande held in the middle, soaked to the skin, and cry until tears can no longer flow.

It is morning before they feel able to move again. But first they dig a grave for Mande, by the oak tree.

They take quite a long detour, through soggy, mushy marsh, to circumnavigate the hippo picnic, which is still continuing in the morning. They see two farmers.

'I will talk to them,' says Rosa, 'they may speak the language I grew up with.'

Rosalind watches her nodding and one of the men pointing. She returns.

'We can head off soon to the Okavango,' she shouts as she draws nearer. 'There is a tributary up here, and if we turn off in the direction we are heading in, which is south, and follow that direction, we should find the river soon enough.'

'Sounds good,' says Tsepo.

'The farmer says "just follow the birds," and this squares with my memory. Birds flocking from everywhere in the wet months.'

'I like the idea of following the birds,' says Rosalina.

* * * * *

They need to carry the raft more in walking across to the Okavango.

Once on the river they enjoy three days on the raft travelling with the flow of the river for the first time, as the mouth of the Okavango is in the desert, not the sea.

This leg of the journey enables them to savour some blissful moments unknown in their lifetimes, with singalong and whistle-along snippets of birdsong at every turn and the most extraordinary and abundant variety of colour, size, scent and shape in the beautiful flowers they pass.

But before they reach the delta, they leave the luxury of the river, and start heading north again, in the general direction of the Zambezi, pulling the raft.

'You are very quiet,' Rosalina says, looking at Rosa as they walk.

'It is unbelievably hard losing Mande. It is equally difficult being so near where I grew up.'

'Let us stop,' says Kanda. They let go of the raft and find a couple of rocks to sit on.

'Mum, what was it like being a little girl here?' asks Tsepo.

Rosa sheds a few tears.

'Mum, don't say if it is too hard,' adds Rosalina, touching her arm. 'We are all deeply upset, but it is worst for you.'

'I was a happy child here,' says Rosa, smiling through the tears. 'I made a friend of a bird. A stork. I would feed it each day, and I would just love its gracefulness flying, and the way it ate. It flew away for part of the year, but then it came back it came to me. I called it Quaw Quaw.'

'Quaw Quaw, that's nice,' says Tsepo.

'My mum and dad worked hard as farmers and fishermen, but they were always very loving to me and my brothers. They taught me and my younger brother how to farm and how to know which fish to catch. Catching was easy then. The life here was harder in the dry months. We had to travel further up the river for water and food. But we and all the other families had a big festival when the water came back into the delta. Those good months were always magical.'

'What do you think? Do you want to go on, stay here a bit, or do you perhaps want to go to the delta?'

'I think I want to go on. I must meet Mande's family, and it is probably even more important now that you do. I can come back if I feel I wish to return to the delta.'

'We would of course come with you.'

They go on.

When they reach the Zambezi, after two difficult weeks, it is a relief to use rather than pull the raft again. It also flows the way they wish to travel.

'The Zambezi is our friend,' says Kanda. 'But from what dad said it is not going to take us to dad's family home. We still have several days of walking before we reach the family home.'

'How will we know it?'

'I know it only in so far as dad described it in detail and described the area around it.' says Kanda.

* * * * *

Twelve days later, they are nearing the great lake. Kanda asks farmers he meets about Mande's family. Mentions his grandparents, great grandparents. They don't know them. He mentions the province of Bunyoro, a name Mande used. They point vaguely north west. They head in this direction.

For two days he asks many farmers, and they do not know.

Then he asks about Mai and Felani, his great great grandparents, and Niambi his greatgrandmother. At last, they meet a woman who knows of Felani.

'Ah, Felani the poet!' she exclaims. 'My great grandmother Nawal talked about Felani the poet with deep admiration. She saw him when he performed in Mombasa. She is long dead now, but my grandmother Zara came to visit your family with her mother, and she still talks about the fine story told by Aneni.'

'Aneni is another of Mande's great grandmothers, I think,' says Kanda, 'This is my mum Rosa, by the way, and Tsepo and Rosalina are my sisters.

'How lovely. My name is Mina, and I live just outside Mombasa.But I am very happy to take you to your family's village. I know the area a little from visiting cousins.'

'This is extremely kind of you,' says Rosa. 'Where is Mombasa?'

'It is by the great ocean. My family has for many generations been traders in Mombasa, from the times before the light fingered Portuguese arrived.'

'Light-fingered?'

'Yes, because they are only here, far from their homes, to steal from us.'

'I like that,' says Rosa.

'Where have you all now come from?' asks Mina.

'My dad Mande was returning with Mande's father to his village, after his dad was taken as a slave decades before,' says Tsepo. 'But when they were trying to reach here on the mighty Congo River, dad was captured and made a slave himself. This was over forty years ago. We escaped to live with freed slaves for a time, while we tried to find a ship. We eventually found one.'

Rosa nods excitedly at that point, and says: 'The children helped sail it to the great river to the west of here.'

Tsepo, Rosalina and Kanda beam with big smiles.

'And we have slowly found our way here, past the place where mum was born.'

'Where was that, Rosa?'

'The Okavango Delta. We got as near as the Okavango River.'

'Such an extraordinary journey, hard to believe. You know, for all the Portuguese like to think of themselves as great explorers, your achievement is greater.'

'No, really it was not so clever; it was a combination of a bit of carpentry and a lot of luck, and fighting off the nasty and dangerous Portuguese' says Rosa.

'Yes. We do not have a happy relationship with these light-fingered ones.'

'I can see why. My father told me that our family left the Mombasa area after a Portuguese attack that nearly killed my great great grandfather,' says Kanda.

'There have been many attacks by these war-like people over the years, I have been told,' says Mina, 'and a lot has changed in my short life. When I was very little, about twenty-five years ago, Mombasa was taken over by a Muslim alliance of Somalis and Turks. My mother tells me that, as we are Muslims, things were better for a while. But then the Zimba came from the Congo, and many Muslims were slaughtered.'

'Then when I was a little girl, the Portuguese took over, and there was again much bloodshed and upheaval. My parents moved to a place just outside of the town then, as it was so dangerous in town. But my father still worked in town. Now, things are a bit calmer, but we all dream of a day when the Portuguese have gone.'

* * * * *

The following day, they are approaching the village at the end of an epic journey.

'I cannot thank you enough, Mina,' says Rosa effusively. 'Do come in for some water.'

As the village is coming nearer, Kanda says, 'I will run ahead and tell them, so they are ready when you come.'

* * * * *

Tucan and Caua half-walk, half-run out of the village to greet them. Maira is behind them, walking slowly.

'Mande? No Mande? Has my soul told me the dreaded truth?' asks Maira.

'Mande was killed by a hippo.' Says Rosalina

'We are his children,' adds Tsepo

'This is our mum Rosa,' adds Kanda

Rosa embraces Maira, and Rosalina, Kanda and Tsepo greet them all with their arms stretched wide and tears flow like the Okavango River.

Maira and Rosa hug until sunset, siphoning each other's pain at loss but also at each other's heart's joy at meeting.

'Forty-four years,' she says. 'Forty-four years! He left me young and you find me old. It's so sad that Otapo couldn't live long enough to meet you, but you know it is many years since his spirit felt unable to remain on this earth and chose to move on.'

'Did he die peacefully?'

'He did, much more peacefully than much of his life was, but he missed Mande until the end.'

'For Mande, it was the hardest thing when he realised in his soul that he would never again know his fatherly arms around him.'

'He was a special man. Much loved here. And much loved in Palmares.'

'Dear Maira. Mande lost half his foot trying to escape to Palmares.'

'You tell me what I feared,' she says. 'The spirits brought me the pain when it happened. It wasn't the pain of death, and it told me Mande was alive. I was strangely happy to know he hadn't died. But it must have been a great discomfort for him.

'He did suffer, sweet Maira, Mande also wanted you to know there is a person who helped so much when we were trying to leave on the ship. This is Tulapu.'

'Oh my beautiful Tulapu! How is she?'

'She asked Mande to send you her love. She also asked him to pass on her thoughts about the Tupi. She feels that the jungle area they have to live in is shrinking all the time, and that Tupi life will more and more be within the world of the cuckoos, the Pink Faces, but without losing what is special about the Tupi.'

'My heart weeps at hearing this, Rosa.'

'And the worst thing was that she was killed by the Portuguese when they attacked us before we left. We were tricked by a blackguard, and she cleverly arranged for the Tupi to ambush the Portuguese. She saved us. But she died.'

'What terrible news you bring, Rosa. The dearest woman, Tulapu.'

'Her funeral was very special, and went long into the night.'

'I am sure. I will think of her all today, spend some time alone.'

Their hands fold over each other.

'My turn!' shouts Tucan, coming in.

'And mine!' says Caua.

'You need to meet my husband, my children, my grandchildren,' says Tucan, with a huge smile, her cheeks glowing, her silver hair flowing. 'The world has turned too many times since Mande was taken.'

'It is wonderful to meet you all,' says Rosa. 'It has been worth all the difficulty of the journey to be welcomed into this extraordinary family.'

'And don't forget my wife and children,' says Caua, also now grey. 'Don't forget them.'

'All in good time,' exclaims Rosa. 'I must spend many days with each and every one of you to discover what has been happening to you all. Let us allow the spirit of each of us to flow through us, and we can get to know each other.'

'And we must meet Rosalina and Kanda and Tsepo,' says Caua.

'And my daughter Anulka is looking after sweet Mina, who brought you here,' adds Tucan.

'It is like we are again in Palmares, climbing a pau brasil tree, or drinking coconut milk,' says Caua. 'And Dad doing his rooster dance at totally the wrong times, and everyone laughing at him.'

'Our gorgeous slightly crazy Dad,' chuckles Tucan.

'The best,' says Maira.

'I wish I had met him,' says Rosa.

* * * * *

The next day, the whole village comes out to welcome Otapo's grandchildren and daughter-in-law. A huge fire is lit, and all the households contribute to an enormous feast. Kanda and Tsepo, who had eaten so little in weeks, eat enough for three and regret it. Rosalina is more restrained.

They make masks. Rosalina and Tsepo particularly enjoy creating intricate patterns, in tropical colours. Kanda is content to be their model.

There is dancing. They improvise a new hop dance for Kanda and Tsepo to represent Mande's one-footedness, which everybody loves. They do the drum dance, and the rooster dance, and Rosa introduces them to dances from the Delta, including one where she mimics flamingos taking off into flight.

They all copy her joyously.

All the local villages come along two days later for a major celebration. They kill three cows.

When the feast is over, and the last neighbours depart, Maira calls Caua and Tucan to her.

'I have had my heart's question answered', she says. 'My life is done. My spirit is preparing its gossamer wings, my sweet children. It seeks to join Otapo.'

She shuts her eyes for the last time.

19.

Slippery Interloper Takes on Early Man

'We are losing too much of our cattle. We have to fight to get them back, if need be,' says Doman.

'Shall we organise a night-time raid, but this time with ten or twelve of us?'

'Perhaps, yes, but not yet. But this time, we need to be prepared for them fighting back. I think the Dutch are getting angry.'

'Not as angry as us!'

'No, but we need to think. They have been training their settlers. I have seen it. For this reason, we need to outsmart them.'

'What do you have in mind?'

'Their firebursts, which they call muskets, are not weatherproof.'

'Not weatherproof, what do you mean?'

'They cannot fire when it rains. So we wait for a good rain, and we go there with our weapons. If they try to attack us when we take our cattle back, then we start attacking them. We should have the upper hand.'

The rain comes three days later. Torrential rain, all day long.

Doman gathers all the men together, and his son Itoi. They head off in the direction of the beach-side grass where the cattle would be, but also the nearby fort.

As they approach, thc Dutch are lined up on the upper level of the fort, with their muskets at the ready. The rain is still ferocious, with strong winds also.

Doman and his men round up about ninety of the cattle, leaving just a dozen or so.

Van Riebeeck orders the military, 'Fire!' and again, 'Fire!' But the muskets do not fire.

Doman orders his men to throw spears at them. Two of the Dutch soldiers die and four are injured.

Doman then leads his men away with the cattle, and his son Itoi follows at the rear.

They make it back to the village, soaked to the skin. Then Doman says, 'Tomorrow, we move two valleys away. They will come after us as soon as the muskets are dry. They may try to kill us.'

At dawn, Doman posts sentries on the top of each hill. He then moves all the village's people and the cattle two valleys away.

Later that day, when a sentry comes to warn Doman that the Dutch are coming, Doman resolves to move one more valley, but to hide in a tree there with his best spear throwers.

The spear throwers are not needed. The Dutch return to the fort and tell Van Riebeeck that the Khoikhoi have disappeared. They even went into the next but one valley but there was no sign of them there. They weren't sure how Doman was eluding them.

Van Riebeeck contacts a scout who had lived with the Khoikhoi. He sends him to locate Doman and report quickly back.

Two days later the scout reports on the valley that Doman is in, along with the cattle, and also reports that Doman has sentries on each hill. He advises sending a small band of armed men, probably four, to go a different route to the valley, avoiding the sentries, and catch the Khoikhoi unawares.

Doman and his family and the rest of his small village are eating when the attack happens. Itoi is killed, along with Doman's wife, and two of his cousins. Doman himself is badly injured in one leg.

Doman sends one of his family to the fort to speak to Van Riebeeck through their Khoikhoi-speaking scout. He says that

Doman wants Van Riebeeck to come to his kraal to discuss peace. They meet the following day.

'You are not from this land,' says Doman through the interpreter.

'No,' says Van Riebeeck.

'You have come here with your strange skin, your strange ways and your very strange language.'

'Yes,' says Van Riebeeck, who cannot avoid a smile.

'But we will agree that you can stay,' says Doman.

'On what terms?' asks Van Riebeeck.

'First, we will agree because you have the firefly's ugly sister, this makes you strong.' And Doman raises his arms to mimic how Van Riebeeck holds a musket.

'You mean by this firefly, our musket? Well of course we have that strength.'

'But this firefly's ugly sister must be used with wisdom. He who kills too easily is not a person to be allowed to take life from someone. My son died this way. It must not continue like this. You need to use more wisdom and show more respect for life. In the end, we are many and you are few, and if you take life cheaply then the fury of the many can become your nightmare.'

'You speak wisely, Doman. I accept and agree that we must be responsible in using our muskets.'

'Taking this into account, you may keep the land you currently have. The rest of the land shall remain ours. There is one condition on this.'

'I am very pleased that your offer allows us to keep our land. What is your condition?'

'Our offer is contingent on us being able to trade with you on the same basis as other Khoi peoples.'

'I am sorry if there has been a disparity. This condition is agreed. My people will be very pleased that you will no longer seek to challenge our right to this land.'

'That is good. Now, the hard part is the cattle.'

'What do you have to say about the cattle?'

'All the cattle are ours, to be truthful. But we will give some to you. You will have thirty for every sixty we have, as the cattle are important to us, as part of our family, and play an integral part in our lives.'

'No, this will not work. The cattle must be divided fifty-fifty.'

'Well, we have given you land which is communal land, and is not land to be yours. I am giving you cattle which is part of our family. It has been part of our family through every generation of our family, going back to when our families came south to these lands. I cannot give you half. Let us agree at forty of every hundred for you, and sixty of every hundred for our families.'

'I agree', says Van Riebeeck.

'So we have a deal, and we can return to peace. This will be better for you. For us, we prefer it to having to fight with you,' says Doman.

'Very good. I will tell my people,' says Van Riebeeck.

* * * * *

In 1660, a ship arrives at Table Bay with one hundred and fifty slaves from Loango, Angola. More arrive later that year, making the total number of slaves one hundred and eighty-seven. The white population is not yet a great deal more than this, at a few hundred. It was to rise to six hundred by 1672.

Doman dies in December 1663.

War, 1673-1677

Gonnema becomes head of the Cochoqua after Doman's death.

'We cannot allow the Chainouquas to benefit from trade on generous terms with Blotchy and Beardy, while we face terms which are unacceptable,' he says.

'So we continue to fight them?' asks his brother Mannema.

'We have no other option, my brother. If we defeat them, we will be able to negotiate better terms with Blotchy and Beardy.'

'But as you know, we face a risk of another war with Blotchy and Beardy. Can we fight with the Chainouquas and with Blotchy and Beardy? What if they gang together against us?'

'We have to be clever. We know the hills, and we have numbers. They have firesticks, Blotchy and Beardy, but lack the numbers. With the Chainouquas, we can pick them off. We are better fighters than them.'

'Well, you are our leader. I will follow,' says Mannema.

A scout comes down from the hill.

'Bearded enemy over hill, Gonnema. Three of them. Firesticks.'

'Good, we will capture them, and gain some firesticks. Mannema, collect eight good men to come with us, with spears and bows and arrows.'

'Yes brother.'

They follow the scout and head over the hill. 'I see them,' says Gonnema.

'If we skirt round the brow of this hill,' says Mannema, 'and head into the little dip, we can ambush them as they come around.'

'Agreed, let's go.'

They surprise the hunters, who are unable to draw their muskets before they are overwhelmed.

'Take their firesticks and their jackets. Bottoms too. Tie their hands together and let them go. They can go and cry to their leader,' barks Gonnema.

The hunters are then allowed to go back to their fort in just their underwear and boots.

'What is your plan with the jackets and bottoms?' asks Mannema, as they walk back up the hill, on the way back to their kraal.

'There is a small Blotchy and Beardy trading post, they call it something like Sad Mannema Bay.'

'Saldanha Bay,' says Mannema, smiling.

'One day we may wish to dress as traders and go there. Not yet, but when the time is right. We have jackets and bottoms. We can surprise them. But, for now, the jackal is not aroused. Let us not poke his nose while he sleeps.'

'You are full of cunning, my brother.'

'In these times, you need to be.'

* * * * *

Months later, the scout comes running to Gonnema, who is outside his hut, having his hair braided by one of his wives.

'There are five plus four Blotchy and Bearded, leader, heading towards high hill with white hat! They have two carts and horse-cows.'

'Come here, young man. What is your name?'

'Doman, leader.'

'Named after the great man! Good. Look at my fingers, how many do I have?'

'One, two, three, four, five. Sir.'

'And with this hand, how many?'

'One, two, three four, five, sir.'

'Do you not know the numbers after five?'

'No sir.'

'So, say after me, six, seven, eight, nine, ten.'

'Six, seven, eight, nine, ten, sir.'

'So, next time you see nine men, what will you say?'

'Six, seven, eight, nine, sir.'

'Just nine is good. And a horse is a horse. A cow is a cow. The two do not go together.'

'No sir, yes sir.'

'Lesson over, Doman. You fetch Mannema for me. Bring him here.'

And the boy runs across the space between the huts. Mannema soon comes across.

'Nine of them, brother,' says Gonnema, whose hair is still half-braided and half-loose. 'On path approaching Eagle Mountain. We need sixteen good men, with our firesticks, and spears and bows and arrows.'

'I have learnt to use the firestick, brother, as have Sukhoi and Wakhoi.'

'Very good. We go as soon as the men are ready.'

They are soon heading for Eagle Mountain, taking a slightly circuitous route to stay out of sight of not only the nine hunters, but also any scouts they may have.

Around two hours later, Gonnema's men are close to the Dutch hunting party. They can hear the men's voices, encouraging a horse to pull the wagon up the slope, with what looks like a carcass on the wagon.

Gonnema sees an opportunity for ambush. They skirt round the mountain the other way, taking a good two hours to find their way past rocks, through bushes, trap and kill the odd snake, and get around the other side. There is a narrow sheep's path here, which they follow for a short while.

'Keep very low,' whispers Gonnema, as they come upon a set of protea bushes by the path.

They can hear the wheels of the cart and the horses. Gonnema waits for the right moment, then raises his hand. They surround the nine men and order them in Khoisan to sit down. Gonnema repeats in Dutch, and most of them sit, with their hands held on their heads.

Mannema spears the thigh of one who tries to run off, and Mannema drags him back, taking his spear out in the process. They spot an antelope in one wagon, with blood pouring from its mostly obliterated head.

Mannema takes his musket from Gonnema, who has been training it on the Dutchmen, along with Wakhoi and Sukhoi. The others are holding their spears aloft. Gonnema walks among the Dutchmen and takes all their muskets, which he puts in the wagon.

They start heading back up the track, with Mannema's son Wamnema guiding one horse and cart, and a friend, Makhoi, guiding the other. The Dutch all have their hands on their heads. When one starts taking his hands from his head, Mannema raps his head with the butt of the musket. The Dutchman whelps and obeys by restoring his hands to his head.

As the light starts to fade, they reach a small copse of trees in a valley. There is a gentle stream there, and Mannema allows the Dutch to get a drink, but only after his men have quenched their thirst. He orders to the men to make a big fire.

Gonnema, like his men, wears little apart from a grass skirt and a belt, plus leopard skin bands on each arm. He takes a knife from his belt. He orders three of the Dutch to take their shirts off, by miming what he wants. One refuses, so gets a thwack round the head with the musket butt.

Gonnema then hands Wakhoi his knife and asks him to cut strips of shirt to tie the nine men.

Wakhoi cuts and Sukhoi and Mannema tie by hand and foot, as tight as they can. Four are tied also to the wheels of one cart, and four to the other cart. One is placed on top in the empty cart and tied to its board.

The fire is now strong, and four of the Khoikhoi men lift the antelope down from the wagon. Wakhoi, having finished on the shirts, starts cutting through the thigh bone of the antelope. One by one, he throws each leg to Sukhoi to place on the fire.

They then fetch plenty of wood, stoke the fire up, and place the carcass on top.

An hour or so later, they are happily tucking into antelope thigh, in the light of the fire, under the moon and stars. Soon after, they have ribs to follow, so there is enough for all of them. They give the bones to the Dutch once they have had all the meat. They leave the Dutch to find a way to munch on the bones with their hands and feet tied.

As the fire dies down, Gonnema asks two of the men, Sinnema and Sandema, to act as sentries, and points to the top of the nearby hill. They head up there. He tells Wakhoi and Sukhoi to take over before sunrise.

At first light, Gonnema is woken by rain and also by the sound of the horses braying and the wagon wheels rubbing on their axles. All the Dutch are on their wagon, except for one by the horse, and are trying to wheel the wagon out of the copse.

Gonnema shakes Mannema, who wakes with a start, and between them they wake the others. They grab their spears. The Dutch have the muskets.

They throw spears at the Dutch, some of whom raise their muskets. But the muskets only give out an angry splutter with the rain dampening the spark. Soon the Dutch are all either dead or seriously injured.

Gonnema looks at Mannema. Nods. Mannema takes the knife to the throats of the two still alive, but barely. One stares at him with a look of dread. Not for long.

'He would have had a worse death if I had left him,' says Mannema.

'They gave us no option,' says Gonnema. 'They could have run home in their vanity pants if they had not tried to escape with the firesticks, but we would have been causing a greater risk to ourselves then.'

'We will need to be extra watchful, though,' says Mannema. 'Now that we have killed some of their number, they will come for revenge. They like to take a nose for a nose.'

'Who didn't bind the bastards tightly, and nearly let them get away? Mannema, Sukhoi, what's your answer?' asks Gonnema.

'Sorry, Gonnema. I realise I put our lives at risk,' replies Mannema.

'Silence from you Sukhoi! You are the dung-for-supper man twice over. Did you fall asleep on watch or what?'

'I will take responsibility,' responds Sukhoi. 'I twice put everyone at risk. I will eat dung tonight as penance.'

'If we are going to deal with these pink faces, with their dangerous weapons and their use of our people as scouts, we must be far stronger, sharper, quicker,' says Gonnema. 'This foe is very different from our fellow Khoikhoi, they are both lion and owl. No more mistakes, all of you.'

'Sorry Gonnema,' says Sukhoi.

'You and Mannema, as a penalty,' barks Gonnema, looking at Sukhoi, 'can take the clothes of the pink faces and carry them to our kraal. We can use them. As for you, Wakhoi, as you also fell asleep on nightwatch ...'

'I whip myself with sorrow,' says Wakhoi.

'Well, you gather up the muskets, and bring those to the kraal. We also need to find their gunpowder.'

'Yes, will do,' says Wakhoi.

'Will the lion and owl wish to strike us hard for this?' asks Mannema.

'They will. But let's go now. We need to prepare a few surprises for them, too. We will see,' says Gonnema.

'Will we get to eat tonight, after our mistakes?' asks Mannema.

'For you, two days with no food, for even asking,' says Gonnema.

They leave the Dutchmen to the hyenas and the vultures, take their knives, muskets, jackets, trousers and boots, and head with the horses and wagons, and the rest of the antelope home.

Two days later, Saldanha Bay

'You know what I was saying about Sad Mannema Bay?' asks Gonnema.

'You mean your weak joke about Saldanha Bay?' says Mannema.

'Yes. Let's go tomorrow. You me, Sukhoi, and Wakhoi, dress as traders. We have all the equipment now. You have good Dutch.'

'I maybe have twenty words of Dutch,' says Mannema.

'That will do. I have about ten. We can be Chainouqua folk who are here to trade with them. The replacement group.'

'Yes, good idea – at least I hope it is. I am with you. I will gather together some goatskins, cowhide, and antelope horns.'

They get Sukhoi and Wakhoi ready. They gather up the goatskins and cowhide, wrapping the muskets and spears inside, and head off early morning.

The trading post is small. It is like a small four-walled port, and there is someone at the gate.

Mannema says, 'We are Chainouqua traders. Can we come in?'

The guard says something in guttural Dutch, but beckons them in.

They lay down the animal skins as two soldiers emerge from a doorway. Wakhoi reaches for his musket and tries to fire it at one soldier, but does not hit him cleanly. The soldier bends over in pain, and Gonnema lunges at the soldier with a knife, killing him instantly. The other soldier runs inside for his musket but

Sukhoi throws a spear at him and hits him in the heart. Meanwhile, Mannema grabs a musket and fires it at the guard at the entrance. He wounds him badly, and he lies on the floor moaning uncontrollably.

One more soldier emerges from the other side of the building and aims his musket at Wakhoi; Mannema dives at Wakhoi and pushes him over just in time to avoid the shot. Gonnema takes a spear from the floor and in the same movement throws it at the soldier. He reacts too sluggishly at first, but then tries to duck. He is too slow, and the spear goes through his eye.

Mannema looks at Gonnema, with the four soldiers all slain.

'You know what you said about not poking the nose of the jackal?'

'Yes.'

'We just have.'

'We have.'

Gonnema has extra scouts on the hills from now. A village many miles to the north is prepared in the event a quick getaway is needed, and some of the women stay there.

When a few dozen Dutch soldiers and a similar number of armed settlers arrive at the Khoi kraal, Gonnema and all his people, eight hundred cattle and nine hundred sheep, have gone. However, the herds leave obvious tracks, and the soldiers follow the tracks until they come across the cattle and sheep.

Their leader, Hieronymus Cruse, considers that the cattle and sheep are a good enough prize, and so they head back with the herds. The cattle and sheep again leave clear tracks, this time for the KhoiKhoi.

Gonnema and his men follow the herds' tracks and catch up with the soldiers and settlers when they stop to camp for the night. This time, the muskets are too much for Gonnema, and after losing about twelve men he withdraws with no cattle and no sheep. This is July 1673.

The following years, the Chainouqas ally with the Dutch against Gonnema and his tribe. The war is suspended for some time, because a disease ravages the Khoisan people generally, causing hundreds of deaths.

The tit for tat between the two sides continues after this hiatus, with the sheep and cattle again changing sides more than once. But Gonnema loses more than he gains.

In June 1677, Gonnema says to Mannema, 'We have to go to the jackal and stroke his ears.'

'I fear you are correct.'

'But we will go there with our head held high, and we will establish trade relations equivalent to the Chainouquas. What the jackal knows is that we have been a worthy foe.'

'That is very true my brother. He will be much happier having you as a trading partner rather than a constant thorn in his anus.'

Gonnema sends messengers to initiate peace negotiations. The talks are agreed.

Sixteen days later, Gonnema, Mannema, Sukhoi and Wakhoi arrive to engage in peace talks.

'You do not want me as your foe any longer', says Gonnema, whose Dutch is by now fairly competent.

'No, I agree,' responds Cruse, whose Khoisan is still almost non-existent.

'So, you will agree it is preferable to agree trade terms with us equivalent to the Chainouquas, rather than to fight with us eternally. If you do agree these terms, we will agree to cease waging war with you.'

'What you say is interesting,' says Cruse, 'but it is not quite what is needed for peace. We need some horns on the sheep that you offer.'

'What horns do you need?'

'The war you have waged has been costly for us. We need fifty head of cattle each year.'

'Ten head.'

'Thirty head is our final offer, if you want peace.'

'Agreed.'

'And we need you to promise to cease stealing back our livestock.'

'No, I will agree to promise to cease taking back *our* livestock.'

'That will do. And you must punish those of your people who take cattle from us.'

'We will punish on our terms.'

'No, on Dutch legal terms.'

'We will punish on the most appropriate terms, whether these are Khoisan or Dutch.'

'Agreed.'

'Well. I think we are all agreed.'

'On this basis, if I put my signature to this agreement, and you add a cross with your blood, then the war is officially over.'

'And so be it.'

'And let me say, Gonnema, that you are a skilful man of war. If I need to fight other tribes in Africa, I will want you by my side.'

'Perhaps,' says Gonnema, 'but for this to happen you will need to return all our cattle and all our sheep.'

Farka and family abducted

'No!' screams Farka, as he becomes aware that the blow is about to fall. His children barely have time to look up before they are also whisked into a cart. Farka has been knocked out, and lies there, a thug trussing him head to toe. His wife Watuso soon follows, and the boys Kwane and Bete are tied too, but less tightly.

When Farka wakes he feels he would prefer to stay unconscious. He cannot believe this can be happening again.

By nightfall they are put in chains and left with a thousand other slaves at the dock in Luango.

20.

Free Slave Community in South Africa

The ship is sailing along the African coastline, awaiting a change in the wind to head east. The ship hits something, it lurches, and soon it stops, trapped on a sandbank and holed.

The slaves discuss running for it, but the soldiers have their muskets trained on them continuously. At night there is a change of shift.

Another ship comes by after a couple of days, with a Dutch flag. They fire shots in the air to show they are armed.

Some of the Portuguese soldiers come out, to see if they can battle the Dutch vessel, but noticing all the armed Dutch slave traders with their muskets and cannons trained on them, they surrender.

* * * * *

The Dutch take half the slaves on board, including Farka and his family. Farka is struck that the majority of the slaves seem to be children. They put them in the hold, still chained up. They leave the other half of the slaves with the Portuguese soldiers in the expectation that they will be picked up by the next Portuguese ship sailing for India.

They sail for three to four days skirting the African coast, until reaching Cape Town, and drop anchor there. As the slave traders head ashore with a long boat they are greeted by the Dutch governor and a few soldiers.

The slaves are bundled out and handed over to the Dutch soldiers, who take them to the fort. There are two hundred of them.

Farka looks at his wife. They are in a dungeon, crushed together with dozens of others. More of them are in the dungeon next door.

'What foul nastiness is this, my love?'

'Is there anything to distinguish their nastinesses?' she answers.

Sleep is impossible, half upright, chains everywhere, desperate to piss, but tiredness has its way in the end. Farka finds himself no less able to be enthused about waking up the next morning.

The plus comes when a soldier opens a door. Light percolates into the dark interior. A gruff voice shouts something unintelligible. Repeats it louder. Some start shuffling upstairs, chains jangling. They all follow. They get to pee outside.

Farka, Watuso, Kwane and Bete are bundled into a cart, with an ox attached. The road is bumpy and uncomfortable, and the journey slow. They are aware of countryside very different from Congo's jungle and savannah. More arid, but also hilly. They stop near a non-African style of building.

A farmer armed with a musket makes them get out and takes them a short distance to a shed. Current residents are chickens and cattle. The doors to this barn are shut. They are in darkness.

Moments later, the farmer returns with some scraggy bits of bony, fatty meat, which he tosses at the family, and closes the door again. Despite the handicap of the chains, they grab the scraggy bits of meat and eat. Watuso makes sure Bete and Kwane get enough. There is a foul bucket of water nearby. Farka shuffles across, takes a handful of water and splashes his face. He takes another handful and tries drinking it, but spits it out.

The door opens again. The man barks an order, and then pulls Farka towards him and takes him outside. He beckons the others to follow. They shuffle out as best they can.

He points at a field, full of weeds. There are two slaves there, each with a hoe. He gives Farka's family a hoe each. He removes the chains from their arms, but they still need to shuffle awkwardly. He points to the other slaves and barks something gruffly. The two slaves across the field beckon them. One speaks a language they don't understand, but the other has a few words of Kicongo. 'Come here,' he says. They go across and he says, 'Do this.' And he watches them hoe the weeds, and then turn over the earth. They try it themselves. Farka shows Bete, and Watuso shows Kwane.

'I Shua. He Makatana. You?'

'I Farka, my wife Watuso, our sons Bete and Kwame.'

Soon they have the hang of it. The sun is beating down, they are hoeing. It might be bearable if not for the hateful chains.

At night, the farmer, a burly man with short blond hair and wide shoulders, comes for Watuso. She screams, and he thumps her in the face. Farka tries to reach for her, but the farmer thumps him.

Shua says, 'Do nothing. Cry silently.'

Farka and the boys can still hear her screams an hour later. Farka feels his anger boiling up.

From this time, Watuso's cheery personality gives way to a silent, withdrawn sadness. She smiles wanly when Bete and Kwame seek assurance. But she has lost all her spark.

The next few weeks, they hoe each day in silence. They finish one field and start another.

Farka knows that they cannot stay with a farmer who rapes his wife every night. He says to Watuso one morning, after she has returned, 'One day we will run for it. Maybe when the boys are a year older, and stronger.'

She looks at him and nods. She remains a shadow of herself.

* * * * *

A year on, Farka and Watuso put a bit of food away each day. They wrap it in a few large leaves they take from a local tree. They have a bit of a store now. It is summer, the best time of year to face nights out in the open.

One night, Farka says to Watuso, 'In the morning. Do you agree?'

She nods.

They head off before dawn, thinking they should have an hour's head start to get away from the farm before the farmer is aware that they have gone. They grab two hoes and half-hobble, half-jog, with the chains severely limiting them.

After a while, when they are at the top of a hill, with the farm some way below them, they hear dogs barking. They keep low and crawl over the other side of the hill and roll down as best they can. Bete and Kwame are the most adept, and Watuso and Farka try to copy them.

There is another farm in the next valley. They skirt round this as best they can. When they come into a small wood a little further on, they try hacking at the chain lock with the hoe. They manage to get Bete's and Kwane's chains off but decide they must keep going for now. The barking gets louder.

Bete and Kwane are now able to go ahead and look for hazards, like pointed stakes, or animal traps. The barking gets louder.

They head over a second hill past the neighbour's farm. In the valley on the other side of this is woodland. They look for fox holes or other possible hiding places. Farka finds a large stake.

As one dog approaches them the boys have now gone ahead. Watuso holds the dog at bay with her hoe, and Farka gives it a mighty thwack with the large stake. They do the same with the second dog, which follows shortly behind.

They venture up through the wood. In the distance are men's voices, they can't tell how near, but they sense that they will be caught up because of their chains.

Farka finds a good-sized rock and now smashes five times into Watuso's chain lock with this rock, and she get free. There is now just his. Watuso cannot break him free, so they go on. They still hear the voices in the distance.

They now cross some open land with some bushes with pretty flowers they do not recognise. There is a baobab tree ahead, and Watuso asks Bete to climb it and look back.

'They are just coming out of the wood now,' he says.

They go on. Watuso is attaching twine she has collected en route around large leaves, so that the leaves can be worn on their feet like socks.

There is another wood ahead, and Farka sees it as their possible salvation.

'If we can find a hiding place, we may get away from them. Failure is not an option.'

Watuso gives the leaf socks to Bete and Kwame, and they slip them on their feet the best they can. She puts them on herself and tries to get one on one of Farka's feet. She succeeds, but she worries that the dragging of the chain may give them away.

The men behind are visible in the distance when they enter the wood. The boys are sent ahead to find a hiding place, preferably well off to the side where their pursuers may least suspect.

A few minutes later, a bird call, three times. It is a way downhill from the track they are following. They head down there, Kwame following. Watuso walks behind Farka, ruffling up leaves so that the dragging of the chain shows less.

Bete has found a deep hole where a large old tree has been uprooted by a storm. Kwame joins them.

They quickly break off some low-slung branches from neighbouring trees, and they cover the hole with these branches and climb in.

They are holding their breath. The men soon enter the wood and are following on the track that they themselves had used. They sound worryingly near as they shout what seem to be expletives, and seem at one point almost upon them. Watuso worries whether their tracks are still visible.

Kwame wants to sneeze. Watuso realises and holds his nose. His face goes red like he is fit to explode, but the moment passes. The voices are still nearby.

Gradually, the voices recede. 'They will need to come back,' says Farka. 'Let's stay here.'

They eat their food. Bete and Kwame wolf it down. The wait still seems like forever. The boys drift off to sleep.

Eventually, some voices again. As before, they hold their breath while the voices seem dangerously near. Again, the voices recede little by little.

An owl hoots, causing Farka to jump. Only when there are no sounds apart from birds does Farka peek his head through a branch. He cannot see anyone. He asks Bete to peek out the other side. He gives the all-clear.

They creep out. But even now they are wary, as Farka's chains still make a noise.

They inch forward. Their confidence grows. They hear a stream, and venture down to it for water. Farka picks up a rock and find a fixed rock by the stream. He puts the chain lock on the fixed rock and gives it several thwacks with his rock. No change. He begins to think it just won't happen.

He has another go, five hefty whacks. It finally gives, and he is free. They all smile.

They head on their way.

* * * * *

There is a sound. A man. A Black man, but with clothes like the Portuguese in Luanda. With musket by his side and standing by a track.

They stop and draw back a little. They do not know what to think.

They have just come out of a particularly large wood, and are on a wider track than usual, which has distinct ruts where a cart has been when muddy.

Farka says, 'I will go ahead. I want you all to go back into the wood.'

'No, we are staying here,' says Watuso.

Farka holds his hands up to signal surrender and walks solely forward.

The man says something with click sounds in his voice. Farka has heard something similar from one of the slaves on the farm, but he does not understand. The man tries another language. Again, Farka looks blankly. The man says in Swahili, 'Friend, not foe.'

The musket remains at the man's side.

'Can you help us?' asks Farka, in Swahili.

'I have very little Swahili.' He points to Farka's feet. 'Your ankles. Ex-slave. I can help.'

'Is there somewhere ex-slaves can be safe?'

'New. Free slaves. Good,' says the man.

'I am Farka,' he says, wondering if there may be something like a quilombo here.

'I am Mahotalese. Call me Ley-se.'

Farka calls the others to come.

'This is Watuso, and these young men are Bete and Kwame. They speak Kicongo but very little Swahili.'

'You will meet men who speak Kicongo. We must walk one and a half days, then take a boat. Eyes always here.' He points to the back of his head.

Farka explains to Watuso, Bete and Kwame.

'It is good news, but we will have to take it slowly,' says Watuso.

'Will we find somewhere to live?' asks Kwame, excitedly.

'With no slave master?' adds Bete.

'We have some little scraps of hope. As we get nearer, the scraps may become a chicken's leg of hope, we will see. We first have to travel through land where people may want to harm us.'

'For me, it will be a whole chicken of hope,' says Bete.

'Me too,' says Kwame.

Ley-se strides ahead on the track. 'Slow him down,' says Watuso, who looks pale.

Farka runs up to Ley-se. 'Slowly, slowly, please. Watuso sick.'

Ley-se looks back and slows down a little.

Farka returns to Watuso.

'Do you need us to stop?' He takes her right hand with his left.

'I want to go on, to get completely away from the rapist blackguards on the farm, and their friends.'

'How do you feel?'

'I think it's the worst of news. It is a type of sickness I know from when Bete and Kwame were inside me.'

'No!'

'I fear so.'

'I find it too hard to bear.'

'Too hard for you is ascending a mountain covered with a sheet of ice for me.'

'I am sorry. Of course. That rapist's seed is inside you'

'We don't have a medicine man near, like at home.'

'No, but that may change.'

'Another scrap of hope for our scrap collection.'

'It is the hardest thing, I agree.'

They walk slowly, the terrain mainly a succession of low hills, some wooded.

As the sun starts its more rapid descent of late afternoon, Ley-se spots a springbok and takes aim with his musket. With its great leap, he misses it the first time. He reloads and steadies himself. Another comes bounding along. This time the shot strikes the deer in its backside. Ley-se strides over, pulls out a knife from a sheaf on his belt, and slices through its neck. He wraps the springbok round his neck, and they continue a little further, until reaching a small copse.

'Eat here, sleep here,' he says. Farka passes the message on.

'I understand that much Swahili,' laughs Watuso.

Bete and Kwame fetch kindling and larger pieces of wood, while Watuso hands over a flint stone she has picked up en route. Farka finds a good-sized branch to sit on, and another dead enough to burn.

'Hangklip,' says Ley-se.

'Hang-clip?'

'Free slaves,' says Ley-se.

'Very good,' says Farka.

They feast well and sleep in the open

The next day, after negotiating a few more hills, they head down a long hill and eventually see a wide stretch of water ahead. The ocean.

The track takes them to a hidden bay, with waves lashing the shore.

Ley-se signals for them to wait, and strides with his long legs to a cluster of bushes. He pushes two bushes aside, and reaches in.

'Farka! Come!'

'And as they pull, the others see a boat. Soon it is out of the bushes, and they pull it down to the water's edge, with Bete and

Contemporary map showing Hanglip (also known as Hangklip) free slave community in relation to Cape Town.

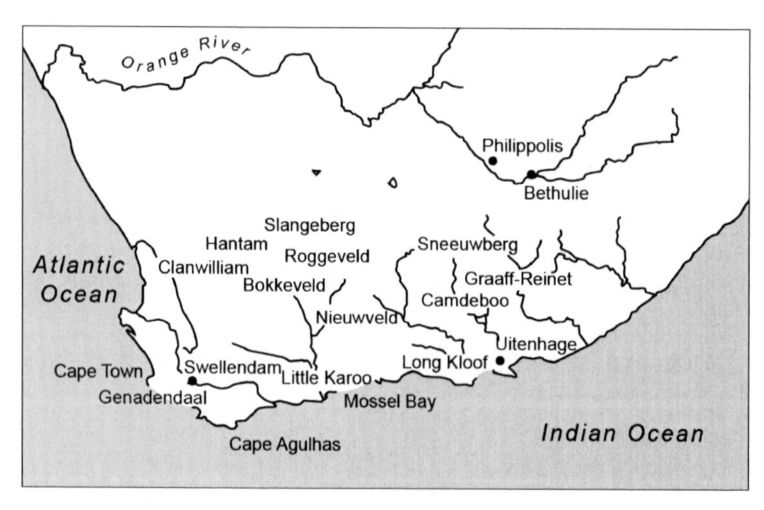

Contemporary map showing white settler communities including Cape Town.

Kwame helping. With one more pull, they bring it to the point where it is starting to float.

'Get in,' says Ley-se. Bete and Kwame help their mother in, then they climb in too. Farka and Ley-se then pull it a nudge or two further into the water for it to float again with them all in, and they jump in.

They now skirt the coast for three to four hours with the sun shining. Ley-se points as dolphins play out at sea, rising up and then joyfully diving again.

Watuso realises for the first time that the tall and thin Ley-se has a very pleasant face, which widens into a broad, full-teethed smile. He has no hair, and a strong forehead. His neck is unusually long.

Ley-se says, 'No Dutch now. Only five hundred Dutch in this land. Big country. Here ex-slaves safe.' Farka translates.

Watuso says, 'If a lion strolls into the midst of a herd of okapis, it causes mayhem far in excess of the risk to each individual okapi. The Dutch do this in this country, in part because, like the lion, they have a weapon that others lack, and in part because of an arrogance.'

'Your upset has not dampened your wisdom,' comments Farka, approvingly.

Eventually, 'Hangklip!' shouts Ley-se.

They see a cove and some Africans walking near the sea. There are a few huts further back from the cove, and what seem to be caves behind.

They row in, with excitement building.

'A full chicken of hope,' shouts Bete, as the boat comes on to the sand, and Ley-se hops out to control it.

'Indeed, a full chicken of hope,' replies Farka, who also now hops out.

The others disembark.

They hear Kicongo.

Watuso shouts, 'Hello, we're from Congo.'

The three Congolese men run down to the boat, and there are embraces all round.

Farka extends his hand to Ley-se. 'We are so grateful for your help,' he says.

'I will have a drink and go again to find more escaped slaves,' says Ley-se.

'If you want to stay the night, I can teach you more Swahili.'

'I will be back, no worry,' replies Ley-se.

'Farewell, good friend.'

Farka looks at the food that is being cooked over a large fire. Several handsome fish, plus pieces of yam.

'You catch fish from the sea here?' he asks the cook.

He answers in broken Swahili. 'Yes, always.' Then says in Kicongo: 'All kinds of fish, and also sea lions and sometimes a whale.'

'You speak Kicongo? My friend, I am Farka. Great to meet you.'

'I am Wakuu, very good to meet you.' Wakuu has a wide circumference, and a cheerful jolly countenance. He is ebony, and has little hair, now grey.

'So you have all the fish you want. Where do you get yams and flour and stuff?'

'A half day from here is a farm. Some slaves there like to help us, and give up some of their food for us. We have a meeting place. Then, once in a while, farmers travel back to their farms from the market in their main town, Cape Town. When we are very short of a few things, we lie in wait for these farmers, and lighten their load a bit by taking what we need. So far, nobody has died.'

'Amazing!' Farka looks around and notices that the cove is hard to access from the land behind, with high cliffs on all three sides, and just a winding path up one less steep incline, in between large rocks.

'Wakuu, is this path the only way for Dutch enemies to attack us here?'

'Indeed, my friend. We can easily repulse any foe trying to come down the path. As for the sea, we are quite hidden from passing boats.'

Farka then notices again the caves which he saw from the boat.

'Do people sleep in the caves?' he asks Wakuu.

'You will see why in the winter.'

'Is it cold?'

'It gets bitterly cold at times, yes,' replies Wakuu. 'But also, the caves are the magic of this place.'

'What magic?' asks Bete, now joining them with Kwame and Watuso.

'There is only one cave that is safe to use. There are many other caves here, each of which are filled with seawater when the tide is in. The sea comes very far in. The special cave is our secret. Before you can access the special cave, you have to pass a series of tests we set you.'

'What sort of tests?' asks Kwame.

'You must spend the night on the beach, and during the night, you will be sent demons, and ghosts, and ghouls and the spirits of dead wildebeest, and if you make it through the night, you get to stay.'

'There is no way I am doing that,' says Watuso.

'Nor me,' says Bete. 'I want to go somewhere else.'

'My friend Wakuu, this is not fair, you can see my son and my wife are petrified.'

'This is only my joke, my friends. You will sleep with us in the special cave.'

'Hooray! No test!' shouts Bete.

'Do you trust us when we are new?'

'You came with Ley-se. He is our best man. We trust you of course.'

'I am so glad we found you here.'

'But not my humour?'

'Not your humour. Well at least, not this time.'

Later

'There is something I wanted to tell you,' says Wakuu, catching Farka's eye after the meal.

'What is that, my friend?'

'I have the misfortune of twice being captured as a slave. The first time I was taken to Brazil.'

'This is uncanny,' says Farka, 'the same thing happened to me. Two captures. The funny aspect of the second capture was that we were meant to be going to Brazil a second time, but the ship was so decrepit that it stopped after a short while. A Dutch ship picked up my family and many others and brought us here.

'When I was taken to Brazil, we went to a quilombo, and I was able to get a ship to Africa, and back home to Congo. I owe it all to a great slave rescuer called Haram and a man called Otapo.'

'This is so strange, here by the Ocean far from everywhere, about as likely an armadillo and a parrot sharing the same experience. The man who brought me back to Africa was called Mande. Mande told me his father was called Otapo.'

'This is remarkable, quite astounding. Do you think perhaps this is the same Otapo?'

'Mande said to me he was from Bunyoro, not far from a very large lake.'

'Yes, Otapo was from Bunyoro. He talked of grandparents Felani and Mai.'

'That's it, then, Mande also talked of Felani and Mai. It must be the same Otapo. How wonderful!

'I mention this because I would like to go home one day. But I feel we have to leave here by the back door. The front door means the Dutch.'

'Tell me more.'

'We need an exit route that quickly takes us north and east, to the lands where the Bantu live.'

'I am sure they will help us.'

'I completely agree. You know, Farka, I am so grateful to Otapo for his role in getting me home. And if I am heading north from here ...'

'Ah, you want to visit Otapo's family further north? It's quite a way, I believe.'

'Well, you guessed the way I was thinking. It is a long way, but what Otapo did was to give me back my life, my family. No distance is too far to thank his family for that.'

'Well, I feel much the same about Mande. Even with one foot chopped off, he was a giant in finding a ship, getting it fixed, and piloting it to Africa. We were also friends for decades. I would happily see him again.'

'Did he lose his foot on a plantation when trying to escape?'

'He did.'

'My friend was hung upside down for twenty-four hours. He looked a fright when he came down, and was barely alive.'

'I just shut my eyes, but the sound of the axe coming down still gives me nightmares.'

'I get nightmares from seeing my friend hanging.'

'I will talk to Watuso and the boys. This would appeal to me greatly.'

'I will keep my fingers crossed,' says Wakuu.

'Not a chance!' says Watuso.

'But it's a good opportunity, we will see Mande, and thank him, and we then get home eventually.'

'Yes, but not with that rapist's deformity inside me. Nothing happens until I am shot of that bastard rapist's seed inside me.'

'Can we not move now and deal with that rapist's baby with the Bantus, with the help of their medicine man?'

'You don't carry that man inside you every day, with his retch-inducing stinking breath, the suffocating stench of his sweat, the hammer and chisel blows of his fist, the baobab branch of his thing forced into me, leaving me constantly black and blue.'

'I did not ...'

'You could not. You are a man. Just let me deliver the thing here, and we can leave it here, and continue with our lives without that reminder of him.'

'Do you think you may be interested in this idea when you are shot of the baby? It will mean getting home in time for Bete and Kwame becoming men.'

'Let us discuss it then. For now, we have good fish or sea lion to eat every day. Bete and Kwame are learning to be good fishermen. We have yam and flour. We have fruit. And the people here are good.'

'Ok, I'll drop it for now. Is there anything I can get you?'

'You never ask me that any other day, so don't ask me now.'

'Why are you arguing?' asks Bete, still dripping after a swim.

'It is just a tiny thing.'

'Is it to do with your tummy getting rounder?'

'It is rude to talk about your mother like that,' says Farka.

'But Kwame and I know that a round tummy like that means a baby. Two of our friends have a tummy like yours, and they smile. Mum, you say nothing all day and scowl like a frog. Are you not happy about having a baby?'

'It is a woman thing,' says Watuso.

'What is happening?' Kwame also now emerges from the sea, pulling sea urchin prickles from the palm of his hand.

'I don't understand why mum will not talk about her baby.'

'Me neither,' says Kwame.

'The farmer raped me. That means he forced himself upon me. Every night. This is his baby,' says Watuso, trying to avoid crying.

'Mum, I understand now why we had to run away like that,' says Kwame.

'I want to kill him,' says Bete. 'When I am bigger, I will go to that farm and kill him.'

'None of that talk here,' says Farka. 'This is a peaceful community. Violence is not always the wise response to violence. It can breed more violence.'

Bete and Kwame hug their mother, and she wets their heads with her tears.

'I love you,' says Bete.

'I love you more,' says Kwame.

'I love you most,' says Bete.

'I double love you most,' says Kwame.

'I know you both love me the same,' says Watuso, through her tears.

* * * * *

Wakuu is cooking on the beach and notices a boat from the corner of his eye. A few escaped slaves are on board, as it approaches the beach. Each looks eastern, he thinks perhaps

Indian, from one or two slaves that have come before. Three are bigger and blacker, and seem very muscular in comparison.

The larger of the three muscular men approaches Wakuu, and asks, 'Hey, are you the cook?'

'We are all cooks here,' says Wakuu. 'Are you new here? I am Wakuu. And you?'

'Bugis, my name. Where do we sleep?'

'There is a special cave amongst the warren of caves. You need to be shown it to find it.'

'Don't worry, I will find out. I am taking control here, with my maroons.'

'We all run it together,' says Wakuu, 'with nobody in charge.'

'That is all going to change soon enough,' says Bugis, brusquely, and marches off towards the caves, with the other two muscular men following him.

* * * * *

Watuso approaches a group of women, two of which are quite heavily pregnant like her. All have beads around their necks that hang over their breasts, and grass skirts. They are each sitting on horizontal logs that have been cut to lengths suitable for one person, or two who snug up together very closely.

'Can I talk to you all, woman to woman?' asks Watuso.

'Fire away, Toosie.'

'It is hard to talk about. But all of you have been slaves, so I am sure that I am not the only songbird here to have been savaged by a feral cat with a twig for a penis.'

'I was, every night,' says one, Safina.

'Me too,' say two of the others in turn.

'Once or twice,' says another.

'The baby I am carrying is the slaveowner's baby. After I deliver it, I want to give it away. Will one of you take it?'

'I have enough on my plate,' says Nkuti, one of the pregnant women, pretty, ebony, small, and wide at her girth.

'I don't want a bastard's baby to look after,' says another.

'Can you not just sit in the sea for an hour and drown it?' asks another.

'Doesn't work,' replies Ntuti, 'water doesn't get in.'

'I may do it,' says Safina. 'I understand your pain.' Safina has a friendly face, the same wild frizzy hair as the others, and with a small frame but a large bump.

'That is sweet of you,' says Watuso, 'just tell me when you know.'

'I may also, if Safina doesn't,' adds Chimananda, tall and thin-boned, deep brown, with sparking eyes.

'Thanks Chimmy, I am grateful.'

'Can we not start a women's army and attack the rapist bastards?' asks Ntuti.

'Nice thought, but not practical,' says Safina.

'Let's go for a swim, while we think of another way of getting our own back,' suggests Watuso. 'Thanks so much everyone. And in particular thanks Safina.'

Half of them take off their skirts and beads and walk down to the inviting gentle waves of the sea. The other half prefer to watch.

Reijnier and Farka

'Have you just arrived?' asks Farka, as a slightly bedraggled, tall bearded Bantu examines his foot blisters. He wears only torn shorts. They are standing where the waves are licking their way up the beach, just caressing their feet.

'Yeah, I am very green,' says the newcomer. 'Can you show me what's what?'

'Well, it's not complicated. We all chip in, fishing, cooking, keeping on top of the mess. Someone will show you later where you sleep. What's your name?'

'Reijnier.'

Farka frowns.

'It was my first slaveowner's name.'

'I am Farka. Have you had a difficult journey?'

'I have slept in pigsties, in cowsheds, under twigs and leaves in a wood. I am a runaway.'

'We are all runaways here, Reijnier.'

'Yes, but It is more complicated for me. My slaveowner Krugel kept beating me. And my wife. And then he started on one of our daughters, Sabina. He beat her day in day out, until she was black and blue. I suggested he sell Sabina rather than beat her, really to protect her, as it would be hard for me and my wife if we no longer saw her. Because I complained, his wife took a sjambok.'

'Sjambok?'

'It is a long whip, made of rhino hide. It is especially painful, even just one lashing. His wife lashed Sabina with the sjambok many times. She then rubbed salt into her wounds. Sabina was unconscious all night. We did not know if she would make it to the morning.'

'Brutish. Did she survive?'

'She did, but she couldn't move for a few days. The other slaves were angry about this terrible beating and made this clear to Krugel. He beat all the slaves as punishment. And this was all because she wouldn't let him fuck her. She was only fifteen.'

'This guy seems a monster.'

'So I went and assaulted him, then ran away.'

'Oh I see. So the authorities want you for this assault?'

'Yeah, they had dogs after me, and soldiers with muskets. That is why I stayed in mucky places like a pigsty, to mask the smell of me from the dogs.'

'I understand.' He now picks up on the pigsty smell.

'The tall guy called Lazy found me just as they were closing in on me, and he took me to a boat he had hidden away and brought me here.'

'Ley-ze found us too. He is a good man.'

'Yeah. I am just worried if I am putting you all at risk by coming here, as the authorities are desperate to catch me.'

'I think we should all come together and discuss this. It may affect us all.'

'That is understandable. Can I get a wash somewhere, and get out of these shorts and my thong?'

'There is a perfect bath right here, where the waves are lapping your feet. It has quite a tide.'

'Will be sore on my blisters but may help in the long run. I will go in.'

Farka and Watuso

'How are you feeling?' asks Farka.

'A bit sore, but if it's anything like with the boys I should be more myself in a day or two,' replies Watuso

'Has Safina taken the rapist's baby?' asks Farka.

'Thankfully, yes. It still inhabits my mind like a woodpecker, but give it time. I am at least past the worst.'

'I am chuffed that you are on the road to recovery.'

'I'm sorry that I have had the charm of a grumpy bullfrog these last months.'

'You must not apologise.'

'I can now start to see more clearly, with Thing out of my body.'

'And what are you thinking?'

'My overwhelming sense if that I must leave this land. For me, it will always be associated with the nauseating stench and the ugly warty purple thing of that man.'

'So, do you want to leave as soon as you feel up to the long march?'

'Perhaps sooner. Let us go in two days. I hope to feel more myself by then.'

'And what do you think about heading north, to find my friend Mande?

'I think so. As you say, we need to go north first, through the Bantu areas. I am not sure of my strength. Not until we try it. But if I am up to it, then it makes sense to go further north to see a man who brought you to me in the Congo. You never stop talking about Mande.'

'Ok, let us suck it and see, as the toothless parrot said. I will tell Bete and Kwame, as well as our friend Wakuu.'

'I think Wakuu will be keen,' says Watuso. 'He has met some new maroons here, and didn't like their bullying manner. He wants to leave soon.'

'That's ideal.'

To the north for Bunyoro and Mande

'Quiet, Bete. It is dangerous here.'

It is just after dawn. They have left Hangklip, and climbed the long, winding path up from the beach, walked for three hours, and are approaching the track that the Dutch use between their farmsteads and the market in Cape Town.

Wakuu is with Farka, Watuso, Bete and Kwane. They each have a gourd with fresh water. They crouch low behind bushes a little before the track. Kwame climbs a nearby baobab tree, and signals to them to wait.

They soon see an ox-drawn cart coming slowly down the track. There are two farmers on board the cart with a dog and two African slaves in a trailer behind.

As they go past, some one hundred metres on, the dog barks.

They see another African further down the track, who seems to be attracting their attention. The farmers stop and the dog runs after the African, who Farka recognises as Reijnier. The latter turns and runs into the woods. The farmers follow the dog in pursuit of Reijnier, the slaves remain in the trailer.

Farka encourages them all to start walking across the track, and they do so, but Bete breaks off and runs towards the cart, ignoring Farka's pleas and shouting at the slaves: 'Run away, run away! Don't stay with those rapist bastards!' He gets nearer, and shouts louder. But they look at him non-plussed. They do not understand Kicongo.

The farmers come out of the woods and move towards the cart. They do not have Reijnier. They see Bete standing near the cart and start raising their muskets. Bete starts running back to the group as fast as his legs can carry him. One farmer fires and the shot flies past his head. The other shot catches him full on the shoulder and he lies there writhing in anger.

Farka starts to move nervously towards him when the dog barks again, and Reijnier comes out from the woods. The farmers follow the dog in pursuit of Reijnier.

Wakuu joins Farka now and they run to pick up Bete, who is in great difficulty and losing a lot of blood. They carry him to

Watuso and Kwame, and quickly move away from the track in the direction of some woods two hundred metres away.

They reach the woods with no further sight of the farmer and find a small copse to draw breath and look at Bete. Wakuu hunts around and finds a baobab, and strips off some bark for twine. Farka has found some large mallow leaves, and they find each other on the way back to Bete, Watuso and Kwame. Watuso places the leaves over the gaping wound and binds it with the twine, taking it around his neck and under his arm.

'We need a village and a medicine man,' says Watuso. 'I am very worried about the wound.'

She places her hand on Bete's forehead. 'Fever,' she says.

* * * * *

The sun is directly overhead when they find a Bantu village, a circle of mud and straw huts with grass topped conical roofs, and a substantial fringe over the circular wall.

The villagers quickly realise what has happened to Bete. They take the family to a communal hut and a woman asks to see him.

'Nguni? she asks.

'Very little,' says Wakuu, in Nguni. 'Swahili, Kicongo.' The woman waves to someone and shouts in Nguni.

Soon, a man comes in and speaks to them in Swahili. He now translates for the woman, who is called Mahotele: 'Your son is very ill. The wound is infected. Mahotele is treating it, but he may not survive the night.'

The family is distraught.

'I shouldn't have told him about the rapes,' Watuso says to Farka.

'You weren't to know he would react like that,' says Farka. 'You said nothing all that time.'

A girl brings some food through, and a soothing drink of rooibos tea.

Watuso and Farka struggle to eat, but enjoy the tea and sheepishly ask for more. Kwame and Wakuu take the opportunity to tuck into the ostrich egg and roast gazelle.

* * * * *

Dawn breaks but has second thoughts. The news is too dark for the sun to rise.

Watuso has been awake all night, but is just drifting off when she feels the sensation she dreads.

She leans over Bete's body and wails; several women in neighbouring huts wail in sympathy. Farka is woken by the sounds, lifts Kwame up, walks with him silently round to Watuso and kisses Bete. As does Kwame.

Farka puts his arms around Watuso. He then lets go to kiss Kwame and hug him, and he then returns to hug Watuso.

Later in the day, they thank Mahotele and all the other villagers. Mahotele insists that they take two spears.

'You will need to kill game to survive on your journey,' she says, through the Swahili speaker. 'And it will give you some protection if you are attacked again.'

Wakuu thanks her.

They bury Bete before they leave. Watuso, Farka and Kwame spend all night squatting by his grave and invoking their spirits.

The walk is much slower from here. Their feet are weighed down by pebbles of pain.

One of the Nguni accompanies them through the next three days. They encounter elephants, rhinoceri, lions, wildebeest. Their companion advises in each case how to avoid being either eaten or trampled.

The giraffes are more friendly but are preoccupied with one thing: eating leaves on high branches.

Kwame stops to admire a weaver bird nest. 'I will miss this place,' he says.

The Nguni man instructs them to keep climbing up and more up to the plateau where the land flattens out again and then heads due north. He bids them good luck and farewell.

'This is much harder than I imagined,' says Watuso.

'It's just up, up and more up,' adds Kwame, misquoting the Nguni.

'We had no idea what to expect, but we can only hope this climb gets us on high, and then we stay high,' says his mother.

'Also, let us dream of getting home, and no longer being in this land of slavery,' suggests Farka.

* * * * *

A moon of tough walking later, they see the ruins of Great Zimbabwe. The mighty stone structures are still standing, but the city has long been empty, and the finely carved owl stone sculptures have long gone.

'How did they make such massive great walls?' asks Kwame.

'The legend is that they had very fine stonemasons, and great architects. No doubt they came from Congo,' says Wakuu.

'Congo?! When has Congo built any great buildings? These were Bantus, and they built a fine city before Zimbabwe, and will build fine cities again.'

'Very touchy about our great rivals,' says Wakuu.

'Indeed, he loves the Bantu more than us,' says Watuso.

'I have learnt much from Mande,' says Farka. 'What he told me made me realise that the Bantu have done more than us Congolese in city-building. We have done more, perhaps, in developing our music and story-telling. But in the end, we are probably all Bantu originally.'

'A tragedy for such a great city to become emptied of its life and soul,' says Wakuu.

'But is our land not a testament to the cycles of life?' asks Farka. 'The small become great, the great become small; the rural becomes urban, the urban becomes rural. The new chimpanzees who have entered our land, and who swing from one port to another causing mayhem, as though they were swinging from lianas in the jungle, may do well to study this cycle. They may not cackle so loudly with their cannons and their muskets.'

'You can be very amusing, when you choose,' chuckles Watuso.

'I agree, Dad,' says Kwame.

'I think we can just continue north from here,' muses Wakuu, changing the subject.

'How long for?' asks Watuso, wearily. 'My patience is no longer that of a sea turtle, it is more that of a fruit bat on heat.'

'Less than a moon, I believe,' says Wakuu, 'if that helps.'

'I think we may need to rest for a day or two at some point, before my fruit bat picks on someone.'

'Thank you for the warning', says Wakuu.

'I will carry you, Mum,' quips Kwame.

'You and whose camel?' laughs Watuso.

* * * * *

Eleven days later, they arrive at the village of Lenje. They stop outside for a long overdue rest.

'We have killed and eaten fish, birds and eland for much of the journey,' says Wakuu. 'I propose to visit the market here, to see if there is something for us to eat today that we don't need to catch. I will take two weaver birds to exchange for a bite to eat.'

'Be careful,' says Watuso.

'I will.'

'I will come with you,' says Farka.

* * * * *

In the village there is a hawker selling beads and ankle bracelets, and another selling ostrich eggs. There are two men examining the ankle bracelets.

Wakuu picks up an ostrich egg, and Farka nods agreement to Wakuu's raised eyebrows. He had enjoyed his egg meal with the Bantu. Wakuu exchanges his weaver birds for four eggs. They each carry two.

'Did you hear those two men? Speaking Portuguese?' asks Farka, as they start heading from the village.

'I did, but they have dirt on their hands and legs, and they are not in soldiers' uniforms. I have only known evil when I have come across Portuguese. I fear them.'

'They have a tool, as though they have been digging soil.'

'In the land of the pau brasil, they only had a nose for wealth equivalent to the riches of gold.'

'Zimbabwe was built on gold from land not far to the south of here.'

'So they are here for gold! That must be it!'

'We must be wary. If they think this land will bring them further riches, they will turn again to butchery.'

'And burning.'

'And slaves.'

'Let us get back with our eggs.'

* * * * *

'We have spoken to a Kicongo speaker,' says Kwame, as they arrive back. 'Bunyoro is north east from here.'

'He says we will find the Luanga River if we head between two baobab trees just at the edge of the village that act as a sentinel to the settlement, and then we head in that direction for three days. After three or four more days on the Luanga River we head due north, and head for Bunyoro. Then we keep asking for directions for the family of Otapo, Felani and Mai, until we find them.'

They stay the night at Lenje, and leave the next morning for Bunyoro. It takes half a moon, softened by the lushness of the Luanga River, which provides them with ample fish and fresh water for a feast, and a beauty that is as much a feast for the eyes.

In Bunyoro they ask many people about the village they seek, but keep drawing a blank in this large province.

At last, an elderly woman remembers Felani, who she heard perform poetry when she was just a girl. She gives them details, but also asks her granddaughter Niambi to take them. Niambi agrees and listens hard at her grandmother's directions.

* * * * *

'I cannot believe we have finally made it,' says Watuso. 'I began to think we would be walking until I died.'

'You will enjoy meeting Mande and Rosa,' says Farka. 'And in no time you will be very pleased you came all this way.'

'At a heavy price.'

'At a very heavy price. But we are here now.'

'I can't wait to meet everyone,' exclaims Kwame, excitedly.

'And look, who is this woman I recognise from long ago coming out now?' shouts Wakuu.

'I am Tucan!'

I am your father's friend Wakuu!

'I remember, a long long time ago!' Exclaims Tucan.

Rosa approaches, Rosalina by her side. 'Oh my, oh my, oh my!' exclaims Rosa, noticing Farka.

'Farka!' shouts Rosa. 'You have come all this way! Who are these lovely people you have brought with you?'

'This is my wife Watuso and my son Kwame.' They all embrace as though they are long lost family, which they nearly are.

Rosa sheds tears.

'Mande died, killed by a hippo,' says Rosa, still in tears.

Then Farka breaks away from the embrace. Heartbroken.

'The poor wee lad,' says Wakuu.

'This is Wakuu,' says Farka, still shaken. 'He came over on the freedom ship with Otapo, and wishes to pay his respects to the family.'

'Of course!' says Caua.

'I remember a much younger you, now,' says Wakuu

Caua and Wakuu embrace for a few moments.

'We must have many conversations about my father,' says Caua, 'as you can fill in some big gaps for me.'

'I would like that very much,' says Wakuu, 'as you can also fill in some gaps for me.'

Tucan, Tsepo, and Kanda also come out. Tsepo, and Kanda recognise Farka and embrace him enthusiastically.

* * * * *

Later, with the sun set, an impromptu feast consumed, the fire golden, the group seated in a wide circle and liquids flowing, Wakuu tells Caua and Tucan about their father's past:

'There was the time in Palmares when you Caus fell off a tree and broke your arm here,' (he points to his forearm) 'and your mum was distraught. Otapo got some wood to make a solid splint, and made up some good strong twine and planed the wood lovingly so it was straight as a giraffe's outstretched neck. He had Maira hold the splint while he held his breath and held your fractured bone in position and attached the splint.'

'Amazing,' says Caua, 'I didn't realise it was so hard.'

'You were under orders to not use the arm for weeks to allow it to heal. You ignored it, so it was forever at risk. Your father was always telling you off, but only because he couldn't face your arm being broken a second time. Of course, you were eight, so you were excitable.'

'I sort of remember Dad being mad with me,' Caua, says, a bit embarrassed.

'And then there was Otapo's dancing. With that sembe music that he loved, he would in no time be high-kicking and fast twirling in ever faster circles, unconcerned how wild he looked. This was even when he was silver grey and losing his teeth, when he was about thirty.'

'Thirty? Silver grey at thirty?'

'No, I jest. At sixty, I mean.'

'And the three of you were right scallywags.' He smiles at Tucan and Caua, who smile back. 'You would find the tallest tree and shimmy up Tupi-style, so high that you would scare Otapo stupid. It was so high that it was beyond an old man like him.

'Mind you, if your mum was at all concerned, she would shimmy up herself and get you down. And Maira would make a particular bird sound and a beautiful red and yellow songbird would come and perch on the end of her finger, and she would feed it titbits. When a bird was killed by a snake, and the hatching eggs were left in the nest, she crocheted a nest for the babies with twine and added dead leaves. She fed the little scrawny, scraggy, needy babies with seeds that she had chewed on, and dabs of cow's milk on her finger.'

'I loved the way Maira fished from the boat,' says Caua. 'She would lean out just far enough so she could see clearly through the water; she would align her hand almost magnetically with the movement of the fish, as it wiggled through the water. Once she was sure she had its movement to a tee, she had this flamingo-like movement where she ducked, cupped, and flipped the fish, and the next thing you knew the fish was in the boat. Magic!'

'But Caua, you learnt that from your mum, and Mande did that for us too, when we were in the boat,' says Rosa. 'It was magic when he did that, too.'

'Dear Dad,' says Rosalina.

They all come together for a big hug. Farka is so upset that tears are trickling down his cheek.

'I was with Mande when he lost much of his foot,' says Farka.

'Do tell us' says Tucan. 'We know so little.'

'Yes, Farka, I would like to know,' adds Caua.

'We were trying to escape with Haram, who had helped your father. A slave called Sando told us he wished to escape too. He tricked us. Otapo's old friend Mwesu, poor old man, was beheaded.'

'No! Dear Mwesu! ' exclaims Tucan.

'Mande had the front of his foot cut off.'

There is a deep intake of breath from Caua and a silent scream from Tucan.

'I nursed him in between my field shifts for two days, then covered for him by working doubly hard for two or three weeks. I fixed a piece of wood to his foot to help him, but he was in agony.'

'You cradled our brother's soul in his time of need, dear Farka. Thank you,' says Tucan.

'I agree,' says Rosa.

'I loved him dearly. As much as I hate that hippo,' replies Farka.

Watuso and Kwame hug him, as does Rosa.

They all drink some coconut milk. Wakuu drinks something stronger.

When they are all again sitting in a circle, he asks to say more about his love for Otapo. They all agree.

'Otapo and your mum Maira developed their skills as carpenters and ironworkers at Palmares almost as they arrived. Even though they were much loved at Palmares and inspired me and others, they were determined to gain skills that may enable them to return home. So when Haram came with his extraordinary news about his damaged ship, it was your dad in particular who fixed it up. Although your mum played her part too.'

'I remember that time a bit,' says Tucan, 'Dad was away, and mum was consulting her spirits as she was in turmoil about whether to leave her people or not. Of course, they advised her to come here.'

'I am not sure if you saw, but there was a ginormous hole in the side of the ship, after it hit a rock that our spirits from Africa must have placed there to sink the ship for our benefit. Otapo used all his skills to fix that hole and make it seaworthy, and that is how I came to be here. On the voyage, Haram was trying to wing it as the ship's captain, with you kids up on the masts to sort the sails in a storm.'

'We could shimmy up the masts as fast as we could trees,' says Tucan.

'Yeah, it was us that saved the sails when that crazy storm came,' adds Caua.

'Well, you were like monkeys on those masts, and you were only little too,' says Wakuu.

'And me and Rosalina did it when we sailed back to Africa!' shouts Tsepo.

'I agree that you all did great on the masts,' says Wakuu. 'It was a wonder to watch Caua and Tucan. But we nearly capsized in one storm. I think that Haram was not a man for a crisis. It was your dad who was the model of calmness throughout, and he got us through, I feel.'

'I've never heard that said about Dad,' says Tucan.

'Me neither,' say Rosalina and Caua together.

'Otapo, for me, was a great man. Nothing was ever too much for him, he would do anything to help. He was lovely at all times with Haram, who really valued his role in looking after all the freed slaves so well. As for your mother Maira, she also made it possible. It was her who helped so much by talking to the local Tupi, and getting their help when needed, as well as food for the journey.

'Let us toast Otapo, a great man!' And they all raise their half coconut shells.

'And,' says Tsepo, 'Mum Maira, who also got us here.' And they toast Maira.

'What about your journey Farka?' asks Kanda. 'The last time I saw you, you were single.'

'That is a question much more full of cracked coconuts than you may imagine,' says Farka. 'There is the good – the very good, the bad – the very bad – and the brutish.

'In Congo, I settled back in my village, found my family, which was very precious. Then magic happened and Watuso and I met. We had Bete and Kwame but we were all taken as slaves. My second time, so beyond the worst thing to happen, after being eaten alive by a lion. There was a moment of farce, when our Portuguese ship went to ground soon after leaving port. A Dutch ship took us to a place at the bottom of Africa where we were slaves to a farmer. He raped Watuso every night.'

'You said brutish. That's as brutish as it comes,' says Rosa, listening in.

'Yes. We ran away as soon as we could. It wasn't as hard as in Brazil to escape, except for the chains. We had a difficult journey, chased for much of the way, and with Watuso pregnant from the rapist. Out of nowhere emerges this miracle-working tall man called Ley-se.'

'What? Lazy? Was he lazy?' asks Tucan.

'Well, it was really Matuley-se, shortened to Ley-se, a nickname. And he was the opposite of lazy, as he worked tirelessly for escaped slaves. Either way, he saved us as he found a boat in the undergrowth and took us by sea to this extraordinary, secluded little place by the sea at a place called Hangklip. It was like an African quilombo.'

'No… really? Come on! A quilombo! South of here?!' exclaims Rosalina.

'Well it was run by maroons like in Brazil, so in a way, yes. As it was right by the sea, you could get fresh fish all the time. They stole other food inland. And the best thing was the enemy couldn't get you, as there was a tiny single-track path to get in, and we had a secret cave.'

'Sounds amazing. So why did you leave?'

'Well it wasn't home, and we wanted home. And weird Wakuu here had the great idea of coming here, on the way home.'

'And the very bad? I guess you don't want to talk about the very bad?' asks asks Kanda.

'You guessed right. But you can also see that Bete is not here, and that's been the hardest thing – by a long, long way the hardest thing – the whole time since being captured.'

'I am so sorry,' says Rosa, holding Watuso tight.

'I am very sorry too,' says Tucan, touching Farka's shoulder.

'You said you were also captured twice as a slave, Wakuu?' asks Caua.

'Well, I was captured in Congo and taken to Brazil, and that is where I met Otapo. And then after Otapo and Haram got me back to Africa and I rebuilt my life, I had sex a thousand times, but then couldn't find anyone who would love my paunch and my lack of teeth and my insecurities. I was captured again in Congo.

'It's gone a bit mad in Congo in recent years, many of the captured being young boys and girls, and young men and women. I was too old for Brazil the second time, but the Dutch bought me, and I was taken to the bottom bit of Africa, like Farka and Watuso, and escaped. Mainly, they thought I was too old and fat to try and run away so they didn't put chains on me. I sat on the back of a cart as it left the farm, and got a few miles before jumping off. Then I walked.'

'And are you now a dad, Caua?' asks Farka.

'I hope soon. My wife is expecting. It should not be long.'

Remembering Palmares

'Remember,' says Caua, 'the three of us sitting there with Mum and Dad.'

'Yes, perfect,' confirms Tucan. 'We played that game.'

'What's this?' asks Farka, joining them in the circle. Watuso arrives, with Wakuu and also Kwame alongside.

'Farka, you can play Mum, Maira. Sit down Wakuu,' says Tucan. 'you can play Dad Otapo.'

'If I sit down there, I am not sure I will get up again,' says Wakuu, making an effort to squat.

'Don't worry, Wakuu, we will borrow a friendly elephant to lift you,' quips Caua.

'Is this the wishing pond game?' asks Tucan, with a broad smile.

'It is,' says Caua. 'For the benefit of Farka and Wakuu, playing Maira and Otapo, this in the middle is an imaginary wishing pond. We each have two imaginary coins, and we take it in turns to throw a coin into the pond and make a wish. We often played it at Palmares as children to keep our spirits up.'

'Can I go first?' asks Tucan.

'You may,' replies Caua, as Rosa and her children come to watch.

She throws her first coin in. 'I wish that we have Farka, Watuso and Kwame with us for many years, and also Rosa, Rosalina, Kanda and Tsepo.' And they all beam smiles at her, and Tucan reciprocates.

Farka throws his first coin in. 'I wish that we all get home safely, and we never encounter slave hunters again.'

'Just stay here with us,' says Caua. 'There is much less chance of slave hunters in these parts than in Congo.'

'That is very kind of you. We will need to think about it, now that it has happened twice to me in Congo, and Watuso's suffered those rapes.'

Caua throws one in. 'I wish that Mande comes back to us.'

'Oh Caua. A precious, beautiful idea,' says Rosa. And tears flow. Kanda, Rosalina and Tsepo join her and all shed a bucketful.

Farka joins them, too, and Caua and Tucan. There is a silence, broken only by sobs. Eventually, Rosa says: 'Please, we must return to smiles. Let's continue.'

It is now Wakuu's turn, and he shakes his imaginary coin between two cupped hands before throwing his coin into the middle. 'I wish I was no longer fat,' he says.

'We love you chubby,' says Tucan. 'Chubby and cheeky.'

'I agree,' says Caua.

Tucan makes her second throw, with her granddaughter mini Aneni now sitting on her knee. 'I wish for Africa to be free of all slavers and all slave hunters, and free of all Dutch and Portuguese who encourage the slave hunting and foster it by buying them.'

'Hooray for that,' cheers Farka.

'Double hooray for me,' shouts Wakuu. 'They've done for me twice, and Farka too.'

'And a triple hooray from me,' shouts Caua, 'as they took my dad, and my brother.

Caua throws his second. 'I wish that we can go back in time, to an Africa with my dad Otapo not taken and my mum Maira finding him, and Mande doesn't get taken and doesn't lose his foot. And Rosa is not taken either, and they still meet and fall in love.'

'I love it,' screams Rosa.

'Me too,' says Tucan.

'Best yet,' says Caua.

Farka throws. 'I wish that Zimbabwe returns as a great city, and one that we can all visit to admire the artistic and architectural skills of the great stoneworkers of the past.'

'A fine idea,' says Watuso.

Caua's turn next. 'I want Grandpa Barawa and his mother Niambi to be still here, with our mum and dad, as we were in Palmares when they were still alive when we were young children, so we missed them.'

'Nice idea, Caua,' says Tucan.

Then lastly, Wakuu. 'It is strange what brings people together,' he says. 'I came here because your father Otapo saved my life and gave me another chance. What I have found is that all Otapo's family are as wonderful as he was. You are like my family now. I have lost my people in the Congo, but I have found you. That is special to me. I wish that it will stay this way.'

'It can and it will,' shouts Tucan. 'Why don't you stay as well?'

Tucan asks mini Aneni if she wants a go. She says yes. And she throws.

'I wish that all the world was like this game,' she says, 'and we could all have a wish when we need it.'

'Brilliant idea,' says Caua.

'Mini Aneni, I think you have done big Aneni proud,' says Tucan. 'What a lovely idea.'

They all agree after the game that Wakuu can stay in their compound. Also, after Farka talks to Rosa and her children, he, they and Watuso agree to stay in the compound too, once a new annexe is built by all of them.

But Rosa has one condition: 'We will do this as long as we make a trip in the next twelve months to the Delta, to the place where I enjoyed my childhood.'

'I would love to do this,' says Farka. 'But we must just be sure that there is no risk of encountering slave hunters. I could not face Kwame being taken. If that can be resolved, we can all go, and maybe others from here.'

'Count me in,' says Caua.

'Me too,' says Tucan. 'I would love to go to the Delta.'

Gonnema and Mannema

'They tricked us,' says Gonnema. 'No more war, they agreed. Leave things as they are, they said. And then they take our land here and take our land there.'

'And take our land everywhere.'

'We have lost so much, but we cannot any longer lead our people into battle against their guns.'

'No we can't. Like sea lions to the slaughter.'

'We have to move to new, barren land. It will not be the life we had.'

'We will have to travel more for water.'

'We will have to travel more for food, for everything.'

'Because we love the land too much.'

'And because we would not give in to the false God of Dutch goods and Dutch money.'

'It is a bad time for the khoikhoi. We have to work for a time when we may rise again.'

'We always have done.'

'We will do so again.'

21.

The End of Palmares

'There is a messenger at the door, Zumbi.'

'Do you trust him, Manu?'

'I do. His face is full of fear, so much so you can smell it.'

'Send him to me.'

'Sir, there is Portuguese army heading here,' says the messenger. 'Fully armed. I fear they plan to destroy Palmares.'

'What makes you say that?'

'It is a large army, with horses, muskets, swords. They are heading directly for Palmares.'

'Thank you, we must take action. Manu, bring me forty free men and women, as quickly as possible.'

Zumbi has only recently become leader of Palmares. He has a strong high brow, a long face, and jutting jaw. He is tall and wiry, but muscular. He looks like he has come through many battles, and probably has. Palmares has been under threat from the Portuguese, and the last leader was removed a few months before, with Zumbi taking over.

The free Africans and Tupis gather. Zumbi, nephew of Ganga Zumba and son of Sabina, speaks in Swahili and in Tupi.

'Listen. I will be brief, and you must act quickly. This is a moment of great danger for Palmares. Ganga Zumba built the Palmares palace with the help of Tupi and freed slaves nearly three decades ago. Palmares is now the home of over twenty thousand, both African and Tupi, but also many mixed race. We have our palace here, home of my family, and courtiers and guards; we have our church in our township of Macaco here, where some of us pray, as well as small chapels.

'We have a true civilisation here, free of slavery. And this they fear above all else.

'Today, Portugal comes to destroy Palmares and destroy freedom. We have our fortress on the mountain side here. We have several walls to protect us; we are above the enemy and can see them below us. We have many traps for them, full of pointed sticks; we have gunpowder, muskets, bows and arrows and spears, and food for a month. With your support, we shall try to hold out and withstand the enemy. They may be too strong this time. If necessary, we can then escape to the west and if necessary over the Sierra.

'Please find five messengers each to spread the message. Ask each person to find five more. Everyone who wishes to fight should come here. The Portuguese are nearly here. Speed is everything.

'There is a quilombo two days to the west. Some can go there if they don't want to be in a long siege. But those who want to fight can join us. Now go!'

In the hours that follow, the whole territory of Palmares seems to be moving, as around fifteen thousand move in a westerly direction, and two or three thousand join Zumbi and prepare themselves in their mountainside fortress.

As the first freemen head through the makeshift fence at the western end, the main part of the Portuguese army breaks through the log barrier at the entrance at the other end, thirty kilometres away, and marches into a town of empty huts.

The Portuguese captain Domingos Jorge Velho assesses the walls blocking the way to the fortress. His Tupi scouts point out the traps full of pointed sticks.

Jorge Velho asks for the cannons to be brought. They were left around twenty kilometres away as they were thought to be unnecessary. Now Jorge Velho realises that all the advantages lie with Zumbi and the free slaves.

Jorge Velho tries one attack after another through the walls of the fortress. Each time, he loses soldiers to the arrows and spears of the freed slaves above.

At night-time, there is constant drumming by the freemen and the Portuguese soldiers cannot sleep.

He arranges for half his force to march around the other side of the mountain to block escapes on the other side.

He instructs his slaves to gather large piles of sticks and to make heaps of mud to construct a long mud wall close to the bottom wall of the Palmarians. He plans to use this new wall to hide behind to better attack the freemen.

The plan does not work. The Palmarian spears and arrows go through the new wattle and daub wall and so it offers no protection.

After eight days the cannons arrive, but the cannon firers are not experienced. Two of the eight cannon balls go right over the mountain and land by the troops of Jorge Velho on the other side. Other cannon balls sail into Velho's new wall, narrowly missing his troops.

Tupi Indians under Jorge Velho's control find ways past the fortress walls and manage to fire poisoned darts at a few of the freemen.

One of the Portuguese commanders copies the Tupi Indians and manages to penetrate the fortress, but three of his men are killed by arrows, and he retreats.

After a month, a wild storm stops the attacks for a couple of days. As the storm subsides, one of Jorge Velho's lookouts sees a few freemen trying to escape along the mountainside. They are captured and brought to Velho.

'Why were you trying to escape?' asks the Portuguese commander.

'We are out of food and ammunition,' they say.

'Kill them!' barks Velho.

'Listen! We have these 'dogs' now. They are hungry and out of weapons. We will attack now. Luis, go to the other side of the mountain to tell General Lopez to use half his force to attack, and half to stop escapees.'

'Yes sir.'

Jorge Velho now launches his offensive, tearing holes in his wattle and daub wall, and starting to batter the fortress walls. As his forces find their way up the mountainside, with arrows raining down on then, a lookout shouts to him, pointing. 'Look there! There is a cave behind the buttress to the mountain there, and several of the escapees are heading there.'

Jorge Velho commands twenty men to stop climbing up the mountain, and to head across instead to the cave.

'Zumbi!' he shouts. 'Zumbi is escaping there! Get him now. Shoot him!'

But before any shot can be fired, Zumbi has disappeared.

'Come here, Indians!' shouts Jorge Velho, to a crack group of Tupi Indian scouts near to him. 'Go after the Palmares king, I must have him, dead or alive!'

The battle rages on the mountain, but the Portuguese have the upper hand now. By the morning, Palmares will be theirs.

Zumbi manages to escape.

A second battalion of Portuguese soldiers reaches the western end before all freemen and women have managed to escape.

The soldiers attack those still leaving indiscriminately, with a volley of shots. As they start to pull out the next cartridge of gunpowder and pour it into the pan to load the musket, a few hundred Palmarians charge them. Some freemen are hit by instantly drawn cutlasses, but some manage to grab muskets and club the Portuguese over the head with the butt. They briefly force the soldiers back, many of them now deprived of their muskets, but there is another musket volley from the soldiers at the back and many more freemen die or are fatally injured. This time, the sheer number of the surviving freemen is able to force the soldiers to retreat, depriving them of their muskets as they try to reload, and many are now able to escape.

Back near the fortress, Jorge Velho searches through the slumped bodies of the many dead bodies, but is unable to find Zumbi. The crack Tupi troop report that he had eluded them, but that they can find him in the jungle if so ordered. He orders them to find Zumbi and kill him, and to bring Zumbi's head to him.

Over a year later, in November 1695, someone gives away his location to the squadron. He is killed and his body mutilated. His head is placed on a stake by Jorge Velho.

Altogether, about two thousand Palmarians die in this attack.

Manu gazes wistfully in the direction of Palmares. He addresses a few hundred Palmarians, who have gathered at a smaller quilombo.

'I am told Palmares is now empty,' he says. 'But it is alive with the spirits of tens of thousands of people who have achieved freedom from slavery by coming here. The spirit of Palmares will always live on.

'You know, our African people and the Tupis will forever be the heartbeat of this country. The sembe music we play here is so infectious you cannot but dance to it. These people can provide this country's rhythms and the energy that will course through its veins. The pink-skinned Portuguese cuckoos will go, others may come, but we will *be* this country. Be its guts. Be its liver. Be its lungs. Be its heart. But, above all, be its soul!'

22.

Khoisan Gather at Blombos Cave, 1700

The Khoisan are pushed ever further away from lands they have looked after for millennia, as the Dutch make ever more extravagant demands for more land for their farms.

The Khoisan know that they will always lose the big battles with the Dutch, as the gun will always defeat their guile, their spears, their bows and arrows.

They spread the word. There is a gathering at the Blombos Cave by the sea on the south coast, which they believe contains the oldest known painting by human hands. They flock from far and wide to share their concerns about the plight of the Khoisan.

Doman Junior, the Grandson of Doman, addresses them.

'We have been here from a time before time. We are the originals, the first artists, the first to think outside ourselves – beyond, to another way of thinking, another life. Would there be art elsewhere had we not sown the seeds from which a great forest grew?'

'Yet, people with no such history, no grace, no soul, and no ability to express the imagining of their souls on a cave wall, come with their guns. They walk on us like they may tread on a slug or a snail. The respect they show us is at best the respect they show a black mamba, as they know we can respond to their killing with spears and arrows. But still they tread on us.'

'Their gun turns them from mouse to elephant. It combines the lethality of a lion's incisor with the game-changing advantage of distance. At times you cannot even see the assailant who has penetrated your body with such life-devouring force.'

'Here, where our ancestors painted with their hands when in the rest of the world they barely knew where their next meal was coming from, and when in the land of the Dutch the closest they came to anything cultural was a school of dolphins and a parliament of owls, we look to the spirits to inspire us.'

'Why not share this land, we ask the Dutch? The San and the Khoikhoi have shared it; the Khoisan and the Bantu have shared it. We were able to continue our way of life, if they would share, for millenia. But these Dutch are voracious. They devour in seconds. Unthinkingly. Blind. For them, to share is to take what is not theirs. They appear to give a little, but only then to bide their time and then say that we cannot have the land they agreed, they want it now.'

'They are the great beast that does not know the limits of its own stomach. It just eats and eats and eats. One day it will get an almighty stomach-ache. And wonder why.'

Itoi speaks.

'We call upon the spirits of our ancestors to guide us as we face our new future. Give us the strength to find a place in the strange and alien world of the soulless Dutch, where we may need to find a way to live our culture among people who understand it so little, and who respect it less. Give us strength as we move to the arid barren lands left us by the Dutch, and bring us rain each year, such that our sheep and cattle may survive, and our crops grow.'

'Give us hope. Give us the wisdom, guile, and fortitude of our ancestors of seventy millennia.'

THE END

BIBLIOGRAPHY

Portugal's Armadas 1487 to 1515 and east coast ports and Brazil

Beaujard, Phillipe: 'The Indian Ocean in Eurasian and African World-Systems before the 16th Century', Journal of World History 16, no. 4, (206, pp 411-465)

Bellingham, Beatrix L: Mombasa: A Guide to Mombasa and Surroundings, Nairobi: Mombasa Times, 1933

Berg, Fred James: 'the Swahili Community of Mombasa 1500-1900,' Journal of African History 9, no 1, 1968, pp35-56

Crowley, Roger: Conquerors, How Portugal Forged the First Global Empire, Random House, 2015

Danvers, Frederick C: The Portuguese in India, Being a History of the rise and Decline of the Eastern Empire, vol 1, Hanse

De Las Casas, Bartolome, History of the Indes, republished W W Norton, New York USA 1971

Greenlee. Frederick B: The Voyage of Pedro Alvares Cabral to Brazil, the Indian continent. From Contemporary Documents and Narratives. Nyan, USA. 2020

Koning, Hans: Columbus, His Enterprise. Monthly Review Press, New York. USA. 1976

Panikker, K M: Malabar and the Portuguese, Topics IIIT collection, India, 1929

Subrahmanyam, Sanjay: The Portuguese empire in Asia 1500-1700. A Political and Economic History. John Wiley, London

Zinn, Howard: A people's History of the United States, Harper Collins, New York USA. 1999.

South Africa history 1487 to 1520

'Remember the Khoikhoi Victory over Dom Francisco d'Almeida at the Cape in 1510', postcolonial Studies Vol 12 no 1, 2009 pp 107-130

'Khoikhoi Warriors Defat Portuguese Thieves', South African History online, Towards a People's History, 2016

Sub-Saharan Africa (Otapo, Mande, etc, family) and slavery

Beaujard, Phillipe: 'The Indian Ocean in Eurasian and African World-Systems before the 16th Century', Journal of World History 16, no. 4, (206, pp 411-465)
Bellingham, Beatrix L: Mombasa: A Guide to Mombasa and Surroundings, Nairobi: Mombasa Times, 1933
Berg, Fred James: 'the Swahili Community of Mombasa 1500-1900,' Journal of African History 9, no 1, 1968, pp35-56
Ellis, Alfred: The Yoruba-speaking People of the Slave Coast of West Africa
Equiano, Olaudah, The Life of Equiano Oludah, or Gustavus Vassa, the African, Thrift Editions, UK, 1789, Re-published as Equiano's Travels, Heinemann, London 1967
F Krug, Jessica A, Fugitive Modernities: Kisama and the Politics of Freedom, Duke University Press, Durham 2018
Meier, Prita, Swahili Port Cities, The Architecture of Elsewhere, Indiana U.P. USA, 2016

African empires

Davidson, Basil: A History of West Africa 1000-1800, Longman Group Ltd, 1977
De Villiers, Marc and Sheila Hirtle: Timbuktu, the Sahara's Fabled City of Gold, 2007
Koslow, Philip, The Kingdom of Africa: Ancient Ghana, The Land of Gold. Chelsea House Publishers, 1995
Martin, JP: AFRICAN EMPRES, Trafford Publishing, 2017
Masoff, Joy: Mali, Land of Gold and Glory, Five Ponds Press 1998
Chirikure, Shadreck: Great Zimbabwe, The Rosen Publishing Group, 1998
Shuter, Jane: Ancient West African Kingdoms, Ghana, Mali, Songhai, Reed Educational and Professional Publishing
Wilson, Thomas H: City States of the Swahili Coast, The Rosen Publishing Group 1998
The Kongo Kingdom, The Rosen Publishing Group, 1998
The Zulu Kingdom, The Rosen Publishing Group, 1998
The Lost World of Nubia, Infobase Learning 2012
The Kingdom of Benin, The Rosen Publishing Group, 2014

Brazil: Tupis encounter the invaders

Fausto, C. Fragmentos de História e Cultura Tupinambá. Da Etnologia como Instrumento Crítico de Conhecimento Etno-Histórico. In História dos Índios no Brasil, org. M.C. da Cunha , 381–396. São Paulo: Companhia das Letras. Brazil 1992

Metraux A: The Guarani. In Handbook of South American Indians. In J H Steward. The Tropical Forest Tribes. Smithsonian Institute. Washington Vol 3

Moore: A Prehistory of South America: Ancient Cultural Diversity on the Least Known Continent. University Press, Colorado. USA. 2014

Noelli F S. The Tupi expansion, in H. Silverman & W.H. Isbell (ed.) Handbook of South American archaeology: 659-670. Springer. New York. USA 2008

Noelli F.S.: Without Tekoha there is no Teko. In search of an ethno-archaeological model of subsistence applied to a Guarani village in a domain area. Porto Alegre. Publ. Springer. New York. 1993

Schiavetto, Oliveira: Guarani; archaeology, construction and deconstruction of indigenous identity; Seal University. Brazil 2003

Website Brazilian mythology | Myths and Folklore Wiki | Fandom

Brazil: Resistance, Mocambos, Palmares

Abreu, Joao Capistrano, de ; Chapters of Brazil's Colonial history 1500-1800, OUP, Oxford 1987

Ajayi, J F Ade, Samuel Ajayi Crowther of Ojo, in Curtin ed, Africa remembered, Narratives by West Africans from the end of the Slave Trade 289-316.

Alpern, Stanley, On the Origins of the Amazons of Dahomey. History in Africa no.25. 1998, pp 9 -25

Araujo, Ana Lucia: History, Memory and imagination: Na Agontime, a Dahomean Queen in Brazil; beyond Tradition, African Women and their Cultural Spaces, 2013

Arens, William: the Man-Eating Myth: anthropology and Anthropophagy

Barcia , Manuel, West African warfare in Bahia and Cuba, Oxford U.P 2014

Bauer, Raymond and Alice Bauer, 'Day to Day Resistance to Slavery' in John H Bracey, American Slavery The Question of Resistance, Belmont, CA, USA 1971

Anderson, Robert Nelson III, The quilombo of Palmares, a new overview of a maroon state I 17th century Brazil. Journal of Latin American Studies 28.

Boxer C R ; Salvador de Sa and the struggle for Brazil and Angola, 1602-1686, University of London, London, UK, 1952

Candido, Mariana: An African Slaving Port and the Atlantic World: Benguela and its Hinterland, Cambridge U P, New York, Howard University. 2011

Cheney, Glenn A: Brazil's Lost Nation of Fugitive Slaves, Hanover CT USA, 2014

Costa, Emilia Viotti da: The Portuguese African Slave Trade: a Lesson in Colonialism, *Latin American Perspectives* 12, 1985, pp 41-61

Da Silva, Daniel B Domingues: The Kimbundu Diaspora to Brazil, *African Diaspora* 8, No. 2 2015, pp 200-219

Dallas, Robert Charles: The History of the Maroons; their Origins until the Establishment of their Chief Tribe in Sierra Leone, 2 vols, Cambridge U P. New York, 2010

Ferreira, Jose Carlos: 'As insurreicoes dos africanus na bahia, Revista do instituto geographico e historico na Bahia, 10, no. 29, pp 103-19

Ferreira, Roquinaldo: Slave fights and Runaway Communities in Angola, *Revista Anos* 90, 21, no.40 (2015) pp 65-90

Fisher, Allan G BB and Humphrey J Fisher: Slavery and Moslem Society in Africa , Anchor, Garden City, NY 1972

Fonseca, Junior: Zumbi de Palmares - A Historia de Brasil que Nao Foi Contada ; Yorubana do Brasil, Rio 2002

Freyre, Gilberto: The Masters and the Slaves: A Study of the Development of Brazilian Civilisation, revised ed 1963

Hemming. John: Red Gold. 1978

Krug, Jessica A, Fugitive Modernities; Kisama and the Politics of Freedom, Duke University Press, Durham 2018

Landers, Jane: Leadership and Authority in Maroon Settlements in Spanish America and Brazil. In Latin America, Interconnections, ed Curto and Soulotre la France, pp 173-184. Africa World Press, Trenton New Jersey, USA, 2005

Lara, Silvia Hunold, Palmares and Cucau: political Dimensions of a Maroon Community in late 17th century Brazil. In American Counterpoint: New Approaches to Slavery and Abolition in Brazil. Yale, 2010

Libby, Jean: 'Technological and cultural transfer of African Ironmaking into the Americas', in Rediscovering America National, cultural and disciplinary Boundaries Re-examined, Baton Rouge, Louisana State Uni 1993

Maia, Luciano Mariz and Francisco Moonen eds; Etnohistoria dos indios potiguara, Joao Pessoa, Secretaria da Educacao e Cultura do Estado da Paraiba Brazil. 1992.

Mannix,D P: Black Cargoes: a History of the Atlantic Slave Trade. Viking Press. New York. 1962

Matson, Henry, Remarks on the Slave Trade and African Squadron, J Ridgway, London 1848

Mattoso, Katia M de Queiros ; To be a Slave in Brazil 1550 – 1888, Rutgers, New Brunswick 2004

Mirzai, B.A., Montana, I M Lovejoy: Slavery, Islam and Diaspora, Africa World Press 2009, pp 37-76

Paiva e Souza, Vania Rocha Filho de; Concelcao das Crioulas Salgueiro, in Quilombos Identidade Etnica Territorialidade, Fun. Getulio Vargas 2002

Price, Richard: Refiguring Palmares, College of William and Mary and Anse Chaudiere, Martinique

Salvador, Frei Vicente Do: Historia da Brasil (1500-1627). Melhoramentos, Sao Paulo. Brazil. 1965.

Schwartz, Stuart B: Resistance and Accommodation in 18th Century Brazil. The Slaves view of Slavery. Hispanic American Histoeical Review, 57:1, Feb 1977, pp 78-79

Thornton, J: Africa and Africans in the Making of the Atlantic World, 2nd ed, Cambridge U P, 1998

Vernet, Thomas: Slave Trade and slavery on the Swahili coast (1500-1750)

Website: www.terrabrasileira.net/folklore/origens/africana/quilomba.html

Overall

W E B Dubois: Black Reconstruction in America: An Essay toward a History of the Part which Black Folk played in the Attempt to Reconstruct Democracy in America, 1860-1880, Harcourt, Brace and Company 1935.

The Invisible Become Visible: A Trilogy

Book Two: Gold, Greed and Insurgency

This represents the second volume in the trilogy of novels on history's forgotten or too little remembered people.

It is the story of the indigenous and enslaved people of Haiti and the indigenous people of Mexico through turbulent but endlessly fascinating and difficult times; it also continues our story of sub-Saharan Africa and Brazil.

It is part of a trilogy that provides:

- A history of peoples who had lived their lives in communities for thousands of years until invaders came and all changed; this seen through characters from those communities
- A history that helps to explain how the profit hungry and powerful in humanity ended up causing a climate emergency in the 21st century

It is also:

- A history that is long overdue, a history from the perspective of the invaded and the enslaved, and a different kind of history that casts a mirror on the invaders.

In Haiti, we follow the extraordinary history of the indigenous Taino people from the arrival of Columbus to their alliance with freed slaves to overthrow both the French and the British invaders during the revolution and wars of the 1790s, prior to the Independence of Haiti.

We see how, in the mountains of Haiti, indigenous people survived in small communities after the Spanish invasion. These mountain communities played a pivotal role in Spain's decision to sell a third of the island to France in around 1700, over 200 years after. The French then brought slaves to Haiti in large numbers. Over several decades, numerous escaped slaves joined the mountain communities. The novel follows in particular the capture of a slave from Benin, who is taken by a British slave ship to Haiti, but later escapes to the mountains, where he finds love. His daughter is the mother of the famed slave leader, Toussaint Louverture, who we follow as a young man working on a slave plantation, until he is partially freed.

Through the eyes of the mountain fighters and of their leader Toussaint Louverture, we experience the historic revolution of the 1790s, the first successful anti-slavery revolution, fought with sticks and the passionate desire for freedom against the biggest armies and navies of Europe, the French and the British.

In Mexico, we experience the life of Aztecs in Tenochtitlan in its complexity. We see the Spanish invasion from the viewpoint of these Aztecs, and the terrible destruction wrought upon Mexico by the Spanish.

We follow two Aztec families, one rich, one poor, and through this we are able to direct a lens towards their history, culture and lifestyle.

We also see, in part through following the same family over nearly three centuries, how different Mexican indigenous communities rebelled through to the mid 18th century, in each case seeking to keep alive a deep and vibrant culture, adapted to the landscape and the climate. We also see how the Spanish used disease as a weapon against the indigenous people.

Book Three: The Great Planet Heist

This represents the third of three novels on history's forgotten or too little remembered people

It is the story of the indigenous and enslaved people of sub-Saharan Africa - in particular peoples that came under the British empire - as well as the story of Brazil, through turbulent but endlessly fascinating and difficult times.

It is part of a trilogy that provides:

- A history of peoples who had lived their lives in communities for thousands of years until invaders came and all changed, this seen through characters from those communities
- A history that helps to explain how the profit hungry and powerful in humanity ended up causing a climate emergency in the 21st century

In this novel, we take up again the dramatic story of our Bantu family from the first novel. We follow it as it faces new Portuguese intruders, seeking gold, then Arab traders, then the arrival in the family's midst of the strange ageing figure of David Livingstone, who takes on as an assistant one of our Bantu family - a teenage son in the 1850s enslaved by Arabs, taken to India, and then rescued by Dr Livingstone. This former slave (Jacob) and two others carry the body of David Livingstone, after his death, 1000 miles to the coast.

Rebellion and fightback. We see further instances of indigenous people rebelling.

- In South Africa, the Zulus (most memorably) fought and at times defeated the Boers and the British, in particular the battle of Isandlwana, a major victory for the Zulus against the British, but with a grim aftermath
- In West Africa, where the Ashanti fought off the European powers for many decades

This novel also tells the story of Cecil Rhodes laying the basis for apartheid in South Africa. Here, as in much of Sub-Saharan Africa, the new 500-round fast-acting Maxim machine gun introduced in 1889-90, laid the basis for military victories by Britain – from South Africa, through Zimbabwe, Zambia, Kenya, Uganda, Ghana etc. In these countries, following military victory, we see all the prime agricultural land being taken at the point of a gun from the indigenous Africans. When the Africans asked for the land back, they were imprisoned and labelled 'terrorists.'

In Brazil, we see the tide of slave revolts that followed the end of slavery in Europe in 1834; the repression of the revolt that presaged ex-slaves being deported back to Africa; and the rise of new Brazilian mocambos and the revolts that culminated in the final emancipation of slaves in 1888.

The stories reflect the current Zeitgeist in two ways:

- Telling the post-invasion story of the indigenous people and the millions of slaves (and how these peoples interacted) in the invaded countries/areas Brazil, South Africa and East Africa and also the extraordinary spirit of rebellion. It represents a forceful anti-slavery drama.
- The Green message of the rich and powerful in Europe and its diaspora gobbling up the planet over four centuries and spitting out its excreta into the air, the sea and the ground.